THERE HANGS THE KNIFE

A JOANNA STARK MYSTERY

MARCIA MULLER

ISBN 0-373-26034-2

9 780373 260348

50350

108340

★

SOMETHING STRUCK
JOANNA AS WRONG

Something she'd seen in the bedroom. No, not something she'd seen, something she *hadn't*. She hesitated and then went over and knelt by the body.

There was no heavy onyx ring on the out-flung left hand.

Joanna reached for the sheet that hung off the bed across the man's face.

She drew it toward her with a shaky hand, then stopped, staring.

It wasn't Matt.

This man had curly dark hair. His skin was pockmarked and dusty.

She yanked the sheet completely aside.

His face was young and fleshy. He wore a growth of wispy beard. His features were Asian or Middle Eastern.

She had never seen him before in her life.

★

THERE HANGS THE KNIFE

MARCIA MULLER

W🌐RLDWIDE®

TORONTO • NEW YORK • LONDON • PARIS
AMSTERDAM • STOCKHOLM • HAMBURG
ATHENS • MILAN • TOKYO • SYDNEY

THERE HANGS THE KNIFE

A Worldwide Mystery/October 1989

First published by St. Martin's Press Incorporated.

ISBN 0-373-26034-2

For Carol and Karl Brandt

ONE

"HOW LONG do you intend to remain in Great Britain?"

"Three weeks, perhaps a month."

"And the purpose of your visit?"

"Just a vacation."

The immigration clerk wielded her stamp and handed back Joanna Stark's passport. Joanna moved past the high desk and along the corridor in Heathrow Airport, searching for the lighted number of the stairway that would take her to the baggage claim and customs area. There it was—thirty-four.

As she started down, clutching at the railing to counterbalance the heavy carry-on bag slung over her left shoulder, she smiled wryly.

I wonder what she'd have said if I'd told her my real reason for coming to England. If I'd said I'm here to trap a thief. And not just any thief....

TWO

As SHE WATCHED the crowded sidewalks of the Mayfair district slip past the windows of the taxi, Joanna felt oddly intoxicated. It wasn't the electrically charged sensation she always experienced upon arriving in New York, or the whimsical, winey high of Paris. This was a stealthy mellow glow, tinged with a nostalgia as sharp as the tang of Devonshire cider.

Seven years, she thought. It had been seven years since her last visit to London. Six years ago her annual trip had been superseded by some event she now couldn't even recall. Five years ago it had been canceled because her late husband, David, had been told he had terminal cancer. And during the past four years she had remained close to home, protected like a creature in a cocoon until the healing process was complete. But with the healing had come the inevitable awakening of emotions—one of them being the obsession she'd come here to lay to rest.

Seven years, she thought again. A mystical number looked upon with favor or suspicion by most of the world's cultures and religions. A lucky number, too. Lucky for me? I sure as hell hope so.

The taxi turned onto Clifford Street and pulled to the curb in front of a small Regency building sandwiched between a men's clothiers and a jewelry shop. Joanna paid the driver the amount they'd settled on for him to continue to the outlying Swiss Cottage district with her bags. He nodded brusquely as she got out, then eased back into traffic. He'd been a good driver, addressing her with the stereotypical British ''luv'' when he'd first spoken, but then refraining from unnecessary conversation—unlike so many New York or San Francisco cabbies, who seemed compelled to rattle on about the weather or sports or their Ph.D. programs. (*Why* were most American cabdrivers getting advanced degrees or engaged in otherwise eccentric and largely unbelievable sidelines?)

Still standing at the curb, Joanna straightened the jacket of her travel-rumpled wool suit and looked up at the building in front of her. It was three stories, gray stone with black iron fretwork. In a district where signs and window displays were quietly tasteful it carried discretion to an extreme. Only a brass plaque by the door advertised its occupants: BLOOMFIELD AND BURGESS ART GALLERY, BY APPOINTMENT ONLY. And, Joanna thought as she crossed the sidewalk, in a city where a five-by-eleven-foot broom closet near Harrod's Department Store had been converted to an apartment and gone on the market for over fifty thousand dollars, these quarters were reasonably spacious. When she and David had patronized this gallery, it had occupied a renovated warehouse in Soho; their old friends must be doing well to have relocated here.

The doorbell's brisk peal was muted, as if the unit was well to the rear of the building. After a minute Joanna was admitted by a gaunt gray-haired woman in a severe black dress who took her name and left her to wait in an anteroom crowded with hulking leather chairs. There was a Persian rug on the floor, two smoking stands complete with humidors, and a coatrack in one corner. Feeling like an interloper at a stodgy gentlemen's club, Joanna perched on the nearest armchair; her feet did not quite touch the floor. It was another minute before she heard hurried footsteps behind the inside door and a man's voice exclaiming, "...should have shown her straight in, for God's sake!" As she stood up, the door opened and Christopher Burgess burst into the room.

He was a man of medium height, and his elegantly tailored tweed suit did not quite conceal a tendency toward pudginess. His head was topped by a bush of curly light hair, and his round face was relatively unlined, in spite of his being in his mid-fifties. Blue eyes sparkled behind brown-rimmed glasses; as he went to hug Joanna the glasses slipped down his broad ski-jump nose and one lens got wedged against her cheek. Christopher squeezed her, then stepped back, took off the glasses, and polished the lens on his handkerchief. When they were once more in place, he regarded her fondly.

"You look as young as ever, now don't you?" he said.

"Except for a few gray hairs." She patted her short dark curls.

"Oh, come now, there's hardly a one."

"I pull them out as fast as they grow in. But how about you? You're looking fit—and prosperous."

"Well, thank you, dear. I do try to keep fit, in spite of my fondness for ale; and the gallery's doing well for us—best move we could have made."

"And how's Richard?" Richard Bloomfield was twenty years Christopher's senior; he'd originally been the sole proprietor of the gallery but had later taken in as partner the young assistant who had shown an uncanny sales ability. The combination of Richard's fine aesthetic sense and Christopher's persuasiveness had been a winning one.

"In good health," Christopher said. "Stays down in the country most of the time and allows me pretty much of a free hand here. Perhaps you could stop in to see him? He knows you were coming and has been asking about you."

"I'd like that." Joanna's husband had been a lawyer whose clients had come from various areas of the visual arts, as well as an avid collector. He had represented Richard Bloomfield's interests in the United States, and in turn Richard had helped him acquire many of his English paintings. Over the years the two men were associated, they became fast friends; over the twelve years Joanna was married to David, she and Richard had also grown close.

Christopher was watching her thoughtfully. "Of course," he said, "you may not have the time."

"I've booked an open return."

"I meant in light of what you're here to accomplish."

"And what is that?"

"It's not completely clear to me yet, but I have an inkling. Three weeks ago you requested that I commission a painting that could be passed off as a recently discovered member of Pieter Brueghel's Proverb Series. I did so, and in talking with the copyist, found that three in the series have been stolen in the past few months. You still own a half interest in that San Francisco security firm that specializes in protecting museums and galleries, don't you?"

"Yes."

"And in the past you've displayed an enthusiastic curiosity about a gentleman who displays his own brand of enthusiasm for Flemish artworks?"

"Yes, again."

"Well, there you are. I heard you had a bit of unpleasantness with that gentleman in your home city last fall, so I don't have to be a genius to guess at your intentions. What I'm intrigued by is how you plan to accomplish them."

"You'll find that out in good time, I promise." It was an unexpected relief not to have to fully explain the background of her plans. Christopher would take them at face value, on the basis of what he'd already figured out, and never suspect any deeper motivation than a spirited professional interest. More important, his showing no trace of disapproval indicated that he could be persuaded to accept and carry through his part in the scheme. She would prefer persuasion to forcing him....

Christopher's glasses had slid down his nose once more. He pushed them back onto their perilous perch and looked sharply at her. "You're tired."

"Yes."

"Why didn't you go to your hotel and rest before coming here?"

Suddenly she felt the weariness from the interminable eleven-hour flight. She ran a hand across her eyes; they seemed gritty, and smarted. When she moved her fingers to the short curls that framed her forehead, she felt a stickiness, as if she'd sweated during the brief sleep on the plane and the moisture had mixed gummily with her hair spray. She let her hand fall limply to her side and shrugged. "I wanted to get started."

Christopher smiled in understanding and motioned at the inside door. "Let's go back to one of the viewing rooms, then, and I'll unveil the work you've commissioned. Commissioned, I might add, not only at considerable expense, but also with considerable wheedling and groveling on my part. Jenny Sherman is both a very good and a very busy copyist."

"She *is* good, and I thank you for getting her to take it on at such short notice."

Christopher's smile thinned. "It took a good bit of convincing, since she wasn't certain of the ethics involved in the situation and, frankly, neither was I. You're fortunate that I'm in your debt. Now...would you care for some tea while you admire the alleged Brueghel?"

Joanna's stomach lurched, a consequence of all the bad coffee she'd drunk during the approach to Heathrow. "No—thank you."

"Sherry, then."

She looked at her watch; she'd neglected to reset it. At home in California it was only a little after six in the morning; the sun would barely be touching the gingerbread curlicues of her Victorian farmhouse in the Sonoma Valley. Here it was after four in the afternoon. "Sherry sounds wonderful."

"Excellent. Come with me, please." Christopher opened the door and ushered her into the inner recesses of the gallery.

"So—*There Hangs the Knife.*"

Joanna set her glass down and went to study the painting that Christopher had just unveiled. Trust him, she thought, to present a blatant fake with pomp and ceremony, velvet drape dramatically flung back to reveal the canvas propped on a mahogany display easel. But really, even if it were the genuine article, it would have very little to recommend such treatment.

It was a small canvas, about eight by twelve inches, depicting a knife hanging from the upper-story window of a typical Flemish cottage. On the sill leaned a woman with a lumpish figure and peasant's dress—also typical, especially for Brueghel. Her face was in shadow, but a suggestion of hope or perhaps anticipation was detectable on her fleshy features. In the foreground several other peasants cavorted around a keg of beer, while pigs rooted in the garden.

The five small canvasses in the Proverb Series had been the sixteenth-century painter's preparation for a larger work—*The Blue Cloak.* A complicated and busy village scene, the *Cloak* had attracted the attention of numerous scholars seeking to identify the more than one hundred Netherlandish proverbs represented there. Looking at it was a bit like trying to decipher one of those cartoons that challenge the reader to find all the rabbits or cats or chickens hiding in the drawing. Many of the proverbs were now outdated and obscure; some were openly scatological or sexual. The title proverb itself denoted a cuckold.

She said, "It's a good fake. An expert would see through it quickly, I suppose, but for my purposes it's perfect. God, it's dreary, though. Brueghel was really into ugliness. What does this particular proverb mean?"

" 'There hangs the knife'? Stands for a challenge. If you looked at *The Blue Cloak*, you'd see a scene very similar to this toward the left-hand side."

"Well, it's appropriate, considering what I'm setting out to do." She sat down and studied the painting from a different angle, which did little to improve it. "Strange proverbs those people had." The genuine paintings in the series had been respectively titled *Tarts on the Roof, The Hat on the Pillar, He Gives the Lord a Flaxen Beard, Horse Manure Is Not Figs,* and *He Who Would Outyawn the Stove Must Yawn Long.* She had no idea what any of them meant—nor did she care at the moment.

"Well, they liked them colorful," Christopher said. "More sherry?"

"Please." While he fetched the decanter, Joanna contemplated her purchase some more. She wondered if the five smaller canvases had been deliberate practice exercises before the artist had attempted the larger one, or if they had merely suggested it to his fertile mind. Then she dismissed the question as one of the chicken-or-the-egg variety. "So how much is this gem costing me?" she asked.

"Fifteen thousand pounds."

"Jesus!"

"I told you Jenny Sherman was good, and for a rush job—"

"I'll have a bank draft for you tomorrow."

"No hurry. I'm sure I can trust you for the money. And I don't suppose you'll be wanting to take the painting to your hotel immediately, anyway."

"I won't want to take it anyplace at all. It's staying here."

Christopher raised his eyebrows. "So my involvement in this scheme is not yet ended," he said softly.

"No. I can't go into the details now. I have things to do and a couple of other people to talk with first."

"Tomorrow, then?"

"Late afternoon."

He looked discomfited—probably more by the fact that she planned to involve him further than by the delay—but merely nodded and sipped his sherry. After a moment he said philosophically, "Well, I can see that the sheer amusement of watching you go about this business will more than make up for any inconvenience caused by you finally calling in my debt."

"Christopher, I've never considered it a debt—not in the sense of my having a hold over you, or being able to ask you to do something you didn't feel was right."

He smiled faintly and flipped the velvet drape back over the canvas. "I'm not sure how I feel at this point. I reserve judgment until you explain what it is you want me to do."

"And if you don't like it?"

The smile faded and he shrugged again, more elaborately.

Joanna watched him as he fussed with the drape, thinking of how Christopher had changed with the years. His genial boyish facade was still intact, but beneath it she sensed a smugness born of success and prosperity. This man was a far cry from the down-and-out friend from her checkered past whom she had run into on a Soho street corner some ten years before.

As she remembered, she'd been trying to get a cab after having lunch with a friend when she'd spotted Christopher. Although she hadn't seen him since they'd lived in the same East End tenement in the mid sixties, she recognized him immediately. His shabby thrift-shop clothing and pathetic happiness at seeing her had made her feel guilty about her own unearned prosperity, and she'd taken him to a nearby pub for a drink. They'd had another, and then another, discussing the bad old times they'd shared in increasingly— and unwisely—louder voices, until she realized she was late for a meeting she and David had scheduled to view some canvasses at Richard Bloomfield's gallery. On impulse, she had invited Christopher to come along.

At first both David and Richard had been annoyed at Joanna and Christopher's giddy intoxication. Then they'd gotten into the Scotch in self-defense. By the time they adjourned to a nearby restaurant for dinner, Joanna could tell Richard was impressed with Christopher's easy charm and enthusiasm for the artworks he'd shown them; when she and David left for their hotel, Richard was questioning him about how fast he thought he could pick up a knowledge of art. She'd had to smile at the discussion, because Christopher had already picked up such knowledge—in very unlikely quarters. But the next day when Richard called her and asked if she thought Christopher Burgess would make a good assistant for him, she answered with an unqualified yes. And Christopher had never given her cause to regret the recommendation.

Still, it wouldn't hurt now to refresh his memory of their shared past. She said, "One of the people I'll be talking with before I go over my plan with you is an old friend—Matt Wickins."

Christopher turned and peered at her over the rims of his glasses, his eyes suddenly cold and flat looking. After a few seconds he said, "Ah, the friend of your youth you asked me to locate. I trust the number I provided was correct?"

"Yes, it's the phone at a pub where he hangs out. I guess he uses it as an answering service." Joanna stood, adjusting her shoulder bag. "But I think you should remember this, Christopher: Matt's a friend of our youth. *Ours.*"

"...Yes...right."

"Will you make time for me tomorrow? At three?"

"Three will be fine."

With an uncharacteristic lapse in manners, Christopher didn't offer to see her out, so she made her own way down the corridor to the front door. The means she had employed weren't exactly blackmail, she told herself. Not after the high-minded way she'd assured her old friend that she didn't feel she had a hold over him.

No, what she'd done was more a test of how deep Christopher's newfound self-satisfaction and respectability ran. She found this crack in his facade extremely satisfying.

THREE

To the northeast of London's Regent's Park lies a district little known to the general tourist trade, called Swiss Cottage. It is an area of quiet tree-shaded streets, many of them lined with tall, dark brick mansions that are in the process of being restored and small, exclusive hotels that cater to a clientele who value peace and privacy. It was to one of these, Primrose Hill Hotel, that Joanna had instructed the taxi driver to deliver her bags.

Named after a nearby park, the hotel was a tidy Georgian structure with a handsomely appointed parlor and dark-paneled bar designed for intimate conversation. Its chief attraction was not the cramped and somewhat uncomfortable guest rooms on the second or third stories, nor the dining room which served frankly mediocre food. What brought Primrose Hill's well-heeled clientele back time after time were the five cottages nestled in the gardens behind the main building, each of which was named after a different variety of the flower. At six o'clock that evening Joanna was settled into Moonlight Primrose Cottage. Settled physically, that is. Emotionally she was more shaken than she'd felt in quite some time.

The problem, she realized, was that this was the cottage where she and David had habitually stayed on their trips to London. When she'd made her reservation, she'd thought she was being wise; it would be a touchstone, a familiar and comforting place from which to mount her unfamiliar and risky undertaking. But now she could see that she'd made a mistake: memories assaulted her, seeming to radiate off every object in the two rooms. The bed was the same one where she and David had slept and made love. The claw-footed bathtub was one they'd often shared. They'd had many breakfasts at the table beside the living room window, had had cocktails on the small patio that bordered the rose garden. The cottage was the same, yet hauntingly different, and the difference was due solely to David's absence.

Joanna hadn't cried over his loss since the night of his funeral, when she'd fled the pack of horrible relatives who were angry because his much younger second wife had inherited nearly everything. Then she had gone to a private place of her own and thrown a wretched, maudlin, spectacular drunk. Now the tears welled up and threatened to spill over.

She shook her head and stepped out onto the brick patio, taking deep breaths of air scented with spring odors of freshly turned earth and early blossoms. The sound of piano music came from the main building. There were voices nearby—light and happy. In the distance, horns beeped and a siren ululated. The balmy late April day had gone crisp; Joanna crossed her arms and rubbed them for warmth.

Tears were the last thing she wanted now . . . would be the last thing David would have wanted for her. She had a job to do, one in which he would have taken a grim satisfaction. Instead of pushing aside her memories, she pictured his face: lean, with hard lines around the mouth and gentle ones around the eyes. She imagined his voice: deep, but with a curious lilting quality that had always betrayed him as a kind—perhaps too kind—man. She pretended she could hear him saying, "Get on with it, my love. It's what you've waited years to do."

After a moment the rising tears subsided. She stood hugging herself for a while more, then turned back toward the warmly lighted sitting room. The memories were there, all right—nothing she could do about that. But now she could live with them; maybe after a while draw the strength and comfort she'd expected them to provide.

Suddenly she felt a strong urge to call home. Six o'clock here, nine in the morning in Sonoma. Her son, E.J., would still be sleeping, tired from his late hours as bartender at Mario's. She hesitated, then thought, What the hell? He'd gripe and grumble about being wakened, but be secretly pleased that she'd called. Besides, she missed him, needed to hear his voice.

The phone rang seven times before E.J.'s sleep-clogged voice answered. Joanna pictured him leaning next to the wall phone in the big country kitchen, his curly blond hair and bushy beard rumpled. He'd be barefooted and wearing one of the flannel nightshirts he ordered in quantity from L. L. Bean and be rubbing his eyes and trying not to yawn in her ear.

"You sure know how to start a guy's day, Jo."

"Don't complain. I haven't been to bed since the night before I left."

"You get any sleep on the plane?"

"Not much. I never do."

There was a pause, then a hissing intake of breath.

"E.J.? Are you smoking dope?"

"What do you expect me to do when you drag me out of bed this early?"

"You'll be walking around stoned all day."

"No I won't—I'll be going back to bed and sleeping until two, like I planned."

Joanna sighed. She'd long ago accepted marijuana as part of E.J.'s life-style, just as he'd accepted wine as part of hers.

"Listen, Jo," he said, "are you okay?"

"Sure. The flight was on time, and I've already seen the dealer who commissioned the painting for me, and now I'm at the hotel. I contacted my old friend Matt Wickins as soon as I checked in, and we're meeting at a pub near his place around nine. I'll touch bases with the Art Squad inspector in the morning, and I have an appointment with Nick's contact on the *Times* at noon—"

"I don't mean are your plans okay. I mean you."

"Oh." She paused, giving it serious consideration. "Fair to middling."

"You sound kind of depressed."

"I am, a little." She hesitated, then laughed ruefully. "I just had an intimate conversation with David."

E.J. laughed too. Thank God, Joanna thought, that her son was used to her flights of fancy.

"So what'd he say?"

"The essence was that I shouldn't weaken."

There was a silence.

"Now what's wrong with *you*?" Joanna asked.

"I just wish you were going into this with more than a ghost for company. At least let me or Nick, or even Rafferty, come over there—"

"No."

"Why not?"

"This is my private affair."

"But Parducci's my—"

"This is between him and me."

E.J. was silent again.

"Besides," Joanna added, "I need you there at home."

"Why, for Christ's sake?"

"Well, to pick up my mail from the P.O. box. To make sure the garden doesn't die before it's barely started. There's that stray cat I took in last week—I don't like the way it's limping."

"I took it to the vet yesterday. Arthritis in the hip. Baby aspirin twice a week should fix him up."

"Then you need to be there to pill him—"

"It cost a hundred and twenty dollars."

"What! For a stray?"

"Needed his shots, X rays. I'm doing you a lot of financial damage by staying here."

"Sorry, you can't pull that on me. And I have to hang up now."

"Jo, wait. I could help—"

"I'll call you again in a few days. Go back to bed." Quickly she depressed the button on the phone. She'd been so close to asking him to catch the next flight....

For a few minutes she remained curled in the corner of the couch, clutching the receiver. She could call Nick Alexander, her partner at Security Systems International in San Francisco. Before she left, she'd asked him to get confirmation that the two remaining canvasses in the Proverb Series were still safe at their respective museums, and the responses might have come in by now. But Nick was rarely in the office before eleven these days, and she wasn't in the mood to listen to Phyllis—their secretary—bitch about his tardiness. On the other hand, Steve Rafferty, her current lover, would have been at his desk in the investigations department of Great American Insurance Company since eight. But Rafferty, like E.J., would try to talk her into letting him come over here, and his pleas would be far more difficult to resist.

No, she decided, no more calls. It would be better to order in a light supper and then rest until she had to leave for her appointment with Matt Wickins at a pub called the Starving Ox.

LONDON'S EAST END was a part of the city that Joanna hadn't ventured into for more than twenty years. Then she'd been barely out of her teens, a runaway from college—and from an upper-middle-class New Jersey suburb—who had gotten involved in some very bad things in Europe and would go on to become involved in more of the same in England. Time and luck had changed her for the better; the

Whitechapel district was just as grim as she imagined it had been a hundred years before when Jack the Ripper had stalked its narrow alleys. Its grimy brick buildings seemed to lean heavily on one another for support. Public housing projects had risen too high and barren to make them decent habitations; even their playgrounds were unfriendly, their equipment rusted and vandalized. Everywhere there was demolition and construction: excavations pitted the ground; cranes rose toward the sky. Modern high rises loomed behind blocks of prewar housing slated to be razed. Vacant lots were mounded with debris; the gutters were littered; abandoned buildings with broken windows and graffiti-smeared walls further blighted the landscape. A cold wind blew unceasingly.

But there was life here, too—and of a different, more hopeful sort than Joanna remembered. The narrower streets—alleyways, actually—teemed with people. Mellow light from shaded windows provided safe illumination for the broken and buckled sidewalks. Many of the people were Asian (which in England meant from India and Pakistan); a large number of the adults wore saris or turbans. Diapered babies rode on their mothers' hips, and older ones in jeans and T-shirts darted between clunker cars lining the curbs. As she drove carefully along one of these alleys in the rental car that had been waiting for her at the hotel, Joanna caught the pungent aroma of Indian cooking and spied a small restaurant with a western-style lunch counter and travel posters of Bombay sprucing its cracked walls.

She reached the end of the block—which she'd turned into by mistake—and reminded herself to keep to the left when rounding the corner. The car was a Ford Fiesta, easy to handle, but the right-hand drive made her feel she hadn't maneuvered an automobile in years. That would pass quickly, she knew: she had always become used to the difference in hours. David had been a nervous driver—nervous because he knew his aggressiveness and quick temper made him a danger—and he'd usually left the task to her, particularly in England. She smiled now, remembering how he—from the passenger's seat—would rail at other drivers and the custom of right-hand drive: "It's the British's arrogant way of showing the rest of us just how goddamned superior they think they are!" But he hadn't really meant it; David had been an ardent Anglophile, down to the toes of his Savile Row shoes.

She had to circle the block to get back to Whitechapel Road and then—God willing—the smaller street where the Starving Ox was located. For a panicky moment she thought she'd misjudged where she was and would be forced to shoot over the Thames into South London on the Tower Bridge. Then the road branched and led her the right way; on a corner in front of her appeared an establishment with dingy amber lighting and a wooden sign cut in a bovine shape. She pulled into the curb lane and looked for a place to wedge the Fiesta. When she found one, it was a bit too far down the deserted street for her taste. Nevertheless, she got out and locked the car, then looked around and started toward the pub, tucking her shoulder bag close under her arm.

Her present reaction to the East End, she thought, was telling of the change more than twenty years had wrought in her. Then she'd been reckless and uncaring, self-destructive and very, very naive. Now she was cautious and forward-thinking; she had a regard for herself and a streetwise sense that the young woman of twenty-one wouldn't have been capable of imagining. It had been born during the next decade, when she'd been forced to grow up and admit her own mistakes and meet the world on her own terms.

Well, she thought ruefully as she paused and studied the shabby facade of the Starving Ox, that wasn't completely true. Nice to romanticize herself, but she was *still* admitting her mistakes, and the world as yet hadn't given in to her unconditional demands. She'd had to face the biggest mistake of all not very long ago when she'd told her son she'd hidden the true facts of his birth from him for his whole life. Coming back here to Whitechapel and dealing with Matt Wickens would only open up one more of those old cans of worms....

Joanna stood outside the circle of light cast by a street lamp and watched the figures that were dimly visible through the windows of the pub. To tourists, a London pub means stained glass, old polished wood, dart games, velvet sofas, and genteel patrons. The Starving Ox was fly-specked mirrors, cracked plastic, a jukebox and video games, rickety stools—and drunks, two of whom were just emerging. Joanna waited until they stopped on the sidewalk, argued about where to go next, and lurched off in the opposite direction from where she stood. Then she went up and stepped into the pub's noisy smoke-filled room.

Its occupants were mostly men dressed in work clothes. They lounged in groups around the tables or stood alone at the bar. The jukebox was playing an incongruous country-and-western song about El Paso; the men at the tables nearest it raised their voices over the wail of mournful guitars. When Joanna entered, a couple of the patrons looked curiously at her, but quickly glanced away. They came here not to meet women but to engage in that brand of male fellowship that seems to flourish in working-class bars the world over.

As Joanna's eyes became accustomed to the gloom, they began to smart, and she remembered how so many more English smoke than do their American counterparts. She made a survey of the bar and the tables, but saw no one who resembled Matt Wickins. Would she recognize him after all these years? she wondered. He'd sounded the same on the phone when she'd reached him here earlier, but often a person's voice was the last thing to change—

A hand touched her shoulder from behind. The familiar voice said, "There you are. I must have followed you in."

She turned and faced Matt. He hadn't changed much. His dark hair was streaked with gray, but he still wore it on the long side with a thatch of it hanging limply over his forehead; his body retained the wiry slenderness of youth. And his eyes...those would never change. They were yellow, like a cat's, and the intensity of their gaze diminished the rest of his narrow, sharp-featured face. Those eyes made Matt at once both memorable and forgettable; after a first meeting a person would remember that unblinking yellow stare, yet come away with only the vaguest impression of his overall appearance. For a man of Matt's pursuits, this was an advantage.

He smiled at Joanna, a tight quirk of narrow lips that elongated his other features; then before she could speak he guided her to a window table that had just been vacated. "What's your pleasure?" he asked, motioning at the bar.

"Lager, a half. No—make it a pint."

"Right." He nodded and went to fetch the drinks.

Joanna shrugged out of the light suede jacket she wore with her sweater and jeans, then rummaged in her purse for a Kleenex. The smoke was already making her eyes tear and was bothering her sinuses; she'd have to remember to pick up a decongestant. Matt returned and set two pints of lager on the table.

"You're looking well." He raised his glass to her, and she saw he still wore a heavy onyx ring on his left hand. Matt had appropriated the ring from a house in the suburbs of Paris during the commission of one of his first jobs, and he'd worn it ever since as a sort of memento of the beginning of his somewhat dubious career.

She said, "You're looking well, too."

"That's a matter of perspective. My back's been acting up lately, and given my old problems with my digestion . . . well, you never know."

Now she smiled, remembering his tendency toward hypochondria.

"Go ahead, laugh," he said moodily. "You always did, anyway."

"Hardly ever."

"Bah!"

"Still, given that it's been over twenty years, you haven't changed much."

"Well, you have. Quite the lady, aren't you? I heard you married rich."

"Where did you hear that?"

"You'd be surprised how word gets around in my circles. Or maybe you wouldn't—after all, you found me, didn't you?"

It was on the tip of her tongue to tell him he hadn't gone far enough to be difficult to find, but instead she said, "My circles aren't all that different from yours."

Matt's eyes flickered in annoyance. "Always the one with the snappy reply, weren't you? No reason that should have changed. But don't think you're about to pull any surprises on me. I know, for instance, that you crossed paths with Tony Parducci last spring."

That surprised *her*, but she wasn't going to give him the satisfaction of seeing it. She merely nodded.

"And I know about that company you own . . . what's its name?"

"Security Systems International." She took out one of her business cards and handed it to him. He stuffed it in his pocket without looking at it.

Matt drained his glass abruptly and stood. "Want another?"

"Not yet, thanks."

The trip to the bar apparently gave him time to conquer his annoyance, because when he returned he wore an expression of faint amusement bordering on the condescending. "You know," he said, "I don't know why I'm even talking to you. Twenty years, and not a word. And suddenly you ring me up and ask to see me. That tells me you want something—and it's neither my witty conversation nor my super body."

Joanna gripped her glass. "You're right. I do want something."

"And why should I even consider giving it to you? You left without a word, without a warning. Not even a ruddy note. If it hadn't been for Christopher running into you at Victoria Station that day, I shouldn't have known you'd gone back to the Continent."

There was a raw undertone to Matt's words that surprised her. She'd never suspected that it mattered to him whether she'd stayed or gone. "I did go to the Continent, but only briefly."

"And then?"

"North Africa. Asia. For a while I worked in Manila."

"And then you went to San Francisco and got yourself a rich husband."

"It wasn't quite that way."

"Wasn't it? Well, no matter. But answer this, just to satisfy my curiosity: Why the sudden departure?"

She thought back to that long-ago day in the dreary tenement room they'd shared. Remembered the cold, the rain streaking the broken and taped glass of the window. Saw herself standing by it, then turning at the knock on the door.

"Why?" Matt repeated.

"Someone came to see me. I had to get out fast."

"Someone. Tony Parducci?"

". . . Yes."

"And he wanted to know what you'd done with his kid—his and yours."

She nodded.

"Why didn't you ask me to help you? You knew how I felt about him; that was the reason you came to me in the first place."

She was silent.

"Why, dammit!"

Joanna reached across the table and put her hand on Matt's arm to silence him. Her fingers tightened on his sleeve as she remembered the rush of shock and fear she'd felt when she looked through the door's peephole and saw Parducci standing in the dark hallway of the tenement.

Matt loosened her fingers none too gently and pushed her hand away. "No matter," he said. "We won't talk of it. It's history—the ancient variety."

"No, I owe you that much—"

"You owe me nothing. Now tell me what it is you want, and I'll see if there's anything I can do for you."

She had just begun to sketch in the general outline of her plan, though, when Matt looked around the pub and silenced her. "This is no place to discuss such matters," he said. "We'd best go."

"Where?"

"My flat."

"No, I don't think—"

"Mrs. Stark"—he made the term of address sound slightly derisive—"I assure you that I have more important concerns than knocking off a quick piece of tail. Besides, you're a grown woman in your forties, and not exactly inexperienced. Surely you'd be capable of fending off one equally middle-aged ex-lover?"

Now that he put it on such terms, her hesitation seemed comic. She smiled wryly.

Matt stood. "Shall we?"

She picked up her jacket and bag and followed him outside.

FOUR

On the sidewalk Matt paused and said, "I assume you came by car?"

"Yes. Did you?"

"No. Don't own one of the bloody things." He stuffed his hands in the pockets of his jeans and hunched his shoulders. It was the sort of motion one might make against the East End's cold wind, but Joanna also remembered him adopting the same posture many times when on the defensive. Matt, she realized, was probably broke and ashamed to admit it.

"My car's this way," she said. "It's a rental, one of those Ford Fiestas."

"Nasty little buggers."

"Yes. Would you mind driving—seeing as you know the way?"

He grunted ungraciously but accepted the keys.

Matt's building confirmed her suspicions about his financial plight. It was one of a block of drab Victorians near the London Hospital and not far from Whitechapel Road. The houses here had had some small claim to elegance seventy-five or a hundred years ago, but now were broken up into small flats or bed-sitters. Several were completely dark and fenced off preparatory to the arrival of the wrecker's ball. The block was a pathetic reminder of a long-gone age; and considering the decrepitude into which it had sunk, one best obliterated.

Stone steps led up to Matt's house behind a set of ornamental front gates. The gates creaked as he pushed them open, and when Joanna touched one to avoid stumbling on the broken sidewalk, flecks of rust came away on her hand. She followed him up the steps and waited as he unlocked the door. When he motioned her into the foyer, a dank, unpleasant smell came to her nostrils; it stirred memories of the odors of poverty and decay that had filled the tenement where they'd shared a room twenty years before. Memories of that, and a vague sense of something else—something more unpleasant, and also associated with Matt.

She glanced up, a question forming on her lips, but he was fumbling with his keys again, apparently oblivious to the fetid air. The foyer was lit by a bare yellowish bulb; its rays made a long V of Matt's lean face, accentuated the dark half circles under his eyes and the hollows of his cheekbones. She had a sudden premonition of what he might look like as a corpse, and drew back, both repulsed and concerned. Matt obviously hadn't been eating well, might even be ill; a residue of long-dormant affection sparked within her.

Before she could speak, he put his hand on her shoulder and wordlessly pushed her toward the long hallway beyond the foyer. They moved down the narrow dingy space, past two doors on the left side and a stairway on the right, to another doorway beneath the staircase. Matt unlocked a dead bolt and said, "Watch your step going down."

He flicked a switch inside the door frame. Another bare bulb came on, showing steps leading to a basement. The air was even worse here, and the once-yellow walls were grayish-green with mold. Joanna began to descend, her boot heels catching a couple of times on the cracked and torn rubber stair tread. She took care not to touch the walls or railing. A feeling of long-repressed fear was rising within her, and she knew she would cry out if she came into contact with anything here.

At the foot of the stairs Matt used his keys on yet another dead bolt. When the door to the flat swung open, the memory Joanna had been keeping in check broke free and rushed to the forefront of her consciousness.

On the surface, what lay ahead of her was a perfectly ordinary flat for this part of the city—drab and depressing, full of thrift-shop furnishings and devoid of any attempts at decoration. What had been the kitchen and scullery of the Victorian were now Matt's living room and kitchenette; beyond the frayed burlap curtain across from the door would be a bedroom and rudimentary bathroom made from what had been the pantry. Overhead piping was exposed and ugly; the walls were a water-stained green; the black linoleum squares curled at the edges. One high window opened in the side wall; when Matt switched on a shadeless floor lamp, its light picked out the shape of bars beyond the glass.

An ordinary room, she told herself, fighting for control. She'd never been here before. Never.

But of course she had—at least to one very like it. Had been there on that terrible night with Matt, and on many other nights as well, in her own miserable, sweat-soaked dreams.

She spun around to leave and stumbled into the door frame.

Behind her Matt said, "Joanna?"

Starting to gag, she grabbed the frame for support. Forced the gagging down. What came out was a whimper.

"Joanna!" Matt's hands touched her shoulders. "What the bloody hell?"

Beads of sweat covered her forehead. She put both hands to her face, fingertips clearing the moisture away.

The pressure of Matt's hands remained the same. He waited.

When she could speak she said, "Oh Jesus, Matt—the room!"

"I admit it's not much, but surely you haven't become so caught up in your wealthy life-style—"

"Matt!" She broke loose from his grasp and whirled. His face was genuinely puzzled. "You don't even see it, do you?" she asked.

"See what?"

"This room! It's exactly like the one...that woman on Worship Street...the night—"

"Jesus God," he said.

She watched as he compressed his thin lips, then turned his head slowly, surveying their surroundings. She saw a comprehension there; he put his hand to his right temple and blinked. "You're right, of course," he said. "I never did see it until now. I wonder why."

"I don't know. You certainly should have. God, that was the worst night of my life."

"It wasn't too lovely for me either, my lady."

His voice was surprisingly gentle, and he'd used the term by which he'd addressed her in those days. It gave her a strange measure of comfort and enabled her to move away from the door toward a lumpy armchair under the high barred window. She set her purse on the floor and sat, pulling her feet up under her.

Matt shut the door and turned the dead bolt. "You all right?"

"I think so."

"I've some brandy. It's not expensive, but—"

"It will do, thanks."

He went to a built-in cupboard—part of the original scullery—that extended the length of one wall and removed a bottle and two glasses. When he held out a full snifter to her, his hand was unsteady. "Gave me a turn there," he said.

"You see the resemblance?"

His shrug was too casual. "It's a basement flat, yes. Otherwise—"

"Matt."

"All right, yes, I see it. But there's no point in reliving all that now, is there? Not any more than there was in my hammering at you in the pub about why you'd left me. So drink up. Not such a bad brandy, is it?"

She sipped the drink. Its flavor was what she imagined a cross between wine vinegar and gasoline would produce. "Not bad at all."

"You always were a liar."

"But a good one." She drank some more. Maybe, she thought, the stuff would grow on her.

"Not anymore." Matt sat on a broken-down hassock. "I find I can read you like a book. But I'm afraid this is the best I can do. Those of us who are recently out of Winson Green must begin at the bottom and work up again, you now."

Joanna sat up straighter. "Winson Green? You mean the prison in Birmingham?"

He grimaced, eyes narrowing and shading to a smoky amber. "Something your contacts didn't fill you in on when they supplied my number, eh?"

"No. What happened? How long were you in?"

"Five years. What happened is a job went wrong—my own bad luck and judgment. Enough said about that; it's why I'm living in this basement and only able to afford bad liquor."

"That will change." But she wasn't so sure: Matt had the look of a man on his way down.

He nodded, apparently not so capable of reading her as he claimed. "You know me that well, at least."

She sipped the awful brandy, suddenly concerned. Having just gotten out of prison, would Matt have the contacts to do what she wanted? More important, could she trust him now? When she'd included him in her plans, she'd been thinking of her former lover as essentially like her: a man with a devious, unconventional turn of mind and a checkered past, but still only a reckless adventurer at heart. But what had his years in prison—and before—made of him?

He was watching her, the planes and angles of his face highlighted and shadowed by the lamp's rays. His eyes were slits, the half circles under them seeming black and sunken.

"Afraid of me now?" he asked.

"No."

"But not so sure."

"When was I ever sure of you?" She tried to make the words sound light. They didn't.

He shrugged and reached for the brandy bottle. "If you're worried about whether I can handle whatever it is you want done, don't be. I've already reestablished myself, I'm back in the game. If you're worried about my dependability... Well, only you can determine whether you want to take that risk."

She hesitated, quickly reviewing her options. None of the others was feasible at this point.

"I'll take it," she said.

Of course, she didn't tell him everything. There was no need, for instance, for him to know that the painting currently residing at Christopher Burgess's gallery was not a genuine Brueghel. Neither did he have to hear the details of her plan after his part in it was finished, nor the identities of the other persons who would be involved. What it boiled down to was that she didn't trust Matt any more now than she had twenty years before. She would use him—but cautiously.

When she spoke of putting an end to the long career of Antony Parducci, Matt's eyes glittered with approval. "You knew I'd stand with you all the way, after what he did to me," he said. "Just as you knew I'd take you in when you came to me from Italy all those years ago."

Joanna didn't like to be reminded of those days, when she'd felt she needed to depend on a man for her survival.

She ignored what he'd said and went on to tell him about the "newly discovered" Brueghel. At the mention of the Bloomfield and Burgess Gallery, Matt's mouth tightened.

"What's wrong?" she asked.

He was silent, reaching for his glass.

"It's Christopher, isn't it? I know you haven't been in touch—"

"It's more than being out of touch, but no matter. A man who goes honest and forgets his friends... Well, you can understand how I feel."

She waited, but Matt said nothing else, and he avoided her eyes. She was certain there was more to the story, but she also knew him well enough not to press for the rest of it.

When she'd finished explaining his part in her plan, Matt said, "Let me ask you this. You claim Parducci's the one who's been arranging the thefts of other paintings in the Proverb Series. I don't dispute that; he specialized in French and Dutch art, and he's the only broker I know of with the clientele and the contacts. But how can you be certain he'll hear of this new one—and come after it?"

"There'll be major publicity on the find."

"Oh?"

"I'm arranging it. Once he hears about *There Hangs the Knife*, Parducci won't be able to resist the challenge. Which, incidentally, is what the title of the painting means: a challenge."

"Well, I expect you'd know what motivates him. And you'd know how to go about the publicity angle. After all, you've got friends in all the right places now."

Matt didn't seem to want to turn loose of the change in their relative circumstances, yet she sensed that needling her about it gave him no pleasure. It was like the masochistic attraction one's tongue finds in a sore tooth: poke at it, cause pain, stop, then return to poke again. Matt continued to harp on the subject as they haggled over the fee for his cooperation, but in the end he agreed to be her liaison in the shadowy world of brokers and middlemen, fagins, and low-level thieves in which he operated. Because of the long chain of complex interrelationships between the highly placed broker—Parducci—and the young and probably impoverished thief who would actually procure the painting, there were bound to be leaks. When Matt ferreted out one of these, his job would be to insinuate himself into the arrangements.

"Remember," Joanna said, "I want the client, as well as Parducci. One well-publicized arrest among the art-collecting elite will scare the hell out of anyone with larceny on his mind—at least for a while."

"And put me straight out of work."

"There'll always be a market for your particular talents, I'm afraid. Besides, I'm paying you damned well."

"Not well enough."

She glared at him.

"All right, Mrs. Stark," he said. "We have a bargain."

WHEN JOANNA RETURNED to the Primrose Hill Hotel at a little after one that morning, she found a message from her business partner, Nick Alexander, shoved under her door. As far as she could decipher the night man's crabbed hand-writing, it said that the two remaining Proverb Series paintings were safe—one at the Rijksmuseum in Amsterdam, the other at Rutgers University Art Gallery in New Brunswick, New Jersey.

Joanna fingered the message slip thoughtfully. New Brunswick wasn't all that far from Tenafly, where she'd grown up. In fact, she could remember a high school field trip to the Rutgers Gallery, although she didn't recall the Brueghel. It had been a warm spring day; she'd dressed up in a floral-printed shirtwaist over a crinoline which—she'd thought—made her skirt sway entrancingly. On the bus she'd held hands with her boyfriend Larry; halfway through the gallery tour they'd ducked out for a special treat—banana splits. God, how the world—and she—had changed.

If she hadn't been bone-tired she would have reflected on those changes for hours. As it was, she crumpled the message slip and dropped it on the coffee table, then took off her clothes and crawled into bed without brushing her teeth or removing what little remained of her makeup.

The cottage was no longer haunted by David's ghost: she had laid it to rest by confronting larger and more disturbing specters.

FIVE

THE EDGAR WALLACE PUB, on Essex just off Fleet Street, is a dark-paneled and mirrored journalists' hangout decorated with playbills and photos and other memorabilia of the 1920s mystery writer, who once was a journalist himself. At noon the next day Joanna bypassed the pub's lower bar and climbed the steep stairway to the second-story dining room, where she ordered a half pint of lager and studied the menu while the barmaid was drawing her beer. There was a good assortment of pub grub—that melange of hearty sausage rolls, pasties, cold plates, and chips that belies the largely false stereotype of unpalatable English food—and her stomach growled in pleasant anticipation.

Pubs and restaurants in London do their most brisk business after twelve-thirty or one, and Joanna had the dining room to herself. She'd suggested an early meeting with Meg Knight, Nick Alexander's contact on the London *Times*, for just that reason—so they could talk without the possibility of being overheard—and now she surveyed the room with satisfaction before sitting at a table in a small private alcove. The room was old-fashioned by design rather than attrition: the dark brown wainscoting was freshly painted; the heavy velvet drapes were obviously new; the fans that turned lazily overhead were of a type currently on display in electrical supply houses. But a serious attempt seemed to have been made at preserving the spirit of Wallace's day, and Joanna imagined rather fancifully that the photo of the writer that stared down from the wall at her wore a benign, approving expression.

She recognized the woman who entered fifteen minutes later from Nick's description: tall and slender, conservatively dressed, with blond hair pulled back in a classic French knot. Knight's prominent facial features were the sort that immediately identified the person as English; her skin had a healthy outdoorsy glow, and only the finest of lines at the corners of her eyes hinted that she was well into her forties. Knight was one of the most powerful figures on the London art scene: favorable notice from her could launch a gallery or an artist's career; negative comment could destroy one. From Nick, Joanna had heard that Meg Knight was a hardheaded woman who placed highest priority on her professional reputation and career. Since a great part of Joanna's scheme to entrap Antony Parducci depended on the reporter's cooperation, it would be necessary to convince her of the advantages of such participation.

Knight offered Joanna her hand and called to the barmaid for a gin. While it was being fetched, they exchanged pleasantries, Knight inquiring after Nick (who had, Joanna suspected, briefly been the reporter's lover). The gin arrived, and Knight drank off half of it quickly.

"You've seen the menu?" she asked.

Joanna nodded.

"They do nice cold plates here, if you like that sort of thing—roast beef, Norwegian prawns, chicken. If we order now she'll bring them after our second drinks."

Joanna agreed to both the prawns and the second drink, then sipped her lager slowly, studying the other woman as she conferred with the barmaid. On her return to the table, Knight removed cigarettes and lighter from an oversized leather bag and lit up, dragging deeply and studying Joanna in return.

"Nick tells me you're here on some pretty murky business," she said. "His words, not mine."

"He would describe it that way. What else did he tell you?"

"He mentioned something about an obsession. It all sounds quite fascinating."

"I suppose so, given Nick's flair for the dramatic." And his disapproval of what she was up to. "Are you familiar with the name Antony Parducci?"

Knight pursed her lips in thought, then nodded. "Italian art thief. Specialized in Dutch and Flemish works for a highly placed clientele. For a long time, beginning in the mid-seventies, he was presumed dead. Now it's rumored he's resurfaced as a top broker. Did I hear something about an abortive theft he engineered in your own city last year?"

"Yes, in the fall. I was the one who performed the abortion."

"Ah." The lines around Meg Knight's eyes crinkled with pleasure. Like most true art lovers, Joanna assumed, Knight had a hatred of thieves, particularly those who assisted a rich clientele in acquiring masterpieces for their private collections—thus depriving the public of the chance to view them.

Fresh drinks arrived. Joanna paused until the woman was back behind the bar. "One of the artists whose work Parducci has always seemed to have a ready market for is Pieter Brueghel," she went on. "In fact, the last theft he was suspected of personally pulling off was of a small Brueghel from a museum in Brussels; that was in seventy-six. Do you follow the news of art thefts very closely?"

"Reasonably."

"Then you've heard of the paintings in Brueghel's Proverb Series that have been stolen during the past few months."

Knight nodded.

"Two disappeared from a gallery in Milan," Joanna said. "Another from a small museum in Vienna. Two are still safe, in Amsterdam and the States."

"And you feel Parducci is responsible for the thefts—and after the entire series."

"It stands to reason. He's one of perhaps two or three brokers who have that sort of clientele."

Knight pursed her lips again. "Well," she said after a moment, "you would know more about that than I, seeing as it's your end of this business. What do you propose to do—trap Parducci?"

"Parducci and his client."

"That I would be delighted to see. It's time someone snared one of those bastards. Seems an excellent one to make an example of, too, since whoever is taking delivery of those paintings has to have unusually large resources."

"Exactly. The bigger the client who gets caught, the better the example to other collectors."

"In theory, it's a good plan. But surely you don't intend to carry it out on your own?"

"Up to a point, but then Scotland Yard will take over. I've a contact on the Art Squad with whom I've been talking all along. I called him this morning, so he knows I'm about to begin."

"Who is that—Evans?"

"Yes."

Knight nodded in approval. The New Scotland Yard Art Squad, formed in 1968 to investigate thefts and other art-related crimes, was considered one of the best in the world, and Evans was their top man. He was a bit of a maverick, willing to take risks and adopt unconventional methods—which was why Joanna had gone to him with her plan in the first place.

Their lunches arrived. They busied themselves with knives and forks and napkins for a moment. Then the reporter came to the crux of the matter. "Now . . . where do I fit into your plan?"

"There is a recently discovered sixth painting in the Proverb Series at the Bloomfield and Burgess Galleries. They'll soon be displaying and auctioning it."

Knight's fork paused above her plate. "Not a genuine Brueghel?"

"No, it's a fake. Do you know of Jenny Sherman?"

"The copyist? Yes."

"It's a genuine Sherman."

"Commissioned by . . . ?"

"Me."

"And?"

"I want you to publicize this find. If you write it up in glowing detail for the *Times*, other major papers and the wire services will pick up the story. And Parducci will also pick up on it. My guess is that both he and his client will find the painting irresistible."

Knight reached for her third gin, eyes narrowed. "It would hardly be to my credit to have it appear that I was foxed by a forged masterpiece."

"But it *would* be to your credit when it came out that you'd been instrumental in apprehending one of the art world's most notorious brokers—not to mention the collector who buys from him. Especially when the inside story was revealed in your own exclusive."

Knight bit her lip, her eyes moving rapidly as she calculated the risk. "I'll have to think about this," she said after a few seconds.

"Of course."

For the rest of the meal Meg Knight's gaze was fixed on her plate, and she ate—Joanna suspected—without really tasting the food. The dining room began to fill; people greeted the reporter and she replied absently. Occasionally she would ask Joanna questions. Where was she staying?

Had she visited London often? Joanna also suspected that it wouldn't have mattered what she replied; Knight was preoccupied with evaluating the proposal. When the dishes had been cleared and coffee brought, Knight leaned back in her chair, lighting a cigarette.

"How do you know this won't become one great, embarrassing failure?" she asked.

"I don't, although I think my plans are solid. But if it does go wrong, you can write your exclusive anyway, and place the blame squarely on me."

Knight shook her head. "Not good enough."

Joanna felt her palms prickle. Time to play her last card. "How about this: if my plan goes wrong, I'll give you a human-interest angle—one that will justify your getting involved, and fascinate even the *Times'* readers."

"Does this have to do with the obsession Nick mentioned?"

"Yes."

"Is he aware of what that is?"

"No. He's only aware that I have what he considers an unnatural interest in Antony Parducci."

"And of course it would do me no good to ask why."

"No."

"Whatever story that comes out of this would be an exclusive?"

"I would do everything I could to protect your exclusivity."

"Your best efforts are all I ask."

Joanna waited.

"Who else is involved in this operation?" Knight asked. "Richard Bloomfield?"

"Only Christopher Burgess."

"I see. Anyone else?"

"Contacts I have in the art underworld."

"Who?"

"Like a good reporter, I protect my sources."

Knight smiled wryly. "Any chance of getting an interview or two?"

Joanna thought of Matt: his self-dramatization, his opportunism—and his knowledge of her past. "Perhaps. I'll have to see how things shape up."

Knight nodded and picked up her cigarettes and lighter, put them into her bag. "I'll need more time to consider this."

"I'll need to know by three."

"Why?"

"Other preparations depend on your answer."

Knight stood. Stalemate, Joanna thought. "Shall I call you?" she asked.

Knight reached into her bag for a card and set it on the table. "I'll be at the office. Call me at two forty-five." Then she turned and went through the glass door to the stairs.

Joanna let out an explosive sigh that made a man at the next table glance her way. Her watch told her it was one-ten now. An hour and thirty-five minutes before she'd know whether this vital element in her plan had fallen into place.

To kill time, she walked down to the Thames and along the Embankment. The air was muggy and sultry today. Debris bobbed on the river: Styrofoam cups, wrappers, cigarette packages—all manner of revolting stuff. A long line of tour buses, both British and foreign, stood near where the excursion boats docked. Bus drivers congregated, smoking and complaining about their passengers. Joanna cut back toward Charing Cross through the Embankment underground station. People rushed by, bound for trains. Many of the younger ones wore thrift-shop clothing and odd spiky haircuts. The ethnic mix was more varied than she remembered it; a great many of the expressions she encountered bordered on the hostile. Except for the style of the surrounding architecture, she could have been in New York or

Paris or Los Angeles, and she reflected on how the great cities of the world were becoming more and more the same; along with their inhabitants, they were losing their individuality and the charm that had once made them distinctive.

The thought depressed her, and for a few minutes she contemplated a visit to the National Gallery to cheer herself up, but she knew its collections were too numerous and comprehensive for the brief time allotted her. Finally she crossed tourist-jammed Trafalgar Square to the section of Charing Cross Road where some of the city's best second-hand bookshops are located. One of those had a wonderful collection of art books; she could lose herself while browsing through them.

At exactly quarter to three she called Meg Knight. The reporter's voice was crisp and decisive. "I've decided to do the story," she said, "provided you take all steps to ensure exclusivity."

"I will."

"And I also want an interview with at least one of your underworld contacts, as you call them."

Joanna hesitated. Perhaps she could stall Knight on that, until it no longer seemed important to her. Or she could coach Matt on what he should say and trot him out briefly for Meg's inspection. After all, she thought, the truly damning things he knew about her past would only put him in a bad light, too. "I'll arrange it," she said.

They discussed various technicalities, and Joanna promised to call Knight with further details at home at nine that evening. She caught a taxi for the Bloomfield and Burgess Galleries with only five minutes to spare.

SIX

"FIRST I'LL NEED to consult with my security man, to see if there's a way to leave the Brueghel relatively unprotected while safeguarding our other stock, and not have the arrangement appear too obvious a trap." Christopher made a note on a ruled pad on the desk in front of him, then looked up at Joanna. "I don't know how long it will take to get him out here."

"Maybe I could help you. I know a fair amount about alarm systems."

"Ah, yes—that firm of yours was originally an alarm installation company, wasn't it? Good, we'll take a look around later. Perhaps we won't need to consult my man at all. It's best to involve as few people as possible."

Joanna nodded in agreement. They were in Christopher's second-floor office, away from the prying eyes and ears of Ivy Harrison, the gaunt gray-haired woman who had admitted her to the gallery the day before. Ivy, Christopher had explained, was his bookkeeper, secretary, and woman-of-all-tasks. She was invaluable to him, and so sure of her position that she didn't hesitate to poke her nose into any and all goings-on at the gallery—her efforts to that end being made more simple by her occupying a third-story flat in the building. "We'll have to watch for Ivy," he'd cautioned. "She's a stern woman and a model of rectitude. You can rest assured she wouldn't approve of what we have in mind."

Now he flipped through the pages of a desk calendar and made a few more notations on the pad. In spite of an initial air of sulkiness—apparently he had considered yesterday's

mention of their mutual past to be a form of blackmail—
Christopher had perked up as she unfolded her plan. His
eyes gleamed wickedly as he looked at what he'd written,
then he circled two things that looked to be dates. Joanna
suspected that the side of his character he'd striven to re-
press all these years—the side that had made him a boon
companion to Matt Wickins in the old days—was finding
welcome release. She realized she liked this afternoon's
Christopher far more than the slick sycophant he'd become
since the day she ran into him on the street corner and took
him to Richard Bloomfield's gallery.

"All right now," he said. "Let's assume for the moment
that you'll be able to make sense of my security system or,
barring that, that I'll be able to get my man out here quickly.
Then Meg Knight will need to run her story on
our...amazing discovery. That should take less than a week.
I know Meg; she acts swiftly, particularly when she senses
career advancements in the offing. A hard woman, Meg."

"I liked her."

"You would. As I was saying, the story will run quite
soon."

"But then the other papers and wire services will need
time to pick it up."

"Never fear—it will take no time at all. And if by chance
they miss it, Meg will whisper a few choice words into a few
carefully selected ears. If anything, she's not without resources."

Joanna smiled at the strong note of disapproval in his
voice when he spoke of Knight. Christopher liked his
women docile and somewhat stupid. "All right," she said,
"how long do you think all that will take?"

He hesitated, pushing his glasses up from where they'd
slipped on his nose. "A week?"

"Sounds about right. Then, of course, we have to allow time for Parducci to find out about the painting and make his arrangements. He'll move fast; he always has."

"You sound quite sure of him. But I suppose you should be. You've been trying to trap the bastard for years."

"Yes. I'm guessing it won't take him more than a week."

"And in the meantime I'll have preparations of my own—notices of the sale will have to go out, as well as a special brochure for my good customers. I can't deviate from the usual procedure, or someone's bound to become suspicious." Christopher's pencil stabbed at the full circled date. "Shall we say May fifth for the preview, and schedule the auction for the seventh?"

"That's reasonable."

"It's a ways off. What do you plan to do in the interim?"

"Take a vacation. I thought I'd drive down and see Richard."

Christopher frowned.

"What?" Joanna said. "You don't want me to tell him about this?"

"There's really no need for that, is there?"

"You're the best judge of what to do. After all, you said he allows you free rein here. If you don't want me to mention it, I won't."

"It might be best. After all, we don't want to involve any more people—"

"Right. But to further answer your question, I plan to travel around the countryside for a few days. It's been a long time since I've visited here, and there are places I'd like to see again and people I'd like to get in touch with. I'll need to touch bases with you, and with Matt. Especially Matt, to keep tabs on what he's found out and what he's been able to do."

Most of the animation had faded from Christopher's face as soon as she mentioned Matt Wickens.

"What is it with you two?" she asked.

He shrugged. "The usual thing that happens to a friendship when one party moves up in the world and the other moves down. Matt's a changed man."

"A changed man living in reduced circumstances, as they politely put it."

Christopher eyed her with interest. "How did you get on with him?"

"Not too badly. He liked the plan. I knew he would, given his past dealings with Antony Parducci."

"Set Matt up, did he?"

Joanna nodded. "It was in Paris. Matt was living there, and he did a lot of jobs with Parducci—that was when Parducci still personally pulled off the thefts. Anyway, there was one job that he knew would go bad, and he let Matt take the fall for it. Matt ran back here before they could prosecute."

"So you knew both of them in Paris?"

"Yes. Didn't Matt ever talk to you about that?"

"No. He merely said you were an old friend from the Continent. Matt always was a talker, but you were the one woman he didn't discuss with anyone. Because of that I always assumed he cared a great deal for you."

Joanna was strangely touched. She'd guessed that Christopher wasn't aware of her association with Parducci, because he surely would have alluded to it at some point had he known. But for Matt to have remained silent, given his penchant for gossip and given the quality of the story he could have told . . .

Parducci had abandoned her when she found she was pregnant with E.J., but later he returned to claim his son. To get the baby safely away from him, she turned to David Stark, her father's best friend from law school, and the one person she'd always known she could trust. But while she was able to depend on David to help with—to adopt and raise—E.J., her pride hadn't permitted her to ask him to help her too. For that she'd gone to Matt—after Parducci had caught up with her in Italy and brutally beaten her. But in doing so, she'd only plunged herself more deeply into trouble.

When she didn't elaborate, the curiosity in Christopher's eyes sharpened, but he didn't ask anything further. Joanna knew that over the years he must have wondered a great deal about her, but he'd never asked for particulars. Part of that unwillingness to pry might have been out of gratitude for her introduction to Richard, but another part could be attributed to Christopher's genuine respect for others' right to privacy.

In order not to further tantalize him with the unsaid, she stood up. "Let's take a look at your alarm system."

"Fine—but first let me send Ivy on an errand."

IT WAS AFTER SIX when Joanna arrived at the Primrose Hill Hotel. Christopher's alarm system had been one she was familiar with, and after some study of the manual she would be able to arrange for whomever Parducci hired to steal the supposed Brueghel to have an easy time of it.

Kind of me, she thought as she kicked off her shoes and scooped up a message slip that had been pushed under the door of the cottage. Kind of me to make the last job he arranges so simple.

The message was from Steve Rafferty; he'd phoned from San Francisco just an hour before. "Hope all is going well. My thoughts and love are with you."

She felt a surge of pleasure, and briefly considered returning the call. But it was morning in California and Rafferty would be in his office at Great American Insurance Company—hardly the place to hold an intimate conversation. She would do better to get up early tomorrow and call him at home during his evening.

Her own evening stretched emptily in front of her. There were old friends—the respectable kind—whom she could call, but the prospect of polite chatter and catching up on the intervening years didn't intrigue her. What did she have in common with such people, anyway? What could she say to them? *I'm plotting to put my former lover and the father of my son behind bars. I've waited over twenty years for the opportunity.*

She smiled, picturing them choking over their gins or sherries. Or better yet, exchanging arch pseudo-sympathetic glances. "The poor dear," they'd say after she left. "She's never recovered from David's death, has become badly unhinged."

Her eyes fell on the burglar alarm manual, but that interested her even less than an evening with incurably stuffy people. Finally she opted for a drink in the hotel bar before dinner in the dining room. The bar was pleasant, dark, and quiet; the food in the dining room was so mediocre that few people ate there. She would have solitude without feeling truly alone, and ample time to consider every facet of her plan—checking and rechecking for possible flaws—before her promised nine o'clock phone call to Meg Knight.

SEVEN

BY THE TIME all the pieces of Joanna's plan were in place and she felt free to leave London, four days had passed and it was Sunday. She drove south through a soft drizzling rain, with no particular destination in mind, eventually ending up at Brighton. It was not a place she had ever visited, and she found it a disappointment. The waterfront attractions were still closed for the season, the elegant hotels facing the pier on King's Road hauntingly deserted. After driving around town for a while, she continued along the waterfront to the adjacent city of Hove and took a room in a Victorian relic with a creaky lift and worn carpet and wallpaper whose roses looked like fat red cabbages. The accommodations suited both her mood and the weather.

While eating a surprisingly good dinner in the cavernous hotel dining room, she alternately glanced at the placid gray sea and paged through a copy of the London *Times*. She was pleased to see that Meg Knight's story on the newly discovered Brueghel had run that morning. The paper had given it excellent placement—on page two, above the fold—since Knight had chosen to play up the irony of one painting in the Proverb Series being discovered in England at the same time that others were disappearing from museums and galleries on the Continent. The story had all the elements for a detective novel, and would be sure to catch the eye of most readers.

Joanna read it twice herself, admiring the reporter's dramatic flair and the way she had turned what might have been news of only limited interest that should be confined to the art page into an item of much wider appeal. But while she felt satisfaction, even excitement, about how smoothly things were going, a discontent that had begun nagging at her somewhere between London and the seaside continued to prickle. She'd long ago come to recognize such feelings as evidence that an unresolved conflict was about to surface; she'd also learned not to force its emergence. The time for dealing with it would come soon enough.

There were old friends in Bournemouth whom she'd planned to phone and visit, but the next morning she decided she wasn't up to seeing anyone. She continued along the coast and cut north at Southampton, finally stopping at Winchester. She avoided the cathedral—English churches depressed her because too many of the long dead were buried under their stone floors; walking over their resting places made her uncomfortably aware of the brevity of her own expected life span. Instead, she spent the rest of the day and part of the next browsing through the shops. Normally she hated shopping; it was something to do through catalogues, or in a quick blitz, list firmly in hand. But now she bought things just for the sake of passing time: a thick handknit sweater for E.J.; an unusual book on textiles for her friend Mary Bennett, who owned the quilt shop near the Sonoma Plaza; a pipe for Nick Alexander, who had recently taken to smoking one; even an absurd pottery figure of a fat pony for herself. Strangely, she could find nothing that seemed appropriate for Steve Rafferty. But then, Rafferty was a man who disliked buying things for himself and didn't much like gifts, either.

The three days she'd spent away from London set a pattern for the rest of the time. She'd start out in the mornings with firm intentions of calling this person or visiting that place, then end up somewhere else, having avoided the phone. She did things that were totally uncharacteristic of her: at Glastonbury she spent hours wandering the ruins of the cathedral; she ate food she wouldn't normally have—a rich chocolate and walnut and whipped cream torte was her entire dinner in Bath; and all the time the discontent nagged....

From Bristol—another place she'd never been and also found she didn't like—she called Matt Wickins at the Starving Ox, as they'd prearranged before she left London. He spoke conspiratorially about "hearing things" and something being "about to happen," but she suspected he was indulging his penchant for melodrama because he hadn't had any success in finding out whether Parducci was in town to make arrangements for the theft. She told Matt she'd call him again in three days when she planned to be at Richard Bloomfield's house in Dorset—one appointment she fully intended to keep.

Later that evening, sitting in a crowded pub and drinking gin and lemon (something else totally uncharacteristic; normally she hated the stuff), she finally put her finger on what was bothering her. In a word, it was revenge: why she was seeking it, and whether it was worth all this time, effort, and money.

In her mildly tipsy state, the concept of vengeance seemed somewhat ludicrous. The picture of a forty-three-year-old woman who had far better things to do with her life setting out to entrap the nemesis of her youth began to strike her as pathetic. Her motivations were altogether too clear—and somewhat shabby. Her scheme seemed merely the device of a fixated woman who wanted to get even with the man who had done her wrong nearly a quarter of a century before.

Of course Antony Parducci *had* done her wrong, had altered her life irrevocably. At a time when she should have been finishing college or holding down her first job or even joining a commune and attending Vietnam War protests, she'd been giving birth to his son in a Paris charity ward. When she should have been carving out a career for herself or marrying and starting a family, she'd given up her son and roamed the world in an effort to escape Parducci, taking meaningless jobs only to support herself at the subsistence level. And later, just when the imagined career or family would have finally become truly rewarding, she had married an older man and played stepmother to her own son. She had loved David Stark, there was no doubt of that, and they had had a good—although too brief—life together. But still, his friends and family had made it difficult for the young second wife whom they resented, and E.J. had acted out a great deal of hostility toward David and her—mainly because he very correctly suspected them of having had an affair for years before the death of the woman whom he supposed to be his natural mother.

"God, what a mess," she said out loud.

The youngish couple at the other end of the table stared at her, then quickly looked away.

It would be nice, she thought, to believe the scenario she'd just constructed. Nice to blame it all on Parducci. What a wonderful justification for her present actions it would make!

But half of the blame, she knew, must rest squarely on her shoulders, in spite of her youth and inexperience back then. And there were no guarantees anyway that had there not been an Antony Parducci, her life would have resembled the orderly one of the scenario. She might not have finished college in any event, and communes and war protests had been shown to be not the glorious experiences depicted in the newsmagazines of the sixties. She might not have carved out a stunning career, either, or the work might have become meaningless and unsatisfying with time. The imagined perfect marriage could have soured; the idealized never-born children could have turned out delinquents or ax murderers. And there would have been no E.J., no David, none of the people and things she now valued.

So much for the happy-ending movie script. What *about* this revenge, then?

Joanna drained her glass and thought about getting another. Then she realized she was more than a little drunk. Too drunk certainly to consider implications, ramifications, consequences. Drunk enough, in fact, that she couldn't pronounce the words right, even in her own head.

Swaying slightly, she got up and made her way out of the smoky pub and down the street to her hotel. If there was one thing life had taught her, it was never to become overly philosophical or to indulge in much deep thinking about something you were too damn drunk to pronounce.

IT WASN'T UNTIL she arrived at Richard Bloomfield's house three days later that she again considered the subject of revenge.

They were seated in his living room and she was—once more uncharacteristically—drinking gin. He had just finished giving her a tour of the place, and she had to admit she was impressed with what he'd done with it. Located outside the two-hundred-fifty-year-old village of Cerne Abbas, the house had formerly been a church. For years it had sat desanctified and deteriorating until Richard had bought it, added a wing, and refurbished the existing building. The room they sat in had been the main section; where the altar had stood was now a stone fireplace; fading sunlight made the four stained-glass side windows glow richly; toward the rear the polished rails of the former choir loft framed a hallway that let onto the second-story bedroom.

Joanna settled into an overstuffed sofa upholstered in a warm nubby brown and glanced appreciatively at the painting on the whitewashed wall above the fireplace. Wisely, Richard had not chosen one with a religious theme that would compete with the windows (wouldn't have anyway, she supposed, since he was the most outspoken of atheists), but instead a worldly Cubist Picasso. Interestingly, the Cubism and stained glass worked perfectly together; Joanna had never realized how similar the two techniques could appear.

"What's the title of the Picasso?" she asked.

Richard turned from the drink cart. He was gray-haired and stooped, with a wizened face that reminded her of a garden gnome—until he smiled. Then he merely looked youthful and elfin. *"The Scorned Woman,"* he said.

"Aha." And then, of course, it came back to her: the discontent, her drunken musings.

Richard's eyes twinkled as he sat down next to her. He was one of the few people she'd ever known whose eyes could actually twinkle. "The title obviously has meaning for you," he said.

"In a way, yes. I was thinking along those lines—not about being scorned, but about taking revenge for it—a couple of days ago."

"And at what conclusions did you arrive?"

"None. I was too drunk."

Richard laughed and toasted her with his glass. "Shall we talk about vengeance—before *we* become too drunk?"

That was one of the wonderful things about Richard: he could engage in endless philosophical discussions without becoming too personal and attempting to link the participants' comments and opinions to their private circumstances. She said, "Sure, why not. What do you think of revenge?"

Never one to speak without reflection, Richard hesitated. "It's fascinating, of course. I'm surprised there haven't been more studies on the subject. Certainly it's been a prime ingredient of myth and reality since the beginning of time."

"A jealous God, and all that?"

"Of course—look at the myth of Creation. God took revenge on Eve for listening to his rival, the serpent, and chucked her and Adam out of the garden. And Medea— there's a double horror. She murdered her husband's lover, then killed her own children to spare them revenge from the dead woman's father."

Joanna grimaced and held out her glass for a refill. She could imagine killing a rival out of jealousy—well, in the abstract she could—but it was beyond her to picture any circumstances that would induce her to harm E.J. Anyone trying to wreak vengeance on him would first have to get past *her*.

Richard brought the fresh drink and sat down again. "To bring it to modern times," he said, "think of some of the relatively recent happenings in your own city; the troubled young man who shot your mayor and the homosexual councilman—the first because he wouldn't restore him to his seat on the council; and the other, as I understand it, because he was gay, a political rival, and 'smirked at him.'"

Joanna was surprised that Richard was so conversant with the Dan White case, possibly the blackest hour in recent San Francisco history. "All right," she said, "I agree that revenge has always been around and is probably here to stay. What else is fascinating about it?"

A long pause. "I'd say the consequences. They're almost always bad."

"Are you certain of that?"

"Take a look at the examples I've given. If there were such a being, don't you think God would rue the day he ran those two out of Eden every time he looked at the world as it is now?"

Joanna smiled and nodded.

"And Medea . . . well, you're a mother."

"Right."

"I don't know a great deal about your councilman—"

"Supervisors, we call them. Dan White."

"He died a suicide, obviously a tortured man."

Joanna was silent. Dan White had shown no remorse during his trial, imprisonment, and parole, but once he was a completely free man, he killed himself.

Richard added, "Of course there's an opposite consequence of vengeance. It's almost always extremely satisfying—at least initially. I suppose it all boils down to whether you're willing to risk satisfaction against possible regret."

"Mmm." She looked down into her drink, feeling regret because she'd gulped the first one so fast. The words *risk* and *against* echoed in a hollow, alcohol-created chamber in her mind.

"Are you willing to risk it, Joanna?"

She looked up into Richard's faded blue eyes. They were keen, inquiring, full of empathy. She hadn't fooled him with pretending theirs was merely an abstract discussion: he suspected she harbored vengeful plans of her own. What he couldn't realize, however, was that they involved the use of his own gallery.

Guilty feelings began to well up. Didn't she and Christopher have an obligation to let Richard know what they were doing—

The phone rang. Both of them started, then laughed self-consciously. In a moment Richard's housekeeper came to the door and announced that the call was for Joanna.

She took it in the cold high-ceilinged foyer, once the church vestibule. It was Matt, phoning from the Starving Ox, sounding extremely agitated.

"You'd best get back here right away," he said.

"Why? What's happened?"

"Don't ask questions, just do as I tell you. Come back to London. The whole bloody thing's about to go bust."

EIGHT

SHE MADE THE TRIP in under three hours, record time. At a little before midnight the pubs and restaurants were mostly closed, the streets of the East End deserted. Abandoned, vandalized buildings stood in darkness, probably harboring squatters. The wind blew cold down the alleyways, rustling the trash in the gutters and setting metal cans to rolling and clanging off the curbs. A swirling fog obscured what few lights remained on, muting their rays until they bled out into the darkness.

Joanna drove directly to the Starving Ox and retraced the route Matt had taken to his building the week before. The narrow lane near Whitechapel Road was clogged with cars on either side. She maneuvered the Fiesta into a cramped space next to some trash cans and walked along the row of dilapidated Victorians toward the one where Matt had his basement flat. Faint light showed around shades in some of the windows, but most were dark.

The gate to Matt's building hung open on rusted hinges. Joanna went through it, stumbling on the broken concrete, and climbed the front steps. The door appeared to be locked, but the knob turned easily; Matt had said he would leave it open for her. Inside the vestibule, the single bare bulb shone harshly. She hurried down the narrow hall, on tiptoe so her boot heels wouldn't click against the linoleum. The door to the cellar stood ajar several inches, but the downstairs light was out.

She sighed in exasperation and started down into the murkiness below, groping her way along the clammy railing, with only a thin line of light that extended from under the flat's door as her guide. At the foot of the stairs she tapped on the door—quietly, so as not to rouse the other tenants. She waited fifteen seconds, but Matt didn't answer.

She clicked her tongue against her teeth, more exasperated now. Matt had probably gone to sleep—which meant this so-called crisis was nothing more than one of his dramatic inventions. She'd cut short her visit with Richard, making a flimsy excuse about a pressing business matter that she was certain he hadn't believed; she'd driven over dark, unfamiliar roads at breakneck speed. And now that she'd arrived, Matt—the sluggard—had gone to bed. She should have known better than to let his agitation infect her, should have questioned him in detail before agreeing to rush back to London.

She tapped again, received no response, and tried the door. As with the one upstairs, the knob turned easily. At least Matt had left it open before dozing off.

The temperature inside the flat was surprisingly cold, and all the living room lights were off. A few rays outlined the tattered burlap curtain that screened the bedroom and bath. The curtain swayed back and forth, as if there was a window open somewhere. Joanna stood in the doorway until her eyes adjusted to the gloom; she glanced at the high barred window in the side wall, but it was closed, and looked to be painted shut.

"Matt?" she said tentatively.

No answer.

"Matt!"

Nothing made a sound, nothing moved except the swaying curtain.

Joanna stepped inside. Over the dank cellar odor she could smell fresh fog-laden outdoors air. She sniffed, standing in the middle of the small living room. There was another odor here—familiar, yet foreign. She remembered it from years before, when a friend of David's had insisted on taking them skeet shooting: cordite, that acrid scent of burnt gunpowder. Outdoors it had been the faintest drifting smell, but here in a relatively closed space it was powerful.

Her skin prickled unpleasantly and her hands caught either elbow, hugging herself. She stared at the rhythmically moving curtain.

"Matt!" This time her voice held an edge of panic. There was no reply. Nothing moved behind that curtain. No one breathed.

After a moment she took a step toward the curtain and put her hand to it. Hesitated, then pulled it aside.

Beyond was a tiny bedroom. A high window in the rear wall was the twin of that in the living room—except it had no bars and stood wide open. Below it on a bedside table stood a garish orange ginger jar lamp; its bulb was of very low wattage and lit only the wall behind it, the tabletop, and the upper half of the bed. Joanna's gaze moved from it and across the rumpled and tossed sheets to a square of carpet between the bed and the door. On it lay the prone body of a man.

"Matt." The syllable came out breathy and hushed. She clutched at the door frame, staring at the splayed blue-jeaned legs. His face was turned away, hidden by a fall of sheet; it looked as if he had grabbed at it and pulled it from the bed when he fell. In the center back of his tan sweater was a blackened hole and a dark stain where the blood had soaked through.

The door frame failed to steady her; she swayed as the curtain behind her had. The prickling of her skin turned to a paralyzing chill and she breathed shallowly.

"Matt!" Now his name came out louder, croaking. She pulled her hand from the door frame and pressed it hard against her lips. For a moment she thought she would black

out. Her vision blurred, cleared, blurred and cleared again.
Then she turned and stumbled into the darkened living
room. The curtain caught at her shoulder, but she yanked it
aside, tearing it from the hooks at one end. There was a
lamp, she remembered, somewhere near that armchair. She
groped toward it, barking one shin on a small table, fumbled for the switch, and turned it on.

The room looked as it had the last time she'd been there.
Everything was the same—except for the man behind the
lopsided and trailing curtain.

She sat down on the armchair, leaning forward with her
head in her hands and her elbows on her knees. As awful as
what she'd just witnessed was, her mind went not to it but
to another scene, a memory from some twenty years before.

Matt had had a job to do not far from Spitalfields Market, in a block of shabby flats very much like this on Worship Street. It was a mission, he'd said, for "a rich chap—
one of these swells, you know, who gets himself mixed up
with a girl not of his class and then isn't able to get out of
it." Matt was to retrieve clothing and other personal items
belonging to "the gentleman" from the flat. The girl was
supposed to be out for the evening, making it an easy in-
and-out job, and Matt had asked Joanna to come along as
a lookout.

She'd sensed something wrong from the first. Matt was
tense, and he'd never asked her to accompany him before.
But, as she'd so often done in those days, she ignored the
warning signs. Even when Matt confessed on the way to the
block of half-burned-out buildings that he felt there was
something wrong with the client, she didn't turn back.

The flat had been a basement one like this. Initially she
stood watch in the foyer, but then Matt—concerned about
the time—asked her to come down and help him. The flat's
layout had been like this one, too, and Matt sent her into the

bedroom to collect any items of men's clothing. It was there that she found the woman's dead and beaten body.

To this day the rest of it was a blur. She knew she'd screamed until Matt had slapped her. She remembered his cool and methodical gathering of the other items that would incriminate his client, and the way he forced her to walk calmly from the building. But as they went down the street, they heard the ululations of police sirens, looked back to see the official cars pulling up to the house they'd just left. They ran then—Matt cursing the man who had set him up, Joanna struggling to hold down the rising bile. Blocks away she was sick in the gutter, and for weeks afterwards she had nightmares of that bloody dead face. The client—who obviously had shielded himself with a false identity—had never resurfaced, and as far as Joanna or Matt knew, the woman's murder was never solved. And in time she'd been able to blot out the memory, had eventually repressed the whole thing.

But tonight it was as clear as if it had only happened yesterday.

After a while she sat up straighter and listened. The building was silent. Why, she wondered, hadn't anyone heard the shot and come to investigate?

Well, for one thing, these old houses were very solidly built. And she didn't know for a fact that the other flats were occupied. Besides, this was a part of London where people strictly minded their own business.

She ran her hands over her face and through her curls. In spite of the chill, sweat filmed her skin. All right, she told herself, figure out what to do now.

Call the police? Impossible. No way to explain what she was doing here. No way to explain without arousing suspicion what Mrs. Joanna Stark of Sonoma, California, and other refined places was doing in the East End flat of Mr. Matt Wickins, formerly of Winson Green Prison.

So what else? Leave as quietly as she'd come. Let someone else discover his body.

For a moment it was tempting. Then she thought, No, Matt was my friend, my lover. I can't just let him lie like that, become a decomposed horror to be discovered by strangers. I owe him that much.

What else, then?

Call Christopher! He'd know what to do. Wait ... there was no phone in the flat. Matt had used the Starving Ox as his headquarters because he couldn't afford a phone.

The thing to do, she decided, was to leave, find a public phone, and then call Christopher.

But before she reached the door, something struck her as wrong—something she'd seen in the bedroom. No, not something she'd seen, something she *hadn't*. Reluctantly she turned and pushed past the curtain. The room seemed colder than before. The smell of cordite had faded; the odor of death replaced it. She hesitated and then went over and knelt by the body.

There was no heavy onyx ring on the outflung left hand.

Joanna reached for the sheet that hung off the bed across the man's face. She drew it toward her with a shaky hand, then stopped, staring.

It wasn't Matt.

This man had curly dark hair. His skin was pockmarked and dusky.

She yanked the sheet completely aside.

His face was young and fleshy. He wore a growth of wispy beard. His features were Asian or Middle Eastern.

She had never seen him before in her life.

NINE

"CHRISTOPHER, I'M NOT JOKING. He was lying there in Matt's bedroom, shot to death!" Joanna gripped the receiver and stared out of the kiosk at a trio of weary train travelers napping on a bench. She'd left Matt's building and driven around for a bit before she realized the best place to find a phone would be at Liverpool Street Station.

At first Christopher's voice had been sleep-clogged, then annoyed. Now his tone sharpened. He said, "And you don't know who he is?"

"I have no idea."

"Where's Matt?"

"I don't know that, either. He called me at Richard's a little after eight, from the pub where he hangs out. That's the last I know of his whereabouts."

"Good God." Now Christopher sounded weary. "A pretty mess, isn't it?"

"Not pretty at all."

"Right." There was a lengthy pause. "I think it would be best if you returned to your hotel. I'll ring the police anonymously—better the caller doesn't have an American accent. Did you touch anything in the flat?"

"I moved a sheet that was draped over him. I thought at first it was Matt, but then I realized he wasn't wearing the ring Matt always has on, so I had to see—"

"Yes, yes. What about in the other room? Do you think you left fingerprints?"

"Oh Jesus, they must be all over the place—both from tonight and from the first time I went there!"

"Would yours be on file with Interpol?"

"No."

"What about in California—for your private investigator's license, for example?"

"I don't have a license. For the kind of consulting work I do, it isn't necessary. I doubt they're on file anywhere except with the Department of Motor Vehicles. You're fingerprinted these days when you apply for a California driver's license."

"Well, I doubt they'll search that far. They'll be looking for Matt first, of course."

The enormity of what had happened was finally coming home to Joanna. "Christopher, do you think Matt killed that man?"

"I've no idea what Matt might do."

"Where do you suppose he is?"

"Again I couldn't begin to guess." Christopher's voice was flat now, with a tight undertone of anger. "Joanna, please go back to the hotel. I'll ring you later."

He hung up and Joanna replaced the receiver. Before she'd talked to Christopher, her main concern had been with the unreported homicide. Now she realized that Matt's disappearance and probable involvement in the killing could jeopardize the entire delicate scheme she'd constructed.

She left the booth and hurried from the station, anger rising that matched what she'd heard in Christopher's voice. When she was inside the car she sat for a moment clutching the keys until they dug into the palm of her hand, then pounded her fists on the steering wheel.

Goddamn Matt! Just as everything was set to happen!

The preview for the auction was scheduled for three days from now. Meg Knight's story, as Joanna had expected, had been picked up by most of the important dailies on the Continent and in the U.S., as well as by the wire services. The preview promised to be well attended. Parducci couldn't help but have heard of the find—and he had had time to arrange for the theft of the painting.

Joanna and Christopher had also made their arrangements for its theft. When the time came, the Brueghel would be left relatively unguarded, but not so much as to arouse suspicion.

And now there was a dead man on the bedroom floor of their underworld informant. And the informant was missing, probably on the run. While it was possible the killing had come about because of some purely personal circumstance of Matt's, Joanna didn't really believe that. It was too much of a coincidence, after Matt's earlier frantic phone call.

What had he meant by "the whole bloody thing's about to go bust"? That he'd killed the man in his flat?

She unclenched her fists, stuck the key into the ignition, and drove swiftly to the Swiss Cottage district. Maybe, she thought, there would be a message from Matt at the hotel. Maybe Christopher would call and say he'd heard from him.

Right—and maybe she would wake up and find this was all one gigantic nightmare.

As Matt would say, not bloody likely.

She'd reserved Moonlight Primrose Cottage for her return, but that hadn't been scheduled until the next day. When she got to the hotel, only the night man—Mr. Stevens—was on duty. There would be no difficulty about the cottage, he assured her. The interim tenants had vacated that morning, and the maid had done the cottage up. He took Joanna back there, his flashlight trained on the brickwork so she wouldn't trip. After he'd set her bags in the bedroom he apologized that the kitchen wasn't open and offered to bring her something to drink. She was about to refuse, but then she reconsidered and asked if he could let her have a bottle of brandy. Stevens nodded and went away; when he returned he brought not only brandy but ice and soda, and a plate of crackers and a pot of Stilton cheese.

"I remember how fond you and Mr. Stark were of Stilton," he said.

Joanna thanked him; when he was gone, she almost cried at the unexpected kindness.

In spite of her agitated state, she ate all of the crackers, a fair amount of the cheese, and began putting a sizable dent in the brandy. At quarter to three she began to pace. There had been no call from either Matt or Christopher. Stevens had promised to put any calls through no matter what time they came in; apparently, he assumed they would be from the States and didn't find the request strange.

Joanna continued to pace, at first around the sitting room, then out into the chill air on the patio. She wondered what had happened with the police. Where Matt was. Why Christopher hadn't phoned. Who the dead man was. Why he'd been in Matt's flat. If he had anything to do with her and Matt's mutual business. . . .

After a while she grew tired of unanswerable questions. She needed someone to talk this out with. Not Christopher, though. He'd known Matt too well to be objective, was too close to the present situation. Besides, there was no telling that she could even get hold of him; he'd said he would call her.

She looked at her watch. Three twenty-three now. Before seven in California. Rafferty would still be at home, and probably awake.

She direct-dialed the familiar number. The phone rang five times before Rafferty picked it up. He sounded sleepy and irritated, but brightened when he heard her voice.

"Janna, how's it going?" Janna was what he alone called her—a childhood appellation that she had never revealed to anyone else.

"Not so well." She sketched out what had happened since she'd last spoken with him—from a small town in Wales where she'd gone after her drunken introspective night in Bristol.

"Christ," he said when she'd finished, "this Wickins really fucked things up, didn't he?"

Strangely, she found herself defending Matt. "Well, I can't imagine him doing it on purpose."

There was a silence. Rafferty must have detected the defensiveness, even though the overseas connection wasn't the best. Joanna thought back to her strategy sessions when she'd laid out the scheme for him, hoping he would spot any flaws in her logic. Surely she hadn't told him Matt had once been her lover, yet he might have guessed....

"I think I should come over there," Rafferty said.

It was the same thing E.J. had suggested. Coming from her son it hadn't annoyed her, had even pleased her a little because he was showing concern. But coming from Rafferty, it gave rise to a prickly irritation.

"Exactly what do you think you can accomplish that I can't?" she asked.

"I could ask around, try to get a line on Wickins, find out who the dead man is."

"I can do that myself, and probably more effectively. I know London, I know these people."

Silence again.

"And besides, you can't very well investigate in your capacity with Great American. You could jeopardize your job by doing that."

"...I guess."

"You've probably got a huge caseload right now, anyway."

"Not so large."

"Large enough; it always is. On the other hand, I can afford to—"

"You can always afford more than I."

It was a perennial bone of contention. Rafferty had an ex-wife and two teenaged children in New Jersey to whom he sent generous support payments; his salary was good, but not so high that those—plus the exorbitant costs of living in San Francisco—were easy to handle. Joanna wouldn't have minded sharing the wealth she had inherited with him. In a way it would have made her feel better about it being un-earned and, to her way of thinking, largely undeserved. But Rafferty was stubborn and proud; he insisted on paying his share—often, more.

"What I meant," she said, "is that I can afford to take the time off. Business is down at SSI right now."

Another long pause. "I still think I should come over there."

"No, Steve." He must be aware of her seriousness now; she never called him by his first name unless something important was under discussion. "I want—no, *need*—to han-dle this myself." ◂

"Why do you always have to be so goddamned indepen-dent?"

"I just do, that's all. I'll call you again in a couple of days, let you know what's developed."

Rafferty didn't respond. She replaced the receiver gently.

She hadn't intended to drink any more brandy, but now she poured herself a thimbleful, looked at the glass, and added a generous dollop. Dammit, she thought, why were all the men in her life so eager to help out when they weren't wanted, so unavailable when she *did* need them? For years when she had needed love from the son she'd given up soon after birth, E.J. had been hostile and combative. After he'd outgrown that, companionable but basically indifferent. Rafferty cared for her, she had no doubt; but when a prob-lem arose—even one so small as the grease fire in her kitchen last winter—he was never around. On that day both he and

E.J. had been wine-tasting with some friends from the city, and she'd fought the blaze alone until the fire department arrived. And Nick Alexander, while in many ways a good business partner, was the worst offender. He had no financial judgment, and she'd had to keep bailing SSI out of trouble every six months for years. Whenever there was an urgent business problem that needed discussing, Nick could generally be found at his girlfriend's home in Tiburon, in the hot tub.

No wonder I'm so "goddamned independent," she thought.

She looked for a cracker, remembered she'd eaten them all, then put her finger in the pot of Stilton, dug some out, and popped it into her mouth. As she resumed her pacing, a sense of guilt washed over her.

Dammit, she thought, Rafferty *was* there when I planned this scheme. He listened to every word, refined a couple of points for me, checked out facts with the companies that insured the stolen Brueghels. Maybe that does give him some right. He's only trying to help....

But still the offer bothered her, and she couldn't quite understand why. Something about his tone, perhaps? Something that said—in spite of all he knew about her—he felt she wasn't capable....

There was a tap at the door. Sucking the last bits of cheese off her finger, she hurried to answer it.

Christopher stood on the brick path. His hair was disheveled—more of a wild Afro now than docile curls—and his glasses had slipped as far down his shiny nose as they could go. His beautifully tailored suit looked ready for the cleaner. He raised a cautionary finger, then pushed past her into the cottage. When she had shut the door and faced him, he said, "You'd best sit down. Is that brandy? May I?"

"Of course." She sat, puzzled. "What's wrong?"

He poured brandy, gulped it, then poured some more. "The painting's been stolen," he said.

Surprise mixed with alarm. "It's too soon! We haven't been able . . . and without Matt—"

"I know. But it's worse than that, far worse."

"How could it be?"

"Ivy Harrison was in her flat on the third floor over the gallery. At about ten, perhaps a few minutes before, she heard a noise from downstairs and went to investigate. She came upon the thief and scuffled with him. He locked her in the storeroom and it took her hours to break out."

"Is she all right?"

Christopher motioned distractedly. "Shaken up, is all, Ivy's a tough old bird."

"But then—"

"What makes it worse is the identity of the thief. Ivy's description of him perfectly matches that of the dead man in Matt Wickins's bedroom."

TEN

"IT'S OBVIOUS TO ME," Christopher added, "that Matt hired the fellow to steal the painting, and then killed him. What I don't understand is why he would go to such trouble for what he knows is a relatively worthless canvas."

Joanna started to speak, but found her throat was constricted. She swallowed hard, then said, "That's my fault. I didn't tell him it wasn't a genuine Brueghel."

Christopher merely stared at her.

"I didn't think he needed to know everything. Matt has a big mouth—"

"He also has highly larcenous instincts." Christopher slammed his glass down on the end table. "Damn it, Joanna! How could you not expect he would come after the painting himself?"

Now that he put it in those terms, she realized she'd been extremely stupid in withholding the information from Matt. The irony was that she'd done so because she didn't trust him—and had made him even more untrustworthy as a result.

"Well, since it was my mistake, I'll just have to try to rectify it." She went into the bedroom and returned with her jacket and bag. "Let's go," she said. "I want to talk with Ivy Harrison."

Christopher shook his head as if her sudden surge of activity had thrown him off balance, but he followed her out of the cottage. As they went along the brick path that skirted the hotel to where his Jaguar sedan was parked at the curb, his movements became more brisk and assured. Probably, she thought, he was relieved that she was taking charge rather than falling apart.

For a long time he didn't speak, except to tell her to watch her step as he helped her off the high curb and into the car. When they were halfway to the Mayfair district he said, "What good will talking with Ivy do?"

"I just want to hear her story firsthand."

"You think I didn't get the facts right, do you?"

"No, it's not that. But I've had some experience in questioning people, in my work at SSI."

"And you expect she'll tell you something she hasn't already told me?"

"Sometimes people see more than they initially realize, and it takes some digging to bring it out."

That seemed to satisfy him, because he lapsed into silence again.

IVY HARRISON had dressed hurriedly in the same sort of black outfit she'd worn when Joanna first saw her. Her tight, iron gray curls looked impeccable, as if they'd just been released from a protecting hair net, but haste showed in an undone button on one cuff and a run in her left stocking. She sat in one of the leather armchairs in the drafty reception room of the gallery, her hands cupped around a china mug of tea. Joanna suspected Ivy had made the tea more to warm her hands than to drink, since she barely sipped it.

"All right," she said, looking down at the small notepad on which she'd jotted the details of Ivy's story so far. "Let's go over what you just told me. You were in your kitchenette on the third floor when you heard the noise. It was . . . what did you say?"

"A sliding. What you hear when a window's being raised."

"Any other sounds?"

Ivy shook her head.

"Then what did you do?"

The older woman compressed her lips, obviously to stifle a sigh of impatience. She said, "I went to the rear staircase and slipped down to the second story. Stopped and listened. Then I heard other sounds. More sliding, as if someone was moving along the floor of the downstairs hallway in his stocking feet."

"And then?"

"I went the rest of the way down, quietly, without putting on a light."

Now Joanna suppressed an exasperated sigh of her own. Ivy was a good witness in that she stuck to the bare facts; so far, she hadn't deviated from the story she'd told the first time through. But that kind of precision could also be less than helpful; it didn't open up any new avenues that would allow Joanna to probe half-realized impressions or temporarily forgotten nuances. It was, she'd found, the results of such probing that often told a completely different—and more useful—version of the events under question.

"And then?" she repeated, her tone a little sharper than she'd intended.

Ivy's eyes flashed, but she said calmly, "A man came through the door from the storage area. He was carrying the painting you and Mr. Burgess have been making the arrangements for these past weeks."

It wasn't what Ivy said so much as her arch look after she'd said it that made Joanna realize the woman was aware of what she and Christopher had been planning. They'd taken every precaution to ensure Ivy be left in the dark, but somehow she'd ferreted it out. Joanna smiled wryly, thinking what a fine spy Ivy Harrison would make.

Ivy, who had thus far demonstrated a singular lack of a sense of humor, frowned.

But there was something wrong, Joanna realized, with what Ivy had just told her. "Back up a minute," she said. "You went downstairs without putting on a light?"

"Yes."

"And there was also no light in the hallway or storage area?"

"Only a little, from the bulb at the rear of the corridor. It was enough to make out the shape of the man carrying the painting."

"Then how did you know it was the Brueghel he had?"

Ivy smiled in triumph. "The frame, of course. It's part of my duties to see that those of our paintings that are framed are properly done up. This one came to us already framed, and it's not a good one. Too ornate, it is, with all those curlicues and whorls. Doesn't fit the subject matter. I took particular notice because of that, and its shape was easy to make out, even in the dark."

Joanna nodded, feeling unkindly bested in a petty game. "Go on with your story, please."

"The man didn't see me at first. He started along the corridor toward the rear—the building backs up on the mews, you know. He was nearly abreast of me when he saw I was there. Then he started and tried to push past me. I grasped the frame of the painting, thinking to take it away from him. My first duty, of course, was to save the painting."

"Of course." Joanna consulted her notes and picked up the interview where she'd left off when she asked Ivy to repeat herself. "What were your impressions of the man?"

"He wasn't very tall. Had curly black hair, a trifle greasy. Face was fattish, scarred—pockmarked, actually—with a straggly little beard. Asian, I suppose."

"What was he wearing?"

"Jeans. A sweater. Bulky one. Light-colored? Yes. Tan, I think."

"What kind of build did he have?"

"Slender. But strong—he overpowered me easily, and I'm no weakling."

"What did he smell like?"

Ivy looked surprised. She closed her eyes and after a moment said, "Like cigarette smoke. And some kind of preparation for the hair. Probably why it looked so greasy."

That didn't tell Joanna much. Many men used hair dressings of one sort or another, and she'd found that her own clothing reeked of smoke every time she set foot in an English drinking establishment.

She asked, "What color were his eyes?"

"I . . . I didn't see them. It was dark."

"But you've described his face in such detail."

Ivy seemed about to lose her composure. She'd been through an ordeal, had attempted to remain calm, but now her nerves were obviously fraying. "It was *dark*! I couldn't observe everything, could I!"

"Of course not," Joanna said. "I didn't mean to imply that you should have." She consulted her notepad, where she'd written "body type/pockmarks/Asian/clothing." Now she added: "Smoke? Hair oil?" The description was enough like the one she'd given Christopher of the dead man that she could understand why he'd assumed they were one and the same. But really, the thief could have been one of any number of people.

"Only a few more questions, Miss Harrison," she said. "How did he get away from you?"

Now Ivy sighed deeply. Joanna couldn't really blame her. Ivy knew Christopher had already told her these details.

"He pushed at me, and I fell onto the staircase. Then he dragged me to my feet and shoved me into the storage area. It locks from the outside, and he turned the key. I heard it drop to the floor, and then I heard him run down the hallway. There were sounds as if he was scrambling through a window—which of course he had, because when I finally broke through the door hours later, I found the open window with a chair pulled under it."

"And then you phoned Christopher?"

"I rang Mr. Burgess immediately."

"Why him, rather than the police?"

Ivy flashed Joanna a haughty look. "Mr. Burgess is my employer. I take my directions from him alone."

And you also knew the painting that had just been stolen was a fake, Joanna thought. You wanted to protect your employer.

She closed her notebook and stood. "Thank you, Miss Harrison. I appreciate your taking the time to talk to me."

"I am always glad to do what Mr. Burgess requests." Ivy stood and moved toward the interior door of the gallery. "I trust you won't need me again tonight...this morning, that is."

"No. And thank you again."

The woman nodded brusquely and went out. Joanna sat down again, letting her breath out in a long sigh of annoyance. Ivy seemed to dislike her thoroughly, probably because she knew Joanna had placed Christopher in a delicate and vulnerable position with regard to the fake Brueghel. She certainly had managed to express that dislike in a variety of humbling but perfectly irreproachable ways.

Christopher stuck his head through the door. "I heard Ivy on the stairs. Are you finished with her?"

Joanna nodded. "What did you find out about the alarm system?"

"I'm not the expert you are, but it's easy to see how he breached it. Using a fairly simple method, too. It's enough to make me rip it out and install a whole new system."

Joanna nodded absently. She kept staring at the notebook in her hand, as if she could see through its cover to the unhelpful facts within.

"Do you want to look at what he did?" Christopher asked.

"Later, maybe. Right now we have things to decide."

"Did Ivy give you anything useful?"

"No. I can't even be sure the thief was the dead man from her description. But I think we can safely proceed on that assumption."

"Proceed?" Christopher balanced on the edge of the armchair opposite her. "There's nothing we can do. You might as well admit it—your plan has failed."

"Not yet, I won't. Do you know anyone at the Scotland Yard CID?"

"No. I thought you did."

"My contact is with the Art Squad. I hardly think he'll be involved in the investigation of a homicide in a sleazy East End flat."

"Well, I certainly can't help you there."

"Christopher, you have all sorts of influential customers. Surely one of them could put you in touch—"

"I can't involve my clients in this!"

"Just ask for a name, an introduction."

"Joanna, how can I explain—"

"You'll think of a way. You've always been good at ... dissembling."

Christopher flushed, as he always seemed to do lately at references to the days when many of his activities had not been legitimate. "What do you want with the CID, anyway?"

"Information about the dead man—who he was, for one thing. What their preliminary findings are."

"Why not wait until it's published in the newspapers?"

"The authorities very seldom release everything they have to the press."

"Well, even if I can manage to find that out—and, mind you, I'm not guaranteeing that I can—what good will it do you?"

"What good will it do us, Christopher. *Us.* You can't divorce yourself from the situation now. What it will do is help us to locate Matt—and my fake Brueghel. I've got fifteen thousand pounds invested in that, and I want it back. Afterwards we'll rethink the scheme and start over."

Christopher groaned and swiped at his slipping glasses. "What about the preview? People will come expecting—"

"Don't do anything about it yet. We've got three days."

He stood, hands thrust in his pockets. "Don't you think it's best to just let it go? I'll cancel the preview, claim I've been taken in by a clever forger—"

"No, don't you do that! If worst comes to worst, we can put it off, but don't cancel it. I'm going to find Matt Wickins and get my fake Brueghel back. And then I'm going to make him very, very sorry he did this to me."

Christopher's eyes narrowed. "What now, Joanna? Is Matt to become your next Antony Parducci?"

For a moment his words gave her pause, made her think of the conversation she'd had with Richard the previous evening. Then she shrugged off the disturbing thought and started for the door.

"Maybe," she said to Christopher.

"Where are you going?"

"Right now? Back to the hotel to rest. Later this morning you can find me at a pub called the Starving Ox, trying to get a line on where Matt might be."

ELEVEN

AT A LITTLE AFTER ELEVEN that morning, the air in the Starving Ox had not yet had time to thicken with smoke; instead, it reeked of yesterday's stale tobacco and beer. Joanna had arrived immediately after opening, while the barman was still removing chairs that had been upended on the tables. She walked gingerly over a linoleum floor puddled with sudsy water, and when the barman caught sight of her, he slipped behind the plank.

"You win the prize for first customer, miss," he said. "What will you have?"

She propped one foot on the bar's battered metal foot rail. "A half lager, if you would. No...make that a bitter."

The man nodded and went to draw the drink. He wiped the overflow away with his hand, then dried it on his already stained apron. "American, aren't you?" he asked, setting the glass in front of her.

"Right."

"We don't get many tourists over this way. Or would you be one?"

"Not really. I come to London often, and have friends here. One of them uses this pub as a sort of headquarters—Matt Wickins."

The expression on the man's face—stubbled with ginger-colored whiskers—became guarded. He picked up a wet rag and began to polish the dull wood in front of him, even though there was nothing spilled on it.

"I'm trying to find Matt," Joanna added.

The motion of the rag stopped, then resumed. "It's true he comes in here," the man said, "but I haven't seen him, not lately."

"He was here last night, before nine. He made a long-distance phone call."

The man glanced at a black instrument resting on the backbar, then picked up a stack of ashtrays and began setting them out at precise intervals. "I'm afraid I can't help you, miss."

"I'm Matt's friend," Joanna said. When he didn't respond, she added, "The phone call was to me."

His gaze flicked to her face. "Where would you have been when you received this call?"

"Cerne Abbas, néar Sherborne."

He nodded slowly. "What did you say your name was?"

"I didn't. Joanna Stark."

He paused at the far end of the bar, evidently thinking it over. Probably, she thought, Matt had told him where he had phoned when he'd paid for the call. The barman might even have overheard him ask for her, or part of the conversation.

"He told me to come to London in a hurry," she added.

The barman seemed to come to a decision. He returned to where she stood and extended a thick hand to her. "Me name's John Grey. I'm the proprietor." He gestured at a sign above the bar that was carved with both his name and the pub's with a pride of ownership that seemed out of proportion to their surroundings.

"It's a nice place," she lied.

"Well, it's homey, and popular with the lads in the district. Not the kind of pub a lady like you would frequent—"

"Oh, don't be too sure of that. My son's a bartender; the place where he works is a good deal like yours." Mentally she made her apologies to Mario's, on the Sonoma Plaza.

"And where might that be?"

"An Italian restaurant and bar in a little town in California—Sonoma, in the wine country north of San Francisco."

"San Francisco...now, I've been there. Years ago, mind you. The wife had a sister married an American army man during the war. After he was mustered out they settled in a place called San Jose—do you know it?"

Joanna nodded.

"A few years ago the wife said we should go for a visit; we'd been talking about it for years, and none of us was as young as we'd like to be. At our age, you never know.... Anyway, they took us to San Francisco one weekend. A beautiful place."

Joanna nodded again, sensing John Grey was rambling on about his trip to the States in order to avoid the central issue. She said, "You feel about San Francisco the way I feel about London. I love this city, and one reason is the friends I have here—like Matt Wickins."

John Grey's lips twitched, either in a fledgling smile or disbelief, but he controlled himself and raised his eyebrows in what he must have thought was an expression of polite interest. "Oh," he said, "have you and Matt known each other long?"

"Over twenty years."

Now he couldn't control his astonishment; he merely gaped at her.

"Mr. Grey," Joanna said, "I know what Matt is."

"What...?"

"I know he's a thief."

"Oh."

"But he's also my friend. It's urgent I locate him."

The publican picked up the rag again and began to polish the bar with a vengeance. "Miss...Stark, is it?"

"Yes."

"I suppose you know what went on at Matt's flat last night."

"Yes, I saw it in the morning paper." It had been a short item, not identifying the victim and merely saying that Matt was being sought "to aid the police in their enquiries". Joanna—not trusting Christopher to carry through on her request—had phoned Meg Knight before coming here and asked the reporter to see if she could find out any particulars. Knight had pressed her about why she needed the information and become sharp when Joanna refused to elaborate. "I hope nothing's gone wrong with your plans," she'd said. "My professional reputation is on the line, you know." Joanna had assured her—with far more confidence than she felt—that everything would be all right.

Now she said to John Grey, "You see why I need to locate Matt, don't you? I want to help him."

Just as he seemed about to speak, a trio of men pushed through the door, calling out greetings and eyeing Joanna with interest. Grey said, "We can't discuss this now. The lorry drivers from the dairy are coming off—"

"I'll wait," she said, looking at the chalkboard that listed what food was being served that day. "Why don't you bring me the chicken with peas and chips, and another half bitter. I'll take one of the rear tables, where I won't be conspicuous."

The three lorry drivers were clamoring for service. Grey motioned for them to be patient. "Like I said, I'll be quite a bit."

"That's okay." She patted her shoulder bag. "I've brought a paperback. I'll amuse myself with it. May I have my drink now?"

Silently he nodded and went to draw it.

When he placed the glass in front of her, Joanna said, "I'll be at that table in the corner. If any friends of Matt's come in, perhaps you could direct them to me."

The publican gave her a "not bloody likely" stare, then went to wait on the lorry drivers.

THE PUB QUICKLY FILLED with men who looked to be drivers or warehousemen and occasional groups of women who were probably clerks or secretaries at the nearby industrial concerns. The level of noise rose, and the air thickened with smoke. Joanna ate her lunch (surprisingly good, so long as she didn't speculate on the cleanliness of the kitchen where it had been prepared), then opened her paperback. From time to time she glanced over at the bar, but John Grey steadfastly avoided her eye.

At quarter after one, the crowd had begun to thin and her interest in the novel had waned. It was a fat family saga that her friend Mary Bennett had liked and given her; Joanna knew such books were popular and occasionally tried to read one to find out why, but she'd never been able to get beyond the first few chapters, and this was no exception. Finally she laid it facedown on the table, open to the point where she'd given up, and scanned the room. About half the tables were still taken, and a group of men in work clothes clustered around the bar. John Grey was at the far end near the door.

As Joanna watched, a slender young man—Indian or Pakistani—entered and approached the proprietor. Grey frowned and shook his head; his gaze slid toward Joanna. Hurriedly he leaned across the bar, grasping the young man's arm, and engaged him in private conversation. After a couple of exchanges, the Asian also glanced Joanna's way, then hurriedly left the pub.

Joanna wanted to follow him, but she wasn't sure she could do so without attracting Grey's notice. Her opportunity came when the phone rang and the publican moved along the bar to answer it, putting the group of drinkers between him and Joanna. She left the paperback conspicuously on the table and stood, looking around as if she were searching for the ladies' room. Grey's back, she saw, was to her; she moved swiftly across the room and out the door into the street.

The young Asian was half a block away to her right, walking fast while he turned up the collar of his leather jacket against the cold, damp wind. Joanna did the same with her own collar, then took a knit cap from her bag; it served the dual purpose of keeping her head warm on this murky overcast day, while making her look quite different from the woman who had been pointed out to him in the pub—an unnecessary precaution, it turned out, because the man kept walking briskly without glancing behind him.

He led her through a maze of narrow streets, deep into an area of small business concerns to the north. It was a circuitous route that only one well acquainted with the district would have taken; after a while Joanna gave up on trying to remember how they'd come. Finally the man turned into an even narrower street next to a vacant lot crowded with junked cars and trucks. Joanna slowed at the corner and then peered around it.

The alley was lined with old dark brick buildings whose slate roofs canted sharply against the gray sky. Some had broken or boarded-up windows, but the majority bore the signs of various small firms. The pavement was deserted save for the man she was following and a stooped old woman picking through trash in a dumpster at the far side. Joanna watched the young man enter a building midway down on the right.

A metal sign hung at right angles to the building above its front door. The wind gusted along the street, flinging particles of grit against Joanna's face and making the sign creak and groan on its hangings. She waited to make sure the man didn't reappear, then stuffed her hands in her pockets and started down the alley. The old ragpicker turned to watch her, eyes black and empty as the windows of the burnt-out building behind her.

Halfway there Joanna could make out the faded lettering on the sign: *Ian Sneath, Wine Merchant*. The building had been fitted with a modern front door—aluminum and glass—that ill suited its otherwise Dickensian appearance. When she went up to it, she looked through the glass; the room beyond was stacked with cartons stenciled with the names of European and American vintners. There was an unstaffed counter that looked to be an order desk, and a few oaken barrels were arranged beside it in a pyramid—for display purposes, she assumed. There was no sign of the man she'd been following.

She hesitated, then pushed the door open and stepped inside. Behind her it shut with a soft pneumatic sigh. The big room smelled of stale wine, as if a bottle might have been broken and the spill not adequately cleaned up. The temperature, while warmer than on the street, was still cold.

There was a bell on the order desk, and a sign taped in front of it said, "Please ring for service." The sign was illustrated with a hand with outstretched forefinger, but the finger pointed the opposite way from where the bell had been placed. Joanna ignored the message and moved around the desk to a corridor that was lined with high-piled cases of Zinfandel. At its far end she could make out the mutter of voices.

She kept close to the stacks of cartons, moving along slowly toward the sounds. At its end the corridor came to a waist-high wooden partition topped by Plexiglas. The glass extended from the partition to the ceiling and muted the voices beyond; but through it Joanna could clearly see an office with three desks, two of them unoccupied. The Asian man stood in front of the third, appearing to be in an argument with a young woman whose punk hairdo was dyed several shades of lavender. He gestured angrily with his hands, but it didn't seem to intimidate the woman; every time he motioned, she merely shook her cockscombed head. Finally she held out a pad of paper to him; he took it, scrawled a note, and thrust it back at her.

Joanna retraced her steps quickly and slipped behind a stack of cartons near the front door. A few seconds later the man came along the corridor and left the building. She followed, noting the stiff, pugnacious quality of his gait. It was a while longer before she realized the route he was taking was the reverse of the one by which he'd come.

By the time he arrived at the Starving Ox and entered by a side door, it was after three. Joanna hesitated on the sidewalk, wondering if she ought to confront John Grey and demand he talk with her about Matt. Then she decided against such foolish behavior and went back to where she'd parked her rental car.

The first phone kiosk she came upon, three blocks away, had been outfitted to accept only phone cards—a recent innovation intended to prevent vandalism. She hunted in her bag for the one she'd bought at the post office shortly after her arrival and finally found it crumpled under her makeup case. For a moment she thought the mechanism might reject it, but with some coaxing it worked. She dialed Meg Knight's office number and waited for the reporter to come on the line.

Without preamble Joanna asked, "Were you able to find out anything more about that homicide?"

Knight's voice bristled with irritation; Joanna had observed that, direct as Meg might be, she liked to observe society's niceties. "I have," she said, "but not a great deal. There's been no identification on the victim. They tell me it might be difficult because he's Asian or Middle Eastern and possibly here illegally. No word on the tenant of the flat, either—at least as of an hour ago."

Nor would there be for some time, Joanna thought. Matt was adept at disappearing when he wanted to, and never before had he had such a compelling reason to vanish. "Will your contact let you know if anything comes up?"

"Yes. Now perhaps you'll tell me—"

"Another question: Have you heard of a wine merchant named Ian Sneath?"

"Sneath? What's he to do with this?"

"I'm not sure. *Do* you know of him?"

"Yes. Sneath is a connoisseur of fine wines, an art collector, and a bit of a shady character. Those who've seen his collection—and there aren't many—say it's mainly pornographic. And it's rumored that he's one of the biggest middlemen in the art underworld."

Joanna was silent, giving that some thought. A middleman was the link between the broker—like Parducci—and the fagin; a person who managed a string of thieves, much like the Dickens character for whom he was named. Usually middlemen were lower level art dealers, but there was no reason one couldn't be a wine merchant, or someone of any other calling. All that was really required was a quasi-legitimate place of business and contacts in the underworld.

"Joanna?" Knight said.

"Hang on a second." She continued with the train of thought. Now that she considered it, she realized that the young man she'd just followed had exhibited that furtive manner so typical of the small-time professional thief. He'd had dealings with John Grey, and Grey had sent him with a message to Ian Sneath. A message prompted by her presence in the Starving Ox . . . ?

"Meg," she said, "does the name John Grey mean anything to you?"

"It's a common enough name. Grey with an *e* or an *a*?"

"An *e*."

"John Grey. Grey. No . . . sorry. Who is he?"

"Proprietor of a Whitechapel pub called the Starving Ox."

"Not an encouraging name, if one were in search of a good meal. Joanna, whatever is going on? I've a right to know."

But Joanna wasn't listening to Knight. Now that she knew about Sneath, it seemed obvious to her that John Grey was a fagin and the pub the headquarters for his stable of thieves. The young man she'd followed earlier must be one of them. The man who'd been murdered in Matt's flat could be another. And Matt? Yet another?

No, that didn't make any sense. Matt was too old and experienced to merely be one of a string of run-of-the-mill thieves. In better days he'd managed his own stable of hungry young men who were willing to take a big risk for thrills and some ready cash.

Matt had been a fagin himself. He probably still was. Like a fool, she'd turned over the plans of her operation to a man who could reap the most benefit by thwarting them.

TWELVE

THE BLOCK WHERE Matt's flat was located was even more depressing in the late afternoon light than it had been on the evenings when Joanna had visited it. The empty houses slated for demolition were gutted shells, stripped by scavengers for every salvageable brick and timber. Even the occupied buildings had a desolate untended air, evidenced by broken windows repaired only with cardboard and tape, and front stoops that were littered with old newspapers. It was as if their residents had merely given up and sunk into squalor while waiting for the inevitable eviction notice.

Joanna left the rental car at the far end of the block and walked along, head bent against the increasingly cold wind, hands thrust deep in the pockets of her suede jacket. She still wore the knitted cap she'd pulled on while following the young man from the Starving Ox, and was grateful for its protection. Fleetingly she thought of home: the soft warmth of spring mornings, her carefully tended garden basking in a hard noonday sun, the evenings when she could sit sipping wine on the patio. She'd discussed putting in a swimming pool with E.J.; he'd been all for it, of course, and had even volunteered to oversee the construction crew. She'd had to admit she could use the exercise it would afford. Riding her bike to the post office every day wasn't working out too well—because she kept falling off it and embarrassing herself....

She wrenched her thoughts away from the Sonoma Valley and surreptitiously studied the row of houses across the street. Matt's looked much the same as it had on her previous visits, except for a police notice stuck to the front door. The houses on either side appeared to be tenanted, although she couldn't tell if anyone was on their premises at the moment. She continued along to the end of the short block, checking the cars that lined either curb to see if any resembled an official vehicle or contained someone who might be watching the house. When she was satisfied that there was no surveillance, she crossed the street and moved down the sidewalk to the house to the right of Matt's.

Its front door stood ajar. She stepped into a musty-smelling foyer similar to the one next door. A metal number "1" hung crooked on an inner door to her left. She knocked, waited, but got no response. The entrance to the basement was padlocked, the lower flat obviously untenanted. Her knocks on the second floor also went unanswered, except for at the rear flat, where a man's voice shouted for her to "get the bloody hell out of here."

Back on the sidewalk she considered trying the other flats in Matt's building, but decided it was too much of a risk. Just because she hadn't spotted anyone didn't mean the place wasn't under surveillance, and she could already be drawing attention to herself—a comparatively well dressed woman in one of the East End's severe pockets of poverty. She walked past the house briskly and entered the building to its left.

Again there was no response at the first-floor flat. No one answered at the basement unit either, but as she turned toward the stairway she noticed the door of the front flat had opened a few inches. Two dark eyes regarded her solemnly through the crack.

"Hello," she said, stepping toward the door.

The eyes continued to regard her. They were on a level with her own, so she guessed their owner was about her height, but otherwise she could see nothing. Then there was a rustling sound and she looked down. The door opened a few inches more as a small boy with a dusky complexion and floppy black hair peered out at her, his body hidden behind a fold of flimsy pink material. Joanna's gaze traveled back up the sari-clad body of the woman whose leg the child clung to; when their eyes met, she saw an expression that was neither fear nor curiosity, but simple resignation.

"Hello," she said again. "I'm trying to get in touch with the man living in the basement flat of the house next door—Matt Wickins."

The woman put her hand on the boy's shoulder and gently pushed him behind her, speaking softly in her native tongue. Then she said to Joanna, "You are with the police?"

"No, I'm Matt's friend. I'm worried about him, and I want to help."

The sari rustled again as the woman stepped into the hallway and shut the door behind her. She moved toward Joanna, peering at her face in the dim light. Then she nodded, "Yes, you were with him, perhaps ten days ago. I saw you arrive in a little red car, and you both went inside his house." There was an emotional undercurrent to her words that Joanna couldn't define.

She said, "You know Matt Wickins, then?"

"Yes."

"And you know what happened next door?"

"Of course."

"Have you seen him since then?"

"No. He . . . has gone."

"Where?"

"I do not—he did not tell me." The undertone was identifiable now: a clear edge of pain that told Joanna more about Matt's relationship with this woman than any number of words could have. She should have known that Matt would have a woman somewhere, and the closer to hand the better. It had always been that way with him—from the lover he discarded only days after Joanna had come into his life, to whomever had surely replaced her soon after her departure.

"Did you see him go?" she asked.

"No. But I knew..." She hesitated, uncertainty clouding her handsome features.

"You knew he was going?"

"Yes." The woman sighed deeply and looked down at her hands. Her fingers were long and delicate, but cruelly roughened by hard work. "I knew because of the car. He had none, you see. But yesterday afternoon he arrived in one and parked it at the curb. It was gone long before the police arrived."

"How long?"

"I do not know. By eleven, perhaps. I last saw him at six. I was angry with him, so I did not go out again until I heard the police sirens."

"Why were you angry with him?"

The woman's eyes focused on a point beyond Joanna's right shoulder. For a moment pain flickered in them, but then they took on their former flat resignation. "He would not explain about the car nor tell me where he planned to go in it," she said. "He laughed at me and said I did not need to know. And he would not tell me when he would come back."

Or *if* he would come back, Joanna thought. Gently she said, "What kind of car was it?"

"I do not know cars. It was small, like the one you and he arrived in that night."

"What color?"

"Blue. A dark blue. I think he may have hired it. There was a sticker on the windscreen, a round one with an emblem that I have seen advertised for a car-hire company."

"Can you describe the emblem?"

The woman wrinkled her forehead in concentration, the motion puckering the traditional daub of red in its center.

"A...I think it is called a chevron. Stripes of red, green, and yellow, shaped like the letter V."

A rental car company advertising with a brightly colored chevron shouldn't be too difficult to locate, Joanna thought. "Do you remember anything else about the car?"

"...No. I am sorry."

"That's all right—you've already helped me a great deal."

The woman studied her face, then stepped forward, placing a hand on Joanna's arm. "It is true, what you said—that you wish to help Matt?"

"Yes," she lied.

"Perhaps you will find him and make him come back here, so he can be cleared of this crime?"

"Perhaps."

The woman nodded, this time in a way that was more in response to some inner dialogue than to what Joanna had said. Then she turned toward the door of her flat. Before she closed it she said, "When you find Matt, tell him I am here, please. Tell him I will be waiting."

Joanna stood for a moment staring at the closed door and wondering what it was about men like Matt that inspired such foolhardy allegiance from women. God knows she'd not been immune to it in her day, and it seemed Matt's superficial charm had survived the years intact.

She *was* immune to it now, however. When he had sent the young Asian to steal her painting, he had created a breach in their relationship that could never be healed—not by charm, nor by nostalgia for the days when they had been lovers. No matter what revenge might cost her, Matt was going to pay for his actions—and pay dearly.

FINDING THE COMPANY from which Matt had rented the car proved ridiculously simple: its name was Chevron Car-Hire, and its tiny ad in the directory was emblazoned with the symbol. Joanna then concocted a story that seemed plausible if not examined too critically: she was Matt's wife and worried about him; since the death of their son in a car crash the year before, he'd been unstable and he'd taken off without telling her where he was going. She needed to locate him before he came to any harm.

Presumably the fear of one of their cars being in the hands of a lunatic was sufficient reason to send the clerk at the company's South London office into her files. Mr. Wickins, she told Joanna, had hired the dark blue Mini at three the previous afternoon, paying a substantial cash deposit. She supplied the license number and then volunteered that he'd inquired about dropping the car in Falmouth.

"You mean in Cornwall?" Joanna asked.

"Yes. We don't have an office there, but we do have an arrangement with Fal Car-Hire. I told him he could leave it there and they would assess the final charges."

Joanna took down the address of the rental agency in Falmouth, thanked the clerk, and hung up. Then she went out to her own rental car and found a map of Great Britain in the side pocket.

Falmouth is a harbor town on the southeast side of the Cornish peninsula. Joanna opened the map and pinpointed it, then stared at the boldface letters, trying to remember what she knew of the place. She'd been there only once, with David, who had been negotiating with an art dealer for the purchase of a group of landscapes by an obscure Cornish painter. The dealer's name had been... She couldn't remember. There had been a hotel they'd liked, the Greenbank, where the writer Kenneth Grahame had penned the opening chapters of his children's classic, *The Wind in the Willows*. What else? The harbor was a large one. They'd taken an excursion boat around it, and the guide had said it was the third largest natural harbor in the world. Two rivers, the Fal and the Helford, emptied into it, but they hadn't had time to take a trip up either. Smuggling claimed a large place in the history of the area, and it was rumored that it went on to this day. . . .

A harbor. Ships. Smuggling.

Joanna replaced the map and went back to her cottage. She sat on the sofa, feet tucked under her, hugging one of the throw pillows and thinking about smuggling. Then she reexamined the subject of Matt and the rental car.

Initially she'd been surprised that he hadn't hired it under an assumed name, but now she realized that rental car companies demanded to see a driver's license. False ones took a while to acquire and cost a good deal for one in Matt's impecunious position. Besides, at the time he rented the car, he probably hadn't expected that anyone but Joanna—and most certainly not the police—would be attempting to find him. A South London agency with only one office had most likely seemed a safe bet to him.

Hence, his leaving a clear trail by asking to drop the car in Falmouth. But why not just abandon it?

Well, she answered herself, if Matt was going to Falmouth for the reason she suspected, he wouldn't want an abandoned car to point to the fact he'd been there. Even if he left it somewhere else in Cornwall, eventually an astute police officer would have noticed its proximity to the port city and figured out what Matt's intentions had been. He had probably reasoned it would be better to return the car and settle the bill, in order not to call attention to himself. And anyway, for someone so unsuccessful in his line of work, Matt had an odd compulsive streak: it would bother him to leave behind such an untidy loose end.

But what about the money—the "substantial cash deposit" the clerk had said he'd paid?

It was cash that had probably constituted the first installment of his commission to arrange the theft of the Brueghel. A commission from whom?

Antony Parducci.

"Double-crossing little prick," Joanna muttered.

She reached for the phone and dialed New Scotland Yard. Her contact there, Inspector Evans, was in his office. When he asked how her preparations were going, she skirted the issue, telling him to expect an update in a couple of days. Then she asked, "What can you tell me about the port of Falmouth—specifically if it's used as a conduit for thieves to ship artworks out of the country?"

"We've long suspected it has. In fact, one of our recent cases came to a dead halt there. Difficult to get a line on who's arranging it, or how, though. The Cornish—do you know them?"

"Only that they're mainly seafarers or miners."

"It's a desolate land. Until modern methods of transportation, it was relatively cut off from the rest of the country. A good deal of illegal activity has gone on over the years: smuggling, deliberate wrecking of ships. They've a closemouthed clannish tradition down there that persists to this day. There's even been talk of a separatist movement. Don't much care for outsiders, the Cornish."

What he said reminded Joanna of a conversation with the Falmouth art dealer: he'd been telling her and David about some fiendish thing "they" (meaning the English) had done to "us." The man spoke with considerable bitterness and anger, and because of that it had been some minutes before she realized that the dirty deed was perpetrated in 1502, rather than the previous year.

"So it's likely," she said to Evans, "that an art thief heading in that direction is planning either to send his loot abroad, or go abroad with it himself."

"Quite likely."

They discussed Cornwall a bit more, but Evans didn't ask the reason behind her inquiries, not even when she requested the name of someone to contact on the CID in the

Falmouth area. Evans, because he had not committed formally to her plan, had no need to keep a tight rein on her; he'd probably found he got his best results by giving those with whom he dealt unofficially a good bit of leeway.

After they'd finished, she called reception. Was it possible, she asked, for them to make a reservation for her at the Greenbank Hotel in Falmouth? For an indefinite stay, beginning tomorrow. Just the room, no meals, unless breakfast was included. Would they call her back and let her know everything was in order? Thank you very much.

She replaced the receiver and looked at her watch. Almost six o'clock. She had a great many preparations to make, and she should also catch a few hours sleep before starting on her journey. First, however, she would go back to the Starving Ox, and then perhaps she would have a talk with Ian Sneath, wine merchant. And before she slept she also must check in with Christopher—it was best to keep him informed on what was happening.

THIRTEEN

AT CLOSE TO SEVEN the Starving Ox was packed. Joanna pushed past a group of spiky-haired young men and women who congregated near the bank of video games, then wove through the older and largely male contingent in front of the bar. John Grey and an elderly female assistant were busy drawing beer and pouring spirits. Joanna edged up to the plank and waited. The publican's gaze flicked to her, moved on, then returned.

Grey carefully topped off the pint of bitter he was drawing and set it in front of his customer. After he had rung up the sale, he ignored the others waiting for drinks and made his way along the bar to Joanna. He tried to arrange his stubbled face into lines of pleasantry, but what purported to be a smile pulled down at the corners and his eyes were cold and watchful.

"It's Miss Stark, isn't it?" he said.

Joanna nodded.

"If you're looking for your Penguin," Grey went on, "I've saved it for you."

"My—?"

"Your book. You left it on the table this afternoon. I thought you'd return for it."

"Actually I've returned for the talk you promised. About Matt Wickins. And Ian Sneath. And Antony Parducci."

When she mentioned Sneath, Grey's lips compressed, but at Parducci's name his head swiveled in alarm, as if he were afraid the man might be standing next to him. "Please, Miss Stark," he said, "this is not the time—"

"When is, then? A man has been killed. A valuable painting has been stolen. Matt Wickins is preparing to leave the country."

Now Grey leaned across the plank, his face close to hers, his hand gripping her arm. "What did you say?"

"He's about to take the painting out of England, leaving you and Ian Sneath out your share of what Parducci paid him."

It was only a guess, but Grey's reaction proved it correct. "I don't believe you. It's true Sneath referred him to a—" Then his jaw went slack and his gaze moved to a point behind Joanna. She turned, but could see no one watching them, only a second barmaid pushing through the crowd with a tray of empty glasses.

"Who did Sneath refer him to?" she asked.

Grey shook his head.

"*Who*, dammit! A collector? Another broker? Or someone who could get the Brueghel out of the country?"

Grey's grip on her arm intensified. "Shut up! You don't know what you're saying, the harm you can do. Here, go back to my office. It's the last door off that rear hallway, beyond the kitchen and the loos. Wait for me there; I'll be along quick as I can."

She nodded and turned, shouldering around a group of men who stood with their backs to her, and made her way to a door marked "toilets."

The office was small, furnished with a bank of old file cabinets and an equally well used desk and chair. Apparently it also served as a supply room, since cartons of bathroom tissue, paper towels, and canned goods as well as large crates of onions and sacks of potatoes were stacked against its walls. The desk was a mare's nest of invoices, order blanks, and scraps of paper with notes scribbled on them; in the center of it all rested a plate containing a half-eaten and crusted meal of fish and chips. The room reeked of cod, grease, and cigarette smoke, augmented by the more subtle odor of fresh onions.

She wrinkled her nose and went around the desk to where a window was covered by crooked venetian blinds. At first the blinds resisted her tugging at the cord; then the window resisted her pushing at its lower half. When she finally heaved it up, the air that entered was surprisingly warm and misted; although fresher than that in the office, it carried the stench of garbage. Joanna leaned out and saw a trash dumpster directly below. The brick wall of the adjacent building was only a few feet away. While it was still early evening, what light that filtered down between the closely set walls was yellowish and muted—

"Good evening, Joanna," a voice said behind her.

Its raspiness and faint accent—so faint that only one who knew the speaker could have placed its origin—touched her with a coldness at the nape of her neck. For a moment she froze, hands still braced on the windowsill. Then she turned to face Antony Parducci.

Her first impression was of how much the years had aged him—even more so than when she'd briefly and violently encountered him in San Francisco the previous fall. Only his eyes were as she remembered them: deep set and an electric blue, the one feature he'd passed on to his son. But while E.J.'s were usually filled with good humor and an intense enjoyment of life, Parducci's were cold and flat. Now as they met Joanna's it was as if some internal switch were flipped on, setting them alight with anger and hatred.

She responded in kind—a visceral repulsion that wiped out all traces of shock and made her feel curiously in control of herself.

"Hello, Tony," she said.

Clearly her matter-of-fact response disconcerted him. He raised his shaggy gray eyebrows a fraction, then shut the door behind him. There was a stack of crates next to it;

Parducci sat on it, drawing his loose Burberry around him. Inside the coat the shape of his tall frame hinted at a nearly cadaverous thinness; his hair had thinned too, and it straggled across the high dome of his head. His facial flesh was drawn tight against the bones, and the hollows around his eyes were dark and sunken. She had thought Matt Wickins might be unwell when she first saw him, but whatever was wrong with Parducci struck her as far more serious. She studied him carefully, wondering.

After a moment he said, "I have seen that look on your face many times before."

"Have you now?" She moved away from the window, putting the desk and chair between them, and gripped the back of the chair with both hands.

"Yes. You are analyzing. You were always analyzing, Joanna."

"Yes. I suppose you're right."

"Is that what you were doing with Mr. Grey—analyzing?"

She recalled Grey's alarmed glance over her shoulder when she began talking about Matt's taking the painting out of the country. "You were out there by the bar, then."

"Yes. I saw you come in, and managed to join the group of jolly topers behind you." He laughed, and the irony was not lost on Joanna: *The Jolly Toper* was the title of a Frans Hals painting, and a Hals was what Parducci had been after the last time they encountered each other. "What were you and Mr. Grey discussing so earnestly?" he asked.

"Not much. I was just trying to find out if he knows where Matt Wickins is. He doesn't."

Parducci's lips compressed into a thin line and he shook his head.

"It's true," she said. "I suspected you had commissioned a middleman to arrange the theft of *There Hangs the Knife*—Ian Sneath, wasn't it?"

He merely watched her.

"And Sneath contacted his fagin—Matt."

Parducci still didn't speak. The burning emotion had faded from his eyes; now they were merely moody.

"But as I said, all that was just guesswork. I was trying to get Grey to confirm it."

Parducci shifted on the crate, crossing one leg over the other and adjusting the knife-sharp crease in his trouser leg. While the man himself seemed to be deteriorating. Joanna noted that his dress was as immaculate and expensive as ever. Finally he said, "You have never been a good liar, Joanna—save for the time when you spirited my son away from me. But we'll speak of that in a moment. First I want to know what you are doing in London."

"That's simple enough. I read about the discovery of this new Brueghel, and about the upcoming auction. It didn't take much to figure out that you'd been responsible for the thefts of the other paintings in the Proverb Series, and I assumed you would turn up here."

"And you saw it as your opportunity to further your personal vendetta against me."

"More professional than personal. People like you have got to be stopped."

"People like me . . . or me in particular?"

"It's one and the same."

"No, I don't believe so."

"Why not?"

"Let me ask you this: Would you be so determined to put an end to my career were I not the father of your child—a son with whom you have allowed me no contact since the day of his birth?"

"Since before his birth. You left as soon as you learned I was pregnant."

"Yes, but I had a change of heart and returned for my son as soon as I learned of his existence. You had already spirited him away. It took me over twenty years to locate him, and when I finally came face-to-face with him, I found he had no idea of my existence.''

''Well, he does now, but he still doesn't consider you his father. Twenty some years is too late to return and try to claim the privilege. You gave that up the minute you walked out on me in Paris.''

Parducci smiled. ''You see—that is what all this is about. It is nothing more than the petty revenge of a woman scorned.''

She started, remembering Richard's Picasso of that title and the conversation they'd had about the high price of revenge.

Parducci was watching her again, his smile gone. ''Why this hatred, Joanna?'' he said. ''Why, after more than twenty years?''

She studied him back, unwilling to trivialize her feelings by giving him a facile answer. What she saw was a man who was about to cross the boundary between middle and old age—should he live that long. Besides the obvious physical debilitation, there was a weariness in his bearing, and he had a grim, inward-looking aura that seemed to be habitual. She wondered suddenly if Parducci was dying and knew it. That would perhaps explain his traveling to California to locate E.J. the previous fall.

Along with that thought she was struck by something else: how mortal the man was; how powerless—in spite of his evil nature—when faced by the greater power and evil of death. In light of that, his question took on some validity. Why all the hatred?

Why all the anger? The nights of waking and brooding until dawn. The hours spent studying the Interpol circulars on art thefts, searching for a thread, a clue, anything that would lead her to him. Lead her to what? This aging, ill, pathetic creature?

As if he sensed a softening in her, Parducci said, "How is the boy, Joanna?"

It was the wrong question. Her protective instincts flared. "Don't ask me about him."

"He is my son. I have the right."

"You have no rights!"

Parducci sighed wearily. "Are we back to this point again?"

"We will always come back to this point. It's the crux of everything between us."

His eyes flickered and their lids slipped over them like hoods. He seemed to be struggling to control a rage. When he spoke his voice was harsher than normal. "For the moment—and only this one—forget the crux of everything. Just tell me how he is."

She gripped the chair back harder, aware she was alone here with him, out of earshot of the bar patrons, perhaps even of the kitchen staff.

She said, "E.J. is in good health."

"Has he found a line of work?"

"In a way. He tends bar at a restaurant."

"Has he married?"

"No, he lives with me. In the house where you visited him last fall."

"Yes, last fall. What was his reaction to my visit?"

"He guessed you were his father, he saw your eyes. Why didn't you tell him who you were?"

"As you say, he doesn't consider me his father. He wouldn't have accepted it. Did he consider David Stark his father?"

"Yes. And he was—in every way but blood."

Parducci nodded. The inward-looking expression was intense now. After a moment he rubbed his hands together—as if washing them clean of the son who refused to acknowledge him.

"Now," he said, "we will return to the matter at hand. Matt Wickins. He has taken delivery of the Brueghel and disappeared. I learned that much from the young man who carried out the actual theft."

Joanna felt a chill creep across her shoulder blades. If Parducci had learned that from the thief, it meant he'd been the one who killed him. "Where did you see him?" she asked. "At Matt's flat?"

"Yes. He was drunk on Matt's cheap liquor, but not so drunk that he couldn't tell me that Matt planned to leave London. I want to know where he went."

"I don't know. Why don't you ask John Grey? Maybe he'll tell you more than he would tell me."

"Grey claims that he knows nothing. I find that hard to believe—given his associations with both Wickins and Sneath—but I can hardly bludgeon it out of him in front of his customers."

"Maybe Sneath knows, then."

Parducci suddenly looked grim. He got up and moved toward the desk. She tensed, ready to move in the opposite direction, whichever way he came at her. "Why don't you talk to Sneath?" she said.

Parducci stopped in front of the desk. "I already have. What he said was of no use. I want the truth from you, Joanna."

She couldn't tell him Matt was headed to Falmouth—not if she wanted to get there first and reclaim her painting. There must be some bit of information that would temporarily satisfy him....

"All right! Grey said Sneath had put Matt in touch with someone. I think it was someone who could help him leave the country."

Parducci blinked. His eyes were still on her face, but they didn't see her at all. They remained fixed for a moment, then flooded with surprise. "Charming," he said.

"What?"

"Never mind." He remained in the same place, fiddling with the belt of his raincoat. His eyes were once again seeing her, and the calculating expression there made her afraid. She looked down at his hand, expecting to see a gun.

Apparently she was easy to read. Parducci laughed mirthlessly. "No, I am not planning to shoot you, Joanna. There are too many people nearby."

"But there weren't many people near Matt's flat, were there?" It was a dangerous question, but she had to know.

"You think I killed the young thief, do you?"

"Did you?"

"Don't you know?"

And then she realized too late what he'd been doing with the belt of his coat—loosening it. Yanking it free, he started around the desk toward her. She should have been more on her guard....

She shoved the chair at him and tried to scramble around the desk toward the door. A sack of potatoes that had slid off its pile and was lying on the floor tripped her.

She fell to her knees, scraping her hand on the rough hemp of the sack. Parducci pushed the chair aside and rounded the desk, only a few feet away.

Joanna pushed up and realized her path was blocked by the stack of crates Parducci had been sitting on. She glanced around, saw a letter opener in the desk. She reached for it, but Parducci was already rounding the corner. He smashed his body against hers, and she fell forward, her hand digging into the slimy fish and chips.

She grabbed up a fistful of the mess and tried to twist her torso. Parducci rammed her flat against the desktop. She kicked back at his shin, and when he grunted in pain she wriggled free and flung the handful of garbage at him. It missed and splattered the door.

Joanna began to scream, even though she was sure the sound wouldn't carry far enough.

Parducci moved in again, the raincoat belt dangling from one hand. His breath came in rasps, his face was a congested red. His eyes glinted aquamarine from beneath lowered lids.

Joanna screamed again. Parducci pushed her back on the desk and got the belt around her neck.

My God, she thought, he's going to kill me....

FOURTEEN

SHE HAD ALWAYS HATED getting up in the morning, but for most of her life circumstances had conspired to force her out of bed. Now something—no, someone—was doing it again: shaking her... slapping her face, for God's sake! An arm supported her shoulders, and then she breathed in foul medicinal air. She gasped, sputtered, and mumbled, "Go away!"

"Coming around now," a female voice said.

"Miss Stark?" This one was a man. "Are you all right?"

Both of these people had English accents. Where was she, anyway? She shook her head groggily and opened her eyes. Faces came into focus. John Grey and his elderly barmaid. What had happened with Parducci also came into focus—fuzzily. She moaned and shut her eyes again. Her head throbbed horribly.

"There, you'll be fine now," John Grey said. "Let's just get you off the floor."

"No." Her mouth was dry, cottony. She swallowed. "Leave me alone a minute."

Grey, the one who had been supporting her shoulders, lay her back against a hard bumpy surface. She kept her eyes closed and touched it with her hand—one of the sacks of potatoes. She said, "What was that God-awful stink?"

"Smelling salts," the barmaid said.

"I didn't know they were even made anymore."

"They are—and they're effective."

"I'll say." After a moment she opened her eyes and looked at Grey. He and the barmaid were kneeling on either side of her in the confined space between the desk and the items stacked against the wall. "What happened?" she asked.

"I was on my way back here when I heard a rumpus. That bloke had you down on the desk and was trying to throttle you."

Her hand went to her throat. There was a slight ridge where the belt had bound, but no abrasions. "What do you mean—'that bloke'?"

The publican avoided her eyes. "The one I caught trying to kill you. He must have followed you back here."

"Are you claiming you don't know he was Antony Parducci?"

"I... All right, I know him."

"Did you send him after me?"

"No."

"See him follow me?"

"If I had I would surely have tried to stop him."

She wasn't sure whether she could believe him, but the fact that he had apparently saved her was a point in his favor. "What happened to Parducci?"

"I pulled him off you, and we had a tussle. He got away from me, went out that window into the alley. By then you'd slipped off the desk and hit your head."

So that was the cause of this awful throbbing. She put her hand to the back of her skull and felt a sore spot.

The barmaid said, "That wants attention."

"I'll see to it later."

"You should see to it now. Head injuries—"

Grey said, "I'll make sure she does, luv. And you'd best go back out front, before those savages commence a beer riot."

The woman looked put out but got to her feet. As she crossed to the door, Joanna said, "Thanks for the smelling salts."

The barmaid smiled ironically. "You're welcome, dearie. Smith's, they're called, sold at most chemists'."

When her footfalls had faded away, Grey said, "She doesn't know about all this, and I don't want her getting ideas."

Joanna thought of Ivy Harrison, who knew far more than *her* employer suspected. If this incident didn't prompt Grey to be honest with her, she could always pump the barmaid. She said, "Parducci got away, then?"

Stupid question. Grey merely nodded.

Joanna braced herself to sit up, trying to remember what had gone on with Parducci. Just before he'd attacked her, she'd asked him if he had killed the thief in Matt's flat. He'd said, "Don't you know?" in that mocking way of his, and then had come at her with the belt stretched tight between his hands. Well, now she knew; there was no reason to doubt it. But why. . . ?

Back up, she told herself. What happened before that? He was questioning me about—

She jerked upright and said, "Sneath! We've got to contact Sneath and warn him that Parducci might be on his way to see him again. Tell him not to say where Matt has gone."

"What's this about Sneath?"

She started to stand. "I told Parducci Sneath had referred Matt to someone. Parducci didn't get anything out of Sneath before, but he might go back and use force."

"We'll ring him. Stay there." Grey went to the desk. There was a phone on the floor behind it. He lifted it and dialed.

Joanna stood anyway. For a moment she felt dizzy; she clutched the stack of crates for balance. Then the sensation passed, and she adjusted her rumpled clothing.

Grey was tapping impatiently on the desk, the receiver pressed to his ear. "Come on, Ian," he said. After an interval he hung up. "No answer."

"Were you trying his place of business or his home?"

"The business. He planned to stay there until at least ten, in the event—"

"In the event Matt tried to contact him?"

Grey dipped his chin in acknowledgement.

"I want you to tell me everything that's gone on," she said. "But first try Sneath's home."

He did so, with identical results. "What shall we do now?" he asked, dropping the receiver in its cradle.

"We'll go over there. It's possible—barely—that we're not too late."

"I can't leave—"

"You've got to."

He hesitated, then said, "Right. We'll leave by the rear door; my car's parked at the foot of the alley."

MATT'S BLOCK had seemed more depressing in daylight, but the block where Sneath's business was located took on a positively sinister aura at night. Few lights showed, although weird atonal music came from one of the boarded-up buildings. Its notes twisted and tangled in an electronic jumble that set Joanna's nerves on edge. The metal sign above Sneath's door creaked in harsh counterpoint. Through the glass the front room showed dark and empty, but the humpbacked shapes of the wine casks were outlined by light from the office area beyond.

Grey had insisted on parking his car a block and a half away. They had then proceeded rapidly on foot, keeping well in the shadows of the buildings. Now he stopped, putting a cautionary hand on her shoulder, and looked up and down the block.

She frowned and cocked her head at the doorway.

Grey moved closer to her. "Lights are on," he whispered, "but there's no sign of Ian's Bentley."

"Where does he usually park it?"

"Here, at the curb." He moved to the door and gave it an experimental shove. It opened. He motioned for Joanna to follow, and together they stepped inside.

The smell of spilled wine was even more pungent than before. Grey moved toward the desk, surprisingly light on his feet for a big man. His graceful stealthiness was the instinctive motion of a professional thief who may have retired but has never forgotten his skills. Joanna smiled faintly: she could guess where Grey had gotten the capital to buy the Starving Ox.

He stopped by the order desk and touched a cautionary finger to his lips, even though she so far hadn't made a sound. He stood listening, and she listened too. The only things she heard were the sigh of the pneumatic mechanism as it closed the door and the rasp and groan of the sign outside. The strains of electronic music had been lost in the wind that swept down the alley.

Grey looked at her and shrugged. Then he moved toward the hallway leading to the offices. Joanna went behind him, wishing she possessed his grace. At any moment she was sure she would bump into something and make a racket—

Her right foot slammed into one of the cartons stacked against the wall, and she stifled a cry. It came out a snort that echoed off the crates around them. Grey froze, flashing her a look of annoyance, and stood with his head high, practically keening the air. There was no response from the rear of the building.

Again the publican shrugged. Then he continued to move toward the half-Plexiglas wall in front of them. Fluorescent lights shone on three unoccupied desks. Two were tidy, their owners' work put away for the night; the other was similar to Grey's, with papers strewn over its surface.

Joanna joined him at the wood-and-plastic partition, peering into the room. Had it not been for the burning lights and the untidy desk, it would have seemed a normal office, put to rights until the start of the next day's business. Then she noticed that the chair belonging to the cluttered desk lay on its side. She tugged Grey's arm to call his attention to it, but he had already noticed.

Grey whirled and went to the door in the partition. It wouldn't budge. He swore and stepped back to kick it in.

Joanna said, "It opens out this way."

"Right you are." He grimaced ruefully. "I guess we'll have to smash in that bloody plastic." He looked around and snatched up a wine bottle from one of the cases behind them. Wielding it like a club, he beat against the top part of the partition. The Plexiglas crunched, and a spiderweb pattern of cracks formed on it. Grey hit it again, but the bottle connected with the solid wood below and broke. Red wine splattered to the floor, splashing both of them.

Joanna stepped back and wiped wine from her face. A drop trickled onto her lips, and she licked it away; it was a heavy burgundy. Already its odor was rising from the floor and her clothing.

Grey motioned impatiently to her. "Lend me a hand."

She stepped into the spreading delta of wine. Grey punched the Plexiglas at the center of the web, and some shards clattered to the floor of the office. Joanna grasped the edge of the hole and broke off a big chunk, dropped it into the wine spill, and broke off another.

When the hole was big enough, Grey boosted himself up on the partition and wriggled through. He dropped to the floor, sprang up, and hurried toward the disordered desk. When he rounded it, he stopped abruptly, then knelt down, his head out of her line of sight.

"What is it?" she called.

No answer.

"Grey!"

Grey stood up, his face ashen. "It's Sneath. He's unconscious—badly smashed up. When I touched him, I thought he was coming round, but he only managed one word and then passed out again.''

''What word?''

''*Charming*. Funny thing for a bloke that's been beaten to say.''

It had sounded strange coming from Parducci, too, she thought. What on earth could it mean? She said, ''Better call an ambulance.''

Grey went to use the phone on one of the desks.

Joanna gripped the ledge in front of her, closing her eyes; the throbbing in her head accelerated. Against her lids a scene replayed: herself telling Parducci, ''People like you have got to be stopped.'' And him replying, ''People like me—or me in particular?''

She said aloud, ''You in particular, Tony.''

FIFTEEN

AFTER HE'D HUNG UP the phone, Grey unlocked the door in the partition and emerged from the office. He said, "I don't think you'd best be here when the ambulance and coppers arrive. I've legitimate business with Sneath—he's my wine supplier—but your presence would be difficult to explain."

"Fine, I'll go."

"Take my car. You can leave it in the alley where it was parked before. Will you be able to find your way well enough?"

"I think so. Are you going to tell them about Parducci?"

"Christ no! I've myself to protect. Let Sneath tell them, if he must."

"But he won't."

"I'd think not. That's why Parducci left him alive—he knew Sneath wouldn't jeopardize himself by talking." Grey handed her his car keys.

She pocketed them but didn't move. "Before I leave," she said, "tell me what's been going on."

"There's no time for that." He began urging her along the corridor, his shock at what had been done to Sneath mixing with his impatience to have her gone.

"Tell me, or I'll stay here and we'll both tell the police."

That stopped him. After a pause he said, "Right, then. You had it figured pretty near. Sneath's a middleman, uses Matt and me to make his arrangements. Parducci contacted him about this job, and Sneath asked Matt to have a go at it. Matt went to and fro a bit, trying to make up his mind whether to cross you by using the inside information you'd given him, or to go ahead and help you nab Parducci. In the end Sneath and I convinced him it was too much money to give up for the sake of an old friendship." Grey paused, looking at her speculatively. "You used to belong to both of them, didn't you?"

"Go on with your story."

"That's answer enough for me. Well, it didn't take any of us long to realize there was even more money to be made if we crossed both you *and* Parducci. And that's just what Matt did. Sneath and I were to pretend we'd been just as ill used as Parducci, but actually Sneath put Matt in touch with a collector who was eager to lay his hands on the painting, and a way to get the goods to him. We three planned to split the profits."

"A collector? Who? Where?"

"Out of the country. South America? It's always a good market."

"And what was the way to get the painting to him?"

"I don't know that. Sneath's very closemouthed about his arrangements. Normally he'd have taken care of it, but he had a business conflict and decided Matt should make the delivery in his place. He didn't even give Matt his instructions until the afternoon of the day the painting was to be snatched."

"Tell me about the thief who was murdered at Matt's flat. Parducci as good as admitted killing him."

Grey held the street door open and practically shoved her outside. "I don't know about that, either; nor does Sneath. Parducci must have done it; he thought he would be collecting the painting at Matt's place that night, but by the time he was due to arrive, Matt would have been on his way. I don't know why Amir was still at the flat when Parducci arrived, though—that's got me done about."

"Amir?"

"Amir Moradi. He was Iranian, new to our stable."

"I think he was probably helping himself to Matt's liquor supply. Parducci said he was drunk."

Grey nodded and gestured impatiently. In the distance the seesawing wail of the sirens had begun. "You'd best be going."

"One more question. The word *charming* doesn't mean anything to you?"

"No. Damned odd thing for Sneath to say."

The sirens were getting closer. There were other things she would have liked to ask Grey, but no time. She started down the sidewalk. "I'll leave your car at the pub."

"Will I be seeing you there?"

"No, but I'll be in touch."

Grey looked as if she wouldn't be doing him much of a favor.

GREY'S CAR was an ancient Anglia, and its gears meshed less than perfectly. Joanna had little opportunity to indulge in speculation as she manipulated the balky machine along the unfamiliar streets. She took several wrong turns—once blundering into a one-way alley—but eventually reached the Starving Ox. It was only when she was back in her Fiesta that she could turn her thoughts to the questions that plagued her.

Had Parducci taken Sneath's car? Grey had said the Bentley wasn't in its customary place, so that seemed likely. If he had, he must have been in a great hurry: stealing a car wasn't his usual style. And if he was in a hurry, it might mean he'd beaten out of Sneath the information that Matt had gone to Cornwall.

But perhaps Parducci had beaten Sneath *before* going to the Starving Ox. If Sneath had lapsed into unconsciousness without giving him any information, it might account for Parducci's savagery against her. But what about the word *charming*, which both men had uttered? It seemed to have had some meaning for Parducci—meaning that he'd only grasped when she mentioned Matt's leaving the country.

Charming. A name? Perhaps a code name?

The question that bothered her most, however, had nothing to do with Parducci's confrontation with Sneath. It centered on Matt's telephone call to her at Richard Bloomfield's house. What had his exact words been? She concentrated, trying to resurrect the memory.

Something about not asking questions and just coming back to London.

No, he'd said, *The whole bloody thing's about to go bust.* How? Why?

She thought over the rest of the conversation. She'd demanded to know what was going on. Matt had refused to tell her. He'd said to come to his flat; he'd leave the door off the latch; they could talk then.

But that had been less than two hours before Amir Moradi had stolen the Brueghel. And long after Matt had rented the car he intended to drop in Falmouth. Even longer after he and Grey and Sneath had conspired to cross not only Parducci but her. *Had* something "gone bust"? Or had that merely been Matt's method of luring her to his flat—where she was likely to encounter Parducci?

No, he wouldn't have done that to her.

But the alternative was even more painful: Matt had planned to kill Moradi and set her up for the crime. Once she'd mentioned the resemblance of his flat to the one on Worship Street where his client had set him up many years before, that old memory might have become an evil inspiration. But why frame her? He would have known she'd eventually be cleared. As a temporary measure to prevent her from coming after him? No, it was too extreme. Besides, even if Parducci hadn't practically told her he'd killed the Iranian, she wouldn't have believed Matt had done it.

Not because he wasn't capable of killing, but because he had no compelling motive.

None of her reasoning made any sense.

Joanna's head throbbed painfully. Every breath she took was filled with the sickly odor of the wine that saturated her clothing. She wanted to go back to her hotel, bathe, and sleep, but she also needed to check in with Christopher. After a moment of indecision, she checked the nearest street sign, calculated her position, and charted a course to Christopher's flat in Bloomsbury.

SHE HAD NEVER BEEN to Christopher's home before, but it was in the Bedford Square area and thus easy to locate. The row of buildings was a prime example of eighteenth-century terrace architecture, with ornamental black iron fences and fanlights over the doors; Christopher occupied a prestigious ground-floor garden flat. In spite of the lights that shone behind the drapes in what she assumed must be his front room, it was a long interval between her ring and the answering buzz that tripped the lock on the door. When Christopher looked out into the foyer, his face registered dismay.

"What are you doing here?" he said.

"Such a warm welcome," she replied.

"And what on earth has happened to you?" His eyes had widened at her disheveled appearance, but he made no move to admit her to the flat.

"I think we'd better discuss that inside."

Christopher glanced over his shoulder.

From the room behind him a familiar voice said, "Christopher, is that Joanna?"

"Richard?" she whispered.

Christopher nodded and rolled his eyes.

"Uh-oh."

"You may as well come in." He held the door open ungraciously.

Richard Bloomfield sat on a brown leather sofa in front of a small marble fireplace where two logs burned. He glanced at Joanna and nodded curtly, then looked back at the flames. Christopher stood behind her, attempting to help her off with her jacket.

"What *have* you been doing?" he murmured. "You positively reek of wine."

"Well, I haven't been drinking it, that's for sure."

Christopher sniffed and carried away the offending garment. Joanna moved toward the still-silent Richard.

The room was a curious eclectic blend of styles, and it was a credit to Christopher's skill as a decorator that the combination worked. The eighteenth-century appointments were enhanced by paint in bright primary colors; the massive modern sofa emphasized the delicate prettiness of the marble fireplace. Twentieth-century sculpture stood in old-fashioned wall niches; a Corot landscape had been placed far enough away from a bold Jackson Pollock that it remained undiminished. Under other circumstances Joanna would have delighted in examining such a room, but at the moment she could only concentrate on the emotional chill emanating from her old friend.

She sat down on one of a pair of leather chairs that flanked the fireplace—far enough away that she wouldn't subject him to the lingering wine smell. "This is a surprise," she said. "When I last saw you, you told me you had no intention of coming to London in the near future."

He turned his head toward her. There was no twinkle in his eyes now, and his wizened face looked more troll-like than elfin. "I saw no need to come to London then."

"What brings you here now?"

"I think you know."

Christopher reentered the room. "A drink, Joanna?"

"Yes—gin, if you have it."

He busied himself at a liquor trolley; Joanna thought she detected a nervousness in the way he rattled the glasses.

"Christopher," she said, "did you ask Richard to come up here?"

He dropped an ice cube on the floor and swore as he bent to retrieve it. "I beg your pardon?" he said.

"Did you ask Richard—"

"Ivy called me," Richard said.

Christopher handed her a drink. She sipped it slowly before she spoke again. "I suppose she told you what she suspects Christopher and I have been up to."

"She told me what she knows. Ivy knows everything that goes on at the gallery."

"And you're here to advise Christopher to have nothing more to do with me, or my fake Brueghel."

A grimly amused expression passed over Richard's features. "I have...advised him, yes. And he has agreed to abide by my wishes."

Christopher sat down at the other end of the sofa, a drink in hand, and stared into his glass, refusing to meet Joanna's eyes. Judging by his flushed complexion, she guessed he'd had quite a number of gins that evening.

To Richard she said, "I realize now that I should have told you what I persuaded Christopher to do."

"Why didn't you?"

"I suppose I knew you wouldn't permit it. And of course you would have been right not to. I was jeopardizing your gallery by using it in that way."

"And presuming upon our friendship."

She bit her lip, then sipped some more gin. "That, too. I'm sorry. I didn't consider—"

"It's difficult to consider others when caught up in vengefulness." Richard's tone had softened, but was still reproving.

Joanna had no reply.

"Remember our decision?" he went on. "The one we had at my house before you received that phone call and had to rush back here?"

She nodded.

"We concluded—or at least *I* concluded—that revenge entails terrible costs. It diminishes one, Joanna. But I suppose our friendship was one of the costs you were prepared to pay."

"You can't be saying we're no longer friends—"

"I honestly don't know if we are or not. I know the quality of the friendship has been changed—perhaps irrevocably."

She felt a sudden wrenching in her breast and lowered her eyes so he wouldn't see the tears that were springing to them.

Richard stood and said to Christopher, "I must be going now. I'll stop by the gallery tomorrow morning to appraise that set of prints and discuss those other matters."

Christopher came to his feet and went to fetch Richard's coat. When he returned with it, he helped him put it on with considerable fussing, as if he were glad to have something to do. Before he stepped out the door, Richard turned toward Joanna.

He said, "What will you do now?"

"I have a lead to where my painting is. I'll try to retrieve it."

"And then?"

She hesitated, then decided the truth could not make things worse now. "Then I'll probably find some other way to use it to set up Antony Parducci. You're not aware of it, but Parducci has killed one man and badly injured another. I've never known him to do that before, and it's an indication he's out of control and has to be stopped.''

Surprisingly Richard didn't seem interested in what she had said. He merely asked, ''Must you be the one to take on the task, Joanna?''

''I not only must—I *want* to.''

He nodded as if he'd known the answer all along. ''Then I wish you luck. I am afraid you'll need a great deal of it.''

SIXTEEN

AFTER CHRISTOPHER SHUT the door behind Richard, he let out an enormous sigh. "That damned Ivy!" he said.

"No," Joanna said, "she was right to call him. And Richard's right, too: I shouldn't have involved the gallery in this scheme. What if the thief had taken some of the really valuable artworks as well as my fake Brueghel? Or what if Ivy'd been seriously hurt—or killed? No, I wasn't thinking straight. I suppose Richard chewed you out?"

"Chewing out's not Richard's style. He merely reasoned with me—which made me feel all the more the heel." Christopher's gaze moved to her glass. "Another gin?"

"Yes, please."

He went to the drink trolley. "What's this about Parducci killing someone? Not the fellow at Matt's flat?"

"It looks that way." She told him about her evening: the violent confrontation with Parducci; finding Ian Sneath unconscious; what John Grey had admitted. As he listened Christopher nervously jiggled the ice in his glass, and when she had finished he went back to the trolley for a refill.

"Nasty stuff you've encountered," he said.

"Very."

"You've found out more than I was able. One of my clients gave me the name of a friend of his on the police, and I spoke with him. What he said confirms the man's identity—Amir Moradi. He'd only been in the country some eight months; was supposed to be employed at an uncle's store, one of these quick food marts that the Asians and other immigrants seem to be opening up all round. The only other thing of interest would tend to support your idea that

Moradi remained in Matt's flat to avail himself of the liquor supply: he had quite a high blood-alcohol content.''

"I wonder if Matt encouraged him to 'avail himself'?''

"Why would he?''

"Well, Parducci was due to arrive and take delivery on the painting. If Parducci thought Moradi knew where Matt had gone, he might have lost time questioning him, been delayed in rushing after Matt.''

"That doesn't make a great deal of sense, considering that Parducci wouldn't have known where to start looking anyway.''

"True. Fuzzy thinking on my part. I guess we can just chalk it up to a young man's fondness for alcohol. I don't suppose you can guess at the significance of the word *charming*?''

He shook his head. They were both silent for a moment. The only sound was the ticking of a French Regency mantel clock. After a moment Christopher sighed and ran his hand through his already disheveled curls.

Joanna asked, "Do you think your business relationship with Richard has been permanently damaged?''

"Let's say he's going to be spending a great deal more time at the gallery in the future. The free rein I spoke of has been tightened.''

"I'm sorry I got you into such a fix.''

He made a gesture of dismissal. "I didn't have to agree to help you, now did I? And if the whole thing *had* come off, it would have made the gallery look good. Anyone who helps put a stop to this bloody thieving is the darling of the art world.''

"Yes, that was what Meg Knight was banking on.'' Just thinking of the reporter made Joanna shudder. "Meg's going to kill me.''

"I'll tell you, I wouldn't want to be the one to face that barracuda.'' After a reflective pause, Christopher added,

"Joanna, did you know that Parducci would go to Sneath, and Sneath to Matt?"

"No. That was pure serendipity—or it would have been if Matt hadn't decided to turn on me. Originally his function was just to keep his ears open and try to find out about the arrangements, perhaps insinuate himself into them. Then Evans on the Art Squad would have stepped in. He planned to put men on Parducci and follow him and the painting clear to the collector. Now we've lost out on both of them."

"Bad luck."

"No, part of the problem was my stupidity in not telling Matt the painting was a fake. I didn't trust him."

"Well, once again he proved worthy of a lack of trust, didn't he?"

Joanna looked at him curiously, remembering the bitterness with which both he and Matt had spoken of each other. "You've had dealings with him recently, haven't you?"

He nodded shamefacedly. "When he got out of prison Matt came to me, looking to borrow some money. He acted as if it was a simple loan, but I thought it had the odor of blackmail and I agreed. It would ruin me, having some of those things about the old days come out now."

"And then?"

"I gave him the money in cash—I didn't want a check going through my account—and told him it was all he was getting out of me, ever. He must have realized I thought him a blackmailer, because he threw the money in my face. Said if that was the sort of person I'd become, he wanted nothing of me. That was the last I saw of him." After a long pause he added. "It makes me angry at him, for forcing me to see myself that clearly."

She nodded. "I guess part of me is angry at Richard because he made me realize how crassly I tried to take advantage of him. Another part of me wants to redeem myself.

And, you know, there may be a way to pull this out yet, and partly set myself square with both him and Meg Knight. If I can find Matt and get my painting back.''

Christopher looked more cheerful. She couldn't tell whether it was a result of the gin or a reflection of her own optimism. "You mentioned that to Richard. Do you really have a lead?''

"Yes.''

"What will you do to Matt when you locate him?''

"What I'd *like* to do involves amputating a couple of his more prized appendages. What I'll actually do is put him to good use—make him work for me in exchange for not turning him over to the police.''

"How?''

"I'm not sure yet. Whatever I work out will hinge on the fact that Parducci's still determined to have that Brueghel.''

With one of those mood swings characteristic of drunken people, Christopher now looked melancholy. "I don't suppose I'll be able to help you.''

"Not if you want to continue in partnership with Richard.''

"I do. But do you know? Sometimes I wish I'd remained free.''

"Free? How do you mean?''

"Oh, you remember how it was back in the old days. We lived hand to mouth, and the digs were ratty, and we were always on the lookout for the coppers. But there was freedom then.... You remember that girl of mine? Sibyl?''

"Yes.'' She'd been a clerk in a cheap dress shop; wide-hipped, overly made up, and not above turning a trick when Christopher's back was turned.

"Beautiful girl. An angel. I wonder what happened to her?''

Joanna suspected, but said, "I can't imagine.''

"And that pub—what was the name of it?''

"I don't remember." It had been even more squalid than the Starving Ox; she'd never gone there without Matt to protect her.

"Neither do I. Great place, though. We had some great times there, didn't we? The fellowship, the darts tournaments . . . people don't play darts anymore, at least not properly. And it was the Beatles era. Songs on the jukebox. 'Ob-la-di, ob-la-da, life goes on . . . '"

It was the most human she'd seen Christopher since the day she ran into him on the Soho street—and the drunkest. She said gently, "I'm sure you have better times now."

"Do I? Christ! Look at all this!" He gestured wildly, and for a moment Joanna feared for the lamp standing next to him. "All I do is pay. To the building society for the flat; to the char that comes in twice a week; to the butcher and the greengrocer and the wine merchant. There's my share of Ivy's salary, and the solicitors. The rates have gone up; I can scarely turn on the lights without cringing. The car wants constant attention. Even to have my hair cut, for Christ's sake . . ."

Joanna had often heard the same complaints from a formerly bohemian friend in Sonoma who had started a little shop on a shoestring and hit it big with the tourist trade. She'd listened critically enough to realize that people who went on that way weren't actually all that dissatisfied: complaining about one's obligations was an inverse way of bragging about one's success.

She said, "Those old times weren't all that good, Christopher."

"Why not?"

"Hand to mouth meant just that: there were whole days when we didn't eat. There were rats in that tenement, and cockroaches, and people who would steal you blind if you stepped out for five minutes and left your door unlocked. And the cops were always there, always watching us." As she spoke, she realized it seemed as if that had been another world, as if those things had happened to another Joanna.

He sat very still for a moment, hands cupped around his half-full glass. Then he shook his head, shuddered, and set the drink on the coffee table. "You know, you're quite right. It must have been the gin talking."

Joanna smiled and got to her feet. Her body felt stiff and sore, but the throbbing in her head had vanished. She stretched and yawned.

"You're going?" Christopher asked.

"Yes. I'm leaving the city in the small hours of the morning."

"Going where?"

"It's best you don't know. But I'll be in touch."

Christopher stood—shakily—and tottered off to fetch her jacket.

It was as she walked from his front door to her car that she sensed that someone was covertly watching her.

SEVENTEEN

A HEAVY MIST was lifting as Joanna crossed the bridge over the Tamar River and drove into Cornwall. She had left London at three in the morning, after a brief and dream-jumbled sleep in which the word *charming* reverberated; and while dawn had broken some time ago, the fog had muted its light. For hours now she had felt as if the night before might have spun out into eternity; it was with definite relief that she greeted the first milky rays of sun.

The road was a good one and even when it narrowed to two lanes she made excellent time. The mist continued to burn off and soon she became aware of the surrounding countryside: low hills spotted with golden-flowered gorse and grazing sheep; erratically rambling walls; small stone houses. Farther south the land became less hospitable, more like the Cornwall of romantic fiction: scrub trees grew at odd angles to the rocky soil, and on the horizon the sky-tips—china clay factories' waste dumps—loomed like great white mesas in some uncharted desert.

As she approached Falmouth the terrain gentled again and she encountered a series of roundabouts—those traffic circles that are the bane of most non-British drivers. Joanna enjoyed roundabouts; they satisfied some latent aggressive instinct in her. She would plunge into the swirl of oncoming traffic and fight for position; and if she missed the road she wanted, she would merely sail around the circle for another try. This morning traffic was light, and much to her disappointment, she proceeded without a single harrowing incident.

At the last roundabout before the town, a road bled off toward the harbor. She followed it to the Greenbank Hotel—a sprawling pea green wood-and-stucco structure set on an incline above the water. The plant-filled entry and dark-paneled lobby were as she remembered them, but across from the registration desk stood an easel holding an architectural drawing. As the clerk looked up her reservation, she went over to examine it; it was a plan for a proposed expansion of the hotel, including convention facilities.

The drawing deflated her spirits disproportionately. Shaking her head, she crossed the lobby and looked into the lounge bar. It had been her favorite room on her previous visit: a relic of the twenties or thirties replete with chintz-covered rattan furniture, fake palms, and lamps whose bases were white china elephants. At least, she thought, that was not about to change. Or was it?

She stepped through the door and glanced into a corner. Years before a plant stand had stood there—a white-robed china male figure with face of black upon whose turbaned head had rested a philodendron. She and David had laughed at this silly anachronism, a harmless reminder of the days when the sun never set on the empire, inoffensive because it could not possibly be taken seriously. But now the planter was gone—banished, because of modern-day sensitivities, to some more remote corner or storeroom. Joanna's spirits dipped further. Even the small towns were following in the footsteps of the great cities; soon all places would be indistinguishable in their standardized humorless mediocrity.

"Mrs. Stark?" the desk clerk said.

Joanna shook off her dismal thoughts and went to sign the register.

The spacious room she was shown to had a view of the harbor. While the porter bustled around doing all the things that bellhops in expensive hotels are supposed to, she went to the window and oriented herself. The Greenbank's quay, flag snapping from its pole, extended into the glassy water; beyond it, bare-masted sailboats and cruisers rode at anchor. Across this narrow neck of harbor whitewashed houses nestled above the seawall on tree-studded hills. The main part of town, she remembered, was to the right. Between it and the hotel were the yacht club and municipal pier, and the shipyards extended farther out toward the mouth of the port. A huge science-fictional metal structure—probably a floating oil rig—dominated the distance; it hadn't been there during her last visit. Her gaze moved from it to the cranes and gantries of the yards, and she thought of Matt. It was probable he had already arrived and made contact with the person who could assist his departure from the country. There was no time to waste.

As soon as the porter departed she found a phone directory in the desk drawer and checked to make sure the address she'd been given for Fal Car-Hire was correct. It was listed on the road by which she'd driven in, near the wharves. She went to the vanity sink, washed her face, and patted it dry. Then she leaned toward the mirror and arranged her expression into what she thought was suitable lines for the wife of a missing and seriously disturbed man— the story that had worked so well with the car-hire clerk in London. While on the surface the painful events of her life had left her oddly unmarked, when the need arose she could call upon her memories to make her face reflect distress and suffering. The need was upon her now.

UNFORTUNATELY, her woeful appearance didn't much impress the spotty-faced youth at Fal Car-Hire. Yes, he said, a Mini with that license tag number had been dropped the day before. No, it hadn't been cleaned up yet. No, he couldn't let her inspect it.

"Why not?" she asked.

"The boss wouldn't like it. Besides, I've better things to do with my time."

She took out her wallet. "I'd be glad to pay for your time."

The youth tried to look offended, but his glance rested on the wallet.

"How much?" Joanna said.

He flicked his tongue over his lips and looked around the office, even though no one else was there. "Five quid?"

"Done." She took out a five-pound note. "It's yours—after you tell me about my...uh, husband and show me the car."

The young man eyed the money. "There's not much to tell. He dropped the car yesterday morning, right after we opened. Paid the balance in cash."

"How'd he seem? Cheerful? Nervous?"

"Nervous, I'd say. He kept looking around, as if he was afraid someone might see him."

"Did he mention where he planned to stay?"

"No, he didn't. Just paid the bill and went out."

"Went out where? Was there someone waiting for him? A taxi?"

He reflected, his somewhat slack jaw firmed by concentration. "Not that I noticed."

"Did he go off on foot?"

"...I don't recall."

"Did he ask you any questions?"

"No. Just paid the bill and went out."

"Okay. Let's look at the car now."

The Mini stood near the back of the lot; dusty, with a bug-splattered windshield. Joanna tried the driver's side door and found it unlocked. Inside, the car was clean except for the floor in front of the passenger's seat, which was littered with soft drink cans, empty crisp packages, and candy bar wrappers. Joanna extracted the keys from the ignition and looked in the trunk. Nothing there, either.

The young man shifted impatiently from foot to foot. Joanna ignored him and got into the driver's seat. There was a side pocket on the door containing a map and the rental car company's instruction booklet. She removed them and dug farther into the pocket, coming up with a dirty Kleenex and a crumpled piece of paper. She replaced the Kleenex and smoothed the paper out on the knee of her jeans.

It was plain white, the kind of sheet that could have been torn off a desk scratch pad. On it were a few curving pencil lines, and the letters *F*, *M*, and *P*. The *F* was at the bottom of the drawing and the *M* and *P* near the top, along one of the left-curving marks. All three letters were circled.

A map? she wondered. *F* for "Falmouth"? *M* and *P* for what?

She motioned to the young man. "Take a look at this and see if you can tell me what it is."

He leaned into the car and studied it. "I couldn't tell you."

"Is it possible it's a map?"

"Might be."

"If *F* were for Falmouth, what would the *M* and *P* stand for?"

He shrugged. "You're asking the wrong bloke. I only came down from Torquay a month ago. Don't really know the area."

Joanna sighed and looked at the drawing again. A map—or something else? What? And whose was it? Could she really assume it had belonged to Matt?

She said, "Do you know anything about the company that owns this car?"

"Chevron? My brother worked for them in Torquay. They're small, but good. I should have liked to get on with them but—"

"Do they clean the cars thoroughly once they're returned?"

He looked miffed at the interruption, but said, "As far as I know. We clean ours well, and we're not nearly as good a firm—" He broke off, looking around as if some invisible ear might hear him.

"So this paper probably belonged to my husband."

"I'd say so."

Joanna looked at it again, then turned it over. On the back was a single word, also written in pencil: Trispin.

"What's this—Trispin?" She held it up for him to see. "Is it a town around here?"

"I don't know. Like I said, I only came down a month ago." The youth paused, looking uncomfortable, then added, "Miss, I don't mean to be rude, but I've left the office unattended. The boss wouldn't like that." He looked expectantly at the five-pound note she still clutched in her hand.

She thought of asking him if the word *charming* had any significance for him, but decided to abandon that line of questioning. It was a common phrase, altogether too vague, and she suspected it would have no real meaning to a person not connected with the art underworld. She got out of the car, folding the paper and putting it in her bag before she handed him the money. "Thanks," she said. "I appreciate your help."

As they walked back to the office, a question that she should have asked before occurred to her. "Tell me, did my husband have any luggage with him?"

"Only a small bag, a weekender."

"What about a package? One about this big." She measured off the approximate size of the painting with her hands.

"Oh, right. He had it on the counter next to him while he settled the bill." The young man paused, then added,

"Funny about that package—he kept his hand on it the whole time, as if it was something valuable. And when he went out he carried it in his arms, the way you would a baby."

Matt might well consider the painting his baby, Joanna thought. Like some people's children, it represented his dreams. Too bad he was in for a rude awakening.

EIGHTEEN

A PAIR OF FRENCH TOURISTS were checking into the hotel when Joanna returned, and she was forced to wait next to the architectural drawing while the clerk finished registering them and answered numerous questions about local sightseeing. The clerk was young and polite in the extravagant but essentially insincere manner that she'd noticed in many service personnel during her stay in the country. As she watched she counted how many times he said "thank you" and "thank you very much" to the French couple: nine, sometimes so fast that the words blended unintelligibly. The pleasantry was reduced to a mere speech reflex; he might as well have been saying "um" or "er."

When the porter had hefted the new arrivals' luggage and escorted them from the lobby, Joanna approached the desk. The clerk showed no surprise at her question, merely said "thank-you-very-much" for the tenth time in three minutes, and took the paper from her hand. After studying it for a moment, he asked, "A map, isn't it?"

"I think so. This"—she pointed to the *F*—"is probably Falmouth. I'm curious about what the other letters might stand for."

He traced the curving pencil lines with his forefinger, stopping at the *P*. "Looks as though they might be villages upriver. There are a number of ones there that are too small to be on the road map."

"Up the Helford or the Fal?"

"From the looks of this, the Fal. Most of the little villages are on its banks to the north, but I'm not familiar with them. Just came down from the Lake District a few months ago. Noreen would know—the barmaid in the harbor pub on the lower level. She's from that area originally.''

''What time does the pub open?''

''Six.''

It was twenty after three. Joanna thanked him and went upstairs to her room, wondering at the influx of new people in this area. The desk clerk, the car-rental clerk, even the barmaid who came from upriver: they were all employed in service jobs, an indication, like the plans for expanding the hotel, that Falmouth might be growing and changing.

Upstairs she took out the number that Inspector Evans had given her for the local CID man. When she called his office, however, she was told he was away and would not return until late that evening. She made an appointment for first thing the next morning, then hung up feeling somewhat at a loss.

It was now three-thirty, still hours before the time when the pub would open and she could pursue her only lead. In the meantime, the possibility of catching up with Matt grew even more remote. What would she be doing in his situation? If she put herself in his place . . . but she couldn't. She wished there was someone she could kick the idea around with, someone like Rafferty. . . .

Three-thirty here, seven-thirty in San Francisco. Joanna reached for the phone again and direct-dialed Rafferty's Telegraph Hill apartment. There was no answer. She hung up and dialed again, this time to the offices of Great American Insurance Company in the Wells Fargo Building.

The man who answered Rafferty's extension sounded irritated. Joanna could understand his annoyance: people go in to work early so they won't have to be bothered by the phones. When she asked for Rafferty, the man said curtly, ''He's out of town.''

When they'd last spoken two days ago he'd said nothing about any travel plans. But it wasn't uncommon for him to have to go out of town on the spur of the moment. "Do you have a number where he can be reached?"

"Sorry. His secretary might, but she's not in yet. Do you want to leave a message?"

"No, it's not important." She replaced the receiver and remained where she was seated Indian-style on the bed, slumping forward now, her chin on her fist, her spirits flagging. Another instance of Rafferty not being there when she needed him. It wasn't deliberate, of course, but it happened more and more lately....

She sat there until the gloom threatened to overwhelm her, then went to the window and stared out at the harbor. Seagulls wheeled in air emitting harsh shrieks. A line of swans swam sedately past the quay. One of the river cruise ships was moving into the smaller neck in back of the hotel; as she watched it stopped and dropped anchor, out of service for the night. She looked to the right, past the yacht club, to where the old stone municipal pier jutted out—and had an idea. Quickly she caught up her bag and jacket and set out for the main part of town.

The sidewalk ended a ways beyond the hotel, so she crossed the road and climbed a set of steps to a raised promenade. It was lined with tall, narrow row houses, most of them in poor repair but commanding an excellent view of the harbor. A calico cat emerged through the bars of an iron fence around one of their tiny front gardens and rubbed against her legs. Joanna squatted and scratched its ears, then continued along the promenade. The cat followed.

"Go back," she said. "I don't want to be accused of cat stealing."

The animal looked quizzically at her, then slithered through the bars of another fence and disappeared into the foliage. Joanna kept walking, feeling ridiculously deserted and alone. The sidewalk went past a small park with benches set on the side of the hill; a woman was walking a pair of fox terriers up there. Across the road was some new construction—condominiums, from what the sign said. In another five years, Joanna decided, Falmouth would go the way of seacoast towns such as Brighton or Torquay; then it wouldn't be such a good place to live or to visit. When the road—called High Street now—dipped down into the town itself, she felt a little better: it narrowed between old-fashioned buildings that she recognized from her last visit. But then she noticed that a great many of the ground-level storefronts were vacant and in the process of being remodeled; soon, she supposed, they would be occupied by chic boutiques catering to the tourist trade. No reason the same thing that she'd watched happen to Sonoma couldn't also happen here.

Progress, she thought. And sighed.

One of the shops on the left-hand side of the street bore the name of the art dealer she and David had visited years ago. Joanna crossed and looked at the painting displayed in the window. A seascape—but not too representational, almost in the style of the Impressionists. She wasn't sure if she liked it or not. Come to think of it, she hadn't much liked the landscapes David had bought from this dealer, either; although she'd never said so, David must have sensed that, because they'd been among the first canvasses to go when he'd begun selling off parts of his collection after he learned he was dying of cancer. Still, it was good to know the dealer was here; if she couldn't get any information about the smuggling of artworks from the CID inspector, this man might be able to give her a lead. She made a mental note to call him in the morning.

A few doors beyond the gallery, the Prince of Wales Pier angled off into the water. It was a wide stone structure with public restrooms and tour and charter-fishing companies' ticket booths at its foot. Most of the posted departure times were earlier in the day, and two of the booths were closed.

Joanna started for one where the window stood open, but paused at a signboard showing the route the River Fal tour took. There was a town called Malpas near the tip of the river.

"Interested in a tour, miss? Last one for today's left, but we've got three on for tomorrow."

The voice came from behind her. She turned. The man had thick black hair and a bushy beard and wore jeans and a pea jacket. "I might be interested," she said. "Is that as far as the tour goes—Malpas?"

He glanced indifferently at the map she indicated and nodded. "But don't take one of their tours, miss. The commentary's not much." He moved as if to put an arm around her shoulders and steer her away. "Now, my company—"

A shout of rage erupted from the booth they were standing next to. "Mind your own territory, Mick! Stop kidnapping my customers!"

Mick responded with a grin and a jaunty middle-finger salute. The window of the booth slammed down. Joanna stepped back out of his reach.

"It's all a game, luv," he said. "Bloke who just shouted is my brother."

Sure, she thought. "The tour only goes as far as Malpas?" she asked again.

"Right."

"What about that other town up there—the one whose name starts with a *P*?"

His eyes flickered slightly, as if in surprise. "Pennack, you mean?"

"That's it."

"Pennack's up where the river gets shallow. Not much there, anyway, at least nothing of interest to tourists. Now, our lunchtime tour—"

"What *is* there?"

"Some shacks, mostly lads in the oystering trade live in them. Some shops. An old wink—"

"A what?"

"Kiddleywink." At her blank look, he added, "Beer-house. Not rightly a pub, they don't serve food nor spirits. Not many of those left, this one's been there in the same place since 1840 or so. But a lady like yourself wouldn't want to go there."

"Why not?"

"Well"—Mick looked uncomfortable—"it's not always frequented by your upright citizens. Now, our lunchtime tour takes you to a lovely pub—"

"And that's all there is at Pennack?"

"That's all." His eyes narrowed. "Odd you should be asking, though."

"Why?"

"Most folks—tourists, anyway—don't know of Pennack. And now I've had two asking about it in one day."

"Oh? Who was the other?"

"Bloke who came by this morning. Wanted to be taken up there. Paid my mate good money for the job."

"What did the man look like?"

He hesitated. "This wouldn't concern any trouble with the law, would it?"

"Why do you ask that?"

"Well, the bloke was awfully nervous. I couldn't locate my mate straight off, and he sat over on the bench"—Mick indicated a number of them farther out on the pier—"and fidgeted. Then my mate couldn't see his way to taking him upriver until this afternoon, and he fretted about that. Arrived an hour early and sat in the exact same place, his package on his knees. Never did take his hands off it."

"A package about this size?"

Mick nodded.

"Well, to ease your mind," Joanna said, "I've got nothing to do with the law. The man's my husband."

"Divorce situation, is it?"

"No, he's emotionally disturbed and needs help. Just to be certain it was him, would you describe him?"

"Slender, about forty. Longish graying hair. Odd eyes—yellow, jumpy. But you'd know about that, then."

Would I ever, Joanna thought. "What time did your mate take him upriver?"

"Round about an hour ago."

"And when will he be back?"

"Not for some time; it's a fair way."

"I'm staying at the Greenbank. Will you ask him to contact me there, in the pub on the harbor level, as soon as he returns?"

"I can ask him, but I don't know if he will."

She took a ten-pound note from her bag and handed it to him. "I'm sure you can convince him."

He grinned as he pocketed it. "I'll try, miss. Now about our tours..."

Joanna had to admire his irrepressible salesmanship. To humor him, she asked, "What's there to see?"

"Prime attraction's the laid-up ships in King Harry's Reach. Cheapest moorings in the British Isles. At the moment there's a couple of ferries, a liquid gas tanker, a freighter, and a cruise ship. Some concrete barges that carried oil and water back in World War Two—they've been there since forty-six, be there forever."

"But why are they all in the—what did you call it?"

"King Harry's Reach, a channel in the Fal. They're waiting until there's work for them, staffed with skeleton crews. The *Devon Pride*—the cruise ship—is due to go back into service any day now. The *Methane Princess*—the liquid gas tanker—will never see duty again: her fate's to be sold for scrap, just like her sister ship that used to be on the river. After that we point out the old smuggler's cottage that your General Eisenhower visited during the war to firm up plans for the Normandy invasion; there's Lord Falmouth's estate...."

Joanna was beginning to be sorry she'd asked. "Maybe I will take tomorrow's tour," she said quickly.

"As I said before, the noon sailing includes lunch at a lovely pub—"

"I'll think about it—after I talk with your friend." She was about to turn away when she remembered the word penciled on the back of the map; she should have thought to show it to the desk clerk at the hotel. "Tell me, do you know of anything or anyone around here called Trispin?"

Mick looked surprised. "What's he got to do with all this?"

"It's just a name my husband mentioned."

"Then he's in more trouble than you know."

"Why? Who is Trispin?"

"Who *was* he, you mean. Alf Trispin had a hand in everything illegal hereabouts—you name it, and old Alf took a percentage. Took it until today, that is. Someone shot him in his office on Trelawney Road round about five this morning."

NINETEEN

THE HOTEL'S PUB was on the same level as the quay and parking lot—a fairly nondescript establishment arranged around a U-shaped bar that dispensed both drinks and snacks. At a few minutes after six, Joanna entered, the map she'd been unsuccessfully studying in hand. Even so soon after opening, the pub had its fair share of customers: locals, she guessed, from the look of them. She recognized the woman she'd seen walking her fox terriers in the park earlier; the dogs were now tethered to a table leg, lying quietly while their mistress enjoyed a solitary gin. Two old men stood at the bar debating the merits of warm bitter versus chilled; they nodded to Joanna and continued their discussion.

Noreen, the barmaid, was a handsome redhead of perhaps twenty-five. As she drew Joanna's bitter, she said, "American, aren't you? A guest at the hotel?"

"Yes."

"Your first time in Cornwall?"

"No, I've stayed here once before. The weather wasn't nearly this beautiful then." She motioned outside, where the sky was gentling over the harbor, the water taking on a pinkish gray sheen.

Noreen put the pint in front of her. "Lucky, you are. The weather's usually bloody awful here. They're saying the fog'll be in tonight." She shivered. "I hate it."

Joanna was about to ask her why she stayed there, but then she thought of the British economy and the scarcity of jobs. People here didn't just pick up and move away in search of better weather, especially if they had good positions. Quickly she dismissed the question and got down to business; even though Mick at the pier seemed to have given her a solid lead to Matt's whereabouts, she wanted confirmation of what he'd said about the villages upriver. "The clerk upstairs said you might be able to help me decipher a map," she told the barmaid.

"Let's have a look, then." Noreen studied it for a moment. "Not much of one, is it?"

"Not really. What do you think it shows?"

"That's easy: Falmouth here"—her fingertip touched the *F*—"Malpas and Pennack here. This line's the River Fal."

"The clerk thought so, too. He says you're from that area."

"Malpas, yes."

"What's it like?"

"Worse than here, even. The fog travels upriver and sits there for days. Chills you to the bone."

"What about Pennack? I hear there's not much there."

"You hear right. Oyster beds—they're all along the Fal. It's a poor place, not a village a tourist would have any interest in—"

"If I wanted to go, what would be the best way to get there?"

"Best? By boat. There are plenty of folks who would hire out to take you. Of course, you can go by road, but it's a roundabout journey."

Joanna laid her map on the bar. "Show me."

The barmaid traced the route: up the main highway the way Joanna had come earlier, toward Truro; then along a series of small roads, mere threads on the map. The last of them wasn't even marked, but Noreen drew it in with pencil. Pennack itself was so small that its name didn't appear, either.

Noreen said, "Might I ask why you want to go there?"

"Just curiosity. I don't like tourist places."

The barmaid looked unconvinced, but she merely nodded and said, "If you want to avoid tourists, Pennack's as good a place as any round here."

A pair of fishermen came through the door. Joanna looked expectantly at them, hoping one might be Mick's friend, but they went straight to the chalkboard listing the snacks without even glancing around the room. Noreen said, "Excuse me," and moved to help them. Joanna took her mug to a small table where she could easily be seen by anyone who entered; as she drank she studied the map.

The *X* that Noreen had penciled in to mark Pennack was on a small inlet on the opposite side of the Fal, very near its tip. The roads to it wound across what looked to be uninhabited countryside. From her drive down to Falmouth, she recalled that the area to that side of the highway had been marshland covered with reeds and scrub trees. It would not be a short drive, nor an easy one, given that dusk was now falling. In an hour it would be full dark, and she couldn't leave until she'd talked with Mick's friend—*if* he showed up at all. Of course, if he did, she might be able to hire him to take her there by boat, as he had Matt....

Two hours passed as she finished her bitter, ordered another, and polished off an indecently huge portion of an oyster and potato and cheese concoction. The pub filled, became noisy and smoky. A darts game began, spirited and hotly competitive. People nodded and smiled at her, accepting a stranger's presence with neither curiosity nor intrusive friendliness. She decided she preferred this bar—which she and David had somehow overlooked—to the rarefied atmosphere in the lounge and dining room upstairs. People dressed for a three-course meal there, and Joanna—who had reluctantly complied with the formal ways of David's sophisticated circle in San Francisco—had in recent years found herself happier in jeans than after-five dresses, more stimulated by real conversation than society chitchat.

At twenty minutes past eight, a man came through the door and stood searching the faces in the crowd. He wore dungarees and a heavy black-ribbed sweater; his skin was the roughened tan of a sailor; and a knitted fisherman's cap was pulled over most of his blond hair. Joanna's eyes met his, and he raised his brows questioningly. She nodded, and he came over to her table.

"You're the lady wants to see me?"

"If you're Mick's friend, and you took my husband upriver this afternoon." Her fictional marriage to Matt was becoming easier to pretend to; she *felt* wedded to him, in one of those unions that has long ago soured and turned to bondage.

"I am. Let me get a pint before we talk." He went to the bar, returned with one of lager, and sat across from her. "Bob Jenkins is the name. Yours?"

"Joanna Stark."

"Not the same as the man you claim you're married to. But then you don't look the kind of lady who would marry that bloke." He lit a cigarette and examined her squint-eyed through the smoke.

"Why not?"

"You've got class. He's an East-Ender if I ever saw one." At her inquiring look, he added, "Yes, I know London. Spent two years there, until I came to my senses and moved back here to run the old man's charter business. But as I was saying, your so-called husband may have money, but it takes more than that to make a gentleman."

"Money?"

"You don't think I took him up for free, now do you?"

"How much did he pay you?"

"Enough."

"How much would I have to pay you to take me to him?"

He was silent, studying the tip of his cigarette.

"How much?"

"...Look, miss, I don't know what your game is. I know what you told Mick about the bloke being daft and you the worried little wife, but I don't buy it. Whatever's going on, I want no part of it."

"How much did he pay you not to talk to anyone about him?"

Silence. Then: "Even if he hadn't, the bloke's got a right to his privacy—"

"I'll double it."

His lips twitched and he picked up his beer.

"How much?"

Bob sighed and set down the mug. Joanna waited.

"All right," he said after a moment. "I'll take a hundred quid. Cash."

It wasn't cheap, but she didn't hesitate. "Done. Half now and half when you take me to him."

He held out his hand.

"First you tell me everything that happened, from the moment you met him until you left him in Pennack. Everything he said or did."

"Mick introduced us, you know that." The man he'd ferried upriver, Bob said, had turned up at the pier that morning and asked at Mick's booth for someone who might be available for a charter. Mick had kept him away from the others who would have been willing to make the trip because he had a deal to refer people to Bob, so it was after two before they got under way.

"He was in a state," Bob commented. "Nervous as my Aunt Sal's Siamese, and a good bit more bad-tempered."

"What name did he give you?"

Bob grinned ironically. "Smith."

Joanna smiled too. "Go on."

"That's about all there was. He didn't say much, just sat next to me in the cockpit with his package on his lap."

"Didn't he talk with you…ask you about the area, or the things along the river? The laid-up ships, for instance?"

"Not that I—Wait a bit. He asked who all the land along the river belonged to. I said Lord Falmouth and pointed out the manor house on the hill. He seemed impressed."

"This Lord Falmouth—is he an art collector, by any chance?"

"Not that I know of."

In spite of his reply, Joanna made a mental note to find out more about the nobleman. "All right," she said, "what happened when you arrived in Pennack?"

"Mr. Smith got off the boat."

"I assumed that. Did he say where he intended to stay? Or ask anything about the village?"

"He wanted to know where the pub was. I told him there wasn't one, not a proper one, anyway. When I went off, he was still standing there on the pier."

"With his package."

"Hanging on to it for dear life."

"You say there isn't a proper pub in the village. What about the kiddleywink?"

"How'd you hear about that?"

"From your friend Mick. Tell me about it."

"Not much to tell. It's just a wink, out on Knackers' Point."

"Could that have been what Mr. Smith meant when he asked about the pub?"

Bob shrugged and drank some beer.

Joanna thought about what Mick had said about the oddly named bar: *It's not always frequented by your up-right citizens.* "What do you know about that kiddley-wink?" she asked.

Silence.

"I'm paying you fifty pounds for this conversation. What about the wink?"

His eyes showed annoyance, but after a hesitation he said, "It's been there for more than a century. Used to be called the Fisherman's Arms, and the point Fisherman's Point. But back in the 1880s some woman who was, as they say, no better than she should have been was murdered there behind the wink. They never found who did it, and after a while folks put it off on the knackers and rechristened both the point and the wink."

"The knackers?"

"Evil spirits from the tin mines. Rather like gnomes, supposed to live underground. No tin mines round Pennack, so these must have crept up from someplace like Pendeen to do the deed." Bob smiled cynically.

"So the wink's now called the Knackers' Arms?"

"Right you are. Otherwise it's much the same as it ever was: you wouldn't want to show money there, and a woman'd be a fool to venture in alone."

From the way he avoided her eyes, Joanna sensed there was something about the wink he wasn't revealing. "What else can you tell me about the Knackers' Arms?"

"Nothing."

"Does it have anything to do with Alf Trispin?"

The intuitive question proved to be a good one: Bob's fingers tightened on his mug—hard enough to make the knuckles go pale. "Mick said you were asking about Alf."

"Well?"

"The wink's been linked to him, yes."

"How?"

"I couldn't say."

"Bob—"

"It's the truth. There are some people and things one keeps one's distance from if he knows what's good for him, and Alf Trispin and his business are among 'em. Besides, the bloke's dead.''

"I know, but he may have had some sort of organization that's survived him. Tell me, was one of his activities smuggling?''

"Ah, you must have been reading one of those romance novels; the wife favors them, too. Smuggling trade died out over a hundred years ago. It's as dead as charming." He smiled, as if at an ironic private joke.

Joanna straightened. "As dead as what?"

He looked startled—whether at her question or at the intensity of it, she couldn't tell. "That's what we call magic, white magic. Cures warts, that sort of thing. Anyway, smuggling never was safe, but now it's not profitable either, what with changes in the excise laws and not so much demand for contraband goods. Not that there aren't those who wouldn't like to revive it: fishing industry's dying too, and we need something to replace it. No, Alf Trispin might have had his hand in at many things, but smuggling wasn't one of 'em."

She sensed his discourse on smuggling was a cover-up for a lie, and that his mention of charming was altogether too coincidental. "What about smuggling things—or people— out of the country, rather than in?"

"I don't follow you."

"Suppose someone wanted to leave the country secretly, without going through immigration? Or get a package out without Customs examining it? Would Alf Trispin have been able to arrange that?"

"I don't know." Now Bob looked wary, eyes once again narrowed behind a shield of smoke from a fresh cigarette. In spite of his casual pose—slumped in his chair, one elbow hooked over its back—his body seemed taut and poised for flight.

She abandoned the line of questioning and asked, "So when can you take me up there? Tonight?"

Surprise wiped some of the caution from his features. "We bloody well can't navigate the river at night, not with this fog blowing in."

"Fog?"

"You can't see it from here—this part of the harbor's protected—but if you went to the end of the quay, you'd notice a bloody great bank of it out there. Be too dangerous going upriver in the kind of craft I have."

"But I need to—"

"Mr. Smith isn't going anywhere, either. If we can't get up there, odds are he can't get out."

His argument made sense. She nodded, and before she could speak, Bob said, "We'll go tomorrow, soon as the fog lifts some."

She nodded and dug in her purse, taking out his fifty pounds. "Call me here, in the morning."

He looked pleasantly surprised this time. Bob, she sensed, was a man to whom life had promised much but given very little; he had probably not expected her to come through with the money. His obvious pleasure pleased her too: she'd always found people to be more trustworthy when they themselves felt trusted.

"I'll call you by noon, latest." He stood, nodded briskly, and made his way to the door.

Joanna watched him go, then drank the rest of her bitter and made a quick decision. The fog might already be affecting river traffic, but it wouldn't as yet pose a hazard on the road. She'd drive to Pennack right away, tonight.

TWENTY

BEFORE SHE STARTED for Pennack she went upstairs to the hotel, intending to get a heavier jacket from her room. In the corridor she encountered the manager, whom she'd noticed bustling about off and on since she'd arrived.

"Oh, Mrs. Stark," he said, "you're just the person I wanted to see. Have you and the man who was asking after you earlier got together?"

"The fisherman? About an hour ago?"

He frowned. "No, this was quite some time before that. Daniel was still on the desk then. A man asked for you and Daniel told him you'd probably be in the harbor bar after six, as you had a question to ask of the barmaid. Afterwards he was sorry he'd said that much; as a rule we don't give out information about the guests, and there was something in the man's manner that made Daniel uncomfortable. He told me about the incident, and I wanted to ask you if everything is all right."

Joanna felt uncomfortable herself. "Describe the man, if you would."

"I didn't see him, and Daniel mentioned nothing about his appearance. I should have asked, but...well, he's young and tends to be overimaginative. Wants to be a writer, spends his free time scribbling in a notebook. You know the sort. Frankly I didn't put too much stock in his story."

"You say Daniel's off duty?"

"Since five."

"May I have his telephone number? I'd like to ask him more about this."

"Of course." The manager led her to the reception desk and wrote the number on a notepad.

Joanna went upstairs and called it. It rang ten times before she hung up. Then she sat very still, thinking about the stranger who had made the desk clerk suspicious. Who was he?

The only answer was Parducci. He might have beaten out of Ian Sneath the information that Matt had gone to Cornwall after all. Or he might even have followed her here. On the long drive down from London she hadn't once given a thought, foolishly enough, to the possibility of a pursuer. For all she knew, Parducci could have been a few car lengths behind her the whole trip.

It made her think twice about going to Pennack tonight, but the urge to try to track Matt down immediately was too strong. Finally she decided to at least start for the village. On the dark, relatively untraveled roads, it would be easy to spot a pair of following headlights.

As she walked to her car, she experienced the same odd sensation of being watched that she'd had outside Christopher's flat the night before. She whirled and looked back at the door of the lower pub, but saw no one. The quay itself was deserted, except for the cars parked on it and in the adjoining lot. Above her, candlelight flickered from the window tables in the hotel dining room; she could see the outlines of heads in the adjacent lounge bar. Probably, she thought, someone in one of those rooms was watching her with mild and innocuous curiosity. But then why did she feel a chill, as if some malevolent force was close by?

It almost drove her back inside to the safety of her room, but she steeled herself and went on to the car. All the way out of Falmouth she kept looking in the rearview mirror; what few cars she saw turned off the main road onto side streets before she reached the city limits.

The first of the narrow roads the barmaid had shown her on the map branched off the A-39, across the marshlands she remembered from her trip south. The patched and potholed pavement wound above the thick reeds—spiky and brown in the Fiesta's headlights—and reminded her of levee roads in the Sacramento Delta. After a few miles she took the next turning and the terrain changed; trees grew thicker and taller until their tender-leaved branches formed a tunnel over the road. Through gaps in them she glimpsed the lights of an occasional farmhouse, saw the silhouetted hulks of what she supposed were barns and other outbuildings. Periodically she glanced in the mirror but saw no headlights—nothing to indicate she was not the only car on the road.

The tunnel snaked along for miles until she saw a stone wall that the barmaid had said would indicate the last turn. When she had gone a mile or so beyond it, the road began to climb in a gradual ascent over gently rounded hills, and at its crest houses began to appear—stone cottages, actually, built far apart. Muted light shone through their small windows, but she saw no one, either inside or out. She passed a pair of dark closed shops, then the pavement made a sharp S-curve and angled down again. The fog had not yet penetrated this far inland, and the moon cut a shimmering, irregular swatch over the black waters of the Fal.

The road descended steeply, paralleling the shoreline. More cottages—frame now, and actually in the category of shacks—were strung out along the concrete seawall. A finger pier—dilapidated and listing to one side—extended into the water, illuminated by a solitary amber light at either end. A few boats that looked to be fishing craft were tied up in the shadows, and others were suspended in drydock in a haphazard boatworks to the other side of the pier. Joanna stopped the car next to a rusted-out panel truck at the bot-

tom of the road, where the pavement petered out into ruts
and gravel.

When she turned off the Fiesta's motor, the night suddenly became quiet. Then she heard water slapping at the
seawall and dock pilings. A dog barked in the distance, and
there was a steady hum of voices from somewhere closer by.
The wink on Knackers' Point, most likely.

After a moment she got out of the car and walked toward the pier. Bob had said you could see the wink from
there. She went midway out on the ramshackle structure,
avoiding a couple of places where the planks were loose and
rotted, and looked around. To her left were faint lights,
masked by a grove of trees. She hurried back along the pier
and looked for some way to reach the point. A path along
the top of the seawall seemed to lead in that direction.

She started along the path, her running shoes crunching
on what appeared to be fragments of oyster shells. To her
right was the hill she'd just descended, lights from the shacks
that clung to it relieving its blackness. The path curved out
toward the thickly forested point. As she followed it, the
voices became louder, their hum broken by occasional
shrieks and shouts of laughter. Finally the path veered away
from the seawall into the trees. Oak, she thought, like those
that covered the hills around Sonoma. Their buds had recently opened, and a fresh growing scent filled the air.

The path rounded a bend, and suddenly she saw a clearing filled with parked cars. Beyond them stood a two-story
black stone house with a steeply canted roof and brick
chimneys at either end. Light blazed beyond the narrow
downstairs windows, but the upper ones were dark. Electri-
fied carriage lamps on either side of the rough-hewn plank
door showed a sign, but its lettering had long ago faded to
a dull wind-scoured gray.

She moved slowly into the clearing, stopped next to the
car nearest the building, and squatted down in its shadow.

The wink looked like a typical pub, and certainly the sounds emanating from it were no more boisterous or sinister than those coming from any drinking establishment at a late hour. But what Bob had said about the Knackers' Arms had made her wary. She remained in the shadows, debating what to do next.

Matt had asked Bob where the village pub was. By that, he'd probably meant this wink. Given that and the short time that had passed since then—as well as the lack of accommodation in the village—there was a good chance he was here. She couldn't just barge through the door and demand the return of her painting, though; she needed to locate both him and it first, then study her options.

A pair of men emerged from the building, talking loudly. Joanna drew farther into the shadows as they staggered to one of the cars. Its motor roared, then hummed steadily, and finally faded to a distant whine. The night was still again, save for the voices from the wink and the chug of a boat motor over near the dock. She moved forward again, examining the layout of the place. To its right the trees closed in, until their branches touched its wall.

She waited, watching and listening, then ran in a crouch to the shelter of the trees. The house wall was windowless here, the brick chimney jutting out from it; the blackness was nearly total. She fumbled in her bag for the small flashlight she always kept there. When she turned it on, she found that the batteries must be going: its beam was a weak thread of yellow, scarcely enough to illuminate anything. She kept the light on the ground, her hand on the stone wall, and groped toward the rear of the house.

Behind it was a yard of sorts—a cleared space of hard-packed earth where a line of garbage cans stood. The windows were dark, but a rectangle of light fell from a door that had been left ajar. Joanna inched toward it, her back pressed against the wall. The voices were more distinct now, though not loud enough for their owners to be directly beyond the door. After a moment she chanced a look, thrusting her head out, then pulling it back quickly. Inside was a storage room stacked with wooden kegs and cases, a hallway with closed doors on either side and extended at its end toward the front of the house, where the drinking rooms must be.

Now what, Joanna? she thought. You can't blunder in there—not unless you want to call a great deal of attention to yourself. Better go around to the front, try to look through the windows. And if that doesn't work, you'll have to bite the bullet and go inside.

As she continued to work her way around the building, the act of coming here alone tonight began to seem extremely foolish. She should have waited until morning; as Bob had said, Matt wasn't going anywhere with the fog building downriver....

Downriver. She stopped, leaning against the wall, and mentally repeated the word. Why had Matt come *up*river if he was planning to leave the country? Wouldn't it make more sense to stay in Falmouth, the port city, closer to the sea? What had brought him to this remote village? Something connected with the late Alf Trispin?

In front of the house people called good night to one another. Car doors slammed and a couple of motors started up. Joanna waited until their sounds had faded, then moved to the corner of the building and looked around. At first she saw no one, but then a man emerged from the trees, the same way she'd come earlier. He wore a heavy oilcloth slicker and his cap was pulled low on his forehead now, but she had no difficulty identifying him.

Bob Jenkins. The boat motor she'd heard over by the dock shortly before she'd begun working her way around the house must have been his. In spite of the fog, he'd made good time in getting here from Falmouth.

TWENTY-ONE

JOANNA DREW HER BREATH in sharply and stepped back into the shadows. Bob walked across the parking lot toward the wink—confidently, as if he'd been there many times before. He opened the heavy front door and let it slam behind him. Joanna came around the corner and moved swiftly to the nearest window, ignoring her fears of being seen looking through it.

Inside, the wink was a typical barroom, dimly lit and murky with smoke. Men and women sat at small tables or clustered near the bar, and for a moment she couldn't spot Bob. Then she saw him moving across the room toward the standing crowd of drinkers. He shouldered through them, speaking to no one, and went directly to a table in a small alcove next to the fireplace at the rear. Only one man sat there: a fisherman, judging from his clothing. Joanna could make out little more about him before Bob's broad back blocked her view. Hastily she glanced around the room for Matt. He wasn't there—at least not within her line of sight. When she looked back at where Bob had stood, she saw he was now seated at the table, forearms propped against its edge, gesturing with his hands as he spoke.

The other man listened intently, nodding from time to time. He wore a cap, and its floppy brim shadowed his features. Joanna strained to see his face, thinking he might be Matt, dressed in borrowed fisherman's clothing. But no, this man was much older than Matt; she could see deep lines bracketing his mouth. After a few minutes he took a pipe from the table and lit it; his hands were gnarled, had seen much hard work.

One of the drinkers near the bar turned to speak with a woman at a table. His eyes rested on the window, moved away, and then returned. Joanna cursed softly and slipped back around the corner, scanning the parking lot as she went. No one was there, and no one came out of the wink; no inquiring head was thrust through the window. After a time she went back for another look inside. The older man was talking now, gesturing as emphatically as Bob had, his pipe in one hand.

Questions crowded her mind. She forced them back, concentrating on her surroundings: the scene inside the window, the door to her right, the parking lot behind her.

The older man stopped speaking. Bob nodded, the firmness of the motion indicating satisfaction. He shifted slightly in his chair and reached into the pocket of his slicker, removing a wad of bills and peeling off two. The other man took them, and then motioned at the empty mug in front of him. Bob picked it up and started for the bar.

A man and a woman near the window also stood up and moved toward the door. Joanna hurried back around the corner. Now she allowed the questions to flood her consciousness: the fisherman—who? Which of the things Bob had told her were true, and which were not? He'd lied about being able to come upriver in the fog, obviously to keep her away from the village until he could...do what? Warn Matt? But what about the exchange of money with the fisherman? And where was Matt, if not at the wink? The wink was connected somehow with Alf Trispin, who had been killed suddenly, in the early hours of the morning. By whom? Was his murder connected with Matt?

The questions went on and on. She had no answer to any of them.

Then she thought of Bob's boat. The sound of the motor had come from over by the dock, just long enough before he'd come out of the trees for him to have tied up and followed the path along the seawall. She'd be able to tell which of the craft it was—the one that hadn't been there before. Searching the boat might tell her something....

The man and the woman had long since departed in a car with a badly misfiring engine. Joanna moved to the window once more and saw that Bob and his companion were drinking beer. Whatever task Bob had paid the fisherman to do had no immediacy; no telling how long they'd remain in the wink. The mugs they held were full pints, and if she hurried she'd have ample time to check out the boat.

She trotted across the parking lot and into the trees. The path was more difficult to follow now; although the trees grew thick, moonlight had shone through their small spring leaves earlier, dappling the hard-packed earth and glowing on the fragments of oyster shell. But now the moon's rays had dimmed. Several times Joanna stumbled, once wrenching her ankle when the toe of her running shoe caught on an exposed tree root. She was afraid to use her failing flashlight: she'd need what little power its batteries still possessed for searching the boat—and besides, its beam might call attention to her.

When she emerged from the grove and started along the top of the seawall, she saw the reason for the sudden darkness: a great towering bank of fog perhaps fifty yards offshore, its upper reaches blocking out all but a sliver of the moon. She began walking faster. Fortunately, the path here was easier to follow, and soon she saw the amber beacons on the dock. At its far end a boat that hadn't been there earlier was moored: white against the black water, a sturdy fishing craft with whiplike radio antennae extending from its cockpit.

For a moment she doubted it was Bob's boat: he'd said he couldn't navigate the river in the fog in the kind of craft he had. But of course he'd lied about the quality of his boat—

again for the obvious reason of keeping her away from Pennack.

Joanna glanced over her shoulder, stood very still listening for footsteps. Nothing moved nearby. There was no sound except for the rumble of voices from the wink. Then from the hillside came the nerve-shattering screams of a cat fight. Joanna started, and ran lightly along the rest of the path and down the dock toward the boat. Her foot landed on a loose board. Her knee started to buckle, and she flung herself to one side, regaining balance. The board raised up and fell with a great clatter. She kept going to the side of the boat, jumped over the gunwale, and fell to the deck.

Her heart was pounding and her breath came in gasps. One elbow throbbed from slamming into the deck. She raised herself up on the other, massaging the injured joint and listening. A dog was barking somewhere near the boat works, but she heard no footsteps, no voices. Probably the crashing board had sounded louder to her than to anyone else; it had gone unnoticed or ignored.

After a moment she got up and took the flashlight from her bag. The boat looked to be a trawler outfitted for the sport fishing trade, with a high cockpit and plenty of room on its aft deck for anglers casting their lines. Joanna remembered Bob's remark about returning from London to operate "the old man's charter business"; it might have been true, or it might not. She moved toward the stern, looking for equipment that would prove or disprove the statement. In a pair of large covered bins near the engine housing she found enough stowed gear for a party of sport fishermen.

Of course that didn't mean this vessel was always used for charter. There were other purposes to which a fast new radar-equipped boat could be put.

She moved forward toward the cockpit, her hands braced on the salt-caked deck rail. The array of gauges and instruments that confronted her was impressive; even though she knew little about boats, she sensed that this was top-of-the-line equipment, expensive and apparently well maintained. There was a door in the middle of the cockpit, probably leading to a forward cabin. Perhaps something down there would give her a clue—

The door was locked.

She turned, frustrated, and moved along the deck to the area where the storage bins were located. The boat, like the scene she'd witnessed at the Knackers' Arms, was raising more questions than it answered.

For instance, *was* the charter business merely a coverup for some sort of illegal activity? Activity such as the transporting of stolen artwork or assisting fugitives in leaving the country? If so, who was involved in it besides Bob Jenkins? How did the clientele contact him? Through Alf Trispin, before he'd met his violent death early this morning? Through the old fisherman at the wink—whoever he might be?

"Dammit!" She realized she was proceeding mainly on supposition. In spite of her earlier reasoning, this might not be Bob's boat after all. Perhaps the name or registry would tell her something; she hadn't seen either as she'd run toward the boat, since the stern hadn't been in her line of sight. She went farther aft, leaned over the rail, and shone the flashlight on the lettering.

Charming, Falmouth.

So that was what the word meant. Not a person's name, or a code word—the name of a boat. It more or less confirmed that the boat belonged to Bob, too; why else would he have smiled so ironically when he'd mentioned it earlier in the pub?

She switched off the flashlight and crouched on the deck, thinking it through.

Parducci had probably beaten the name out of Sneath— that and not much more. Then he'd gone to the Starving Ox to see what he could get out of John Grey. Except he hadn't had to threaten or injure the publican because he'd seen Joanna there, followed her to Grey's office, and gotten the information from her... or more correctly, gotten the catalyst he'd needed to make the connection.

If the *Charming* was used to smuggle stolen goods or fugitives, if it was connected with the late Alf Trispin, chances were Parducci knew of it. Good brokers like Parducci kept track of such resources, were up on the various ways in and out of a country, knew whom to call if they needed such services. When she told him Sneath had sent Matt to someone, the word *charming* had led him directly to Alf Trispin.

Parducci would then have had plenty of time to contact Trispin, either with some story designed to keep him from making arrangements for Matt, or with the truth—that Matt had crossed him and should not be permitted to get away. Trispin would have complied: Parducci was a respected and feared man in their dubious circles. Then Parducci would have driven or flown to Cornwall to confront Matt. But something had gone wrong, because Trispin had been shot.

Had Matt found out about Trispin's deal with Parducci and killed him? No, she doubted that. Matt's style would be to run. Perhaps, after Parducci had arrived, Trispin had refused to cooperate with him. Or perhaps he *had* cooperated, but Parducci had not wanted to leave anyone alive who might know he had come after Matt. Joanna had no doubt that once Parducci caught up with Matt, he would kill him. He'd tried to kill her, hadn't he?

Now that she considered it, Parducci's attempt to kill her seemed strangely out of character. The last time she'd encountered him, when she'd foiled his attempt to steal the Frans Hals painting in San Francisco, he'd been enraged, but not enough to kill. Yet, last night—in an abrupt turnaround after he asked why *she* nurtured such hatred for him and implied that he'd put such emotions behind him—he'd turned violently on her.

She'd kept tabs on his career over the years; there had been no indication that he'd killed before. But she was certain he'd murdered Amir Moradi, beaten Sneath within an inch of his life, and shot Alf Trispin. Why such a change in him, such a loss of control?

There was one answer that occurred to her immediately: Parducci had gone insane.

It fit with what she'd observed of the man last night. She'd thought him ill, perhaps riddled with some fatal disease. But a warped, obsessive mind can destroy the body and soul as surely as cancer, a faulty heart, or AIDS....

If Parducci had begun to lose his grip, Joanna knew neither she nor E.J. would be safe until he was apprehended. Nor would any number of other people who might step into his relentless path—people such as Moradi, Sneath, and Trispin, who had committed their share of crimes but surely hadn't deserved what he'd meted out to them...

Footsteps crunched on the path. Joanna raised up enough to see Bob walking along the seawall, his oilcloth slicker billowing out around him. Panic rose in her; she pushed it down, considering her alternatives. She could run down the dock to her car, hoping to drive away before he could stop her. She could go over the side into the black, seemingly bottomless water. She could stand up and confront him. Or...

It was a rash action—that much she knew—but also the most appealing of all. Before Bob reached the dock, she had opened the nearest storage bin, burrowed into the nets and line, and closed the lid over her head.

TWENTY-TWO

JOANNA LAY CURLED in a fetal position, a coil of heavy line digging into her right hip. The air in the bin was stale and smelled so strongly of fish that she gagged and pressed her hand against her nose, breathing through her mouth. Outside there was a thump, and then footsteps moved along the deck; from their direction, she guessed Bob was casting off the mooring ropes.

She heard him pass very near the bin, going forward, and held her breath until he was gone. The coiled rope's pressure was becoming painful, but she resisted the urge to wriggle around. It was very dark in the bin, but above she saw a line of gray where the lid fitted improperly; at least some air would enter so she wouldn't suffocate.

When the boat's engine started, the roar from the adjacent housing was deafening. Joanna jerked her hand from her nose and jammed both fists against her ears. The vibration made the rope's pressure especially painful; she gave up on her resolve to stay still and wiggled around until she slumped on a pile of nets, resting on the base of her spine, her shoulders propped against the wall. A churning, rocking motion began as the boat moved away from the dock.

After a few minutes the engine noise didn't seem so loud—or maybe she was just getting used to it. She lowered her hands and felt through the pockets of her jacket until she found a couple of wadded-up tissues; after balling them up more firmly, she stuffed them into her ears. They worked as well as her fists had.

The boat settled into a steady, slow motion, the engine thrumming rhythmically. She found she could tell from slight shifts and rolls when Bob was correcting its course. After a while she decided they must be well into the river, heading for Falmouth—she hoped. Now that she had time to reflect on what she'd just done, she was extremely sorry she hadn't chosen to make a break for her car. She wasn't going to find out anything from inside this bin, and it might be hours before she could get off the *Charming* unobserved. And what about the Fiesta? Eventually she'd have to find someone who would drive her to Pennack to retrieve it. But before she did that, she would get in touch with her contact on the CID here, tell him what she knew, and let him take over. She was through playing the role of sleuth in a game whose rules she didn't understand.

Her left knee—the one she'd badly sprained back in the days when she still fancied herself a bicycler—began to throb. She tried to shift to ease it, but slipped down and banged the back of her head on the wall. Normally she didn't suffer from seasickness, but she didn't often ride on this small a vessel. Now the motion and the fishy odor began to make her queasy.

All you need, she told herself shortly, is to throw up. You've gotten yourself into a fine mess, haven't you?

Her mood became blacker as the boat progressed on its unknown course. She began to reflect on all the mistakes of the past weeks; her poor handling of Matt; her betrayal of Richard; her tipping Parducci, however inadvertently, to where Matt had gone; her rash actions tonight. She knew from her years with SSI that it was natural for things to go awry in the very best planned of operations. But what one did then was correct for the error, much as Bob was correcting the course of this boat. She'd thought she'd done that, but each time the correction had not quite worked.

Maybe Rafferty's right, she thought. Maybe I shouldn't have taken this on alone. Maybe I shouldn't even be let out of the house without a keeper!

And maybe Richard was right, too: maybe she was so obsessed with revenge that she had not thought clearly or acted wisely. Revenge *did* have its price, and she was paying an installment on it right now.

Here in the dark, deprived of any outside stimuli but the monotonous sound and motion, she experienced a subtle alteration in her perception of time and distance. It was too dark to see her watch, and she didn't dare use the flashlight. At first the minutes had seemed extended, as she coped with fear and discomfort. Now there seemed to be no minutes at all—just a continuum that could have been hours. She had no way of judging where the boat might be or how far it had come—they might be only miles from the Pennack dock, or well beyond Falmouth on the open sea. Strangely, the disorientation didn't bother her; her emotions were as dulled as her senses. After a while even the recriminations about her failures ceased to interest her, and she merely slumped there, her attention stupidly focused on the pain in her knee, the uneasiness in her stomach.

At first she barely noticed the decrease in the boat's speed and the cutback of engine power. Then the state of suspended awareness shattered, and she jerked upright. The motion of the vessel had changed, as if it were cutting across a strong current. In a short time the power was cut back further, and the *Charming* bumped against what must have been a dock. The sudden cessation of the engine was as much of a shock as its starting up.

Footsteps moved aft on the dock again—Bob tying up, most likely. Then he moved forward, and she heard him jump over the side. The sound of the footsteps changed: hollow and echoing, as if on wooden planks.

She stirred her cramped limbs and shifted onto her knees. Bob's footsteps were fading, and the night seemed abnormally quiet. Then she remembered the tissues in her ears and pulled them out. The night was still quiet: the footsteps had halted, and the only sounds were the creak of the mooring lines and a distant foghorn. She straightened and cautiously raised the lid of the bin.

The air was misty, but not like the blowing, swirling fogs she'd become accustomed to in San Francisco. This was more like the tule fogs that rose from the marshes and flatlands between there and Sonoma: white and thick and eerily still. Joanna dragged in deep breaths; there was a brackish odor—fishy, but nowhere near as pungent as the stale air in the bin. The foghorn brayed once more, then fell silent.

She pushed the lid all the way open and stood. Straightening her body was a relief, but also painful; her joints protested the sudden demands on them. Quickly she stepped over the bin's side and crouched down on the deck. She crept to the rail and pulled herself up enough to peer over.

Along the boat's side lay a narrow expanse of dock—more ramshackle than the one at Pennack, with a great many missing boards. The fog screened whatever was on the other side of it, but to her right, where she supposed the land must be, a light glowed weirdly. She turned her head and saw a man's figure, a hulking silhouette, and realized the light came from a powerful torch that he held aloft. He stood very still, surveying the scene ahead of him.

In the distance, where the snaggletoothed dock met the land, was a concrete boat ramp. The man—Bob—stood at its foot, his torch illuminating a trio of dilapidated stone buildings surrounded by a tangled encroachment of shrubbery and a thick overhang of tree branches. The larger of them, to the left, was built on pilings over the water; the other stood at the top of the ramp, its arched entry seeming to swallow the concrete; the third was between them, nearly hidden in the wild undergrowth. Even in the scanty light Joanna could see sunken holes in the thatched roofs; the building on pilings tilted dangerously toward the water; the concrete of the ramp was broken and buckled by tree roots. It looked as if no human being had come here in decades.

What was it? she wondered. Probably an abandoned oyster farm; there were supposed to be oyster beds all up and down the river. But *where* on the river? And—more important—what was Bob doing here?

He started to move then, up the ramp toward the building with the door like a gaping mouth. Joanna slipped over the side of the boat, letting herself down quietly on the dock. She removed the flashlight from her bag; its batteries had some life yet, but not much. Training the weak beam on the boards, she moved as silently as possible toward the land, sidestepping places where the planks had fallen away. When she reached the ramp, Bob had already entered the building. His torch shone inside, outlining the arch.

There was a sudden stirring sound and a great flap of wings. A huge cloud of black birds soared out of the archway and scattered, frantic missiles against the white fog. Joanna threw her hands over her head, then smiled faintly; the birds were probably more frightened than she.

The torchlight swung around inside the building, briefly picking out the shape of an old skiff. Joanna switched off her flash and stepped to the side of the ramp, into the low underbrush that bracketed it, and moved up the incline. Ahead she could hear Bob's voice, the words indistinguishable. Then, as she reached the shelter of a spiny bush a few yards from the building, she was able to make out what he was saying.

"Smith! Smith, where are you?"

No answer.

"Smith! Ruggles sent me."

Joanna froze in the shelter of the shrub. The foghorn brayed once, twice. Footsteps sounded in the building, and Bob emerged, torch held high. It illuminated his features: knotted with displeasure, or perhaps apprehension. He swung the light to the side, then started for the building that was partially hidden in the undergrowth.

Joanna stayed where she was, breathing shallowly. In a minute she heard Bob calling Smith—the name Matt had given him—again. There was no reply. Then she heard a noise over by the dock, and whirled.

Nothing moved over there now. Probably only a bird, or a fish jumping in the water.

But as she turned she heard it again: a splashing and a thump. Was Matt hiding from Bob? Was he in the water, perhaps trying to get away with the boat? She began to retrace her steps, moving closer to the dock. Matt Wickins was going nowhere without her.

Behind her twigs snapped near the smaller building. Light flared, making a tracery of the plant growth between her and Bob's torch. She dropped to a crouch as she heard his voice, loud and angry now: "Where the bloody hell are you, Smith?" Its echo died away into silence.

"Goddamn it, Smith, Ruggles sent me. Ruggles—the fisherman in the wink. I'm to take you to the barge. The crewman from the *Devon Pride*'ll be there at one, but he won't wait."

Devon Pride. Like the *Charming*, she'd heard of that ship before. It was one of those moored at King Harry's Reach; Mick had mentioned it when he'd explained about the laid-up vessels. It was a cruise ship, due to go back into service any day now.

So that was how they managed it.

Briefly she flicked on her flash and checked her watch: only a little after eleven, almost two hours before the scheduled meet at the barge. This place must be a considerable distance from King Harry's Reach.

Bob moved through the underbrush, more surefooted now; he'd probably found a path. Joanna moved parallel to him, following the light from his torch. He was going to the building that listed on its ancient pilings over the water. Soon its age-blackened walls were highlighted by the up-thrown rays. Bob's tall figure hesitated at the door, as if he were reluctant to enter. Then he disappeared into the blackness.

"Smith—" His voice broke off as abruptly as if someone had clapped a hand over his mouth.

Joanna plunged through the underbrush, heedless of the noise she made. A cry cut through the air, coming from the building: It was guttural and inhuman, more like an animal's than a man's.

Joanna kept running toward the source of the sound, pulled now by both the instinct to help Bob and the need to cut off the terrible noise. She stumbled through the trees, branches raking at her skin, and broke out into a clearing some twenty feet from the building.

As suddenly as it had begun, the screaming stopped, and Bob burst through the door. He still carried his torch, was swinging it wildly; its beams glanced off his twisted, horrified features.

Joanna ran toward him. He saw her and lurched forward, his knees giving out as he reached her. She staggered under his weight, and they both collapsed to the ground.

As they lay there panting, the sound of the *Charming*'s engine ripped through the silence.

TWENTY-THREE

JOANNA TRIED TO SIT UP, but Bob's weight pinned her to the ground. She shoved at him, but he seemed oblivious both to that and the sound of the boat's engine. He kept saying, "Don't go in there. You mustn't go in there."

"Bob!" Finally she managed to push him aside. "Bob, your boat!"

He raised his head, at last seeming to hear the engine. By the time he was halfway to his feet, the sound had begun to recede. He froze, listening as it gradually became fainter, and when it was no more than a distant drone, he fell back to the ground and lay with his face pressed into the weeds.

"To hell with the bloody boat," he muttered. "After what I saw in there, it doesn't much matter."

Joanna sat up, pulling leaves and twigs from her curls, unwilling to ask the necessary question.

Bob said, "Whoever's on that boat has got to be a bloody animal. What he did to that bloke in there—butchered him like a hog. Don't go in there. You mustn't."

"Who is it, Bob? Matt Wickins?" At his puzzled look she added, "That's the real name of the man you brought upriver earlier."

"That's who it is, all right."

"He's dead?"

"Christ yes, he's dead!"

Joanna felt cold. She got up onto her knees, arms crossed over her breasts, hands cupping her elbows. The old stone building was a hulking black shape in the strange stationary fog. This was where it had ended for Matt, the friend of

her youth, who had survived all the chancy intervening years
to wind up "butchered like a hog...."

She started to stand. Bob's hand caught her wrist and
wrenched her back to the ground. "Don't."

"I have to."

He released her and rolled over onto his back, blank eyes
staring up into the mist.

Joanna took the torch and started across the clearing. The
night seemed to have turned icy, but she knew it was her own
dread that made her shiver. At the building's door she
paused, swallowing hard. Then she stepped into its dank
black interior.

She raised the torch, her hand shaking spasmodically. At
first its light wavered over nothing more than high stone
walls, wooden beams, and a hole where the thatch had caved
in. Then she lowered it, steadied it with her other hand, and
aimed it at the floor. There was a heavy spattering of a
gouted dark liquid. It had sprayed in a semicircle from over
there—

The bloody body that the torchlight illuminated jolted her
senses, made her grunt and jerk her eyes away. She gagged,
recognizing the death odor that underscored the brackish
fishiness. Her breath came swiftly and her pulse raced and
she spun around, face against the frame of the door. For a
long moment all she could think of was getting her body
under control. But when she had managed that, her emotions still raged.

She wanted to speak to the corpse, as if words would form
a bridge between them, somehow bring him back to life:
Matt, I'm sorry I got you into this. I never suspected such a
thing would happen. For all the things we never were to each
other, I cared for you in some odd way. But I used you, too,
and I'm so sorry.

But then she felt a flash of anger: it's your own damn
fault, Matt. You're a victim of your own greed. You never
could keep from taking more than what was offered you,

but you just weren't smart enough to play the game well. Matt, you got yourself killed.

All of it was true. None of it would help him—or her—now.

Finally she steeled herself, turned, and raised the torch again. She swung it around the room, searching every inch of it. She saw no newspaper-wrapped package, just an open canvas flight bag a few feet from the body. Her eyes averted from the bloody mess on the floor, she picked up the bag and inspected its contents.

Socks and underwear. A couple of rolled-up shirts and a pair of jeans. Toilet articles and sneakers. Some stamps and a package of cheap paper and envelopes, only one of which appeared to have been used. A well-thumbed copy of J. D. Salinger's *The Catcher in the Rye.* It had always been Matt's favorite novel, showing an oddly youthful and optimistic side of him. The contents of the bag were not much to be starting a new life with, and their paucity brought tears to Joanna's eyes. She dropped the bag where she'd found it and stumbled outside.

Bob was sitting up now, his back against the trunk of a tree. When she approached he said, "Are you okay?"

"I think so."

"Do you know who did it?"

"Yes. A man called Antony Parducci."

The name didn't mean anything to Bob; he seemed to be waiting for her to explain.

She went over to the tree and leaned next to him, her shoulder against his upper arm, as if the feel of another human being would bring some measure of comfort. It didn't; the vision of Matt's body kept flaring up before her like bloody red neon against a pitch dark night. She said, "We have to get out of here and call the police."

Bob didn't answer.

"How do you suppose Parducci got here?" she asked. "He took your boat, so that means he didn't have one of his own. Did he drive? He must have."

Bob shuddered; he was having visions of his own.

She picked up the torch and shone it full on his face. His eyes were dull, his mouth slack. She said, "Is there a road leading to these buildings?"

He blinked and jerked his face away from the light. "Back beyond the boat house. I think I can find it."

"Then let's go. Parducci probably left a car there. We'll go back to the wink and call the CID, the harbor patrol—whoever has jurisdiction."

He sighed deeply. "I suppose they've got to be notified. Can't cover up a thing like that." His gesture was directed at the building where Matt's body lay. "It's not the boat I care about—it mostly belonged to Trispin, anyway. What I care about is stopping the swine who took it."

As they tramped through the underbrush looking for the road, Bob told her the full story of where the late Alf Trispin, the fisherman at the wink, and he himself had fit into Matt's ill-conceived—and ultimately fatal—plans. The sight of the bloody corpse had apparently removed any inclination for secrecy; he talked long and freely. In the end, it was not much more than she'd already suspected.

Bob's association with Trispin had begun several years before when he'd returned, as he'd told Joanna, from London to run his father's charter fishing service. He had even less of a head for business than his predecessor, however, and Bob—newly married and with a baby on the way—was unable to turn the failing concern around. He was becoming desperate when Trispin had approached him with a lucrative proposition.

"It went this way," he said. "He was to buy me a good boat—fast, radar-equipped, all the latest gadgetry. I was free to use it for my charters—the two the old man had were tubs—and each year I'd earn a certain percentage of ownership, in exchange for carrying out errands for Trispin.''

"Such as?"

"Well . . . pickups and deliveries."

"Drugs?"

"Packages; I never saw what was inside. And people."

The people, he explained, were fugitives wanting to leave the country. Trispin had worked out a deal with members of the skeleton crews on a few of the ships periodically berthed at King Harry's Reach, to help his "clients" stow away when the ships went back into service. The fugitives were directed to the kiddleywink on Knackers' Point, and from there were taken to the oystering shacks, where they would wait for Bob. He would pick them up late at night and rendezvous with a crew member from the designated ship at the World War II cement barges, which marked the beginning of the moorings, not far from the shacks. It was then the crew member's responsibility to get the client safely aboard the ship.

"Wait," Joanna said. "If those shacks are so close to the barges, why were you calling out to Matt to hurry up? Surely it wouldn't have taken nearly two hours to get there."

There was a lengthy pause. "I'll explain that later, when I come to that part."

With the new boat, Bob continued, he'd finally gotten the business off the ground. Things were going well until his father—"He's not really my old man, just the bloke who married my mam when I was ten; mean old bastard, too"—had found out about his arrangement with Trispin. Instead of going to the authorities, as Bob had feared he would, the old man demanded a piece of the action. He had retired when Bob took over the business, up near Pennack, and he reasoned he would be in a better position to handle the fugitive-smuggling operation from there.

"It was blackmail, all right," Bob said, "but I was relieved in a way because I was spending more and more time on Alf's errands and less on the charters. I saw it as a way to cut back. I talked to Trispin, and he liked the idea, so the old man got a boat out of him and took over that end of things."

"And?"

"That's all."

"Not quite. You haven't told me about today, yet. Things started to fall apart when Trispin was shot, didn't they?"

"Yes, and God knows what he was doing in his office at five in the morning—"

"I think he was meeting with Antony Parducci, the man who killed Matt Wickins."

Bob's look of comprehension was illuminated by the torch. "That might explain things. Wickins told my—No, I'm getting ahead of the story. Let me tell it straight on."

Bob had been scheduled to have a conference with Trispin about a new series of pickups late the previous evening, when he was due back in port from a two-day charter. But when he'd arrived at home, he received a message that Trispin was cancelling; Alf had said he had an early morning meeting the next day with an important client, and wanted to retire early.

"That client must have been your Antony Parducci," he added.

"I think so. He must have phoned Trispin from London and asked to see him as soon as he arrived here."

Bob waited, again seeming to expect some explanation of who Parducci was. When it wasn't forthcoming he went on with his story.

Matt Wickins, aka Mr. Smith, had turned up at the Prince of Wales Pier around nine that morning, looking for someone to take him to Pennack. Bob's friend Mick routinely steered individual charters to him, and it was by pure happenstance that Bob encountered a would-be client of Trispin.

"Right off I suspected he was someone who had wanted to make connection with old Alf and arrived too late," he said. "I was leery of taking him upriver, what with the way Alf had died, but I was also thinking ahead. The coppers would be looking into Alf's affairs soon enough, and they'd find out the boat mostly belonged to him. At best I'd need the money to buy out his share; at worst I'd need it for a solicitor, so I agreed to take him."

"The same way you agreed to sell me information."

"It's a living."

"But you didn't give me my fifty pounds' worth. And you lied to me about not being able to make the trip in the fog."

"Well, I had to, didn't I? I figured I'd hold you off until the next day when Smith... Wickins would be on his way. Then I'd take you to Pennack, you wouldn't find him, and I'd have my other fifty quid. Never dreamed you'd drive there on your own."

After he'd left her at the pub, Bob went on, he started thinking about Matt, and the large wad of cash he'd noticed in his flight bag when he'd paid him for the ride upriver. "Seemed to me he'd be willing to part with all of it to make that meet with the bloke from the *Devon Pride*. He was in a fix, and he knew it. That was why I came here early, in case it took a while to persuade him."

"But first you went to the kiddleywink. Why?"

"I had to check with the old man, about who the meet was with and when, make sure the bloke was already at the oyster farm. Old bastard held me up for twenty quid before he'd tell me the details, and demanded half the take, too." Bob laughed harshly. "He's in for a surprise, he is."

"You mean that man you were talking with in the wink is your father?"

"*Step*father—Ben Ruggles. Like I said, he's a mean old bastard. Made me buy him a pint, too."

Joanna smiled wryly, thinking that natural parentage was no guarantee against being a bastard, either. Her own relationship with her father was virtually nonexistent, although E.J. kept in touch with him, and she'd recently spoken with him on the phone for the first time since she'd run away from home over twenty years before. And E.J.'s feelings for his own father... he'd been the first to applaud her plan to put Parducci behind bars. For the first time she thought about what she would have to tell E.J. when she returned to California. How do you inform your son that his father has turned into a vicious killer? Somehow she suspected E.J. would handle the revelation far better than she would handle making it.

Bob batted away a low-hanging branch and motioned for her to move in front of him. Ahead, a rutted path snaked away into the tangled shrubbery. "There's the road. Car had better be around here, or we're in for quite a walk."

He turned to the left, where the undergrowth was the densest, and she followed. "Did Matt tell your stepfather anything?"

"Just that an associate in London—Sneath, I think he called him—had referred him to Trispin. But when he got to Falmouth and called him, Alf kept putting him off. When Wickins heard Alf was dead, enough time had gone by that he was getting desperate, so he decided to make his own connection. This Sneath had told him about the wink and the village, so he knew to go there."

And Trispin had told Parducci about the wink and the village and the oystering shacks. He might even have mentioned the imminent departure of the *Devon Pride*. Somehow Parducci had found out Matt had gone to Pennack and guessed what the plan was. He might even have been waiting for Matt at the shacks when he arrived....

"Well, damn me. You were right," Bob said. "There she is—as pretty a Bentley as you'd hope to see."

A Bentley was what John Grey had told her Ian Sneath drove—the car that had been missing from its usual spot in front of Sneath's shop. Parducci had taken it and driven to Cornwall.

Bob went ahead of her and checked inside the car. "We're in luck—keys are here."

She ran to join him and soon they were on their way— along dark lanes surrounded by hedgerows that blocked out all lights and other signs of human habitation. Bob drove silently, hunched over the wheel, eyes intent on the road. Joanna sensed he was having regrets about telling her so much, but she doubted he would try to keep her from contacting the authorities: something about the way he'd told his story indicated he knew his life had been moving toward an encounter with them ever since he'd allowed his greed to overrule his good sense.

There were only a few cars in the parking lot of the wink when they arrived. Bob stopped near the door and let the engine die. Joanna jumped from the car and hurried inside, scanning the dim room for a telephone. Two men at a nearby table stared at her; the barman halted in the process of drying a glass.

Bob came in behind her and said, "Lady needs the phone, Bill." To her, he added, "It's behind the bar. Go round; he'll hand it to you."

She crossed the room, digging in her bag for the number of the Falmouth CID man she'd tried to call earlier. The barman put the phone in front of her. As she picked up the receiver a man who sat at a table in the far corner got up and walked toward the bar. She didn't realize who he was until he said, "It's about time I caught up with you, Janna."

Steve Rafferty.

TWENTY-FOUR

"WHAT THE HELL are you doing here?" she said.

"A nice welcome, after I've come all this way." Rafferty was smiling, but his eyes were watchful. His trim, muscular body was clad in a thick down jacket and jeans, and his prematurely silver-gray hair was tousled. He stood with his hands thrust in his pockets, making no move to touch her.

Normally she would have felt a rush of pleasure at seeing him; now she was aware of a creeping distrust. "What did you expect?" she said. "I asked you not to." She turned back to the bar, reaching for the phone.

"You'd better tell me what's happened before you make that call, Janna." She'd never heard him use that tone before—stony and sharp. She glanced at his lean tanned face and saw his mouth set matched his voice. Questions began to form in her mind. How had he found her here? How long had he been in England? Before she could ask them, he added, "You've made a mess of things. I can't allow you to screw up anymore."

Again she faced him, anger rising. "*You* can't allow—"

"Be quiet and sit down. I need to know what's going on."

Out of the corner of one eye Joanna saw Bob backing away from them. She said, "Don't you run out on me now, Bob Jenkins!"

In a voice full of wounded dignity he replied, "Didn't plan to. Was just going to get myself a pint. Man's got a right to one after what we've been through, hasn't he?"

"Of course. Get me one, too."

Rafferty was studying Bob. Now he looked questioningly at Joanna. She cut him off, turned, and dialed the number for the CID. There was a weird whistling on the line, which quickly degenerated into static. "Damn!" she exclaimed and hung up. When she redialed, the static was even worse. The British phone system had never been good; and although some improvements had come about in the last ten years or so, they apparently had had little impact in rural areas such as this.

Rafferty pulled out a chair from the nearest table and motioned for her to sit. She looked at the phone, sighed, and flopped down. He straddled the chair next to her. "Now," he said, "tell me."

"First *you* tell *me* what you're doing here."

"Later."

Later. She glanced at her watch. In about fifty minutes the crewman from the *Devon Pride* was due to pick up his passenger at the cement barge. She had no doubt that that passenger would be Parducci. "There's no time to talk. I've got to get through to the CID." She started to get up, but Rafferty's hand clamped on her arm and he pulled her back into the chair.

"Give it a few minutes; the line'll clear. I want to know what's wrong. Christopher said you'd gone after Matt Wickins and the fake Brueghel. Have you found—"

"Christopher!" She remembered leaving his flat the other night, and her strange feeling of being watched. Up until now she'd assumed the watcher was Parducci, but by then he'd been on his way to Cornwall. "That was you at Bedford Square."

"When you weren't at your hotel that night, I looked up Burgess's home address and went there, to see if he knew where to locate you. You were just leaving, and I decided to check with him on how things were going. He filled me in—"

"I was just leaving, but you decided to talk with *Christopher*, rather than me. Why?"

"Let's face it, Janna, you would have been furious with me for coming over here. You'd made that plain during our last phone call. I thought the best thing for me to do was watch from the sidelines and help you out when you needed me. And it looks like you do now."

Bob set a pint in front of her. It was all she could do to keep from hurling it in Rafferty's face. She bit off a sharp retort and went to the phone. This time the line was clear. Her contact wasn't in, however, and it quickly became apparent that the officer on duty was extremely leery—if not downright unbelieving—of her story.

"You'd best come in, miss, and talk to us in person," he said.

"But a murder's been committed, and the man responsible will get away—"

"All the more reason to come in straight away."

"Can't you alert the harbor patrol, at least?"

"I can't be asking them to go out in this fog on the strength of a phone call. If you come in and bring identification—"

Joanna hung up on him.

She turned to Bob, who was standing next to her. "They want me to go all the way back to Falmouth and *talk* about it, for God's sake! That could take hours, and by that time Parducci'll be aboard the ship. What time do you think it's scheduled to leave?"

"Early enough that she might clear the harbor before they could get an order to search her."

"Damn! How long would it take us to get to the barge?"

"Us?"

"You and me, in a boat."

"Now wait—"

"How long?"

"Perhaps twenty minutes, half an hour. But we don't have—"

"What about your stepfather's boat? Can you get hold of it?"

"Not likely. He's a tight old bastard."

"I'd pay."

"You'd pay dearly. Like I said—"

"Never mind the cost. See if he will."

"Doesn't matter if he will or not. I'm not going up against that swine who killed—"

"Do you want the *Charming* back, or don't you?"

Bob hesitated.

"At least you'd have your boat back. And if you help apprehend Parducci, the authorities might go easier on you when your connection with Trispin comes out."

He set his pint down and started for the door. "I'll be back in ten minutes, latest."

Rafferty said, "What's all this about Parducci? What boat was stolen?"

"Never mind. Just stay out of my business."

"You're so fucking stubborn and independent."

"And you're so fucking patronizing and untrusting."

"I only wanted to help."

"Right. Well, you can help by leaving me alone."

"I can't."

"Why not?"

Rafferty looked away.

"Why not?"

"Janna, this trip has cost me a lot of money. I've taken valuable time off from my other cases."

"Your *other* cases?"

Rafferty suddenly seemed to feel too warm. He unbuttoned his jacket and took it off, tossing it on the chair next to him. A sense of betrayal, as cold as Rafferty's discomfort was hot, spread through Joanna.

She sat down and said, "You cut a deal with one of the insurance companies holding the policies on those missing Brueghels, didn't you?"

Silence.

"Doesn't Great American frown on independent contracting by their investigators? But I suppose the finder's fee would be large enough to justify the risk."

"All right!" Rafferty said. "I need the money! You know how hard it is to live in San Francisco on my salary, plus make my support payments."

"And you know I've offered to help out. But no, you've always been too proud for that. It's wrong to take the money I'd freely give you, but it's all right to use me without my knowing. Tell me this—did you make the deal before I came over here, or after?"

"... Before."

"How long before?"

"A while, I don't know."

"About the time I thought of my scheme to trap Parducci?"

"After that."

"Oh, I see. After I'd talked it out with you and you were sure it was feasible. After you'd given me all the helpful hints to refine it."

"Janna—"

"I thought you were helping because you cared about me. But in reality it was because you cared about the profit you could make. And then you came over here and spied on me, sneaking around like some cut-rate James Bond. That was you watching me at the hotel tonight, wasn't it? You asked the desk clerk about me, didn't you?"

"Yes."

"How'd you find out I'd come to Falmouth? Christopher didn't know."

"You made your reservations through the Primrose Hill Hotel."

"Ah. And I suppose you found out I was asking about Pennack from the barmaid in the Greenbank pub."

"Yes."

"Good detective work, Rafferty. Too bad you don't apply it to your regular job. Because you're going to need that job. There isn't going to be any profit here. Matt Wickins is dead, and if Bob can't get hold of that boat, Parducci will leave on the *Devon Pride* before we can convince the authorities to get an order to stop and search it."

"What the hell are you talking about?"

She told him, omitting none of the unpleasant details of Matt's death. When she finished, Rafferty had gone pale under his tan. He went to get a beer, his hand shaking and spilling the liquid down the sides of the glass before he set it on the table.

"How long before that fellow comes back?" he asked, glancing at his watch.

"I don't know. He may never come back at all; I know I'd run out on us if I were he. But somehow I think he'll be here soon. He wants his boat back and... Well, he saw what was done to Matt."

Rafferty took a large swallow of beer. "All right, if he gets hold of a boat on time, we still may be able to stop Parducci."

"You don't give up, do you?"

Rafferty didn't reply.

Joanna would have liked to refuse to take him along, but she knew she was no match for Parducci, and Bob would mainly be occupied with handling the boat. With Rafferty, they might stand a chance of apprehending him. "All right, but I want to make this clear: that will be the end of it for us."

"You're being unfair." -

"No, *you've* been unfair. You used me. No matter how you rationalize it—to me or yourself—you aren't here to help me or protect me or whatever else you want to call it. You're here for your own financial gain, nothing more."

Rafferty was silent.

At least, she thought, he didn't think her enough of a fool to be swayed by further rationalization or an apology.

They sat quietly, sipping their beers, within a foot of each other but miles apart emotionally, until Bob returned and announced he had the keys to his stepfather's boat.

Rafferty stood up and grabbed his jacket. "Let's go," he said.

Joanna stood more slowly. "Does your stepfather have a weapon on the boat?" she asked Bob. "A gun?"

"Neither of us ever carries one."

"And I don't suppose you have one, either," she said to Rafferty.

"I didn't suppose things would be so fucked up that I'd need one."

She ignored the barb. "We'd be fools going up against Parducci unarmed. He's shot two men that we know of."

Bob nodded and looked over at the bar. Then he went up to it and held a hurried private conversation with the barman. When he came back, he held out his hand to Joanna and said, "Give me fifty quid."

"Fifty—"

"Come on!" He snapped his fingers impatiently.

Joanna dug in her bag and pulled out a handful of pound notes. When she'd counted out two twenties and a ten, she had exactly five pounds left.

Bob went back to the bar, gave the man the money, and tucked something inside his slicker. Then he motioned for Joanna and Rafferty to follow him outside.

In the parking lot, he reached inside his slicker and extracted a long-muzzled handgun from his belt. He extended it to Joanna.

She recoiled; she'd always hated guns. "I don't want that thing!"

"I'll take it," Rafferty said.

Bob shook his head and pushed the weapon at Joanna.

"She doesn't know how to shoot," Rafferty said. "it would be better if I—"

"No." Bob's voice was cold. "I don't know you, mate. The lady holds the gun, or we don't go."

Joanna looked inquiringly at Bob. Sharing an intense emotional experience as she and he had often makes relative strangers intimate, able to intuit each other's feelings. She supposed Bob had picked up on her distrust of Rafferty.

"I tell you, she doesn't know how to—"

"Shut up, Steve." Joanna took the pistol. "Let's go," she said.

BEN RUGGLES'S BOAT was berthed in a makeshift slip some distance beyond the boat works, which was why Joanna hadn't noticed it earlier. It was a cabin cruiser, trimmer and faster looking than the *Charming*, with the same expensive array of gadgetry. They all clambered on board, and Joanna and Rafferty cast off the lines while Bob started the engine. It rumbled and burbled, then began to purr; Joanna could understand why Trispin had chosen such a sleek, quiet boat for late-night clandestine expeditions.

As they churned away from shore, Joanna went into the cockpit and took the seat opposite the wheel. Bob glanced over at her and tried to grin reassuringly. She pulled her own lips back in what she supposed was an unconvincing parody of a smile. Rafferty came up behind her and steadied himself by placing his hands on the back of the seat. She moved to one side, out of his reach, ignoring him.

Odd, she thought, how one man—who had been a total stranger six hours ago—could have become her ally, while the other—who had held an intimate place in her life for over six months—had now become something just short of the enemy.

The boat moved slowly away from Pennack, the few remaining lights on the hill and the faint glimmers from the wink disappearing in the fog. The running lights of the boat barely penetrated its milky thickness.

"How can you see?" she shouted to Bob over the steady thrum of the engine.

"Can't, but don't worry yourself. I know these waters better than I know my own mind, and besides, I've these lovely gadgets to help me." His hand swept along the rows of gauges. "Of course," he added, "it may get rough once we approach that barge. Your Mr. Parducci's bound to be leery of any craft that comes near. We'll have to run without lights for quite some ways. I take it Parducci is armed?"

"Probably. As I said before, he shot two men—Alf Trispin and a fellow in London."

"Christ." But then Bob brightened. "Maybe he's got rid of his gun. Wasn't any pistol did for that bloke Wickins."

Joanna felt her mouth go dry at the memory. "I think," she said, "that he slashed him that way because he enjoyed it, not for the lack of a weapon."

Behind her Rafferty grunted.

After a few seconds, Bob said, "This lad Parducci—he's some sort of thief, right?"

"An art thief. I've been after him for years."

"Is he daft?"

"I didn't used to think so, but now I do."

"Bloke'd have to be, to do someone like that." He paused, then added in a lower voice, "*I'm* daft, to have gotten myself into this."

Rafferty said, "You're not going to back out now."

"No. I suppose, as the lady suggested, I might get my boat back. And redeem myself in the eyes of the law." In the light of the instrument panel, Joanna could see his small, self-mocking smile.

Bob spoke no more, staring out at the fog, checking the instruments and making minute corrections. After a moment Rafferty moved over to stand behind him, Joanna leaned back in her seat, trying to empty her mind and relax before what she assumed would be a violent confrontation. The thought of Rafferty's treachery kept nagging at her, however; there was something wrong with what he'd admitted to her, or perhaps something unsaid. If her scheme had worked as laid out, Parducci and the fake Brueghel would have been turned over to New Scotland Yard's Art Squad; they would have been the ones credited with apprehending the collector and recovering the stolen paintings. How had he expected—?

Well, she wasn't going to ask him about it now. It was all water over the dam, anyway. *Over* the dam? Hell, the dam had burst: the destruction of their relationship was total.

She closed her eyes and let the misty air cool her face. She saw only merciful darkness behind their lids, rather than bloody neonlike images. Although she'd had very little sleep since she'd discovered Amir Moradi's body in Matt's flat two nights ago—and what rest she had snatched had been dream-haunted and broken—she felt curiously alert and clearheaded. Fear and betrayal and death: none of them could touch her inside, where she really lived.

And where was that? What *was* at the core of her? Revenge, as Richard Bloomfield seemed to believe? Had she really become an obsessed woman who might one day be consumed by this most debilitating of emotions?

Maybe—but there was nothing she could do about it. For over twenty years she'd played with the fantasy of apprehending Parducci. Then, when she'd come face-to-face with the man last fall, the fantasy had turned into a real possibility. Now it was necessity: neither she nor E.J. nor anyone else she cared about would be safe from him, as long as he went free.

Call it vengeance, she thought, call it obsession. Even admit to yourself that it's probably, as Parducci suggested, the overly long-nurtured sour grapes of a woman scorned. The label doesn't matter anymore. The results do....

Bob said, "I'm cutting the running lights now. Fog's lifted some. That's the *Methane Princess* to starboard."

Joanna opened her eyes and was shocked to see the bulk of the doomed liquid gas tanker. Although they were at some distance from her, her enormous prow towered above them—rust red below the road line, black as it thrust out and skyward. Chains as big around as a man's body held her fast to her moorings; her white superstructure gleamed in the glare of its security lights.

Joanna swiveled in her seat and looked behind them. A line of ships, the far ones looking to be no more than bathtub toys, was strung out along the curve of the river. "How come I didn't see them before I closed my eyes?"

"Weren't there yet. You'd dropped off by the time we reached them, and I thought you needed your rest."

"Dropped off? For how long?"

"A good ten minutes."

And she thought she'd only been resting her eyes for a minute or two. Again, as in the storage bin on the *Charming*, she was conscious of an odd shifting in her sense of time.

Bob motioned in front of them, and she went to stand by his seat. "Those two white ships riding side by side are ferries. The barges start perhaps a hundred yards to their bows. I'm taking us in closer to shore and cutting back on power until we see what the situation is."

"Where's the *Devon Pride*?"

"Back the way we came, last in the moorings. I think we're on time—early, perhaps, because I haven't seen her skiff."

Joanna stood next to Bob, studying the great white shapes of the twin ferries and, as they passed them, straining to see the barges to their bows. Rafferty had moved over and taken the seat she'd vacated; he seemed as eager as she to put physical distance between them. Bob brought the cruiser close to the shore and cut the throttle to an idle.

"I don't see the barges," Joanna said. Her voice seemed to boom in the relative silence. She lowered it. "Where are they?"

Bob extended his arm and she trained her sight along his outstretched finger. "Four of them, linked bow to stern. If you look carefully you'll see a rectangular chain, something like freight cars on a track."

She could make out its shape, just barely. "How come there aren't any lights on them?"

"Don't require any. For years no one's been interested in them but the waterfowl. They're merely channel markers."

"Which one is the meet scheduled for?"

"The first...and I think I can make out the *Charming*, pulled alongside."

Joanna could hear the quick excitement in his voice; Bob wanted his boat back more than he would admit. Rafferty must have heard what he'd said, because he came to stand with them. "No boat from the *Devon Pride* yet?" he asked.

"No," Bob said. "We may be in luck. Something's delayed him."

Joanna said, "Bob, would Trispin have told Parducci what kind of boat would be making the pickup?"

"I doubt Alf himself knew. He merely collected the fee and sent the client on to the wink. Only the old man—and me before him—would know who to expect."

"Then I suggest we take over the crewman's job. Rafferty and I will go below so Parducci won't spot us, and you'll pick him up. When he's aboard and we're into the channel, send him below and we'll deal with him."

Bob looked dubious, but Rafferty said, "it's a good plan. We'll have to move fast. I think I see another boat coming the way we did."

Joanna looked back, but she couldn't see anything. She decided to take Rafferty's word for it, though, and said, "We'd better hurry."

Bob pulled the throttle back, his teeth set in a grimace that was part determination and part fear. "Right. We'll go now. And hope Parducci isn't still in possession of his gun."

TWENTY-FIVE

JOANNA SAT on one of the berths in the cruiser's tiny cabin, the .32 Bob had bought from the barman clenched in her hand. Rafferty crouched under the ladder that descended from above. The boat rocked as it cut across the current, making her vaguely nauseated, and she kept swallowing. It was warm in the cabin, and very dark; she could just make out the silver of Rafferty's hair.

It was also tense in there. Neither of them had spoken since they'd firmed up their plans on how to deal with Parducci. Every now and then Rafferty made a small noise, trying to clear his throat quietly. It was a nervous habit that Joanna had noticed before, and it had never bothered her, but now she wanted to snap at him, tell him to quit it. Then she realized that her repeated swallowing was probably having the same effect on him, and she prudently kept quiet.

The cruiser's speed decreased abruptly, and Joanna dug her fingernails into the rough cloth that covered the bunk. They must be nearing the barge, close enough for Parducci to see them. Would he suspect something was not as it should be? Perhaps fire at them? Or would he merely accept Bob as the crewman from the *Devon Pride*—

And then a terrible thought came to her: what if Parducci had seen Bob at the oyster farm? It had been dark, but Bob had had the torch; she herself had seen his features highlighted by it, clearly enough to read his expression. Where had Parducci been at that moment?

The idea made her suck in her breath. Rafferty's head swiveled toward her, but he quickly turned back, cocking it in a listening position. She strained her hearing, too, trying to catch a hint of what was happening above.

There was a thump; the cruiser making contact with the barge, she supposed. The engine's power dropped to an idle, and the boat rose and fell the way one does when it pulls up to a dock. She heard shouted words: Bob's. There was an answering cry, but it came from farther away, and she couldn't tell if it was Parducci's voice. She dug her fingers harder into the mattress.

Nothing but more bumps. The boat banged into the barge and bobbed on the current.

An exchange of words, not so loud now. Parducci must be close enough to see Bob's face.

She swallowed, shut her eyes, held her breath. Put all her effort into hearing what went on above.

More thumps, but different than before. The sound of someone boarding the cruiser. A thud, as if he might have dropped something. And then footsteps, coming forward.

Joanna let her breath out softly. Her pulse began beating faster, and adrenaline set her limbs atingle. She opened her eyes, and in the shadows saw Rafferty's silver mane nod once in the affirmative.

So far, so good.

The engine's power increased gradually, and the cruiser began to move. That was the next step: get away from the barges, into the open channel.

The change in motion must have taken Rafferty off guard; she saw his hand grab one of the rungs of the ladder, steadying himself.

Get your hand out of sight! she thought. *Move—now!*

The hand disappeared.

Now it was her turn to act. She scrambled along the bunk, into the V-shaped space at the bow where the two bunks met and the darkness was deepest. A relatively safe place, hard to reach should Rafferty fail to restrain Parducci and her shot miss him—or if she couldn't muster the nerve to fire. She slipped into the deep cavity, curling herself into a cramped position, gun in both hands now and braced against her knees. She was glad she'd decided to wait until the last minute; limber as she was, her joints and muscles began to throb immediately.

Come on, Bob, she thought, *get us into the channel and send him down here.*

Minutes passed. Impossibly dragging minutes.

Then there was an exchange of voices above them. Bob, telling Parducci to go below and not turn on any lights. The cabin door opened, showing grayness at the top of the ladder. A pair of long legs started down, clumsily, as if their owner was not accustomed to boats. The rest of the body followed, and she saw that part of the clumsiness was due to the newspaper-wrapped package he clutched to his chest.

She had to stifle a sigh of relief when the gray light from above showed her Parducci's hollow features.

He descended all the way into the cabin and stood uncertainly. Then he groped toward one of the bunks and set the package on it. At the top of the ladder Bob shut and locked the door. Parducci's head jerked that way, as if he was becoming aware that something was amiss.

Joanna said, "Hello, Tony."

Parducci whirled at the sound of her voice.

Rafferty came out from behind the ladder and grabbed him, pinning his arms.

Joanna waited until Rafferty said, "Okay," then wriggled out of the V-shaped cavity. She crawled along the bunk and felt at the bulkhead for the switch that would turn on the cabin lights. When they flashed on she looked up at Parducci.

He stood pinned in Rafferty's grasp, blinking at the sudden glare. When his gaze first rested on her and the .32 she held, his face was flaccid with shock; then his lips quickly drew back in a snarl.

Rafferty said, "Janna, the rope."

With her free hand she took the coil from where it lay on the opposite bunk and approached them. A physical aversion—what she supposed people meant when they spoke of their skin crawling—made her stop.

"Come on," Rafferty said. "Frisk him first."

As she slid the rope up her arm and moved to touch him, Parducci turned his head and looked down at her. His sunken eyes blazed with hate. A chill washed over her; her palms were sweating.

"Janna!"

Parducci wore a windbreaker over a heavy sweater. One pocket of it sagged. She reached inside with her left hand and her fingers encountered oily metal. She extracted the gun; it was snub-nosed, heavier than the .32. Again her flesh rippled unpleasantly.

She stepped back and handed the rope to Rafferty. As she trained the gun on Parducci, Rafferty released his hold and tied Parducci's hands behind him. Then he said, "Janna, put the guns down and help me tie his feet."

She hesitated. Parducci was silent and passive, but his behavior didn't reassure her; it had always been his style when cornered to conserve his energies, study his options, and wait for a break. Rafferty made an impatient sound, and she reluctantly set both guns on the floor.

"Shove him onto the bunk so we can get at his feet," Rafferty said.

She moved to do so, but Parducci whirled on her, eyes burning blue like the tiny ellipsoid at the very core of a flame. His lips flattened against his teeth, and then he spat at her face.

Her hand flew to her cheek and she drew back, crying out in shock and disgust.

Behind her Rafferty moved suddenly, to shove Parducci himself, she supposed. She stepped away, wiping at her face. And then realized something was wrong.

Rafferty now held Parducci's gun in his right hand. With his left he stuffed the barman's .32 into the deep pocket of his jacket. Then he leaned against the ladder, pointing the weapon. At both of them.

For a long moment she was unable to speak. Couldn't comprehend what was happening, then couldn't believe he was serious.

Parducci broke the silence, laughing harshly and cynically. "What a fine choice of confederates you've made, Joanna!"

"Shut up," Rafferty said, "and sit down."

Parducci sat.

"You sit down, too, Joanna," Rafferty added, "and we'll talk about what's going to happen next."

The use of her given name, rather than the nickname, convinced her of his seriousness. She stepped backward and sat on the edge of the bunk opposite Parducci. When she looked up at Rafferty, he wouldn't meet her eyes.

"Steve," she said, also using her serious form of address, "why are you doing this?"

"You know why," he answered. "You're stubborn, and a monomaniac when it comes to Parducci. Since you won't cooperate, I have to insure that you won't be a hindrance. If you and Bob do as I say, it will all work out and no one will be hurt."

Parducci's posture had become straighter, his eyes alert and calculating. Rafferty glanced at him and shifted the gun slightly in his direction.

"In a few minutes," he went on, "we're going topside— all of us. We'll wait until we see the boat from the *Devon Pride* approach the barge and leave again. When it's gone Bob will pilot us back there and tie up. He'll then disable this boat, and I'll lock you"—he nodded at Joanna—"and him down here. Parducci and I will leave aboard the *Charming*. In the morning the harbor patrol will spot the cruiser tied up at the barge and release you."

Joanna was about to protest that he couldn't pilot a boat like the *Charming*, but then she remembered he'd grown up around boats, spending his summers on the Maine Coast; one of the things he'd promised but never gotten around to was taking her sailing out of Port Sonoma. She asked, "And when we're released, where will you be?"

"Parducci and I will be in a safe location. He doesn't know it yet, but he's going to tell me the identity of the collector who has the other Proverb Series paintings. I'll notify the insurance carriers; they'll deal with the authorities; and when the paintings are recovered—and I'm assured of my finder's fees—Parducci will go free."

Parducci was now watching Rafferty intently.

"Why not turn him over to the authorities, too?"

"Because from what you've told me of him, he's the strong and silent type. I don't think he'd reveal the name of that collector without some incentive."

Parducci said to Joanna, "How kind of you to have extolled my virtues."

"Shut up," Rafferty said.

Parducci smiled mockingly.

Joanna said, "You must realize that when I'm released I'll go to the authorities. Bob will back up my story."

"I doubt that. You won't want to look like a fool, and Bob will have no reason to. Reason not to, actually: he'll have his boat back, and if the story of what happened tonight doesn't come out, neither will the details of his illegal activities."

"What about Matt Wickins's body? Even if we don't go to Scotland Yard, someone will discover it."

"I doubt that, too. No one but Bob's stepfather and Trispin's clients ever goes to those oystering shacks—nor are they likely to now."

Joanna's anger rose at his callous dismissal of Matt's death. "I warn you—I'll tell Scotland Yard what you're planning to do!"

Rafferty shrugged. "I'll take that chance. It'll be your word against mine. After the way you've been running all over England like a woman possessed, I don't think they'll believe you. Too many people know of your grudge against Parducci."

Parducci gave her an arch smile. "You see, Joanna?"

She glared at him. "There are a couple of other things you haven't considered. What if the crewman from the *Devon Pride* reports that the *Charming*'s been abandoned at the barge?"

"It's not likely. Why would he want to admit to having gone there?"

It was all so damned logical—and defeating. Her remaining hope was to drive a wedge between him and Parducci. "How does Parducci know you won't turn him in?" she asked. "After all, he's only got your word for it."

"And no other alternative. Mr. Parducci is pragmatic, you've told me that."

Joanna glanced at Parducci. His face was quietly thoughtful. She'd seen that look before when he was weighing the pros and cons of a situation, and she was certain he would react characteristically—by cutting his losses.

Rafferty said, "Shall we go?"

Joanna remained sitting.

"Get up, Joanna."

"You wouldn't shoot me."

"Don't force my hand."

She looked searchingly at his face, willing him to meet her eyes. Finally he couldn't resist the pull of her gaze, and what she saw there shocked her profoundly. The openness and often self-deprecating good humor that she'd always taken as hallmarks of Rafferty's character were gone; in their place was a cold determination. She wondered what had happened to change him like this, or if she'd only been imagining those qualities from the beginning. Perhaps during the past six months she'd been involved with a man she'd created in her mind, but who wasn't really like that at all.

"Let's go," Rafferty said.

Joanna got to her feet and started toward the ladder, her body feeling clumsy and leaden.

"No, let Parducci go first."

Parducci stood and looked at the parcel on the bunk. "Don't you want to take that?"

Rafferty smiled faintly. "No, let Joanna have it."

Parducci frowned.

"You haven't taken a look at it yet, have you?" Rafferty asked.

Parducci shook his head.

"If you had, you'd have seen it's a fake."

"A forgery?"

"No, Brueghel never painted anything called *There Hangs the Knife*. It was specially created by an excellent copyist—at the request of Joanna Stark."

"Then it was all a trap." Parducci looked at Joanna. As in the office at the Starving Ox, his eyes were devoid of emotion. He merely looked old and tired.

There was no reason for her to reply.

They went above then, Parducci needing to be boosted up the ladder. When Rafferty pounded on the door for Bob to let them out, the boatman looked surprised. Then he saw the gun in Rafferty's hand and exclaimed, "What the bloody hell?"

Rafferty explained, as he had to Joanna and Parducci.

As he spoke, the color drained from Bob's face, and when he had finished he said, "You're not going to let that scum go free?"

Rafferty merely nodded. Parducci didn't react at all—merely stood at the edge of the cockpit staring out at the distant ships.

"Jesus Christ!" Bob said. "Do you know what you'll be doing? The bloody swine's killed three people."

Rafferty said, "Forget about him, Bob. You'll have your boat back soon—I'm a good pilot, and nothing will happen to it. More important, there's a good possibility no one will ever look into your illegal activities."

Bob hesitated, his eyes fixed on Rafferty.

Joanna said, "Don't listen to him, Bob. Remember what Parducci did to Matt Wickins."

Bob's gaze met hers, then pulled away. He hesitated, and then nodded, as if he'd come to a decision. "We'll go back to the barge," he said. "That's the cutter from the *Devon Pride* just pulling away from her."

Joanna looked out and saw the small craft's lights moving toward where the ferries were moored.

Rafferty shoved Joanna into the cockpit seat and motioned for Parducci to sit beside her. She tried to shrink away from the touch of his body, but there was no place to go. Through his thick clothing he felt shrunken, almost skeletal. A sour odor emanated from him: fear, and something else. The creeping moral and physical decay that sometimes accompanies madness?

Parducci kept shifting in the seat, apparently trying to find a comfortable position. After a moment Joanna stood, wedged against the bulkhead. Rafferty noticed but didn't object.

The cruiser moved slowly toward the barges. The fog had thinned, was drifting now, and through it Joanna could make out the shape of the *Charming*. Helplessness descended on her; she sighed, and it came out a forlorn whine. Parducci looked up and smirked at her.

Bob cut the throttle and the cruiser drifted toward the barge. Rafferty said, "Turn the engines off."

He did so.

"Now tie her up."

Bob crawled onto the forward deck and cast a line around a stanchion on the barge. When he returned Rafferty said, "I want you to disable the ignition. I'll be watching you. I know boats, so don't try to fake it."

Bob nodded silently and went toward the cockpit. Joanna watched, thinking there was something deliberately slow about his movements. He stopped, snapping his fingers. "I'll need tools," he said. "Don't want to screw up the old man's boat. Box is back there in the bin." He motioned behind Rafferty.

"Get it, then."

Bob went aft, edging carefully around Rafferty. Rafferty kept the gun trained on Joanna and Parducci, then seemed to realize his dilemma—but too late. He was just beginning to turn toward Bob when the boatman's fist connected with his right temple.

Joanna shoved around Parducci and flung herself at Rafferty. He fell, his shoulder smashing against the rail. The gun crashed to the deck, and there was a clatter and then a splash as Bob kicked it overboard.

Rafferty pushed up, palms flat on the deck, then went for the other gun. Joanna grabbed his shoulders and knocked his hand away from his pocket with her knee. For a few seconds she was carried along piggyback as he stumbled toward the cockpit. She reached into his pocket and fumbled the .32 out while kicking at his legs. Rafferty bucked her off his back and she landed on her side on the deck, the gun still firmly clutched in her hand. Pain knifed through her ribs.

There was a heavy smashing sound, and she looked up in time to see Rafferty stagger backward from a blow that Bob had struck to his head. Rafferty bounced off the bulkhead, fell to the deck in the cockpit. And stayed there.

There was a sudden loud splash to the starboard side.

Joanna realized Parducci wasn't in the cockpit. She glanced around, didn't see him anywhere.

"Bob! Where's Parducci?"

Bob was standing over Rafferty, breathing heavily. When she called out he whirled and ran to the rail. He leaned out, head moving frantically back and forth.

"Bob, don't let him get away!"

There was no further splashing—nothing but the slap of the water against the boats and barges.

"Bob!" Joanna tried to get up, but the searing pain in her side prevented it.

Bob turned, his shoulders sagging, hands upturned helplessly. "He didn't get away. His hands were tied. Must've sunk like a stone." He stood there for a moment, looking sick, then went back to where Rafferty lay. "This one's out cold, thank Christ."

Joanna tried to sit up again. The pain in her side made her cry out. Bob came over to her. "You hurt?"

"I think I've broken a rib."

He knelt, probed gently with his fingertips. "That you have. Perhaps two."

"Oh hell!" The pain brought tears to her eyes as Bob helped her to a sitting position. "What about you? Are you okay?" she asked.

"I'm all right."

"What made you do that? Change your mind, I mean?"

"My mind was made up from the beginning. I wasn't going to let that scum Parducci get away." He looked toward the starboard rail, his face pained and vastly older than when he'd walked into the pub the previous evening. "And he hasn't, I'll wager."

But Joanna wasn't sure of that. She never would be—nor feel—safe again until she had actually seen Parducci's body.

TWENTY-SIX

IT WAS A HOT AFTERNOON in late June, and Joanna was preparing the soil for a pair of citrus trees she intended to plant on the far side of her patio. On the other half of the double lot E.J. was supervising the workers who were staking out the foundation for the new swimming pool. From the annoyed looks the other men kept giving him, Joanna had concluded that he made a better bartender than general contractor, and she was glad when he went off around the house and she heard his motorcycle start up. Probably going to the post office for the mail.

She added a couple of handfuls of bonemeal to the soil and mixed it in with a trowel. Then she took some more of the coarse beige powder from the sack and slowly let it trickle through her fingers. In the past she would have been the one to go to town, pick up the mail, perhaps have lunch at one of the restaurants at the plaza or stop in to chat with her friend Mary Bennett at her quilt shop. But now E.J. had assumed the postal responsibilities, seeming to sense—although they never spoke of it—her need to stay close to home.

It wasn't fear that kept her there, she told herself now. Not exactly. Although Parducci's body had not been found, the CID had assured her that she could safely assume him dead. After all, the man had jumped or fallen into a deep, swiftly moving river with his hands tied behind him. But Joanna wondered if indeed his hands *had* been tied: she remembered him shifting on the seat in the boat's cockpit, working out of his bonds, perhaps. But even if he was alive, even if he could have gotten into the States somehow, she didn't expect he'd try to abduct her from the middle of a busy tourist area at high noon. No, it wasn't fear that kept her at home. Not really.

She sat back on her heels, dusting the bonemeal and dirt from her hands then wiping the sweat from her forehead. The temperature was in the nineties, with no breeze to relieve it. Her shorts and tank top stuck to her damp skin. Her cracked ribs had healed nicely, and now her body cried out for exercise. She wished she'd decided to have the pool put in before she'd gone to England.

The thought of England and the dreadful cost of the trip made her shudder. Not financial cost—although there had been plenty of that—but cost in terms of lives, friendships, and her own self-confidence. Three men had died; her relationships with Richard Bloomfield and Christopher Burgess had been permanently damaged; and while Meg Knight had gotten the inside story of an art thief who had turned into a cold-blooded killer, the reporter had been cuttingly scornful of Joanna's mishandling of the scheme. And Rafferty was lost to Joanna forever.

Rafferty. She took up the trowel and began digging furiously, trying to blot out thoughts of him. But as usual they wouldn't be banished. When they'd finally contacted the CID in the early hours of that cold foggy morning, Joanna had made a decision and followed through on it. She'd sent Rafferty away, and she and Bob Jenkins had said nothing about him to the authorities. As far as Scotland Yard knew, she and Bob had been alone on the boat when Parducci went over the side.

Perhaps the decision had been based on foolish sentiment; perhaps she made it in reaction to the terrible results of her hatred of Parducci. But whatever momentary weakness had prompted it didn't stop her from telling Rafferty that if he ever attempted to see her again, or if she ever heard of his doing anything outside the ethics of his profession, she would bare the whole story. After she'd returned to San Francisco, she found out from Nick Alexander that Rafferty had arrived some twenty-four hours ahead of her, quit his job, given up his apartment, and vanished from the Bay Area.

In a way, she supposed, it was punishment enough. Rafferty would live his life in fear that she wouldn't keep her silence. That fear would prevent him from ever returning to San Francisco, and perhaps from taking another job in the profession he loved.

As for her own penance, she'd brought *There Hangs the Knife* back from England and hung it in her front hall, where she'd have to see it every time she entered or left the house. She'd rechristened it, too: *Stark's Dark Star*. The title was symbolic of a plan born under a dark star and ending in disaster. It would serve as a warning to her, should she ever be tempted to indulge in such a thing again.

The roar of the motorcycle announced E.J.'s return. In a minute he called to her through the kitchen window. "You want a wine cooler, Jo?"

"Yes, thanks." She threw down the trowel, wiped grit from her bare thighs, and went toward the house.

The country kitchen was cool, insulated by the sturdy construction of the big Victorian farmhouse. The stray cat she'd taken in before leaving for England napped on one of the counters, next to the coffee maker. The cat, unnamed as yet, no longer limped and had developed a disgustingly healthy appetite. Joanna took pleasure in lifting it off the counter and depositing it with a thud on the floor.

E.J. stood at the chopping block, pouring red wine and club soda over ice. "Your mail's on the table," he said.

She went to the round oak table in the breakfast nook and riffled through the stack of envelopes. Something from the county tax assessor, her American Express bill, a notice that she might already have won ten million dollars in a sweepstakes, an envelope from SSI. E.J. set her drink in front of her and flopped in one of the other chairs, pulling his sweatband from his blond hair and running a hand through his sweat-streaked beard. "Jesus, it's hot," he said. "I wish that pool was done now."

Joanna slit open the envelope from SSI with her index finger, giving herself a paper cut. She put the finger in her mouth and said around it, "It might get done faster if you'd leave the workmen alone."

"You think so?" E.J. stuck his feet on the table support and tipped his chair back. "I was thinking the same thing. Construction work's not my forte."

"What is?" She opened the envelope and found it contained another smaller one.

"Well, it's not bartending, either. Mario chewed me out again last night."

"Why, this time?"

"Same thing—too familiar with the female patrons."

She frowned at him.

He smiled disarmingly and spread his hands wide. "What can I tell you?"

"You'll be fired if you keep it up."

"I know. That's why—Jo, what's wrong?"

She was staring down at the envelope SSI had forwarded, and supposed she'd gone pale. It carried no return address; the stamps were British; its postmark was Falmouth. Apparently it had been sitting in her in-box for some time before SSI's secretary had realized Joanna was taking one of her frequent sabbaticals and thought to forward it. The postmark was early in May, the day before the debacle at the barge on the River Fal.

"Jo?"

"I'm okay. Just let me read this." She broke the seal, took the piece of cheap paper out, and scanned it, looking for the signature. When she saw the boldly scrawled name, she felt a hollow pang deep below her breastbone. Then she read and reread the letter slowly.

> *Joanna: By the time you receive this I'll be safely away from here with the Bregle. I'm not writing to apologize for that—it's a risk you take when you deal with my kind. What I do want to apologize for is the fix I got you into when I called you back to London the other night. I knew if I sounded panicked you'd come, and by the time you arrived Parducci was supposed to be at my flat. You wanted him badly, and I thought I could at least give you that. I didn't know he'd be armed, or that Moradi would be there, or that he'd kill him and you'd be stuck finding the body. But I guess you did because the paper said some unknown caller reported it. I'm sorry for the trouble it caused you.*
>
> *Matt, who once loved you*

How on earth had he known where to write her? she wondered. Then she remembered giving him her business card that first night at the Starving Ox. It was so like Matt: he'd acted with the best of intentions, but had not thought things through. None of the pitfalls he'd mentioned had occurred to him, nor what she would have done when—totally unprepared—she came face-to-face with Parducci.

Her eyes suddenly filled with tears, and she looked up at E.J. Illogically she said, "The poor thing couldn't even spell Brueghel." And then she began to cry.

E.J. was used to her sudden mood swings. He merely got up and refreshed her cooler. The action made her cry harder; for years her son had been an irresponsible and undependable wanderer. Now, at twenty-three, he was rapidly becoming her mainstay. Perhaps E.J. would disprove her conviction that the men in her life were never there when she needed them.

He must have correctly interpreted her renewed burst of weeping, because he let her go get her own Kleenexes. When she came back to the table he was reading the letter. "So," he said, "your last question about what went on over there—why Wickins called you back to London—has been answered. Eerie, isn't it? Like a voice from the grave."

"Don't say that!"

"Jo, he's not coming back."

"Obviously."

"I don't mean Wickins. I mean my father." There was no hesitation before he spoke the word *father* as there always had been in the past. E.J. believed Parducci was dead; that death had made him free. She would say nothing to shake his belief.

"Now," he added, "I've got a proposition for you."

"Oh? And what's that? You want me to hire you to dig the hole for the swimming pool by yourself?"

"No, I want you to fire me from supervising those guys. You see, what I started to tell you before is that while I'm not much of a bartender, I do know wine. And there's this little vineyard a ways up the valley that's for sale. Run-down and just dying for attention. We could take a drive up there this afternoon, and if you think it's a good deal, maybe I could hit you up for the down payment. I'd give you twenty-percent ownership, of course."

She just looked at him in surprise.

"We could go now," he added. "If you're ready to leave the house again."

It was time. One learns to live with fear. She said, "Offer me a thirty-percent interest, and you might have a deal."

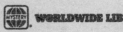

Return to the scene of the crime with Worldwide Mysteries

COLD TRAIL—Dell Shannon $3.50 ☐
Detective Luis Mendoza marks the rising heat in Los Angeles by
the crime and violence raging through the streets—a thug is shot
to death, the body of a woman is found and a mysterious string
of robberies continues—all without a clue.

ALL BOOKED UP—Terrie Curran $3.50 ☐
A professor and his wife find themselves up against a brilliant
criminal when rare books mysteriously disappear from the
Boston University library and members of the staff turn up dead!

NO HARM—Wendy Hornsby $3.50 ☐
A young woman's life becomes endangered after she inherits a
palatial estate. Several near-fatal accidents fuel her growing fear
as she searches through generations of buried secrets to find the
portrait of a family killer.

Total Amount	$	_____
Plus 75¢ Postage		.75
Payment enclosed	$	_____

Please send a check or money order payable to Worldwide Library Mysteries.

In the U.S.	In Canada
Worldwide Library Mysteries	Worldwide Library Mysteries
901 Fuhrmann Blvd.	P.O. Box 609
Box 1325	Fort Erie, Ontario
Buffalo, NY 14269-1325	L2A 5X3

Please Print

Name: _____

Address: _____

City: _____

State/Prov: _____

Zip/Postal Code: _____

 **WORLDWIDE LIBRARY**

MYS-10

Worldwide Mysteries make murder—most intriguing!

MURDER-BY-THE-SEA—Layne Littlepage $3.50 ☐
Opening night for the Carmel Playhouse was a killer—especially
when the body of an actress washed ashore. A former Hollywood
starlet investigating the death finds herself amidst a strange cast
of characters and someone in a murderous mood!

CRY AT DUSK—Mignon Ballard $3.50 ☐
A woman comes face-to-face with her darkest nightmare when
she returns to her small hometown to investigate the death of
her cousin and learns the secret of not one murder but two!

SPIT IN THE OCEAN—Shelley Singer $3.50 ☐
Private Eye Jake Samson becomes entangled in a strange case
involving a theft from a sperm bank in California. When a body
surfaces and attempts are made on Samson's own life, it
becomes apparent that someone wants him off the
case . . . permanently!

Total Amount	$	_____
Plus 75¢ Postage		.75
Payment enclosed	$	_____

Please send a check or money order payable to Worldwide Library Mysteries.

In the U.S.

Worldwide Library
Mysteries
901 Fuhrmann Blvd.
Box 1325
Buffalo, NY 14269-1325

In Canada

Worldwide Library
Mysteries
P.O. Box 609
Fort Erie, Ontario
L2A 5X3

Please Print

Name: _____

Address: _____

City: _____

State/Prov: _____

Zip/Postal Code: _____

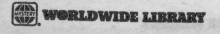 **WORLDWIDE LIBRARY**

...ward from the Mystery
...alisbury Davis
...equals in setting up a puzzle, complete
with misdirection and surprises.''
— *New York Times Book Review*

Julie Hayes Mysteries

LULLABY OF MURDER $3.50   ☐
When an infamous New York gossip columnist is found
murdered, reporter Julie Hayes starts digging and discovers a lot
of people are happier with him dead! As murder takes center
stage, Julie finds herself caught in a web of hate, deceit and
revenge, dirty deals and small-town scandals.

THE HABIT OF FEAR $3.50   ☐
New York columnist Julie Hayes struggles to regain her

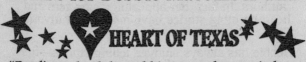

Debbie Macomber is one of America's most popular authors. In fact, her appealing characters and heartwarming stories have made her a favorite around the globe.

Debbie has always enjoyed telling stories—first to the children she baby-sat as a young teen and later to her own kids. As a full-time wife and mother and avid romance reader, she dreamed of one day sharing her stories with a wider audience. She sold her first book in 1982—and that was only the beginning!

Today there are more than 40 million copies of her books in print.

Debbie loves to hear from her readers. You can reach her at P.O. Box 1458, Port Orchard, Washington 98366

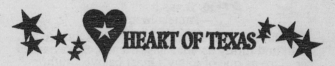

HEART OF TEXAS

Books in order of publication:

Lonesome Cowboy
Texas Two-Step
Caroline's Child
Dr. Texas
Nell's Cowboy
Lone Star Baby

DEBBIE MACOMBER

NELL'S COWBOY

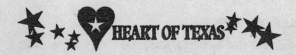
★ ★ ★ ♥ HEART OF TEXAS ★ ★ ★

Harlequin Books

TORONTO • NEW YORK • LONDON
AMSTERDAM • PARIS • SYDNEY • HAMBURG
STOCKHOLM • ATHENS • TOKYO • MILAN
MADRID • WARSAW • BUDAPEST • AUCKLAND

ISBN 0-373-83346-6

NELL'S COWBOY

Copyright © 1998 by Debbie Macomber

Dearest Friends,

After the success of MIDNIGHT SONS, and those stubborn Alaskan men, Harlequin approached me about doing another six-book series. But where was I going to find heroes to match those strong, endearing bush pilots? The answer wasn't long in coming. I've always had a weakness for cowboys, and no place on earth grows 'em quite like Texas.

So, my friends, here they are: the men and women of Promise, Texas. Situated deep in the Texas hill country, Promise is truly a town with heart, populated by people like you and me—hardworking, proud and just a little sassy. A town with an interesting past and an exciting future.

For the MIDNIGHT SONS series, my husband and I traveled to Alaska. This time around, I conned my editor, Paula Eykelhof, into exploring Texas with me. With a rental car, a map and the sense of direction of a pet rock, Paula and I toured the Texas hill country. We met the people, sampled the barbecues, tasted the wines and gazed endlessly at cowboys. If this wasn't heaven, then we were pretty darn close!

So I invite you to sit back, put your feet up and allow me to introduce you to a few of those Texan cowboys. The men of Alaska started this craziness, but the men in Texas refuse to be outdone. They're just as stubborn, just as ornery, just as proud. And just as lovable.

Enjoy.

Debbie Macomber

THE PEOPLE OF PROMISE: CAST OF CHARACTERS

Nell Bishop: thirty-something widow with a son, Jeremy, and a daughter, Emma. Her husband died in a tractor accident.

Ruth Bishop: Nell's mother-in-law. Lives with Nell and her two children.

Dovie Boyd: runs an antiques shop and has dated Sheriff Frank Hennessy for ten years

Caroline Daniels: postmistress of Promise

Maggie Daniels: Caroline's five-year-old daughter

Dr. Jane Dickinson: new doctor in Promise

Ellie Frasier: owner of Frasier's Feed Store

Frank Hennessy: local sheriff

Max Jordan: owner of Jordan's Towne & Country

Wade McMillen: preacher of Promise Christian Church

Edwina and Lily Moorhouse: sisters. Retired schoolteachers.

Cal and Glen Patterson: local ranchers. Brothers who ranch together.

Phil and Mary Patterson: parents of Cal and Glen. Operate a local B&B.

Louise Powell: town gossip

Wiley Rogers: sixty-year-old ranch foreman at the Weston ranch

Laredo Smith: wrangler hired by Savannah Weston

Barbara and Melvin Weston: mother and father to Savannah, Grady and Richard. The Westons died six years ago.

Richard Weston: youngest of the Weston siblings

Savannah Weston: Grady and Richard's sister. Cultivates old roses.

Grady Weston: rancher and oldest of the Weston siblings

Chapter One

Nell Bishop barreled down the highway, heading home, racing against the approaching storm. The March winds whipped against the pickup as she hurried toward Twin Canyons Ranch, thirty-four miles south of Promise, Texas.

Her mother-in-law was with the children, but Jeremy and Emma would have difficulty getting the animals into the barn without help. Ruth would do what she could, but the older woman's heart wasn't strong and... Nell didn't want to think what might happen if she didn't make it back in time.

Her life had been on a fast-moving treadmill for the past three years, ever since her husband died in a tractor accident. Storms were the least of her worries, considering the financial challenges she'd faced working the ranch without Jake. Not a day passed that her husband wasn't in her thoughts. Twenty years from now, *forty* years from now, he'd still be a part of her.

Ruth and others had encouraged her to remarry, at least to date, but Nell had resisted. She never expected to love again— not the way she loved Jake. Their

love was the kind that happened only once in a lifetime, and no other man could compare to her Jake.

Nell had always known she wasn't any candidate
for homecoming queen, but Jake had made her feel
like one. He'd understood what it was to be big-boned
and just plain big. Dainty or elegant would never describe her; at six feet, Nell was as tall as most men.
Jake had been six feet four inches by the time he was
a high-school freshman, and the only boy in school
taller than Nell.

They'd lived in the same town all their lives, but
it wasn't until high school that she'd noticed him. The
very first day of high school, as a matter of fact. She
was a freshman to his senior, and the minute his eyes
met hers as she walked down the hall, she knew she'd
found her life's mate. He was the only boy she'd ever
dated. When he enlisted in the army and became an
Airborne Ranger, she'd written him every day. He
served his time in the army and was discharged a
week after her graduation. Despite her family's protests, she'd married Jake while still a teenager.

Neither was to know that ten years was all the time
they'd have together. It was Nell who'd found her
husband trapped beneath the tractor, Nell who'd held
him in her arms as the life flowed out of him, Nell
who'd screamed in anguish, helpless to do anything
to save her husband's life.

Now it was Nell who struggled to hold on to Twin
Canyons Ranch, tended what remained of the herd,
raised their children and cared for Jake's aging
mother. The ranch had been Jake's dream—and hers;

it was a small spread that they'd bought together, shortly after their marriage. But she was so very tired, weary to the bone with her financial struggles and other worries. The past three years had drained her mentally, emotionally and physically. For that reason she'd sold off most of the herd and started a new venture. A dude ranch.

Bless Jeremy's heart. Her son had been the one to give her the idea. Last year, she'd promised him a reward for acing his spelling test and he'd chosen to rent a movie. Of all the movies available, he'd picked *City Slickers,* and to Nell it was like a revelation.

After seeing the movie, Nell hadn't been able to sleep all night. She was certainly familiar with dude ranches, but it had never occurred to her that this might be a solution to her own dilemma. She couldn't say she understood it, but people actually paid for the opportunity to eat food cooked in a chuck wagon, ride around on horses and drive cattle. Why these people would prefer to live in primitive circumstances when they could experience the luxury of some fancy resort for basically the same price was beyond her. Apparently she had a lot to learn—but learn she did. After months of research Nell was convinced that a dude ranch really was the answer. With a portion of her profits from the sale of last year's herd, she'd had brochures printed and she'd contacted several travel companies. Now she was almost ready for business, and in a couple of months she'd be entertaining her first bunkhouse full of greenhorns.

In many ways she was a natural for this kind of

work. After these few years without Jake, there
wasn't a ranching chore she couldn't accomplish with
the speed and dexterity of a man. At this point, she
knew as much about ranching as any cowboy. Not
only that, she'd heard the great stories of Texas all
her life—stories about the state's settlement and the
Alamo and the early cattle drives and many more.
She'd always loved those stories, and if she could
make money telling them now, romanticizing the Old
West, all the better.

Heavy black clouds darkened the sky. Pushing
thoughts of Jake from her mind, Nell focused her attention on the highway. Driving well above the speed
limit, she rounded a turn in the road and saw a sports
utility vehicle parked along the side.

Some damn fool had stopped to take pictures of the
approaching storm. The man obviously wasn't a local.
Anyone from Texas would know to take cover, and
fast. Like the state of Texas itself, storms tended to
make an impression, especially spring storms like this
one.

Despite her hurry, Nell applied her brakes and
pulled over. With the engine running, she leaped
down from the cab. The wind slapped her long braid
against her face as she raced toward the stranger.

The greenhorn lowered his camera. "Howdy," he
greeted her cheerfully. He was taller than she was and
clean-cut. His clothes were new-looking but rumpled.

"Listen, I don't mean to be rude, but any idiot
knows to head for cover in a storm."

His smile faded to a frown.

"I don't know where you're from or where you're going," she went on, "but if I were you I'd get my butt back into that fancy car of yours and drive into town as fast as those tires will take you." Having done her duty, she started back to her truck.

"Hey," he said, "Got a minute? I have a few questions."

"I have to go." Nell didn't mean to sound abrupt, but she didn't have time to waste. She'd said her piece and whether or not he took her advice was completely up to him.

"Are you from around the area?" he called after her.

"Yes! Now listen, we get hail the size of golf balls and if you don't want to pay to have the dents removed, then I suggest you make tracks for town."

"This will only take a minute..."

"I don't *have* a minute, I've got horses and calves to worry about," Nell shouted into the wind. "And I don't have time to convince you a storm is about to break." She raised her hand toward the threatening sky. "It's going to cost you plenty if you don't get that vehicle under cover."

"I'm insured."

"Hail is an act of God." Whether he caught her last words or not she didn't know. Nell leaped into her truck and put the pickup in gear. One glance in the rearview mirror proved that giving this stranger advice had been a wasted effort. He hadn't moved. Furthermore, he wasn't snapping pictures of the dark horizon anymore; he was taking pictures of her!

Shaking her head in wonder, Nell dismissed him from her thoughts, and drove home at breakneck speed.

When she pulled into the ranch yard, she saw Jeremy chasing chickens in a futile attempt to lure them into the coop. Emma and Ruth led the horses toward the barn, yanking on the reins as the two geldings battled the wind. The scene right before the tornado in *The Wizard of Oz* flashed through Nell's mind.

She parked the truck near the barn, where it would be protected, and hurried toward her family. With her help, Ruth and Emma managed to secure the animals before the storm broke.

By the time they scurried into the house, the rain had started and they were breathless and excited.

"We did it!" Twelve-year-old Jeremy said, exchanging a high five with his sister. Unlike most siblings, Jeremy and Emma rarely fought. Sure, they squabbled now and then—all kids did—but these two were close in age and temperament. They'd also been through the devastating experience of their father's death, which had created a strong bond between them.

Jeremy was large for his age, like his father and Nell, too—big-boned, muscular and tall. Two years younger, Emma was small and delicate, resembling Ruth, her grandmother.

"I'm glad you made it home in time," Ruth said, pouring Nell a cup of hot tea before filling a second cup for herself.

Nell gazed out the kitchen window at the ferocity of the storm. The wind propelled the rain at an almost horizontal angle, pelting the trees and flowers. Smaller trees were bent nearly in half. Many a new crop would see ruin this afternoon.

Sighing, she turned away from the window. "I would have been a couple of minutes earlier if it hadn't been for some greenhorn," she said. "The silly fool stopped at the side of the road to take pictures."

"Anyone you recognized?" Ruth asked.

"Never saw him before in my life." Nell would have remembered him if she had. He was big like Jake, sturdy and broad-shouldered. Unfortunately— unlike Jake—he didn't seem to possess an ounce of common sense.

Ruth shook her head. "Probably one of those tornado chasers."

Nell frowned. "I don't think so." He wasn't the type. Too soft, she decided, and although it might sound unkind, not all that bright. Anyone with brains knew to seek shelter in a storm.

"What's for dinner?" Jeremy asked.

"Not chili," Emma pleaded.

Despite herself Nell laughed. "Not chili," she assured her. Her family had been good sports, sampling different variations of her chili recipe for the past few months. Nell was perfecting her recipe and had used her family as taste-testers.

The Chili Cook-off was being held that weekend as part of the Promise Rodeo. These festivities launched spring the way the big Cattlemen's Association dance in June signaled the beginning of summer.

Nell held high hopes that her chili might actually win this year. Her talents in the kitchen were legendary, and she believed she made a great pot of chili. For weeks she'd been combining recipes, adding this, subtracting that. After feeding her family chili twice a week, she was finally satisfied with her recipe.

"Are you going to win the cook-off?" Emma asked.

"Of course she is," Ruth answered before Nell could respond. "I don't see why she shouldn't, seeing she's the best cook this side of the Rio Grande."

Both children nodded enthusiastically, and Nell smiled. "How about porcupine meatballs for dinner?" she suggested. The meatballs, made with rice and cooked in tomato soup, were one of the children's favorites. Jeremy and Emma instantly agreed.

"I'll peel the potatoes," Ruth said. As usual her mother-in-law was willing to lend a hand.

The lights flickered just then, and the house went dark.

"That's okay," Jeremy said. "We don't need electricity. We can roast weenies in the fireplace, can't we?"

"Yeah," Emma seconded. "We could have hot dogs."

"Sounds like a good idea to me." Nell reached for a candle, grateful her children maintained a sense of adventure. They were going to need it when the first dude ranch guests arrived.

CAL PATTERSON shook the moisture from his jacket as he stepped inside out of the driving rain. He removed his Stetson and placed it on the hook just inside the porch to dry. He'd done what he could to protect his herd, gotten his horses into the barn and battened down the shutters where he could. Glen, his brother and business partner, had left for town early in hopes of beating the storm. Cal had worked alone, listening with half an ear for his wife's arrival. He didn't like the idea of Jane driving all the way from town in this kind of weather.

"Cal, is that you?"

His heart rate accelerated at the sound of her voice. "Jane? What the hell are you doing here? Where's your car? I didn't see it."

"I live here, remember?" she teased, joining him in the kitchen porch while he removed his boots. She'd obviously just had a bath and now wore a flannel bathrobe, belted loosely about her waist. "And I didn't park in my usual place because Glen's truck was still there."

"You should've stayed in town," he chastised, but he was delighted she'd managed to make it home. He didn't relish the idea of a night spent without her. Two months of marriage, and he'd grown accustomed to sharing his home and his heart with this woman.

"The clinic closed early," she informed him, "and I've got my beeper. Anyone can reach me in case of a medical emergency."

Cal shed his jacket and slipped his arms around her waist, pulling her close and urging her into the kitchen. His wife was the town's only physician, so there were constant demands on her time. "I don't know if I'll ever be able to stop worrying about you."

"Hey, I'm a big girl."

"Sure you are!" He was about to kiss her when the lights went out. Not that he minded. A romantic interlude wasn't unwelcome.

"I've got a fire going in the fireplace," she whispered, pressing against him, reminding him of the benefits of married life. She looped her arms around his neck and kissed his jaw.

Cal shut his eyes and inhaled her fresh sweet scent. This was about as close to heaven as he expected to get in his lifetime. "I don't suppose you're wearing that see-through nightie of yours?"

"No," she said, "but that could be arranged."

"Now you're talkin'."

Cal felt her smile against his skin. "I love you, Rebel."

Growling, he swung her into his arms and carried her into the living room. Sure enough, a small fire flickered in the fireplace. This had become their favorite room; he'd lost count of the number of times they'd made love in front of the fireplace. The room had a special significance for him, since it was here that he'd first realized how much he'd come to care about her. It was here in this very room that Dr. Texas, as he was fond of calling her, had taken his freeze-dried heart and breathed life into his lonely existence.

Cal was happier than he'd ever thought possible.

With each passing day he loved Jane more. Their love had demanded plenty of adjustments on both sides. Sacrifices. But for everything he'd given up, he'd gained so much more.

The storm raged outside and a fair one was building on the living-room carpet when Jane's beeper went off.

Cal groaned and rolled onto his back, inhaling several deep breaths. "That damn well better be important," he muttered.

"Cal!"

"I want someone *real* sick."

Giggling, Jane scrambled for her beeper and read the message. "It's Laredo Smith," she said.

"Wanna bet he's phoning about Savannah?"

"She's just over eight months," Jane said, sounding concerned.

"But Laredo's acting like she's three weeks overdue."

"He's worried, that's all."

Cal figured he would be, too, in Laredo's situation. This was the Smiths' first child, and Savannah was over thirty; as well, Cal knew there'd been some minor complications with the pregnancy. Despite that— and unlike her husband—the mother-to-be remained calm and confident. Savannah had insisted on a home delivery, overriding Laredo's protests.

"This shouldn't take long," Jane promised. She hurried over to the hall phone.

Cal cupped his hands behind his head and watched his wife move through the room, bathed in firelight.

Her hair was mussed and her bathrobe hastily tied—
and he couldn't recall a time she'd looked more beautiful. It never ceased to amaze him that Jane had
agreed to be his wife.

Cal had begun to wonder if someone had spiked
the water supply last summer. In less than a year most
of his friends had married. First, Savannah Weston
had met a stranger to Promise named Laredo Smith
and subsequently married him. His own brother had
married Ellie Frasier, owner of the local feed store,
last September. No sooner had *that* wedding taken
place when Grady Weston asked the postmistress,
Caroline Daniels, to marry him—all within the space
of a few short weeks. Even Sheriff Hennessey had
married his longtime sweetheart, Dovie Boyd.

It hadn't been long before Cal fell in love himself.

At one time Cal, Glen and Grady had been confirmed bachelors. With Cal, it had been a form of self-
protection, he realized now. He'd been jilted by a
former fiancée and the experience had left him bitter,
determined never to fall for a woman again.

But that was before he'd met Jane. Their first date
was arranged by Ellie. At the time Cal had been annoyed and frustrated that his brand-new sister-in-law
was matchmaking. By the end of the evening, however, Jane had managed to pique his interest. To his
surprise he discovered he was looking forward to seeing her again. Before he could help himself, he was
deeply in love with her.

A city girl. Worse, one from California. If anyone
had told him six months ago that he'd marry a woman

like Jane, he would have run screaming into the night. Now he couldn't imagine living two minutes without her.

With the phone against her ear, Jane caught her husband's eyes and blew him a kiss. He grinned, content to wait. Relaxing on the rug, he listened to one-half of the conversation.

"Don't worry," Jane was telling Laredo, "you didn't interrupt anything important."

Cal sat upright at that, raising his eyebrows. *Didn't interrupt anything important?* He saw that his wife could barely hold in her laughter at his expression.

But her smile faded as she continued to listen to Laredo. "No…no you were right to phone. How long ago did you say her water broke?"

The smile left Cal's face, too. This was more serious than either of them had anticipated.

"How far apart are the contractions?" Jane reached for a pad and pencil and noted the information.

Cal had delivered enough calves to know the signs of imminent birth. Savannah and Laredo were about to have their baby during the worst storm of the year.

"I'll be there within the hour," Jane promised, and replaced the receiver. "Savannah's in labor," she told Cal.

"So I heard." He stood and she walked over to him and caressed the side of his face. "Looks like we'll have to put our romantic interlude on hold."

"I'm a patient man," he reminded her. He caught her fingers and pressed a kiss into her palm. "What time are we leaving?'' he asked, snapping his shirt closed as he spoke.

"We?" Jane asked, arching her brows expressively. "I'm perfectly capable of delivering this baby."

"I never doubted it for an instant." He opened her bathrobe, kissed the valley between her breasts and refastened it.

"I can drive in a storm, too."

"I realize that," he said, "but how good are you at keeping two strong-willed ranchers out of your hair?"

"Two?"

"Laredo and Grady." Cal knew his best friend, and Grady would be as nervous as Laredo at the birth of his first niece or nephew. Jane was going to have her hands full, and it wasn't with Savannah or the baby, either. It wouldn't surprise him if father *and* uncle made damned nuisances of themselves. "Trust me, darlin', you'll thank me later."

"Oh, all right, Cal Patterson, you can tag along, too. Now I'd better go change."

He grinned, pleased he'd been able to convince her she was going to need him. Truth be known, he wouldn't miss this birth for anything. It was about time something good happened in that family, especially after Richard Weston's trial and sentencing.

A baby was just what the Westons needed to put their troubles behind them. Cal was determined to celebrate the blessed event with his friends.

TRAVIS GRANT rolled into Promise at precisely the moment the storm struck. He drove down Main Street, peering out between the constantly beating windshield wipers, but he couldn't locate a single hotel. Seeing as his last meal had been aboard a plane and hadn't amounted to much, he decided to stop for dinner and inquire about a place to stay. By the time he found a parking space and raced to the restaurant through the pounding rain, he was soaked to the skin.

He gulped down a glass of water and started on a bowl of tortilla chips with salsa before he even looked at the menu. His stomach growled and he ordered *arroz con pollo,* his favorite Mexican dish.

Gazing out the window, he decided the town was just the way Richard Weston had described it. This was something of a pleasant surprise. Men like Weston weren't exactly known for their truthfulness. Travis had interviewed him shortly after he was sentenced to twenty-five years in a New York prison. No possibility of parole, either. He wouldn't have talked to him at all if it hadn't been for his ex-wife, who'd been Weston's state-appointed attorney. As far as Travis was concerned, Weston was the ultimate sleaze—an opinion that the interview only reinforced.

Knowing his interest in Western ghost towns, Valerie had told him about Weston, a man who'd hidden from the law in an abandoned town buried deep in the Texas hill country. Weston had agreed to an interview—in exchange for certain concessions. The warden of the prison, however, hadn't approved of the idea that Weston should have a TV and sound system in his cell. Weston had consented to the interview, anyway—because it was another opportunity to be the center of attention, Travis figured. Their meeting continued to leave a bad taste in his mouth. If it hadn't been for Valerie, Travis would have abandoned the entire project, but his ex-wife seemed to have a way with the man.

Valerie. Travis frowned as he thought about her. She'd dumped him and their marriage for another man five years earlier. His lack of malice seemed to disappoint his friends. Frankly, he considered life too short to waste on ill will. He'd loved her, still did, but as she'd so eloquently put it, she'd fallen out of love with him.

She'd remarried as soon as the ink was dry on their divorce papers and seemed content. For that matter, he was, too, although it had taken him longer to achieve peace and he hadn't become involved in another serious relationship. Also, to his friends' surprise, he and Valerie had stayed in touch.

The waiter, a kid of maybe eighteen, delivered a plate heaped with rice and chicken and covered with a thin tomato sauce and melted cheese. "Could you give me directions to the closest motel?" Travis asked him.

"Brewster's got a motel."

"Great." Travis reached for his fork. "How far away is that?"

"About a hundred miles."

He laid his fork back down. "You mean to say a town the size of Promise doesn't have a motel?"

"We've got a bed and breakfast."

"Fine." A bed was a bed, and at this point he wasn't picky.

The waiter lingered. "You might have trouble getting a room, 'cause of the big festivities this weekend."

"Festivities?"

"The rodeo's coming, and then there's the big chili cook-off. I thought that was why you were here."

Apparently the town was small enough to recognize him as a stranger. "Where do the rodeo cowboys stay while they're in town?"

The youth stared at him as if the answer should be obvious. "Motor homes."

"All of them?"

"Unless they got family close by."

"I see," Travis murmured. He hadn't considered that there wouldn't be a motel—but then that was one of his problems, according to Valerie. He didn't think ahead.

"If you'd like, I could write you out directions to the Patterson's B and B."

"Please." Famished, Travis dug into his meal, devouring it in minutes. He'd no sooner finished when the waiter returned with a hand-drawn map listing streets and landmarks. Apparently the one and only bed and breakfast was off the beaten path.

Thunder cracked in the sky, followed by flashes of lightning. No one seemed to pay much heed to the storm until the lights flickered. Everyone in the restaurant paused and waited, then sighed with relief when the lights stayed on.

The storm was bad, but he'd seen worse off the New England coastline five years before. Holed up in a rented cottage in order to meet a deadline, Travis had watched storms rage as he fought his own battles. It'd been shortly after the divorce.

He thought of that sassy ranch woman who'd spoken to him today and wondered what she'd say if she knew he'd stood on a rocky bluff overlooking the sea, with the wind and rain pounding against him, and openly defied nature.

Remembering the way she'd leaped out of her truck, eyes flashing with outrage, brought a rare smile to his lips.

She'd been an attractive woman. Practically as tall as he was and full-sized, not some pencil-thin model. A spitfire, too. Definitely one of a kind. Briefly he wondered if he'd get a chance to see her again and rather hoped he would, just so he could tell her he'd managed to survive the storm.

Following the directions given him by the waiter at the Mexican Lindo, Travis drove to Pattersons' Bed and Breakfast, which turned out to be a large older home. He rang the doorbell.

Almost immediately a tall gray-haired lanky man opened the door and invited him inside. "Welcome to Promise." The man extended his hand and introduced himself as Phil Patterson.

"Travis Grant. Do you have a room for a few nights?" he asked, getting directly to the point.

"Sorry," Phil told him. "We're booked solid."

Travis had left New York early that morning and didn't relish the thought of traveling another hundred miles through a storm to find a bed for the night. "I'm tired and not difficult to please. Isn't there any place that could put me up for a few nights?"

Phil frowned. "The rodeo's coming to town."

"So I understand."

"I doubt there's a room available in Brewster, either."

Travis muttered a curse under his breath.

"Phil." A woman's voice called out from the kitchen. "You might try Nell."

"Nell?"

"Nell Bishop."

Phil sighed. "I know who Nell is."

"She's opening her dude ranch in a couple of months, so she's probably got rooms to rent."

Phil's face relaxed. "Of course, that's a great idea."

Travis's spirits lifted.

"I'll give her a call." Phil reached for the phone, punched in the number and waited. After a minute or two he covered the receiver. "Nell's busy, but her mother-in-law's there and she said you'd be welcome to drive out, but she feels obliged to warn you there's no electricity at the moment."

"They have a bed and clean sheets?"

"Sure thing, and Ruth—that's her name—said she'd throw in breakfast, as well."

He named a price that sounded more than reasonable to Travis. "Sold."

Phil relayed the information, drew him a map, and soon Travis was back on the road.

Patterson had told him that the ranch was a fair distance out of town; still, by the time Travis pulled off the highway and onto the gravel drive that led to Twin Canyons Ranch, he suspected he was closer to Brewster than Promise. Approaching the front door, he felt as though his butt was dragging as low to the ground as his suitcase.

A kid who looked to be about twelve answered his knock and stared blankly at him while Travis stood in the rain.

"Hello," Travis finally said.

"Hello," the boy answered. A girl two or three years younger joined him. Good-looking children, but apparently not all that bright.

"Most people come to the back door unless they're selling something, and if you are, we're not buying."

Despite feeling tired and cranky, Travis grinned. "I'm here about a room."

The two kids exchanged glances.

"Who is it?" He heard an older woman's voice in the background; a moment later, she appeared at the door. "For the love of heaven, young man, come out of the rain." She nudged the children aside and held open the door.

He stood in the hallway, which was all gloom and shadows except for the light flickering from a cluster of candles. Travis glanced around, but it was impossible to see much.

"Mom's in the barn," the boy said.

"I know that," the older woman told him. She put the candle close to Travis's face. "You look decent enough."

"I haven't eaten any children in at least a week," he teased, eyeing the two kids. The little girl moved a step closer to her brother.

"I'm Travis Grant," he said, turning his attention to the woman.

"Ruth Bishop, and these two youngsters are my grandchildren, Jeremy and Emma."

"Pleased to meet you." He shifted the suitcase in his hand, hoping Ruth would take the hint and escort him to his room. She didn't. "About the room..." he said pointedly.

"You'll need to meet Nell first."

"All right." He was eager to get the introductions over with so he could fall into bed and sleep for the next twelve hours straight.

"This way." She led him through the house to the back porch, where she pulled on a hooded jacket. Then she walked down the back steps and into the rain, holding her hand over the candle to shield the small flame.

Travis wasn't enthusiastic about clumping through the storm yet again, but didn't have much choice.

"Ruth?" a new voice called into the night. A low pleasant voice.

"Coming," the grandmother answered.

They met halfway across the yard in the pouring rain. "I got us our first paying guest," Ruth announced, beaming proudly. "Travis Grant, meet my daughter-in-law, Nell Bishop."

It took Travis no more than a second to recognize Nell as the woman who'd called him an idiot.

He liked her already.

Chapter Two

Nell located an old-fashioned lantern for Travis Grant. It had probably been in the family for fifty years and was nothing if not authentic. Next she gathered together fresh sun-dried sheets, a couple of blankets and a pillow. She tucked everything inside a plastic bag and raced through the storm, holding the lit lantern with one hand. When she arrived at the bunkhouse, Nell discovered Travis sitting on the end of a bed, looking tired and out of sorts.

The initial group of tourists was scheduled to show up the first week of May, and almost everything in the bunkhouse had been readied. It was primitive, but then this was the real thing. A genuine ranch, complete with enough cattle to give would-be cowboys the experience of dealing with a herd, horses for them to ride and plenty of land. Nell was as determined as Curly in the movie *City Slickers* to make real wranglers out of her guests. It was what they were paying her big bucks to do, and she firmly believed in giving them their money's worth.

"Thanks," Travis said when he saw her. He stood

up to remove the bag from her arms, and she placed
the lantern on a small wooden dresser opposite the
bed.

"I realize this isn't the Ritz," she said as she
spread the crisp sheet across the thin mattress.

"Hey, beggars can't be choosers," her guest reminded her. "I'm grateful you're willing to take me
in at all."

Actually no one had thought to ask her. It was her
mother-in-law who'd agreed to put him up for the
night when Phil Patterson phoned. But to be fair, Nell
suspected she would have agreed herself.

"With the rodeo coming, the Pattersons didn't have
any vacancies," he explained unnecessarily, leaning
over to help her with the top sheet and blanket.

The lantern actually gave a fair amount of light,
much to Nell's chagrin. She chose to pretend she
didn't recognize him. And either he was too tired to
remember the way she'd harangued him at the side
of the road or he'd decided to forget. Whatever the
case, she was grateful.

"Does the Texas hill country generally get storms
like this?"

"This one's worse than some," she told him, lifting the edge of the mattress to tuck in the covers.
Given his size, she wondered if the bunk would be
big enough for him. Well, there was no help for it,
since this bed—or another exactly like it—was the
only one available.

"What about losing your electricity?"

"Happens now and then," she said, not looking at

him. She reached for the pillow and stuffed it inside the case, then plumping it up, set it at the head of the bed. "Is there anything else I can get you?" she asked, ready to return to her family.

"Nothing. I appreciate your putting me up," he said again.

"No problem."

"Mom." Breathless, Jeremy burst into the bunkhouse, his face bright. He carried a blue-speckled tin coffeepot in one hand and a matching cup in the other. Emma followed with a covered plate.

"Grandma sent us over with hot chocolate and—"

"—one of Mom's cinnamon rolls," Emma finished for her brother. Travis could see a black-and-white dog waiting patiently at the door.

He took the pot and cup from Jeremy and set them on the nightstand. "Hey, no one said anything about room service. How'd I get so lucky?"

Emma handed him the plate. "My mom's the best cook in the world."

Nell grinned and put an arm around each of her children. "Now probably isn't the time to mention we roasted hot dogs in the fireplace for dinner."

"Are you staying for the chili cook-off?" Emma asked their guest.

"I wouldn't miss it for the world." Travis sat on the side of the bed and poured himself a mug of steaming cocoa.

Nell wasn't sure how Ruth had managed to heat the cocoa—the fireplace, she supposed—but was pleased her mother-in-law had made the effort.

"Mom's going to win. Her chili's the best."

"Emma's opinion might be a little biased," Nell said, steering the two children toward the door. "Let us know if you need anything."

"I will. Good night," Travis said as they left to go back to the house.

Nell turned and smiled when she saw that he'd already started on the cinnamon roll with the appreciation of a man who rarely tasted anything homemade.

The children ran across the yard ahead of her. Lucky, their border-collie mix, followed at their heels. Ruth waited for Nell in the kitchen, holding the candle and looking inordinately pleased with herself.

"Travis Grant seems like a nice young man," she said the moment Nell entered the kitchen.

"He's from New York City," Nell said, wanting it understood right then and there that he was a big-city boy and only drifting through Promise. It just so happened that he'd ventured into a strange town and needed a place to sleep; there'd be plenty of guests just like him in the months to come.

"We have a big day tomorrow," Nell said. "It wouldn't hurt any of us to get to bed early for once."

As she'd expected, her children put up token protests, but they didn't argue long. Both were tired and, without electricity, there was little to entertain them. The lights probably wouldn't be coming on soon, especially with the rain and the wind still so intense.

"Did our guest mention what he's doing in Promise?" Ruth asked. She held her hand protectively in front of the flame of the candle she carried and led the way across the living room.

Nell wondered, too. "He didn't say."

"You could've asked."

"Well, I didn't. That's his business, not mine."

"Weren't you curious?"

"A little." A lot actually, but Nell wasn't willing to admit it.

"He's probably here for the rodeo," Jeremy suggested, heading up the stairs, Lucky at his side.

"Maybe, but I don't think so." Nell wasn't sure why she thought that, but she did. Her guess was that when morning came Travis Grant would pack up his bags and leave.

"He reminds me of someone," Emma said, and yawned.

"Me, too," Jeremy murmured.

Jake. Nell had seen it, too, not in looks but in build. Travis Grant was a lumberjack of a man, just the way her beloved Jake had been. Sadly the children's memories of their father had dimmed with time into vague recollections.

The family stood at the landing at the top of the stairs, where they exchanged good-night hugs and kisses. Even Jeremy let his mother and grandma kiss him tonight. Ruth guided the children to their bedrooms while Nell retrieved a candle for herself.

Once everyone was in bed, she undressed and put on a full-length white cotton nightgown. She unbraided her hair and brushed it out, the thick dark tresses reaching halfway down her back. Jake had loved her hair, had often gathered it in his huge hands and run it through his fingers. Nell missed those moments, missed everything about Jake.

Time, she'd discovered, was a great healer, just as Pastor McMillen had told her. The grief became duller, less acute, with every month and year that passed. But it was still there, always there. Now though, her grief shared space with all the good memories, the happy moments they'd had together.

Nothing would ever erase those ten wonderful years she'd shared with the man she loved.

Setting her hairbrush aside, Nell pulled back the covers and climbed into bed. She leaned against the headboard, her back supported by two pillows, and opened the drawer in her nightstand. She took out a pen and her journal.

By the light of a single candle, she wrote down the events of the day, pausing now and then to collect her thoughts. When she'd finished, she reread what she'd written, something she rarely did, and was surprised to note she'd mentioned Travis Grant in the first line. It didn't take her long to figure out why.

It was because he was like Jake and meeting him had shaken her. Not the first time on the road into town, when she'd stopped and read him the riot act, but later. It hadn't hit her until they stood across from each other to make the bed. He was the same height as Jake.

Nell reached for the framed photograph of Jake taken on their wedding day. It was a rare shot of him without his Stetson. Fresh from the military, his hair

had been cropped close. He looked strong, capable—
and oddly vulnerable.

Her heart clenched as it always did when she studied the photograph, but the usual tears didn't come.

"Good night, my love," she whispered, and placed
the photograph back on her nightstand. As she did,
Nell saw a light come on outside the window. Tossing
the blankets aside, she peered out and noticed a bright
even glow coming from the bunkhouse. The electricity was back on.

"I DON'T KNOW how much longer this is going to
take," Laredo Smith said as he reappeared to give
another update on Savannah's progress. He'd practically worn grooves in the carpet from the bedroom to
the living room where the men had gathered. Rain
continued to beat against the window and there were
occasional flashes of lightning, although the storm
had begun to let up.

Grady smiled indulgently at his brother-in-law,
grateful that the electricity was back on. "Babies take
as long as they take," he said wisely. He reclined in
the leather chair and laced his fingers behind his head,
rather pleased with his insight.

"That's easy for you to say," Laredo snapped in
a rare display of temper. "It's not *your* wife in there
giving birth to your child. Let's see how calm you
are when Caroline delivers."

The grin faded from Grady's face. Laredo had a
point.

"Birthing babies is a whole lot different from

bringing calves into the world," Cal said. Grady's best friend leaned forward and rested his arms on his knees, then glanced at his watch.

Grady was surprised when he checked the time. It was already past midnight, and it could be hours more before Savannah's baby was born. Not one of the assembled group showed any sign of being tired, much less leaving. Caroline and Jane were with Savannah, and his daughter was in bed upstairs. Six-year-old Maggie had tried to stay awake but fell asleep in his arms around ten.

Laredo had been with Savannah from the first, but returned to the living room periodically to make his reports. Grady watched his brother-in-law with interest. Laredo was so pale he looked in danger of passing out.

"I had no idea it would be like this," Laredo mumbled, ramming all ten fingers through his hair.

"That it'd take this long?" Grady asked.

Laredo vigorously shook his head. "No—that I'd feel this scared, this nervous. Savannah and I must've read ten books about pregnancy and birth, and I thought I was ready. Hell, man, I've been around horses and cattle all my life, but this is nothing like I expected."

Those books were the very ones Grady and Caroline were reading now. His wife was two months pregnant. Grady had been walking on air from the moment she'd told him. He'd thought about the baby a lot, his excitement building as he watched his own sister's pregnancy progress. He and Caroline had told only a few people, since she was months from showing.

To Grady, his wife had never looked more beautiful. Maggie was pleased and excited at the prospect of becoming a big sister. What Grady hadn't considered was this strange emotion Laredo exhibited.

Fear.

He hadn't thought of his child's birth as a frightening event. He'd imagined himself a proud father, holding his infant son or daughter. He enjoyed the prospect of people making a fuss and giving their opinions on which parent the baby resembled. Friends would come to visit and it would be a time of celebration and joy.

But tonight Laredo had destroyed his illusions. In his imaginings, Grady had glossed over the actual birth. Until now. Beyond any doubt, he knew that when it was Caroline's time to deliver their child, he'd be as bad as Laredo. Pacing, worrying, wondering. Praying.

"I'm going back in there," Laredo announced as though he couldn't bear to be away from Savannah a moment longer.

Grady stood, slapped his friend on the back to encourage him, then sank into his seat again.

"We're going to be just like him, you know," Cal said.

Grady nodded in agreement. "Worse, probably."

Cal grinned. "When's Caroline due?"

"The end of October."

"You two certainly didn't waste any time, did you?" Cal teased.

"Nope." Their wedding had been the last week of October, and Caroline was pregnant by the first week of January. They'd hoped it would happen quickly, seeing as Grady was already well into his thirties and Maggie was going on seven. It made sense to start their family early.

As the wind howled, Cal looked out the window. "Why is it babies are always born during a storm?"

"It probably has something to do with barometric pressure."

Cal scratched his head. "You think so?"

The hell if Grady knew, but it sounded good. The phone pealed in the kitchen and the two men stared at each other.

"It's probably Glen and Ellie again," Cal said.

Cal's brother and his wife lived in town and would have been with them, Grady suspected, if not for the storm.

Grady answered the phone. "Nothing yet," he said, instead of his usual greeting.

"Why didn't anyone phone me?" Dovie Boyd Hennessey demanded. Dovie and Savannah had been close since the death of Savannah's mother, Barbara, seven years earlier. Dovie owned and operated the antique shop, which sold everything from old scarves and jewelry to valuable china cups and saucers, all arranged around antique furnishings. The women in town loved to shop at Dovie's; she was universally admired and treasured by the town.

"Savannah's in labor and I only *now* find out," Dovie said, as though she'd missed the social event of the year.

"Who told you?" Grady asked. The women in Promise had a communication system the CIA could envy.

"Frank, naturally," Dovie told him. "I guess he talked to Laredo earlier this evening. He just got home." She paused for breath. "Has the baby come yet?"

"Nope, and according to Jane, it could be hours before the blessed event."

"How's Savannah?"

"Better than Laredo," Grady said.

Dovie's soft laugh drifted over the line. "Give her my love?"

"Of course."

"And call me the minute you hear, understand? I don't care what time of day or night it is."

"You got it," he said on the tail end of a yawn.

"Don't let me down, Grady."

"I wouldn't dream of it," he assured her.

By the time he returned to the living room, Cal had picked up a magazine and was flipping through the pages.

"You read that one an hour ago," Grady reminded him.

"So I did."

A few minutes later Caroline came into the room, and Grady leaped to his feet. "Sit down," he urged his wife. "You look exhausted." She should have been in bed hours ago, but he knew better than to suggest it. Caroline was as stubborn as they came, but then so was he. They understood each other, and he could appreciate her need to be with her best friend.

"It won't be long now," she told him as she slid her arms around his waist. "The baby's crowned."

Grady nodded. "Wonderful. How's Savannah?"

"She's doing well."

"And Laredo?"

"He's holding Savannah's hand and helping her with her breathing." Grady sat down, pulling Caroline onto his lap. She pressed her head against his shoulder, and he kissed her temple.

Grady glanced in Cal's direction and found he'd folded his arms and shut his eyes. Caroline's eyes were closed, too, and Grady decided to rest his own. Just for a few minutes, he told himself.

An infant's cry shattered the silence. Grady jerked awake and Caroline jumped to her feet and shook her head. "Oh, my goodness!" she gasped.

Grady hadn't a clue how long they'd been out. Cal straightened and rubbed his eyes with the heels of his hands.

"The kid's got one hell of a pair of lungs."

A few minutes later the bedroom door opened and Laredo emerged, carrying a tiny bundle in his arms. Grady noted that his friend's eyes were bright and his cheeks tear-streaked.

"We have a daughter," he said, gazing with awe at the baby he held. "Laura Rose, meet your family," he whispered to the newborn. "This is your uncle Grady and aunt Caroline."

"Hey, don't forget me," Cal said, stepping over to gaze down at the baby.

"That's Cal," Laredo continued. "His wife's the one who coaxed you into the world." Laredo gazed at the small group gathered around the baby. "Isn't she beautiful?" he said. "Doesn't she look like Savannah?"

Grady studied Laura Rose carefully and decided she looked more like an alien, but he certainly didn't say so.

Another hour passed before Grady and Caroline were in their own home and their own bed. Fortunately the rain had ended. Grady had carried a sleeping Maggie from Savannah's place to the car and then into her room; she never did wake up. He was exhausted, too. This had been a night to remember. His sister was a mother, and for the first time in his life he was an uncle. Damn, but it felt good.

Caroline pulled back the covers and joined him. She sighed as her head hit the pillow. "Did anyone phone Dovie?" she asked.

"I did," Grady said as he reached for the light.

"Good." Caroline rolled onto her side. "I think I could sleep for a week," she mumbled.

Grady drew his wife close, cuddling her spoon-fashion. His arm went around her and he flattened his hand against her stomach and grinned, feeling extraordinarily happy. Soon Laura Rose would have a cousin.

TRAVIS AWOKE and lay in the warm bed, unwilling to face the bright morning light. Not just yet, anyway. Something warm nestled against his feet, and he was content to stay exactly as he was for a few more minutes.

Despite his exhaustion, he'd had a hard time falling asleep. It didn't help that his legs stuck out a good six inches over the end of the bed. Those cowboys must've been pretty short guys, he thought wryly.

His eyes flew open as his toes felt something damp and ticklish. He bolted upright to find a goat standing at the foot of the bed, chewing for all it was worth. It didn't take Travis long to realize that the animal had eaten the socks clean off his feet. All that remained were a few rows of ribbing on his ankles.

Obviously, once he'd fallen asleep, he'd slept deeply—the sleep of the jet-lagged. He laughed and wiggled his toes just to be sure the socks were the only thing the goat had enjoyed. So far, so good.

"Yucky, what are you doing in here?"

The door flew open and Nell's boy—Jeremy, if Travis remembered correctly—rushed inside.

The boy planted his hands on his hips and glared at the goat.

"Morning," Travis said.

"Hi." Jeremy smiled and must have noticed Travis's feet for the first time because he burst out laughing. "Yucky ate your socks!"

"So I noticed."

"Sorry," Jeremy said, sounding anything but. He covered his mouth to hide a giggle, which made the situation even more amusing. "Mom said to tell you breakfast will be ready in twenty minutes if you're interested."

Travis didn't need a second invitation. His stomach growled at the mere mention of food. If the cinnamon roll the night before was any indication, Nell Bishop was one hell of a cook.

Travis dressed, showered and shaved, entering the kitchen just as Nell set a platter of scrambled eggs and bacon on the table.

"Morning," he greeted her.

"Morning," she returned, and poured him a mug of coffee.

Travis gratefully accepted it and pulled out a chair. Nell joined him and the children, and the three bowed their heads for grace. The instant they were through, Jeremy reached for the platter.

His mother sent him a warning glance and Jeremy immediately passed the platter to Travis. "Here," the boy said. "You're our guest. Please help yourself."

Travis was impressed with the boy's manners. So many children didn't seem to have any these days. He forked some fluffy scrambled eggs onto his plate and took a piece of toast from a bread basket in the center of the table. He gave Nell a sidelong glance as she buttered her own toast. She was obviously doing her best to be a good mother. The owner of the B and B had told him Nell was a widow, and he admired her for the loving manner in which she schooled her children.

"You collected all the eggs?" Nell asked Emma, interrupting his thoughts.

"Yes, Mama."

"Did you check under Bertha?"

The little girl grinned and nodded.

"I understand," Nell said, turning to Travis, "that we owe you a pair of socks."

He glanced up from his plate and saw that her mouth quivered with the beginnings of a smile.

"Best darn pair I owned."

"Your feet must've been pretty ripe to attract Yucky's attention," Jeremy said.

Travis couldn't help it; he burst out laughing. Nell, however, didn't take kindly to her son's comment. Jeremy read his mother's look and mumbled an apology.

Breakfast was wonderful, the food even better than he'd expected and the company delightful.

As soon as the kids had finished, they excused themselves and set their plates in the sink, then rushed out the back door.

"The children have animals to tend before they catch the school bus," Nell explained before he could voice his question.

"I see."

"Jeremy's got rabbits. Then there's Yucky, whom you've already met."

"We have a close and personal relationship," he said, leaning back in his chair, savoring the last of his coffee.

"Currently we have twelve horses, but I plan on

buying several more. Jeremy feeds them grain and alfalfa, and Emma makes sure they have plenty of water. I'll be mucking out the stalls later this morning.''

Travis could see that they had their chores down to a science and admired the way they all worked together. Briefly he wondered about Ruth, but guessed she reserved her strength for later in the day.

Nell cleared the remaining dishes from the table. ''Take your time,'' she said as she put on a sweater and headed toward the door.

''Can I help?'' he asked.

''Not at all. Just enjoy your coffee.''

Travis did as she suggested and watched from the window as Nell and the children worked together. They were a real team, efficient and cooperative. Half an hour later Jeremy and Emma raced into the house and grabbed their lunch boxes from the counter.

''We gotta go to school now,'' Emma said, staring at Travis as though she'd much rather spend the day with him.

Jeremy was on his way out when he paused. ''Will you be here tonight?''

Travis had to think about that. ''Probably.''

''I hope you are,'' the boy said. ''It's nice having another man around the place.'' And with that, he flew out the door.

Travis rinsed his mug and set it beside the kitchen sink. He met Nell as he left the house. ''Do you mind if I plug my computer into an outlet in the bunk-

house? I want to get some work done while I'm
here.''

"Not at all," she said, her smile congenial.

Whistling, Travis returned to the bunkhouse and
retrieved his portable computer from his bag. With a
minimum of fuss, he located an outlet and set up
shop. The computer hummed its usual greeting as the
screen saver reminded him that he was one hell of a
good writer—a message he'd programmed in to battle
the deluge of self-doubts all writers faced.

The note was just the boost his ego needed before
he dug into his latest project. He'd achieved indis-
putable success with his series of Western stories for
preadolescents and young teens. The book he planned
to write next might possibly be his best; he could feel
that even before he wrote the first word. A main-
stream novel set in a Western ghost town—his editor
had been ecstatic over the idea.

Travis never did the actual writing while he was
on the road, but he wanted to document facts about
the storm from the night before. One of his characters
was sure to lose his socks to a hungry goat, too. He
prided himself on the authenticity of his details, although in his past books, most of that background had
come from research.

Rarely did anything happen to him that didn't show
up in a book sometime, one way or another. He used
to think he kept his personal life out of his work, but
that was a fallacy. Anyone who really knew him
could follow his life by reading his books. The con-
nections weren't always direct. Take the end of his

marriage, for example. Of the two books he'd written the year of his divorce, one took place in Death Valley and the other on the River of No Return. Those locations had corresponded to his emotional state at the time.

He didn't want to stop and analyze why a ghost town appealed to him now. Maybe because his life felt empty and he struggled with loneliness. Travis realized without surprise that he envied Nell her children.

He entered notes about Texas, the drive from San Antonio, his impressions of the landscape and the people. The storm was described in plenty of detail. He made notes about Nell and her children. Ruth, too.

The next time he glanced up, he was shocked to discover it was midmorning. He stored the information onto a computer file and headed for the kitchen, hoping Nell kept a pot of coffee brewing during the day. He didn't expect to see her, since she had stalls to muck out and plenty of other chores, many of which he knew next to nothing about.

He was pleasantly surprised to find her in the kitchen.

"Hello again," he said.

"Hi."

The spicy aroma of whatever she was cooking made him instantly hungry, despite the fact that he'd enjoyed one of the finest breakfasts he'd eaten in years.

"What are you making?" he asked. He noticed a can of beer sitting by the stove at—he glanced at his watch—10:35 a.m.! He wondered with some concern if she was a drinker...but then he saw her add it to whatever was in the large cast-iron pot.

"It's chili," she said. "Would you like a taste?"

"I'd love it."

Nell dished up a small bowl and brought it to the table where Travis sat. "This might sound like a silly question, but did you happen to mention to Ruth how many nights you intend to stay?"

He delayed his first sample, wondering if Nell was looking for a way to get rid of him. He'd be keenly disappointed if that was the case. He happened to like Twin Canyons Ranch. His visit would add texture and realism to his novel. And being here was so much more *interesting* than staying at a hotel, or even at a bed and breakfast.

"I'm not sure yet," Travis said in answer to her question.

He tried the chili. The instant his mouth closed over the spoon he realized this was the best-tasting chili he'd ever eaten, bar none. The flavors somersaulted across his tongue.

"What do you think?" she asked, her big brown eyes hopeful.

"If you don't win that prize, I'll want to know why." He scooped up a second spoonful.

"You're not just saying that, are you?" Her eyes went from hopeful to relieved.

"If I was the judge I'd award you the prize money without needing to taste anyone else's. This is fabulous."

Nell's freshly scrubbed face glowed with a smile. Travis had seen his share of beautiful women, but he felt few would compare with Nell Bishop and her unspoiled beauty. The kind she possessed didn't require makeup to enhance it. She was as real as a person could get.

"I made a terrible mistake when I saw you on the road yesterday," she said, suddenly frowning a little.

"How's that?"

"I implied you were...not too bright.." She pulled out a chair and sat across the table from him. "I was wrong. You're obviously very bright, indeed!"

Chapter Three

"How come *you* were asked to be one of the judges for the chili cook-off?" Glen asked Ellie as they walked toward the rodeo grounds. The air was charged with excitement.

"Just clean living," his wife replied, and did her best to disguise a smile. Actually it had more to do with her participation in the Chamber of Commerce. But her husband had done nothing but complain from the moment he learned she'd been asked to judge the chili. It was a task he would have relished.

"I'm the one who happens to love chili," he lamented—not for the first time.

Unable to help herself, Ellie laughed out loud. "If you want, I'll put your name in as a judge for next year," she said, hoping that would appease him.

"You'd do that?" They strolled hand in hand toward the grandstand. Luckily the ground had dried out after the recent rain. The rodeo was one of the most popular events of the year, along with the big summer dance and the Willie Nelson Fourth of July picnic. The town council always invited Willie to the picnic, but he had yet to accept. With or without him, it was held in his honor, and his music was piped through the park all day.

"Sure will. I'll let Dovie know you want to be a judge next year," Ellie promised. "Consider it just one of the many benefits of marrying a local businesswoman."

Glen wrapped his arm about her waist and gave her a squeeze. "I know all about those benefits," he said, and kissed the top of her head.

He raised his hand so that it rested just beneath her breast. "Glen," she warned under her breath.

He sighed and lowered his hand to her waist.

Ellie saw Jane and Cal and waved. Dr. Texas immediately returned her wave, and the two couples sauntered toward each other.

"So you're going through with it," Glen said when he saw his brother.

"I can't talk him out of it," Jane said, rolling her eyes.

"I've competed in the bull-riding competition for ten years," Cal argued. "Besides, if I'm injured, I know one hell of a fine physician who'll treat me with tender loving care." He winked at his wife.

From the look Jane tossed her husband, Ellie suspected she'd be inclined to let him suffer. Grinning, she reflected on how well her matchmaking efforts had worked. She gladly accepted credit for pairing Cal with Jane; the match had been brilliant, if she did say so herself. Jane had moved to Promise as part of a government program in which she agreed to work for three years at the community health clinic in exchange for payment of her college loans.

Cal, of course, had been burned in the romance department several years earlier when his fiancée had dumped him a few days before their wedding and skipped town. In addition to the hurt and rejection he'd suffered, Cal had been left to deal with the embarrassment and the questions that followed. For years afterward he'd refused to have anything to do with women.

Until Jane.

She'd moved to town after living her entire life in California. Poor Jane had been completely and totally out of her element until Dovie took charge. One of the first things Dovie had done was introduce her to Ellie.

In the beginning Ellie wasn't sure it was possible for them to be friends. Jane had an attitude about all things Texan, and it rubbed her—and just about everyone in town—the wrong way. Everything she said and did had an air of superiority.

Jane's start had been rocky, that was for sure. Ellie smiled as she remembered that first lunch in which she'd suggested Jane take her wine-sipping, quiche-eating butt and go back where she'd come from. She was grateful now that Jane had decided to stick it out.

When Ellie set up the date between her distrustful brother-in-law and the doctor-with-attitude, she knew she was taking a chance. It would have been just like Cal to take one look at the setup and walk out of the restaurant. He hadn't. In fact, he'd shocked both Glen and Ellie when they discovered that he'd agreed to give Jane horseback-riding lessons.

They were married within six months and Cal was happier than she could ever recall seeing him. He hardly seemed like the same person.

"I have a feeling I could win this year," Cal said.

"He's been claiming that every year since he first entered," Glen muttered just loudly enough for everyone to hear.

"I'm gonna win," Cal insisted, defying his brother to challenge him.

"This is a man thing," Ellie explained to her sister-in-law. "Glen competes in the calf-roping event."

"I have the *blue* ribbons to prove it."

Cal winced at the small dig. "Ouch, little brother."

"Calf roping I can tolerate, but watching Cal on those huge bulls is something else again." Jane looked at her husband, and Ellie saw a spark of genuine fear in her friend's eyes. She had to admit she was grateful Glen wouldn't be competing on the bulls.

"I've done everything I know to talk him out of this," Jane confided as the two women made their way to the grandstand and found seats in the second row. Both men were by the chutes, chatting with their friends and making small talk with the professional rodeo riders.

Jane clenched her hands in her lap.

"It'll be fine," Ellie assured her. "Cal's no fool."

"How can you say that?" Jane said, biting her lip. "Only a fool would risk his neck riding an ill-tempered beast who weighs as much as the state of Texas.''

Ellie laughed.

''If...if Cal happened to get hurt, I don't know if I'd be able to treat him.''

''You love him that much?'' Ellie asked.

''Yes, but that's not the reason. I don't think I could stop myself from clobbering him for worrying me like this.''

Ellie laughed outright, although she understood.

The grandstand quickly filled to capacity as the competition time neared.

''I heard a wild rumor,'' Ellie said, hoping to distract Jane from her worries. ''Someone told me Willie Nelson might make a surprise appearance at the dance later this evening.''

''You're joking!''

She shook her head. ''I don't know if it's true, but that's what people are saying.''

''That would be wonderful. What brought it about?''

''I've heard he likes surprising people now and then.'' She gave a slight shrug. ''He knows this is Willie country and he's never been able to come to our Fourth of July picnics. Maybe that's why.''

''My parents went to hear him recently,'' Jane said. ''They said he isn't going to replace the Beach Boys in their eyes, but the music was entertaining.''

''Give 'em time,'' Ellie said.

The calf-roping event was one of the first on the program, and Ellie wasn't surprised when Glen took first place. She loved the way he raced after the calf, roped him on the first try and maneuvered the animal onto its back. He made it all look so easy. But when he tied the animal's legs, then tossed his hands in the air and leaped back, his eyes didn't go to the time. Instead, they zeroed in on Ellie and he'd smiled that secret little smile meant for her alone. Only then did his gaze go to the clock.

When his time was announced, Ellie jumped to her feet and applauded loudly. Pursing her lips around her index finger and thumb, she released a piercing whistle. Jane stood with her and the two of them made several victory punches in the air.

"How long before Cal rides?" Jane asked after they sat back down.

"Pretty soon."

Jane placed her hands between her knees and took several deep breaths. Ellie gently patted her shoulder. "Hey, it's only eight seconds."

"A bull like that could kill him in one."

Ellie let the comment slide. "Cal knows what he's doing."

Jane nodded, but she looked pale. Ellie realized how difficult this was for her. Not having been raised around cattle ranches, Jane must view these competitions as barbaric. Ellie decided she hadn't given her sister-in-law the credit she was due for marrying into this whole new way of life.

When the competition had begun and Cal's name was announced, Jane bit her lip and closed her eyes. Cal sat high in the chute on the bull's back, his concentration intense. The door opened, and man and beast plunged forward. The bull snorted, shaking his massive head, determined to dislodge his rider.

Jane leaped to her feet and covered her mouth with her hand. Ellie had just stood up, too, when Cal went flying off the bull's back. There was a collective drawing in of breath as the crowd waited for him to jump out of the bull's way. The clowns diverted the bull's attention, but Cal remained on the ground.

"Dear God!" Jane cried. "He's hurt. I knew it, I knew it." She was already stumbling past everyone in the row, Ellie right behind her. "I swear if that fall didn't kill him, I will."

By the time they made it down to the steps, Cal had been carried off the grounds on a stretcher. Just as they reached him, they heard the final contestant's name being called.

Glen, who was with his brother, took Ellie's hand. Jane knelt beside her husband, tears in her eyes.

"It's all right, honey," Cal said, clutching his ribs. He gave her a smile but was clearly in pain.

"He's had the wind knocked out of him," Glen said.

Jane began to unfasten Cal's shirt.

"Jane—not in front of all these people," Cal said in a feeble attempt at humor.

"Be quiet," she snapped.

"Best not to cross her in this frame of mind," Cal said, then groaned when Jane lightly pressed her fingertips against a rib.

"I'll need X rays, but my guess is you've broken a rib."

"It won't be the first."

"But it'll be the last one you'll ever get riding bulls," Jane said in a voice few would question.

"Whatever you say."

"You might want to take this with you." Max Jordan, a local business owner, hurried over to join them.

"Take what?" Glen asked.

Max grinned broadly and handed Cal a blue ribbon. "Congratulations, Cal! You stayed on longer than anyone."

Despite the pain it must have cost him, Cal let out a loud triumphant cry.

TRAVIS HAD BEEN WRITING for years. He'd researched rodeos and even written about them—but this was the first one he'd actually attended. Jeremy and Emma had volunteered to be his guides, and he welcomed their company. Nell was busy adding the final touches to her chili; judging would take place later in the afternoon. The last time he'd seen Ruth, she'd introduced him to two friends, Edwina and Lily Moorhouse, sisters and retired schoolteachers. One of them had mentioned something about cloves—cloves?—a special cordial, and the next thing he knew, all three women had disappeared. Made no sense to him.

Now that the rodeo was over, Jeremy and Emma decided it was time to show Travis the booths. It seemed everyone in town had something on display. All new to Travis. The closest thing New York had to this was the farmers' market, in which everything from rip-off brand-name running shoes and "real" French perfume to home-grown vegetables and spicy sausages was sold.

Travis and the kids wandered by the long tables where the chili was being cooked. "Hi, Mom," Emma called.

At the sound of her daughter's voice, Nell turned. She wore a pretty blue cotton dress with a white bib apron over it.

"I wondered where you two had wandered off," she said.

"The kids are playing tour guide," Travis explained. "They're doing a good job of showing me the ropes." He ruffled Jeremy's hair, and the youngster grinned up at him.

"I hope they aren't making a nuisance of themselves."

"On the contrary." They were likable kids, and seeing the rodeo and other festivities through their eyes had been a bonus.

"I'll get my purse so you can buy your lunch," Nell told her children.

"That's all right, Mom," Emma said. "Travis already fed us."

Nell's gaze briefly met his.

"We didn't ask," Jeremy added, apparently recognizing the look in his mother's eyes.

"It was the least I could do," Travis said, not understanding why she'd be disturbed about something so minor.

"My children and I pay our own way, Mr. Grant," she said before he could say anything else.

"It was my pleasure, Nell—honestly. Without Jeremy and Emma, I would've been lost." Both kids had taken delight in tutoring him in each of the rodeo events. They'd also shared tidbits about the community and its traditions, and the education he'd gained had been well worth the price of a couple of hamburgers and ice-cream bars.

"When are the judges going to be here?" Emma asked.

Nell glanced at her watch. "Not for another hour."

"You're gonna win," Jeremy said with confidence.

"I'm crossing my fingers for you, Mom." Emma held up both hands to show her.

"Good luck," Travis tossed in.

"We're headed for the carnival now," Jeremy said. "I promise I won't spend all my allowance."

Nell nodded and glanced at Travis. "Listen, everyone, I'm sorry, I didn't mean to snap at you earlier. I guess I'm more nervous than I realized about this contest."

"That's all right, Mom."

"No apology necessary," Travis said, thinking it was unusual these days to find anyone willing to apologize. It was a sign of maturity and inner strength, and he admired her for it. In fact, there seemed to be quite a bit to admire about Nell Bishop....

"Have fun at the carnival," she said, stirring her chili.

"We will."

"If they don't mind, I'll tag along just for the fun of it," Travis said to Nell. He couldn't recall the last time he'd been on a Ferris wheel—probably when he was younger than these two; and maybe he could convince Jeremy and Emma to go on it with him.

He'd never spent much time around kids, although his books were geared to them. Life was full of ironies such as this, he reflected. Valerie used to say he related to children because he'd never grown up himself, and he supposed it was true. She'd meant it as an insult, but Travis had considered it a compliment.

They had a wonderful afternoon on the midway, and he loved every minute. He let Jeremy and Emma spend part of their allowance, but he paid for most of the rides. They went on the octopus, a ride he remembered from his boyhood, and Emma covered her eyes, screamed the entire time, then insisted they do it again.

"Don't spend all your money on us," Emma said when he bought them each a huge cotton candy.

Travis was half-tempted to say there was plenty more where that came from, but decided it would be a crass comment. "Don't worry..." he began.

"Be happy," Jeremy completed for him.

"Right," Travis said, and chuckled. He enjoyed children, always had. That was one reason he'd chosen to write for the age group he did. His overwhelming success had surprised even him.

"In that case, could I have some popcorn, too?" Emma asked.

Laughter bubbled up inside him. Both of these children were forthright and honest, hardworking and appreciative—and they had a sense of humor. It would be unfair to compare them to children in New York, since he knew so few, but he was sure these two were special. As special as their mother.

"Have you met Dovie?" Emma asked a short while later between mouthfuls of popcorn.

Dovie—not dove. A name. "No, I haven't."

"You gotta meet Dovie," Jeremy said, directing him away from the carnival rides.

They led him to a large booth set up close to the chili cook-off area. A friendly slightly rotund older woman stood in front of a colorful patchwork quilt.

"Hi, Dovie," Jeremy said.

"Hi, Dovie," Emma echoed.

"Hello, Dovie." Travis figured he didn't want to be left out.

Dovie looked at him and blinked, as if she was afraid she should've recognized him and hadn't. Jeremy and Emma burst out laughing.

"This is Travis," Emma said, and reached for his hand. It was an innocent gesture, but it tugged at his heart.

"He's staying at the ranch," Jeremy added.

"From what I hear, I'm the first paying guest," Travis explained.

"Pleased to meet you," Dovie said, holding out her hand. "I don't mean to be rude, but I'm wondering if I could interest you in a raffle ticket for this fine quilt."

"Of course." Travis reached for his wallet.

"The Dorcas Group at church is raffling it off to raise money for missions."

"How much?"

"A dollar each, or six for five dollars."

Travis pulled a ten from his wallet. "Give me twelve tickets."

Dovie flashed him an appreciative smile.

"He's a good guy," Jeremy said proudly.

"I like him, too," Emma added.

Travis tucked the ticket stubs securely into his hip pocket and wished Dovie luck with the quilt.

"Thank you. How long will you be in town?" she asked.

It'd been a common question all day. "I'm not sure yet."

"I hope you enjoy yourself."

Emma took his hand again. "You ready?" she asked. "For the chili judging?"

"Sure," he returned.

"Is it time?" Jeremy asked.

Emma nodded.

A crowd had gathered around the chili cook-off area and the judges, five of them, stepped forward to do their taste tests. The samples were numbered so it was impossible to tell who had cooked which chili.

"That's Ellie Patterson," Jeremy whispered. "She owns the local feed store." A pretty brunette sampled the first taste and nodded in approval.

"I hope that was Mom's," Emma said.

So did Travis. The taste she'd given him the day before was fabulous and nothing like any chili he'd tasted before. He'd accidentally discovered her secret ingredient was beer but had been sworn to secrecy.

In his short visit he'd learned quite a bit about Texas chili, which was different from anything he'd tasted in New York City or on his previous travels. In Texas the chili was thick with meat and spices and it wasn't made with beans.

"That's Mr. Jordan," Jeremy said, identifying the next judge. "He owns the Western-wear shop."

Someone called Billy D, owner of the local tavern, and Adam Braunfels, a restaurateur, tasted next.

The last one to try the chili samples was a large rancher type.

"Who's that?" Travis asked.

"Pastor McMillen," Jeremy whispered back.

That surprised Travis. The man looked like he'd be more comfortable on a horse than in a pulpit.

After all the judges had sampled the entries, they cast their votes. The crowd grew quiet with anticipation as the town sheriff, Frank Hennessey, stepped forward with the results of the voting.

Emma stood next to Travis with her eyes tightly shut, her hands raised and fingers crossed.

Sheriff Hennessey cleared his throat. "It was a difficult decision this year, but it appears that one entry stood out as the most flavorful. The voting is unanimous. The winner is—" the faint sound of a drumroll could be heard in the background "—number five."

Travis frowned, not knowing who the winner was until he noticed Nell. She stood there as though in a daze.

"Nell Bishop," Frank Hennessey shouted cheerfully as a stunned Nell moved slowly toward the microphone. "It gives me a great deal of pleasure to present you with this check in the amount of five hundred dollars."

Nell might be in shock, but Travis noticed that she snapped out of her stupor fast enough when it came to reaching for the check. The crowd loved it.

Following the competition, spoonfuls of chili, dished up in small paper cups, were left for the crowd to taste. People surged toward the table that held the samples labeled "number five."

"Yay, Mom!" Emma said, rushing forward and hugging her mother.

"This is really cool," Jeremy said. He exchanged a high five with his mother.

Travis barely knew Nell Bishop, but he was as thrilled that she'd won the cook-off as if the success had been his own.

NELL WAS EXHAUSTED. Exhilarated but exhausted. Adam Braunfels, one of the judges and the owner of the Chili Pepper, the best restaurant in town, pulled her aside when the competition was over. He told Nell her chili was the best he'd ever tasted and that he'd like to talk with her later about the possibility of buying her recipe. He wanted to serve it in his restaurant. Nell could hardly believe her ears.

Following their conversation, Adam handed her a ticket for a free meal and suggested she stop off at his booth for dinner. Nell sat at one of the picnic tables at the far end of the rodeo grounds and savored a barbecued-beef sandwich and a heaping cup of cole-slaw. It was the first time she'd eaten all day; she'd simply been too nervous before.

Jeremy and Emma were with their grandmother, who'd taken them home. The kids had chattered in-cessantly about Travis Grant. Apparently he'd shown them the time of their lives and they sang his praises to all who'd listen.

"Do you mind if I join you?"

Her thoughts seemed to have conjured up the man. Travis stood directly across the table from her, hold-ing a cup of coffee.

"Please." Nell gestured toward a chair, and Travis sat down.

"Congratulations again," he said.

"Thank you." She was dying to tell someone about her conversation with Adam Braunfels, but held her tongue. Nothing was definite, and she didn't want to say anything until the details were settled.

"From what I understand, I owe you a debt of thanks," Nell said. "The kids told me this was the best rodeo of their lives, and all because of you."

"I was just about to thank you for sharing them with me. They're terrific kids, Nell."

"I think so, too."

She pushed aside the rest of her dinner and reached for her coffee. After being on her feet all day, she was grateful to be sitting. "Ruth drove them home," she said unnecessarily. She'd stayed to clean up the kitchen area and talk to Adam, but was so relaxed now she wasn't sure she'd find the energy to move.

"I heard someone say Willie Nelson was coming for the dance later," Travis mentioned.

"Don't believe it." Nell hated to be the one to disillusion him. "This is Willie Nelson country. We love him, and we send him an invitation to a picnic in his honor every single year."

"He's never come?"

"No, but then, we don't really expect he will. He's got bigger and better places to perform. We understand that and love him, anyway." Whether or not Willie showed, the people of Promise would continue to enjoy his music. Willie Nelson represented everything they loved about country music.

"Tired?" Travis asked.

"A little." An understatement if there ever was one.

"Too tired to dance?"

It took a moment to understand the question. Travis Grant was asking her to dance with him. She stared at him, unsure how to respond. It was kind of him, offering to be her partner. With anyone else she would have found an immediate excuse to decline. Not with Travis. For one crazy moment she actually considered it.

"Thank you, but no," she finally said.

If she'd disappointed him, Travis didn't let on.

Nell checked her watch, thinking it was time—past time really—to head home. The band, a popular local group, was playing in the background. The stage wasn't in sight, but well within listening range.

"They sound good," Travis said.

They did. Much better than Nell remembered, but then, it'd been more than three years since she'd stayed for the evening festivities.

All at once a crazed cheer rose from the audience and the announcer's voice came over the microphone. "Ladies and gentlemen, it's a pleasure to introduce the good people of Promise, Texas, to *Willie Nelson.*"

Nell's gaze flew to Travis. "This has got to be a joke," she said.

But even before the words were out, the opening strains of "Whiskey River" echoed across the grounds.

Her fatigue gone, Nell leaped to her feet and hurried toward the dance area. So did everyone else within shouting distance. Travis was right behind her.

Nell and Travis never did get to see him. The crowd grew so thick they couldn't do more than listen. Willie sang three numbers to wild applause, then suggested everyone dance. The music flowed, smooth and easy. People around her paired off, even though they weren't anywhere near the dance floor.

Travis smiled down at her. "Shall we?" he asked, stretching out one hand.

Nell couldn't stop looking at him long enough to decline. It wasn't that Travis was a handsome man. His face was too angular, his features too rugged to be considered pleasing.

He took her lack of response as answer enough and

slipped his arm around her waist. His hold was loose and gentle. A lifetime ago Nell had loved to dance. Jake had possessed two left feet, but he'd made an effort for her sake.

Travis danced as if he knew exactly what he was doing—and as if he enjoyed it. What surprised her was how well they moved together, how gracefully.

"Don't look so shocked," he said with a laugh. "Big men aren't all klutzes."

"The same applies to big women."

"You're not big," he countered. "In fact, I'd say you're just about perfect." He brushed a stray lock of hair from her forehead, and his fingertips lingered a moment longer than necessary.

Nell didn't know what madness possessed her, but she closed her eyes and allowed herself to indulge in a fantasy. She didn't pretend that the man holding her was her dead husband. That would have been too painful. Instead, she fantasized that she was a different kind of woman, willowy and lithe, petite and beautiful. Like the young Audrey Hepburn of *Sabrina,* a movie Nell had loved all her life.

It was the night for such dreams.

The dance ended almost as soon as it had begun. Too soon. Nevertheless, she didn't dare to continue. Didn't dare to indulge in any more fantasies.

"Thank you," she whispered. "I've never enjoyed a dance more."

"Me, neither," Travis said, his voice low and sounding vaguely unlike him.

Of one accord they turned and walked across the grounds, toward the parking area.

''Nell.'' He stopped her in the shadow of the grandstand.

''Yes?''

''Don't be angry.''

''Angry? Whatever for?''

''For this,'' he whispered. He turned her around to face him, then lowered his mouth to hers.

Chapter Four

His kiss left Nell feeling lightheaded, as if she'd been out in the sun too long. His lips lingered on hers, his arms firm about her waist. He would have kissed her a second time, she sensed, if she hadn't moved her head just then. She needed a moment to compose herself, to gain perspective and deal with what had happened—what she'd allowed to happen. At any point she could have stopped him...and hadn't.

"I...wish you hadn't done that." Her voice trembled, shaky with shock and wonder. What astounded her as much as his kiss was how much she'd enjoyed it.

"Are you looking for an apology?"

His voice was close to her ear and she realized that he still held her.

"I could give you one if you wanted," he went on, "but it wouldn't be sincere."

She smiled at his words and eased away from him. There was definitely something in the air tonight that had caused her to behave so completely out of character.

"It's because of today," she said aloud. "The whole day." One of the best days she'd had in three years of grief and struggle.

"The day?" Travis repeated, walking at her side as they continued toward the parking lot.

She glanced at him, surprised she'd spoken aloud. Since she had, she couldn't very well leave him in the dark. That would be rude and unnecessary. If he was to continue paying for room and board, then she had best set boundaries between them now. Kissing was definitely *out* of bounds.

"Naturally I'm flattered that you'd want to kiss me."

"I'd like to do it again, if you're not opposed."

She shook her head. "I'd rather you didn't."

He was quiet after that, but not for long. "What did you mean when you said it was because of *to-day?*"

She exhaled slowly. "Winning the chili cook-off. The kids having such a wonderful time. Willie Nelson showing up like that. Dancing in the moonlight... I wasn't myself. I wasn't thinking—otherwise that kiss would never have happened."

"How weren't you yourself?" he prodded.

Nell was much too tired to endure an inquisition. "I just wasn't."

"How?" he pressed.

"I was happy, excited..."

He couldn't seem to leave it at that. "You aren't normally?"

"No," she returned shortly. "Not for the last three years."

A silence followed her words. Nell heard his sigh.

"You must have loved him very much."

She didn't hesitate. "More than life itself. In many ways I died with my husband. Nothing will ever be the same again."

They paused in front of her battered pickup. The Dodge was well past its prime. It'd been ready for the scrap heap when Jake was alive, but Nell had coaxed three more years from it; she prayed the truck would last another year.

"I disagree," he said.

His words cut into her thoughts. She raised questioning eyes to him. "What do you mean?"

"You loved Jake, and it's obvious you two shared something very special. But you didn't die with him. The woman I kissed is alive and healthy. She's vital and lovely and passionate." He raised his hand as if to touch her face, but changed his mind and slowly lowered it. "I felt your heart pound against mine. The woman I kissed is *alive*, Nell. She has a lot to live for."

"I—"

"You might prefer to think of yourself as dead, but you aren't."

His words surprised her more than his kiss. She didn't know how to respond, how to react. Ruth had been saying the same thing to her, but in different words. All this time she'd resisted, afraid she'd lose even more of Jake than she already had. This was dangerous stuff, too dangerous to think about right now. She'd leave it for another time.

"You haven't dated since Jake died?" Travis asked.

She shook her head.

"What's the matter with the men in this town?" he asked in a way that suggested they were idiots.

"Grady Weston asked me to the big summer dance last year."

"And?"

"And I turned him down. Glen Patterson, too."

"Nell, no." He planted his hands squarely on her shoulders. "Wake up. Look around you. Breathe in the cool night air and let it fill your lungs. Let yourself *feel*."

He spoke with such intensity all she could do was stare at him.

"You don't believe anything I've said, do you? I can see it in your eyes."

Instantly she lowered her gaze. "I'll never have with anyone else the kind of love I had with Jake."

"Of course you won't," he said.

The man said and did the most shocking things.

"Jake was Jake," he continued. "Any relationship you might have with another man will be different from your marriage to Jake because that man will be different from Jake." He paused. "The problem, Nell, is that you haven't seen it this way. The way you see it, any other man is destined to fall short because he can never be a replacement for the original."

She had to admit Travis made sense. It was exactly

what Ruth and Dovie and several others, Savannah included, had been trying to tell her. Either she hadn't fully understood or she hadn't been ready to listen.

It hit her then that Travis spoke as if he was familiar with this type of loss. "You lost your wife?" she asked him.

Now it was Travis who looked away. "In a manner of speaking."

"What manner?" He'd prodded and pried, now she did the same.

"I'm divorced."

"You loved her?"

"Very much," he said, "and I assumed she loved me. But apparently I was wrong."

Nell waited for him to go on, and after a moment he did.

"She met someone else." Travis buried his hands deep inside his pockets as though he felt a need to suppress his anger, even now. "Someone who could give her the things she needed, the things I couldn't—and I'm not just talking about money." He sounded philosophical, but beneath his matter-of-fact statement, she recognized his pain. Recognized it because she'd experienced a similar pain.

"Tony, Val's new husband, sets her on fire," he said, his voice dripping with sarcasm. "I didn't."

Nell might have accepted the words at face value if not for one thing. He'd held her and kissed her. There was definitely fire in him, and it was burning strong. Maybe his ex-wife hadn't provided enough kindling, she mused—and felt some amazement that such a thought had occurred to her. "Bitterness wouldn't solve anything, so I decided to do what I could—go on with my life, put the past behind me."

"Have you?"

"I like to think so." He said this as if he expected her to challenge him. "How is it we're talking about me? You're the one who's still living in the past, not me."

"Really?"

Travis chuckled and held up his hand. "Enough. Your point is well taken. We're both among the walking wounded."

Nell smiled. "Perhaps we could learn from each other," she suggested.

Travis nodded. "Perhaps we can."

They drove back to the ranch in separate vehicles. Travis pulled into the yard seconds behind her.

"Good night," she called, offering him a friendly wave as she headed toward the house. A single light shone above the back porch door. In all likelihood Jeremy and Emma were sound asleep; it would surprise her if Ruth was still up.

"'Night, Nell."

Once inside the house, she climbed up the stairs to her room, undressed in the dark and sat on the edge of her bed, reviewing the events of the day. When she turned on the bedside lamp and took out her journal, it wasn't the five-hundred-dollar prize money she thought of. Instead, she found herself writing about Travis's kiss and the discussion that had followed.

JEREMY AND EMMA had been up for at least an hour by the time Nell got out of bed. Sundays were just as hectic as schooldays because chores needed to be finished before they left for Sunday School and church.

Nell had coffee brewing and was cracking eggs for French toast when the kitchen door opened and Travis strolled casually inside. "Morning" he said, helping himself to coffee.

"Good morning," she said, whipping the eggs into a frothy mixture before adding the milk. The griddle was ready and she had six slices of egg-soaked bread sizzling in short order.

"You coming to church with us?" Jeremy asked as he and Emma dashed in.

"Ah…" Travis glanced at Nell.

"It's the Lord's day," Emma said severely, as if there should be no hesitation on his part.

"You're welcome to join us if you wish," Nell said.

He didn't show any sign of reluctance. "I'd enjoy that."

At breakfast Jeremy sat on one side of Travis, Emma on the other, the children accepting him as easily as they would a much-admired uncle.

"We're lucky Mr. and Mrs. Patterson didn't have any rooms left to rent," Jeremy said.

"Real lucky," Emma agreed.

"With the rodeo over, the Pattersons should have plenty of room," Ruth muttered as she walked into the kitchen, yawning.

The news landed like a bombshell in the kitchen.

The children stared at each other as though they'd just learned the horrible truth about Santa Claus. Nell felt an immediate sense of disappointment, but Ruth was right. Phil and Mary would have space available for Travis now, and the accommodations would be far more comfortable than a too-short mattress in the bunkhouse. At Phil and Mary's, Travis wouldn't need to worry about a goat eating the socks off his feet, either.

"That's true. Mr. Grant could move into town," Nell said, trying to sound as though it made no difference to her. It shouldn't, but hard as she tried to convince herself it would be best if Travis left, she hoped he wouldn't.

Every eye went to their guest. "Move into town?" he repeated, glancing at each in turn. "Would anyone mind if I stayed on here? Your goat and I have recently come to terms. It would be a shame to leave now."

She shouldn't be this happy, Nell decided, but she was. She really was.

"WHAT TIME IS IT?" Frank Hennessey mumbled as he rolled over in the large feather bed and stretched his arms to both sides.

"Time for you to be up and dressed," Dovie said. "Church starts in less than thirty minutes."

"Church," Frank groaned. "Dovie, you know how hard it is for me to sit through Sunday service." But he eased himself up in bed to enjoy the sight of his wife fluttering about the room, hurriedly dressing.

Dovie was a fine-looking woman and he took pleasure in watching this woman he loved.

It'd taken him long enough to make the leap into marriage. Not many men waited until they were sixty years old—maybe that was why the decision had been so hard. He might have remained single all his life if not for a woman as wonderful as Dovie. Their arrangement was perfect, he'd thought. Twice a week he spent the night. Two of the best nights of any week.

Dovie, being the kind of woman she was, had wanted them to get married. He'd led her to believe that eventually he'd be willing, and for ten years he'd believed it himself. Then all at once Promise experienced a rash of weddings and Dovie became possessed by the idea of marriage.

That was when he'd realized he simply wasn't the marrying kind. Painful though it was, he'd confessed to Dovie that he just couldn't do it—and she'd promptly ended their relationship. Those weeks apart had been agonizing for him.

He loved her, but he'd broken his word to her, and although he hated himself for hurting the woman he adored, he couldn't give up the comforts of his life as a bachelor. For instance, the fact that his house was a mess. It was *his* mess, though, and he knew where things were. Dovie wouldn't tolerate the unsightly stack of magazines by his recliner or the pile of laundry beside his bed.

Marriage meant more than making a commitment to her, he'd thought; it meant he'd be forced to alter his entire life. At sixty such a drastic change didn't come easy.

Things had looked hopeless—and grew even worse when he made the mistake of taking Tammy Lee Kollenborn out one evening. That was the night he'd known he could never love anyone but Dovie. Afterward, when Dovie had gone away on a short cruise, he'd been terrified she'd meet another man. It seemed inevitable that he was going to lose her, and the knowledge was destroying him.

The solution had come from an unexpected source. From the man he'd assumed would be the least understanding. Reverend Wade McMillen. Frank owed him big time. The local preacher had suggested that Frank and Dovie get married but maintain separate households, the same as they were already doing. Then they could both have what they wanted. What they needed. Dovie had the commitment she craved, the wedding band on her finger. And Frank was free to eat baked beans out of a can in front of the television, wearing nothing but his underwear, if he so desired.

"Dovie," he whispered softly, watching a silk slip float down over her breasts and hips. "Come here, love."

"Don't you use that tone of voice with me, Frank Hennessey. I'm running late as it is."

"Dovie," he coaxed, and sat up. He held out his arms to her. "How about a good-morning hug?"

"Not now."

"No?" Frank was surprised. Dovie rarely refused

him anything, especially when it came to what she called "the delights of the flesh." He'd never met a woman like her. Dovie was a lady to the core, but when it came to lovemaking, she was both lusty and generous.

"It won't stop with a hug and you know it," she chastised.

He did know it, and he sighed deeply.

Dovie disappeared into her closet.

"Where are you going now?" he called.

"Out of sight, out of mind," she called back, giggling.

Frank tucked his hands behind his head and closed his eyes. He didn't bother to tell her it didn't work that way, at least not with him. The time they'd been apart, he'd done nothing but think of her. Thoughts of Dovie had tormented him day and night, until he was sure he'd lost his mind.

"Do that again," he said, savoring these moments in bed.

"Do what?" came her muffled question.

"Giggle."

"That's a silly thing to ask." But she did.

Frank loved the sound of it. He had to smile every time he heard her giggle. Or laugh. Or just heard her, period.

Dovie reappeared a minute later in a royal blue dress that buttoned up the front and belted at the waist. She braced one hand on the bed post as she slipped into her pumps.

"I'm going to do something with my hair and then I'm heading for church."

"No hug?"

One outraged glance answered the question. Frank laughed.

"I'm driving out to see Savannah, Laredo and the baby after church," she said.

"Do you mind if I tag along?" he asked.

Apparently his question caught her by surprise because she abruptly stopped brushing her hair and met his gaze. Her eyes softened. "You want to see the baby?"

Frank nodded. "That surprises you?"

"Yes. Do you like babies?"

"Actually I'm quite fond of children." It was his one regret in life. He'd give anything to have met Dovie as a young man and had children with her. She would have been a wonderful mother, just as she was a fabulous wife. "I would have liked kids of my own," he confessed with a hint of sadness.

She continued to stare at him and he noticed a sheen in her eyes—as though she was about to weep.

"Dovie?" he asked gently. "What's wrong?"

"Oh, damn," she said, sniffling. "I'm going to ruin my makeup and I don't have time to fuss with it now."

Frank climbed out of bed and reached for his robe. "What is it, Dovie?" he asked again.

"I always wanted children," she whispered. "So badly."

"I assumed you and Marvin decided not to have a

family," he said. They'd never discussed the subject, and it seemed strange to be doing so now.

"We couldn't have children," Dovie said. "Marvin...had the mumps as a teenager. I never complained, but..."

"Couldn't you have adopted?"

"Marvin wouldn't hear of it. I asked him to reconsider many times, and he refused. As much as I wanted to be a mother, I couldn't bring a child into our home when my husband felt the way he did."

"I'm so sorry, Dovie."

She attempted a smile. "It was a long time ago. I don't even know why I'm crying. But when you said how much you regretted not having children, I realized...why I love you so much."

The hug he'd been longing to collect all morning was now given with spontaneity. Frank held her tight and closed his eyes.

"Perhaps Savannah and Laredo will allow us to be substitute grandparents for Laura Rose," he whispered.

"I was thinking the same thing," Dovie said. She cradled his face and smiled, her eyes bright with unshed tears. "I love you, Frank Hennessey."

"I wish we'd met years ago," he said, voicing his earlier thoughts.

"We met at exactly the right time," she told him. "Any sooner and I would've been married."

"Any later, and you might've been with that judge you met on the cruise. The Canadian guy."

"Perhaps," she admitted, but skeptically. She

dabbed at her eyes. "Frank, I really must rush. You know how compulsive I am about being on time."

Frank checked his watch and knew if he hurried, he'd have time to dress and join her.

"I'll go with you," he said.

"Any reason?" she asked.

"Several reasons—but if I take the time to list them, we'll be walking in during the middle of Wade's sermon."

TRAVIS WAITED until Jeremy and Emma had left for school on Monday morning before he approached Nell, who was in the barn. "Ruth said I'd find you here," he said, feeling a bit awkward.

She was busy tending a newborn calf, but glanced up and smiled when he entered the barn. Kneeling in the straw, feeding the animal with a large baby bottle, she explained that the calf was one of twins and had been rejected by its mother. Once again Travis found himself admiring her compassionate capable nature.

They exchanged a few pleasantries as she worked, and when she'd finished, he opened the stall gate for her.

"Thanks," she said, walking over to the barn faucet where she washed and dried her hands. "So what can I do for you?"

"Do you have time to talk for a few minutes?"

"Why?" she asked bluntly.

"Well, I'm a writer," he explained, "and I'm working on a project that has to do with this area."

"All right," she told him, "but I haven't got time

to stop now. I need to go out and check the fence line. Tag along if you want."

"I'd enjoy that."

It wasn't until Nell led a gelding out of his stall that he realized she didn't intend to use the truck. Travis had ridden before—in Central Park. Years ago.

"You're going on a horse?" This probably wasn't the most intelligent question he'd ever asked. But he had to weigh his decision; on the one hand, he wouldn't mind some Western riding experience and it would be a chance to talk to her. On the other, he didn't want to risk looking like an idiot in front of a woman he found *very* attractive.

"You don't ride?" she asked in a voice that suggested she should have thought of that herself. She expertly placed the saddle on the gelding's back.

He hesitated before he answered. "A little."

"You're welcome to join me if you want. I've got Jake's saddle and you'd fit that comfortably."

"Is Jake's horse still around?" He figured that would have to be an older horse, which could only help his situation.

"Yup."

"Does he take to strangers?"

"Some."

"That's encouraging."

Nell tossed back her head and laughed, her long braid swaying. "Come on. It'll be fine."

Within minutes she'd brought a huge quarter horse out of his stall. Travis watched her saddle him, amazed at her ease with animals.

"Twister, meet Travis," she said, handing him the reins.

Travis found it amusing that she'd introduce the horse to him and not the other way around.

She led the two geldings outside into the sunlight. With a swift graceful motion, she mounted. "Do you need help getting up?" she asked when he stood there, unmoving.

He tried to look as if the question had insulted him; actually he wouldn't have objected to her holding the reins while he swung his leg over the saddle. With a mighty effort he did manage to scramble onto Twister—appreciating the fact that Nell didn't laugh at him.

As they started out, she set a slow easy pace, for which Travis was grateful.

"You wanted to ask me about the area?" she reminded him.

"Yeah," he said jerkily as his butt bounced against the saddle. "Te-ll m-e wh-at you kn-ow abou-t the gh-ost town."

Nell eased to a stop. "Ghost town?" she asked, frowning.

Twister, following the other horse's lead, stopped, as well. "If I remember correctly, it's called Bitter End."

"That's why you're here?" she asked. "Why you came to Promise?" She nudged her horse into a trot. "I thought you were a writer!"

"Yeah." Travis managed to keep pace with her,

but not without a price. If he survived this with all his teeth intact… "I am. And I w-want to—"

"Who told you about Bitter End?" she asked, stopping her horse again. The warmth she'd shown him had cooled noticeably. "You're from New York," she said. "You know Richard Weston, don't you?"

"I met him once, yes, but, Nell—"

"What did he tell you about Bitter End?" she demanded. "We were afraid of this," she muttered, not looking at him. "Everyone was."

"Afraid of what?"

"It doesn't concern you."

"Nell, if you'd give me a chance to explain." He shifted in the saddle, wishing he could touch her, reassure her in some way.

"You've already said everything I need to know. You're a friend of Richard's—"

"No, I'm not! Don't even think that. I met the man *once,* Nell. Just once. For a couple of hours. But it only took me a couple of minutes to see the kind of person he is."

That brought her up short. Her gaze returned to him, cautiously, as if she wasn't sure even now. But he could see she wanted to believe him, wanted to trust him. He yearned for that as much as he did her kisses.

"Valerie, my ex-wife, defended him—his state-appointed attorney. Richard mentioned the ghost town to her, and she told me. I was intrigued. A ghost town from the Old West, one that's basically undiscovered and hasn't been commercialized. I wanted to see it for myself, as background for a project I'm working on."

Nell said nothing. Then she said, "So you came all this way because of Bitter End?"

"That's what initially brought me here. Yes." But he liked the people of Promise, especially Nell and her family.

"Now I suppose you're looking for someone to take you there?"

"Yes—I want to see the town." He wanted to learn the history behind it, too. It was more than just a ghost town, if what Weston said was true, and Travis was hoping to unravel its secrets, include them in his book.

"I'm afraid you've made a wasted trip."

Her unwillingness to help him took him by surprise.

"I won't take you to Bitter End. And no one else will, either."

She sounded stubborn about it, but he could be stubborn, too. "I'm going there," Travis said. "I'll find it, Nell. Others have and so will I. But I'd rather we did it together."

"I can't...I won't. You don't understand."

"Then explain it to me."

"That town has done nothing but bring Promise grief. We just want to forget about it."

"What aren't you telling me?" he asked.

His question seemed to catch her off guard. She was silent for a long time; when she spoke again, it was with the seriousness of a woman who knows more than she wants to. "Nothing good has ever come out of that place. Nothing. The best thing for you is to forget you ever heard it mentioned."

"You've been there?"

"No," she admitted reluctantly.

"Then how do you know? Who told you? How many people have actually been in the town?"

Nell shrugged, not answering him.

"Then how can you be so sure if you've never been there yourself?"

"Everyone knows," she whispered.

"But you've found out where it is?"

She hesitated. "I have a vague idea where it might be."

"Where?"

Nell made a sweeping motion with her arm. "It's out there somewhere. Exactly where, I couldn't tell you."

"And even if you could, you wouldn't."

She nodded.

"This is a historic site. Doesn't anyone understand that?"

"Bitter End?" Nell laughed without amusement. "Why is it so important to you?" she asked again.

"Curiosity, mainly," he told her. "Like I told you, I'm a writer and I'm using a ghost town in my book. I wanted to make it as authentic as possible. I'm also intrigued by the mystery."

"Well, you'll have to ask someone else to take you, because I won't."

"Who, then?"

"I doubt that anyone will. But you might try Grady Weston."

Richard Weston's brother, Travis remembered.

"I wish you well, Travis. If you ride back to the house, Ruth will give you the Westons' phone number." Having said that, she galloped off, leaving him to make his own way back to the barn.

"All right, Twister," Travis said, doing his best to sound calm. "It's you and me, boy. We're friends, right?"

He pulled on the reins to reverse their direction. "See the barn, Twister?" He pointed toward it. "Let's walk there...slowly." Apparently the horse didn't care for Travis's tone of voice, because he took off at a gallop. It was all Travis could do to stay in the saddle.

When he reached the barn, he managed to dismount, then, legs shaky, succeeded in removing the saddle; the bridle he left for Nell. He coaxed Twister into the stall with his name on it, then tottered back to the house.

That afternoon when he phoned Grady Weston, he learned Nell wasn't the only one with strong feelings about Bitter End. It took him several hours to reach the other man; once he did, Weston practically bit his head off. In no uncertain terms, he made it clear that he'd have no part in satisfying Travis's curiosity. Travis supposed Grady's aggression could be attributed to his negative feelings about his brother.

Nell sought him out in the bunkhouse an hour or

so later. "Did you speak to Grady?" she asked, her mood more conciliatory, or so it seemed.

"Briefly."

"And?"

"And he isn't willing to show me where Bitter End is, either. Just like you predicted."

She nodded. "You'll be leaving, then?"

"No."

It wasn't the answer she'd expected; he could tell by the way her eyes widened. "No?"

"I'm going to locate Bitter End, Nell, with or without this town's help."

Chapter Five

Nell was furious with Travis, but she didn't know why. That morning, as she'd ridden across her property, checking the fence line, she'd thought about him. And she'd thought about Bitter End.

Just when she was beginning to like Travis, really like him, she'd discovered that he had an ulterior motive. He'd made friends with her children, kissed and flattered her, pampered Ruth. All this because he wanted her to take him to Bitter End.

He'd been open enough about telling her he was a writer. Now everything was beginning to fall neatly into place. His job was what had brought him to Promise, probably with all expenses paid by his publisher. She should have suspected he had an ulterior motive for befriending her and her family. He was planning to write about Bitter End—although she didn't really know why. He'd told her he was working on a book. What kind of book? she wondered, and what, exactly, did he hope to achieve?

What *really* infuriated Nell was his comment about Bitter End being a historical site. He seemed to be implying that Texans were a bunch of hicks who didn't appreciate their own history. Well, that was the furthest thing from the truth! She knew as much about this state's history as anyone around here. In fact, she thought grimly, maybe she respected history *more* than that...that Easterner. That wannabe cowboy. Because at least she recognized that the past still had power over the present—the way Bitter End had power over Promise.

Everything she'd ever heard about the town had been negative. Her family's roots went back to the original settlement, which had been founded shortly after the Civil War; so did Jake's. Something ugly had happened there, something horrible. Whatever it was, it'd been disturbing enough to cause everyone to vacate the town. No one knew why, and for years and years the town was rarely mentioned. When people did discuss Bitter End, they spoke in hushed whispers. Now some ignorant Yankee wanted to turn it into a historical site!

When Richard Weston was fleeing the authorities, he'd holed up in the town, and that made sense. He belonged there, if anyone did. Richard had figured out where the town was partly because of Savannah. Despite Grady's objections, she'd explored the countryside to find Bitter End in her quest for lost roses.

Nell had asked Savannah about it, and she'd watched a shiver move down the other woman's arms as she recounted her visit. Savannah had mentioned an impressive find in the cemetery—Nell had forgotten what the roses were called. Savannah had gone on to describe the eerie feeling that had come over her; she'd hurriedly taken the rosebush and left.

Later, convinced she'd allowed her imagination to run away with her, Savannah had returned, hoping to rescue other roses. She'd told Nell the most astonishing fact. Nothing grew inside the town. Not even a weed. The town was completely without life.

Yet all Travis saw was a money-making opportunity. He'd come to Promise to dig up information about a place best forgotten. Despite everything she'd said, everything Grady had told him, he'd insisted he was going to find Bitter End. Then he'd write about it and attract more people, strangers, to the town. Soon tourists would pour into Promise and their lives would no longer be their own. No one here knew why the settlers had abandoned Bitter End—and Nell thought it was better to leave things that way, to let whatever secrets were buried there lie forgotten. She wasn't the only one to feel this way.

She wished now that Travis had chosen to move into town, to the bed and breakfast. Phil and Mary would know better how to handle his curiosity.

Nell closed her eyes and groaned at the memory of how pleased she'd been when he decided to stay on at the ranch. She felt lost and inadequate; worse, she felt foolish for having allowed this man to weave his way into her life.

She understood now that he had his own reasons for kissing her, for encouraging her kids, for staying at her ranch.

Reasons that had nothing to do with *her*.

SAVANNAH HAD JUST PLACED Laura in her crib when someone knocked on the back door.

"Anyone home?" Unexpectedly her brother stepped into the kitchen.

"Grady, come in." Savannah didn't bother to hide her surprise. It was unusual for him to drop by the house on his own. Her home was only a short distance from the ranch house, and while Grady visited often, it was almost always with Caroline and Maggie.

"How are you feeling?" he asked.

"Wonderful." The birth had been the most incredible experience of her life. Savannah had known there'd be pain and had prepared as best she could for labor. What she hadn't known was how she'd feel afterward—that sensation of stunned joy and amazement, that surge of accomplishment and pride.

In her arms she'd held living proof of her love for Laredo. Together they had created this new life, this beautiful child.

"I was just about to have a cup of tea," Savannah said, crossing to the stove. "Would you care to join me?"

Grady removed his hat and set it on the oak table. "Sure."

He'd get around to explaining his visit in his own time. Savannah could see no need to rush him.

She filled two cups and carried them to the kitchen table, then sat across from him. He asked her a few questions about the baby, but she noticed that he wasn't really paying attention to her responses. He was thinking, weighing his next words, wondering if he should approach her about whatever he'd *really* come about. After living with Grady all those years, Savannah knew him well, better than he realized.

"Nell's guest called me," he said casually as he stirred a second spoonful of sugar into his tea.

Nell's guest! That was the reason for this visit. The sugar had given him away. Grady seldom added sugar to anything, and two teaspoons was particularly telling.

"I don't believe I've met him," she said.

"His name's Travis Grant. Seems nice enough—Caroline and I met him at the rodeo."

"Oh?"

"Like I said, he phoned yesterday."

"Really?" She remained calm, unaffected.

"He knows Richard."

The words hit her without warning and Savannah stared at her brother. A sinking sensation came over her, and a deep sadness. Her younger brother had been sentenced to twenty-five years in prison without parole. It hurt to think of Richard locked behind bars. She'd written him twice, once shortly after he'd been taken back to New York to stand trial and then after he'd received his sentence. He hadn't answered either letter.

"Actually it was Grant's ex-wife who introduced him to Richard," Grady added. "Apparently she was the court-appointed attorney who defended him."

"Did this Travis Grant tell you what he wanted?" It went without saying that if Richard was involved, their brother was looking out for his own selfish interests.

Savannah often wondered what had turned Richard into a man who acted without conscience or compassion. Her heart ached every time she thought about him. *Why?* She would never understand why he'd used his family, why he'd betrayed good people, why he'd exploited the vulnerable.

Twice he'd stolen from her and Grady. The first time had been the day they'd buried their parents. While Grady and Savannah stood beside the grave, Richard was sneaking away with the forty thousand dollars in cash left them by their father. Six years later he'd returned with a hard-luck story, needing a place to stay.

Savannah blamed herself for what happened next, since she'd been the one who convinced Grady to let him stay. But Grady wouldn't let her accept the blame. He insisted they were equally at fault because he'd known what kind of man Richard was and had closed his eyes to the obvious. Both of them felt an obligation to family, and they both wanted to believe their brother had changed.

Within a few months of arriving back in Promise, Richard had charged thousands of dollars at various stores in town, using the Weston accounts, the Weston name. When it was all uncovered, Richard had conveniently disappeared, leaving Grady to foot the bill. Only after he was gone did Grady and Savannah learn the whole truth. Richard had been on the run—from his unsavory creditors and "partners" and from the law. The New York City DA's office had a list of charges long enough to put him behind bars until he was an old man.

What hurt Savannah most wasn't the fact that Richard had destroyed her faith in him; it was learning that her brother was guilty of bilking immigrants. He'd helped get them into the country illegally, then forced them to live and work in deplorable conditions. If that wasn't bad enough, he'd confiscated their money. He'd been one of several men accused and convicted of a crime so heinous she cringed every time she thought about it. That her own flesh and blood had hurt innocent people in this way had devastated her. Men, women and children had suffered because of her brother.

"Richard told Travis about Bitter End," Grady continued.

Savannah exhaled a deep sigh. "So Travis is here to find it?"

"That's what he says."

"For what purpose?"

"I don't know for sure. He's a writer, so I imagine he's doing research for an article about Bitter End."

Savannah thoughtfully replaced her cup. "What did you tell him?"

Grady scowled, then met her eyes.

"Grady Weston, what did you do?"

He gave her a wry smile. "Now I know where Caroline gets that tone of voice. I should have recognized it was from my very own sister."

"You were rude, weren't you?"

He shrugged. "I told him to mind his own damned business. I said there wasn't a soul in this town who'd help him, and advised him to give up his search now."

"Oh, Grady."

"I don't think he's going to take my advice."

Savannah mulled over this information for a couple of minutes. "I'm beginning to think it might be a good idea to put the past to rest."

"What do you mean?"

"No one knows what happened in Bitter End," Savannah reminded him. "No one's sure why the entire town up and moved. It almost seemed to take place overnight. From what Ellie told me, there were still cans on the shelves in the mercantile store. People left furniture, clothing, all kinds of valuables behind. They were in such a hurry to leave they couldn't get away fast enough."

"It was probably some disease or something to do with the water," Grady reasoned.

"Perhaps. I'm sure there's a logical explanation for what happened. All I'm saying is it's time to find out what went wrong and why. And who better than a writer? Someone who knows how to research and how to separate fact from legend. A stranger. Someone who can approach this without the emotions and fears we all have about Bitter End."

Grady didn't look convinced. "As far as I'm concerned, it's best not to disrupt the past."

Savannah considered her brother's words. "A year ago I would have agreed with you."

"But not now?" he asked, sounding surprised.

"Not now," she said. "Having Richard home was a painful and bitter lesson. It taught me that turning away from the truth, ignoring trouble, is a dangerous thing to do."

"It isn't like we're hiding anything," Grady insisted. "No one knows what went wrong in Bitter End."

"Then don't you think it's time we did?"

"Why?"

"Because, as the Bible says, the truth shall make you free."

"I'm free now," Grady said. He stood up and walked over to stare out the window above the sink.

"We aren't free, Grady," she offered gently. "Otherwise we wouldn't be this afraid."

"I'm not afraid," he countered sharply.

She didn't contradict or challenge him, but she knew that wasn't entirely true. Whatever had happened all those years ago in Bitter End still haunted them. In Savannah's opinion, it was time to bring it into the light, expose it and deal with the consequences. Each generation has been influenced by Bitter End, whether they admitted it or not.

Savannah recalled the first time she'd heard about the ghost town. Grady had been the one to tell her. He'd heard their parents talking when he was a teenager, discussing this secret place and its mysterious past. Afterward Grady, Cal and Glen had decided to find the town and, in the manner of boys, went about making it their own private adventure. Savannah had wanted to join them, but they didn't want a girl hanging around.

She would have gone to look for it on her own, except that Grady had said he'd take her to Bitter End once he knew where it was. Naturally she had to promise not to tell anyone, especially the Patterson brothers.

The three boys had eventually located the town. But Grady never did take her there; it was the first and only time he'd broken his word. All he'd tell her was that something horrible must have happened in that place. She remembered how he'd closed his eyes and shivered, and vowed he was never going back.

His words had remained with her for a long time.

About a year ago she'd sought out the town herself. According to an article she'd read, abandoned cemeteries and homesteads were often a good source of nineteenth-century roses. That motivation was strong enough to let her put aside her apprehensions about the place. After weeks of searching, she'd stumbled upon the town, hidden deep in the hills. Only then did she understand what her brother had meant.

The instant she'd stepped onto the main street of Bitter End, a feeling had come over her, an eerie sensation of anxiety and dread. And yet she couldn't have named the reason, couldn't have said what she feared.

Afterward she managed to convince herself that she'd imagined the entire episode. So she returned. But she'd been right the first time. Something was there—not a ghost, but a persistent feeling of intense sadness, a haunting sorrow.

"Let him do it, Grady," she said, releasing a pent-up sigh. "Let him find out what happened in Bitter End. Let Travis Grant expose whatever wrongs were committed there."

"You think a stranger can do that?"

"He can start."

Her brother pondered her words, his face thoughtful. Then he slowly shook his head. "It isn't often I disagree with you, but I do now."

"You're not going to help Travis find Bitter End?"

"No."

She accepted his decision, but deep down, she wondered how long it would take him to change his mind. Grady was having second thoughts already; otherwise he wouldn't have come to her in the middle of the day. Especially during the busiest time of the year.

Savannah knew she was right, and she knew Grady would eventually see it. Beneath his doubts he, too, felt a need to lay this matter to rest once and for all.

TALK ABOUT STIRRING UP a hornets' nest, Travis mused as he sat and stared at his blank computer screen. Nell had avoided him all day. And after speaking to Grady Weston, it wouldn't surprise him if the other man was busy rounding up ranchers to tar and feather him. All this because he'd asked a few questions about a ghost town. Why were they so intent on keeping this secret, whatever it was?

He wondered if the people here even knew what

had happened in that town. Perhaps they were being influenced by fears and vague suspicions rather than facts.

Travis preferred to face problems, not let them fester. He believed in knowledge and the power of truth. Shutting down the computer, he leaned back in the chair, hands behind his head, reviewing his options. Soon, however, he discovered that his thoughts weren't on Bitter End anymore.

Instead, he was thinking about Nell. Despite her disapproval of his plans, he admired her strength and courage. He was attracted to her, he admitted that, and he sensed she felt the same way. Even if she preferred to ignore it.

Travis decided to get a breath of fresh air and he reached for a sweatshirt. He walked out of the bunkhouse and around the yard, stopping to say hello to Yucky. As he neared the front of the house, he was pleased to find Ruth sitting outside in a rocker, crocheting.

"Travis," she said with a friendly smile. "Come join me."

After Nell's silence and Grady Weston's explosive anger, Travis was more than grateful for a cordial greeting. He climbed the steps and leaned against the porch railing.

"Was that you I saw on Twister yesterday morning?" Ruth asked.

"Yeah," he said, not mentioning that he considered himself lucky to be in one piece.

"That gelding's got a mind of his own."

"So I discovered."

Ruth laughed, and he grinned himself. The older woman's fingers agilely worked the yarn, never slowing. It amazed him that she could carry on a conversation without disrupting her work.

"What are you making?" It wasn't what Travis wanted to ask—he had questions about Nell. However, any inquiries would have to be a natural part of the conversation. Unobtrusive.

"An afghan," she answered. "I find crocheting relaxes me."

He started to comment, but Ruth broke in. "You're curious about Nell, aren't you?"

Her directness surprised as much as pleased him. "I won't deny that I am."

Ruth nodded. "She's interested in you, as well. I haven't lived with her all these years not to understand the way she thinks. Have you kissed her yet?"

Slightly embarrassed, Travis laughed. "Yes."

"And?"

"And it was very good."

"You plan on bedding her?"

"That's none of your business," Travis said. He wasn't accustomed to discussing his love live with elderly women, or with anyone else, for that matter. However, he'd certainly fantasized about making love to Nell. She was a passionate woman. Their one kiss had given him a glimpse of that. She was also a woman who didn't believe in half measures; it was all or nothing. He knew that when it came to love, loyalty or friendship, she held nothing in reserve.

For that very reason, she was reluctant to become involved with another man. The potential for pain was too great.

That was something Travis understood. The breakup of his marriage had been one of the most painful ordeals of his life. He'd loved Valerie and been stunned to learn that she wanted out of their marriage, that she'd viewed their lives together as a temporary thing until someone "better" came along.

She'd been intrigued with Travis because he was a writer. Later she'd urged him to give it up and get a real job. Everyone knew there wasn't any real money in publishing. Not unless you were Stephen King. She'd been scornful about his financial prospects.

The irony was that she'd left him too soon. Not long after their divorce, he'd hit it big and his books had been selling almost as fast as the publisher could print them. She laughed about her lack of insight now. Once, a year before, she'd tried to lure him into bed, saying she'd made a terrible mistake and wanted him back. It'd flattered his ego, but in the end he'd told her he wasn't interested in sleeping with a married woman.

In the years since the divorce Travis had rarely dated. Friends had tried to match him up and he knew he was considered a catch. But he preferred the comfort of solitude; being alone was better than being with the wrong person.

The next time he fell in love, it would be with a woman who loved him back, heart and soul. A woman willing to make as strong a commitment to him as he did to her. In the years since Val had left him, he hadn't met such a woman.

Until Nell.

"She's a bit prickly at the moment," Ruth said, and for the first time since he'd joined her, the older woman's fingers paused. "Did you two have a spat?"

"Not really," Travis said. He didn't bring up the ghost town for fear Ruth would respond the same way Nell and Grady Weston had.

Ruth scowled. "I don't know what's wrong with her, then, but she'll come around. Be patient, you hear?"

Suddenly the screen door burst open and Nell stuck her head out. "Ruth, have you seen—" She stopped midsentence when she noticed Travis.

"Seen what?" Ruth asked, looking almost gleeful at Nell's reaction to him.

"My kitchen scissors."

"Top drawer, left-hand side. Look under the church directory."

"Afternoon, Nell," Travis said.

"Oh—h, Travis."

It shocked him how his heart raced, how exhilarated he was by the sight of her.

"I'm putting a chicken on to roast," Nell said, her voice unmistakably nervous.

"Let me help," he insisted, and didn't give her a chance to object.

"Yes, let Travis help," Ruth murmured, sounding as if she was about to burst into laughter. "Nell's never cooked a chicken in her life."

Nell marched into the kitchen with Travis following, and just the way she walked told him she wasn't
pleased. "I don't need any help roasting a chicken,"
she announced brusquely.

"I didn't think you did. I just wanted to talk to
you."

"If it's about Bitter End, there's nothing to say."

"At least explain to me why everyone reacts this
way the minute I say the name."

"I already have."

"Tell me again."

"No." She paused. "Bitter End's the only reason
you came here, isn't it?"

"Yes." He wasn't going to lie.

"Then there's nothing to talk about."

"There's everything to talk about."

She stared at him, her expression wary.

"I want to know what it is about this ghost town
that evokes this type of response. Don't you want to
find out what caused everyone to leave? Aren't you
curious?"

"I don't need to know—no one does," she said,
then dragged in a deep breath. "You don't understand."

"Then explain it to me."

"I'm afraid," she admitted reluctantly. "Afraid
it'll be like opening Pandora's box. I really believe
that in this case, ignorance might be bliss."

He frowned.

She shook her head. "Leave it, Travis...please?"

"Fine. I'll leave it—but just for the moment." He

lowered his voice. "Right now I'm more concerned with settling this matter between you and me. We were on the brink of getting to know each other."

"No, we weren't," she denied vehemently. "You're reading more into one kiss than you should... You caught me at a weak moment."

"I want to catch you again."

"No," she said with such force she appeared to surprise herself. "Don't even try."

It took a moment for her words to sink in, and when they did, a slow satisfied smile appeared on his lips. "You liked it that much, did you?"

"No!" she said. "I...I wish it'd never happened."

"It frightened you half to death, didn't it?"

She shook her head, which sent her braid flying. "This is the most ridiculous conversation I've ever had. It'd be best if you left now."

"Not on your life. Oh, Nell, sweet Nell, don't you realize I felt it, too?"

"There was nothing to feel, dammit!" She whirled around and headed for the sink. A chicken rested in a pan on the countertop. Reaching for it, she thrust it under the faucet.

"It's only natural for you to be afraid," he said in low soothing tones as he slowly advanced toward her. He rested his hands on her shoulders, but the instant she felt his touch, she jumped.

"Nell, sweet Nell," he whispered, and kissed the side of her neck.

"Don't do that!"

"Then what about this?" He ran his tongue around

her ear and felt a sense of triumph at the almost imperceptible sound of her moan.

"Not that, either," she said, obviously struggling to put some starch in her voice.

"And this?" he asked as he wrapped his arms around her middle.

The chicken fell unheeded into the sink.

"No one's going to help you..."

"Help me what?"

"Look for the town."

"Fine, I'll look for it on my own." He spread a series of nibbling kisses along her neck.

"You won't find it."

"That's okay, because I've found you."

A shiver moved through her. "I think you should go."

"Where?" He was far too involved in kissing her neck and her ear to pay much attention. Her words said one thing and her body another. Her hands hung idle at her sides and she let her head fall back, exposing her throat to his mouth.

"Somewhere else..." Her words were barely audible.

He turned her carefully to face him and smiled at her tightly shut eyes. "Open your eyes, Nell," he instructed. "I want you to know who's kissing you."

"I don't want you to..."

He laughed softly and cupped her face with both hands. "I'd expect you to be honest, if not with me, then with yourself."

She opened her eyes, and he knew his words had

hit their mark. "Good, very good," he whispered, and gently lowered his mouth to hers.

His lips had just made contact when the phone on the kitchen wall rang. The sound startled them, broke them apart.

Travis groaned. Every nerve, every sense had been readied to enjoy their kiss.

After two rings, Nell answered it. "Hello," she said, her voice trembling, but only a little.

It surprised him how close to normal she sounded. Travis wasn't sure he could have pulled it off nearly as well.

He watched as her gaze revealed surprise. "It's for you." She handed him the receiver.

"Me?" Only a few people knew he was in Promise. "Travis Grant," he said into the mouthpiece.

"This is Grady Weston."

Grady Weston. Travis didn't think victims were normally contacted in advance of a tar and feathering.

"I've changed my mind," the other man said gruffly.

"About what?"

"Taking you to Bitter End. Be ready by noon tomorrow."

"Fine... Great!"

Travis replaced the receiver. Nell stood a few feet away, with arms crossed, her eyes worried.

"Grady's decided to help me find Bitter End, after all," he said.

Chapter Six

Only eleven-thirty. Travis glanced at his watch, pleased that Grady Weston had agreed to show him the way to Bitter End. He wasn't sure what to expect once they got there, especially considering people's reactions every time he mentioned it.

Killing time, he walked over to the paddock outside the barn where Jeremy's horse, Dot Com, ran free. Earlier, Jeremy had told him proudly that he'd come up with the name himself. Now Travis stood and watched the young animal racing back and forth, kicking up his hind legs, running for the sheer joy of it.

The air was clear and Travis inhaled deeply. Until now he hadn't spent much time in Texas other than book signing and media tours in cities like Dallas and Houston. He'd written several stories set at least partly in Texas, but his research had been limited to libraries. The greater his success, the tighter his schedule and the less time he had for personal investigations. A shopping center in San Antonio or an airport in Dallas hadn't prepared him for what he'd discovered here in the hill country. He found the vast openness awe-inspiring and the life so dissimilar from his existence in Manhattan he felt as though he were visiting an alien planet.

The silence was perhaps the most profound difference. Without even realizing it, Travis had grown accustomed to city noise. Taxis honking, buses, shouting, street musicians, the clang and clatter of vendors. He'd lived in Manhattan for almost fifteen years now and hadn't realized how loud it could be. These few days in the country with Nell and her family had changed his whole perspective.

To his surprise he'd slept all night, every night. He never drafted his books while on the road, but the tranquility here had both relaxed and inspired him, and he was overwhelmed with ideas. He'd started to jot down a few thoughts on his laptop last night, and before he knew it four hours had passed. It'd felt like fifteen minutes.

His great-grandparents had been farmers, he remembered. He wondered if he'd inherited some of his ancestors' love of the land, though he'd never experienced country living. His parents had divorced when he was young, and he'd lived in New York state for most of his life.

He heard a sound behind him and glanced over his shoulder. Nell. A smile automatically came to his lips. He was convinced she didn't have a clue how beautiful she was. His attraction to her was as strong as anything he'd known; it still surprised him.

Ruth's probing questions of the day before hadn't

helped, either. Thoughts of making love to Nell had begun to fill his dreams, and while the physical attraction was intense, he found Nell compelling in other ways. He loved her determination, her sense of family, her pride in the ranch and the sheer grit it'd demanded to keep Twin Canyons afloat.

"Do you have a few minutes?" she asked, coming to stand beside him.

"For you, always," he said.

She rested one arm on the top rail of the paddock fence and studied Dot Com as though she needed to compose her thoughts before speaking.

"Problems?" he asked.

She shook her head, and the long braid swung back and forth.

One day he'd enjoy undoing that braid of hers, letting her hair slip unrestrained through his fingers. He imagined filling his hands with it and drawing her face to his and kissing her.

"I...I don't know if Jeremy and Emma know about Bitter End," she said, her voice low. "Naturally there was some talk after Richard was found, but mostly everyone kept it as hush-hush as possible."

"And you're afraid I'm going to tell them?"

"Yes."

"I take it you'd rather I didn't?"

"Please..."

But as she spoke, Travis noticed the hesitation in her voice, as though she wasn't sure this silence would be right for her children.

"You really feel it's right for them not to know?"

A small smile trembled at the edges of her mouth. "Am I that readable?"

"No." He placed his boot on the bottom rail next to hers and, leaning forward, rested his arms on the top one. "I'm beginning to know you."

She smiled. "You think so, do you?"

Her eyes went serious then, and Travis knew this matter of the ghost town and whether or not her children should know continued to bother her.

"They'll hear about Bitter End one way or another," he said.

"The children and I have never discussed it," Nell told him, "although I'm almost convinced they heard something about it after Richard's accident. But they didn't ask and I didn't volunteer any information. For all I know, Jeremy and Emma know everything there is to know about the town."

"I won't say anything in their presence if that's what you think is best." He wanted to reassure Nell that he was worthy of her trust, that her confidence in him was well placed.

"There's something else," Nell said, her expression growing truly somber now. She turned and looked away, as though she found Dot Com's antics of sudden interest.

"You can speak to me about anything you want, Nell."

"I have no right to ask you this."

"Ask me, anyway," he insisted gently. He suspected she was wondering about his divorce. She glanced at him, and he saw the gratitude in her eyes.

"It's natural to be curious about me," he encouraged. "I feel the same way about you. I like you, Nell, a great deal, and I'd welcome the opportunity to deepen our friendship."

She hung her head, and he was sure he'd embarrassed her.

"Ask me," he urged.

"Travis...please, don't go. That's what I'm asking."

"You don't want me to go to Bitter End?" He couldn't fathom why, after everything that had been said.

"I've never told anyone this—not even Jake." She faced him, meeting his eyes steadily. "Once, as a child, I heard my parents talking about the town. I was young and impressionable, and I've never forgotten it."

"What did they say?"

She shook her head. "I don't recall exactly. All I can remember is they were worried that one day I'd ask questions about it and find it myself. They'd decided not to mention it until I came to them."

"Which is what you've planned to do with your own children."

Apparently she hadn't made the connection because her eyes widened as she recognized the truth. "You don't understand, Travis, my father was a big man. Nothing intimidated him—but he was terrified of Bitter End."

"He'd been there?" Travis asked.

Nell nodded. "Once, with a bunch of his friends.

Whatever he saw or experienced disturbed him, and he was anxious to protect me."

"Is that what you're trying to do for me, Nell?"

She nodded, then shrugged. "You're from New York City—what do you know about the Old West? There are dangers you wouldn't understand."

"I'll be with Grady."

"Yes, but..."

"Does this mean you care about me?" He wanted to hear her admit it.

"Of course I care about you," she returned impatiently. "I care about everyone."

"It'd do wonders for my ego if you'd admit you cared for me in a more...personal way," he said, loving the way her cheeks instantly filled with color.

She frowned, dismissing his remark. "Call Grady and tell him you've changed your mind," she pleaded urgently.

It hurt Travis to refuse Nell anything.

Her eyes held his, and her fingers squeezed his arm.

"I have to go," he told her with genuine regret. "I'd do almost anything for you, but what you ask is impossible." Even as he spoke, he knew he'd disappointed her.

Another woman might have responded with anger. That had been Val's reaction when she didn't get her way. Not Nell's. Instead, she offered him a resigned smile, as though she'd expected him to refuse. He could tell from the closed expression on her face that she'd retreated emotionally.

He was about to argue, explain himself, when the

screen door opened and Ruth appeared, holding the cordless phone.

"For you, Travis," she said. "It's Grady Weston."

Travis took the phone and lifted it to his ear. "Hello," he said crisply, damning the other man's timing.

"Problems," Grady said, skipping the usual chit-chat. "I've got a water pump down. Which means I'm not going to be able to take you out to Bitter End this afternoon."

Damn, Travis thought. It wasn't Grady's fault, but his time here was limited; not only that, he felt as though he'd just fought—and won—a dreadful battle asserting his need and his right to go there, and now the opportunity had been snatched away.

"Savannah's been though," Grady continued.

Travis was shocked. Surely Grady didn't expect a new mother to go traipsing all over the countryside!

"She could draw you a decent map," Grady said, "and give you some directions. Then you could find it on your own."

Travis's sagging spirits buoyed. "Good idea. I'll give Savannah a call."

"I apologize if this puts you out any."

"I'll find it on my own, don't worry."

They ended the conversation in the same abrupt way they'd started it.

Ruth and Nell were both watching him when he finished. "Grady's got problems with a water pump."

"But you're going, anyway," Nell said, and her lovely face tightened.

"Yes, I'm going, anyway."

Nell nodded sadly, then turned and walked away.

GRADY WAS LATE getting back to the ranch for dinner, and Caroline found herself glancing out the window every few minutes. Shortly after she'd arrived home from the post office, Savannah had phoned, explaining that a water pump had broken. Both Laredo and Grady were working on it, and neither man was likely to be home soon.

Caroline hadn't been a rancher's wife long, but she'd lived around cattlemen most of her life. Caring for the herd took priority over just about everything. The herd was the family's livelihood and their future.

Savannah had mentioned something else, too, and that was the reason Caroline awaited Grady's return so anxiously. Her sister-in-law had told her Nell's dude-ranch guest knew Richard.

Caroline was astonished by the apprehension those few words could bring her. She hadn't realized Richard held such power over her. It'd been months since they'd last heard news of him. Richard had been nothing but a source of heartache for the family—and for her.

The fact that Nell's would-be cowboy was an acquaintance of Richard's explained a great deal. Grady had been restless and short-tempered the night before, tossing and turning. Caroline had awakened around two and found him sitting on the porch in the very spot his father had once favored. He hugged her close, kissed her, then after a few minutes, sent her back to bed.

Caroline had known something was troubling him, but not what. He'd tell her, as he always did, when he was ready. That was how Grady operated. But now she had reason to suspect that his recent bout of restlessness was somehow connected to Richard.

At six Caroline ate dinner with Maggie and put a plate aside for Grady. Maggie was playing with her dolls in her bedroom when Grady and Wiley, their foreman, rode into the yard.

Caroline moved onto the porch and savored the sight of her husband, sitting his horse with natural ease. His dog, Bones, trotted along behind. Bones was the grandson of Grady's beloved old dog, Rocket, who'd died the previous year. He looked a great deal like his granddaddy. The minute he'd been born, Grady had picked him out of the litter and trained him personally.

Her heart swelled with pride and love as she watched her husband dismount and head into the barn.

"Welcome home," she said when he returned a short time later. His steps were slow and heavy and she knew how tired he must be.

Grady's face revealed his pleasure at being home and finding her waiting for him. Caroline held her arms open. Grady didn't hesitate to walk into them and hold her tight.

"The pump's working?" she asked.

"Good as new," he said as he released her.

"You hungry?"

"Starving," he growled.

"Then wash up and I'll warm dinner for you."

When he came back into the room he seemed revived. Wearing a lazy grin, he said, "Maggie's decided on a name for the baby."

Months earlier Grady had allowed the child to name a new born colt—which he'd subsequently given her for her sixth birthday—and she'd chosen Moonbeam. When they learned Caroline was pregnant, Maggie had assumed she'd be naming her little brother or sister, as well. No amount of explaining could convince her otherwise.

Caroline could just imagine the name her daughter had chosen. "I'm afraid to ask."

"For a boy, she's decided on Buckwheat."

"Buckwheat?"

"And for a girl, Darla."

"Ah." Caroline understood now. The television had been on earlier that afternoon and Maggie had been watching reruns of "Our Gang."

"I'll talk to her again," Caroline promised, thinking she'd let Maggie go through the baby-name book with her. She wanted her daughter to feel part of things, but Maggie needed to understand that the ultimate decision rested with her and Grady.

"I don't know," Grady said with a thoughtful look. He pulled out a kitchen chair and sat down. "Buckwheat has a nice ring to it, don't you think? Buckwheat Weston. And we wouldn't need to worry about any other kids in his class having the same name."

"Grady!"

Her husband chuckled, reaching for his fork.

Caroline poured herself a glass of iced tea and sat down across from him. "I talked to Savannah this afternoon," she said, hoping he'd bring up the subject of Richard.

Grady didn't so much as blink as he took his first bite of pork chop.

If anything bothered him, he didn't show it. Nothing, it seemed, would deter him from enjoying his meal. A man had his priorities, thought Caroline with wry amusement. He'd wait until he'd finished his meal.

"Did Savannah mention that Travis Grant knows Richard?" he finally asked.

Caroline nodded.

"You weren't going to say anything?" He regarded her quizzically, as though her silence had surprised him.

"I knew you'd mention it eventually."

Grady reached for his coffee and held the mug between both hands. "It bothers me knowing my brother's in prison," he admitted. "God knows it's what Richard deserves..." He leaned forward, set the mug aside and reached for Caroline's hand. He looked into her eyes and she felt his love, stronger than anything she'd ever known.

"I couldn't sleep last night," he told her.

"I know."

"I didn't understand it, not at first. Every time I closed my eyes, Richard was there. Dammit, this is my brother, my little brother. Mom and Dad would have wanted me to look out for him, but—''

"No." Caroline shook her head and tightened her fingers around his. She believed that Grady's parents would have wanted Richard to accept responsibility for his own actions. She told him so.

"Deep down I realize that," Grady said, and released a deep sigh. "But last night I realized something else." He lowered his gaze. "I'm afraid of Richard."

"Afraid?"

Grady nodded. "It's idiotic, I know, but those fears seemed very real in the dead of night."

"But why? He's locked away. He can't hurt us or—''

"My greatest fear," Grady said, interrupting her, "is that one day he'd try to take away what is most precious to me. You, Maggie and the baby."

"Oh, Grady, it'd never, never happen."

"I know it doesn't make sense. But remember that one of Richard's great pleasures was grabbing whatever he thought anyone else wanted," he said bitterly. "Especially something that was important to me."

"Grady, don't you know how much I love you?" she demanded. Had the situation been reversed, though, she suspected she'd feel exactly the same. All she could think to do was reassure him.

Standing, Caroline walked to the other side of the table and sat on his lap. She draped her arms around his neck, then lowered her mouth to his. Their kisses grew in length and intensity, stoking fires of need.

"I've changed my mind," Maggie announced as she stepped into the kitchen. She clutched some small stuffed animals in her arms. "Buckwheat is a dumb name for a boy."

Caroline sighed and pressed her forehead against Grady's shoulder.

"I was just getting attached to it," he said, sounding almost like his normal self. "Do you have any other ideas?"

"Beanie," the six-year-old suggested next. "We're gonna have our own Beanie baby."

Caroline groaned and Grady chuckled.

DINNERTIME CAME and went and Travis had yet to return. Nell did the dishes, but kept her eye trained on the dirt road that wound down from the two-lane highway. He'd been gone the better part of seven hours.

"Are you worried?" Ruth asked as Nell dried her hands on a dishtowel.

"About what?" she asked, pretending she didn't know what Ruth was talking about. She hated being this transparent, but she couldn't stop worrying about Travis. He'd gone in search of Bitter End all on his own, despite her request that he give up this stupid search. It hurt that he'd refused to heed her advice. It'd taken every ounce of pride she possessed to ask him to stay away.

Now this.

"You've been looking at the clock every five

minutes," Ruth pointed out. "Travis will be back any moment—there's no need to worry."

"How can you be sure?" Nell asked in a rare display of temper. Anything could have happened. Anything. The scenarios that flashed through her mind saw him dead and bleeding at the side of the road. Or inside a collapsed building, like Richard.

"Did you phone Savannah and Grady?" Ruth returned.

In her panic Nell hadn't thought to contact them. It made all the sense in the world that Travis would stop off and discuss what he'd discovered with Grady. She was surprised she hadn't thought of it herself. Foolish, that was what she'd been. Foolish and histrionic.

Her heart leaped with renewed hope. Casting her mother-in-law an apologetic glance, Nell reached for the cordless phone. Caroline answered on the second ring.

"Hi, it's Nell," she announced cheerfully. "I don't suppose Travis Grant is there?"

If Caroline was surprised to hear from her, she didn't let it show. "No, Nell, we haven't seen him."

"Not at all?" Nell couldn't hide the apprehension in her voice.

"Is everything all right?" Caroline asked.

"I'm sure it is," Nell replied, making light of her concern. By sheer willpower she forced her pulse to return to normal. This not knowing was hell. *Hell!* "I expected he'd be back before now, that's all. I'm sure everything's all right."

They chatted a few minutes longer and Nell promised she'd phone back if Travis hadn't shown up at Twin Canyons by nine.

Nine o'clock. Nell glanced at the clock on the stove. Two more hours. The day's light was already beginning to fade. She didn't know what Ruth thought when she said she was going out to look for him herself. But she figured she'd go stir-crazy waiting another minute; another two hours was out of the question.

She grabbed the truck keys off the peg on the back-porch wall and was out the door. A sense of urgency filled her, a combination of anger and fear.

If anything had happened to him, she swore she'd give every pair of socks he owned to Yucky. The man was a fool to traipse across unfamiliar territory.

It wasn't until she was at the top of the drive, the truck's headlights stretching across the paved highway, that she remembered she didn't know where Bitter End was or how to get there. Making a quick decision, she headed south toward the Weston spread. From what Caroline had just told her, Travis had gone to Savannah for directions.

Nell left the engine running when she arrived at Savannah and Laredo's home. She leaped out of the cab and raced across the yard.

Savannah met her at the door and said, "Caroline phoned and said no one's heard from Travis."

"Not a word?"

"No. But I drew him a map," Savannah said.

"Can you draw me one, too?" Nell asked.

"Of course." Savannah led the way into the kitchen.

Nell followed, her heart pounding.

"You're worried, aren't you?" Savannah asked.

Nell nodded, afraid if she said anything, her voice would crack. Dammit, she was beginning to really care about that greenhorn. Which infuriated her, because she didn't *want* to care about him. He'd drifted into their lives and would drift out again. A few weeks after he left, Jeremy and Emma would probably have trouble remembering his name.

Not Nell. It would take her much longer to forget Travis Grant.

"That map took a long time to draw, and I don't want to keep you waiting," Savannah said, reaching for a pad and pencil. "I'll have to give you a rough sketch." She bent to her task, and in a minute the job was done. "You should be able to figure it out from this."

Savannah's hurried map wasn't ideal, but it gave Nell something to go on.

"Would you like me to come with you?" Laredo asked, joining the two women.

"No." Nell couldn't see any reason to drag him into the night.

"You're sure?"

"Positive. Thanks for your help," Nell said. She bounded out of the house and back into the truck.

Savannah and Laredo came to the stand by the back door silhouetted in the light that spilled from the kitchen. Nell realized she hadn't been able to hide her feelings from them any more than she'd concealed them from Ruth. Heart still pounding, she waved goodbye, then turned back up the drive.

In situations like this, she knew she had to face her worst fear. Recognizing what it was came easy because she'd encountered it once before.

Her greatest fear was finding that Travis had been hurt or killed.

"Dear God, no," she pleaded aloud, her mouth dry with horror. *Not again.* Finding Jake crushed beneath the tractor had forever changed her. It had nearly destroyed her, too.

The tears gathering in her eyes infuriated her, and she roughly swiped them away with the back of her hand.

She came to a juncture in the road and checked her map to choose which way she should turn. According to the directions, Bitter End was inaccessible by car. Which made sense, otherwise the town would have been found and explored much earlier.

If the makeshift map was at all accurate, Bitter End wasn't anywhere close to the road, and the turnoff point was some distance yet. She inhaled deeply, forcing herself to remain calm and in control of her emotions. As she drew near the section of highway where she'd need to drive onto unpaved land, she slowed to a crawl.

Her heart flew into her throat when she saw tire tracks that turned off the road. She was sure they were made by the vehicle Travis had rented.

She remembered again what had happened to Richard. Cal had found him in Bitter End, near death, half-crazed from thirst and his injuries. A stairway had collapsed on him, and he'd been two days without water or medical attention. It was described as a miracle that he'd survived. He'd been airlifted to Austin and hospitalized.

Nell shook off the memory and concentrated on driving. The terrain was hilly and uneven and the truck pitched and heaved first one way and then another. Fortunately it was a clear night and a bright three-quarter moon had risen; at least she could see where she was going.

Why Travis was in such an all-fired hurry to find the town she'd never know. He was probably on deadline. Here she was, desperately worried about a man who was no doubt planning to make a laughing-stock out of the entire community.

He'd urged her to see the town herself, and now he was getting his wish. Nell slowed, squinting into the distance, convinced she'd seen a flash of light.

She eased the pickup to a stop and opened the door. Standing on the narrow running board, she peered in the direction she'd seen the light. It wasn't visible now.

"Travis," she yelled at the top of her lungs. She waited for a response and thought, just for a second that she'd heard one.

Getting back into the truck, she sped ahead, heedless of the terrain. Sure enough the light reappeared.

"Travis! Travis!" She slammed on the brakes

when he was caught in the farthest reaches of her headlights.

Jumping out of the cab, she shouted. "Travis?"

"Here!" As he raced toward her she stumbled in his direction.

He held a flashlight, which he dropped when she neared. He threw open his arms. She wasn't sure which to do first, kiss him or slug him.

She fell into his arms with a force that might have knocked a slighter man to the ground. All at once nothing mattered, except that he was alive, uninjured, and she was in the warm security of his embrace.

"What happened? Where were you? Dear God in heaven, did you have any idea how worried I was?"

He shut her up with a kiss, then explained everything in five simple words.

"I ran out of gas."

Chapter Seven

"You ran out of gas?" Nell shrieked.

Travis felt foolish enough without her yelling at him, then figured it was what he deserved. He didn't know how he could've let something like that happen. His only excuse was his unfamiliarity with the vehicle—pretty lame as excuses went.

"I'm sorry," he told her.

"Sorry—all you can say is you're *sorry?*"

To her shock and dismay, Nell broke into sobs. She covered her face with both hands and half turned from him. Stunned that he'd driven her to tears, he moved to reach for her, but stopped, not sure how she'd react to being held when she was in such distress. The sight of her weeping was more than he could bear. He gently drew her to him, comforting her, holding her loosely. She struggled at first and he let her.

"You're right, Nell, sorry just doesn't cut it," he whispered soothingly.

"You're a fool," she told him, wiping the tears from her face.

"I know."

"You're not supposed to agree with me."

He cradled her face between his hands. "You were worried sick, weren't you?"

Even in the dark, with only the headlights behind her and the glow of the moon, he read Nell's fear.

"I...I was the one who found Jake," she said. "I was so afraid you..."

She didn't finish; she didn't need to. Travis wrapped his arms completely around her, his heart pounding with an emotion so overwhelming it made him weak in the knees.

"I'm fine. A little chagrined but fine."

"I'm not," she said, and clung to him.

Holding her like this was worth every moment of anxiety he'd endured, every second he'd floundered around, hoping he'd headed in the right direction. Common sense said he should have remained with the vehicle, but he'd felt compelled to make his way back to the road. Back to Nell.

She sniffled and raised her head to gaze up at him. Their eyes met, and something warm and wonderful passed between them. A recognition, an acceptance, a consent.

It was a profound moment.

Travis lowered his mouth to hers, and when their lips met, he barely managed to stifle a groan, it was that good. His lips lingered on hers as he prolonged the kiss, not wanting it to end.

She slipped her arms around his neck. He'd been the one to initiate the few kisses they'd exchanged to this point. She'd allowed his kisses, even enjoyed them, but she'd always remained slightly aloof, tentative.

That restraint was gone now. Her fingers were in his hair and her mouth clung to his, warm, demanding, erotic. By the time the kiss ended, Travis felt weak, drained—and at the same time exhilarated.

"Nell...sweet Nell." His voice was barely audible.

As she buried her face in his shoulder, he closed his eyes and breathed in her scent, the scent that belonged only to her. Equal parts soap and hay...and Nell. A cool breeze rushed against his face, and he silently prayed it would clear his head. At the moment all he could think about was making love to Nell. Not here, he told himself. The timing, the location, everything was wrong, but his body seemed intent on convincing him otherwise.

"Let's talk," he murmured.

"What do you want to talk about?"

"I have a few thoughts I want to discuss with you."

"Now?"

He nodded. "It won't take long."

He slid an arm about her waist and they walked toward the pickup. Nell turned off the engine and lowered the tailgate. They sat on it side by side.

Now that he had her attention, Travis wasn't sure where to start. He reached for her hand and held it between both of his; unable to resist, he kissed her knuckles. A heavy sigh worked its way through his chest as he gathered his thoughts.

"Travis?"

"First of all," he said, "I'm sorry I worried you."

She made a small sound as if to say now that he was found, all was forgiven.

"You came looking for me." His respect for her multiplied a hundredfold, especially now that he knew she'd been the one to find her dying husband. She'd had no idea what to expect tonight, but she'd put aside her fears and gone in search of him. "I don't think I've ever met anyone braver than you."

"Me?" She laughed softly. "I'm the biggest coward who ever lived."

"Not true."

"If I was as brave as you suggest, I wouldn't have asked you to stay away from Bitter End."

He smiled, following her thoughts. It didn't surprise him that they aligned with his. "That leads nicely into what I wanted to discuss with you."

"Bitter End?"

He felt her stiffen and searched for the words to reassure her.

"Did you find it?" she asked.

"Unfortunately, no. I got lost. My map-reading abilities leave much to be desired. I haven't a clue how close I was or wasn't."

She made no comment.

"Next time I want you to come with me."

"This is a joke, right?" she burst out.

He shook his head. His hands continued to hold hers. "You came looking for me—"

"Yes, but..."

"Don't you realize how much courage that took?"

"But I couldn't bear not knowing—"

"You also need to know what happened in Bitter End. You and everyone else in this community. The truth is long overdue. It's time to uncover the past, place it in the proper perspective, stop pretending Bitter End doesn't exist. Once everyone knows what happened there, the allure will be gone. You won't need to worry about Jeremy and Emma sneaking away to find it on their own."

"They wouldn't do that," she insisted weakly.

"Didn't you say your own father did? And Grady and the Patterson brothers searched for it when they were kids."

"Who told you that?"

"Savannah," he said. "This afternoon. They aren't the only ones either."

Nell turned away from him.

"Why me?" she asked, her voice weary.

"I need someone who knows the history, someone who'll help me understand it. According to Savannah, your family was among the original settlers. All I know is what Richard Weston told me and—"

"I wouldn't believe a word that snake said!"

"Right. So will you help me?" he asked quietly. "Come to Bitter End with me. Together we can solve this mystery once and for all."

Nell's shoulders rose with a sigh. "I...need some time to think it over."

"All right." He suspected that in the end she'd agree.

"You ready to go home now?" he asked.

"Home," she repeated. "Yes." She glanced at him. "We'll get your car tomorrow."

When they were in the truck cab and Nell had started the engine, it suddenly occurred to him that he'd referred to Twin Canyons as home.

Home. That was how it was beginning to feel.

RUTH SAT IN HER ROCKER and worked the crochet hook and yarn. While her fingers were busy with their task, her mind sped off on its own course. Nell had been gone more than two hours now, worried sick about that tenderfoot.

The children were upstairs asleep and the house was quiet. Calm. A cat nestled in Nell's chair, and Lucky, Jeremy's dog, slept on the braided rug in front of the fireplace. Yet Ruth's mind raced.

She'd been a youngster herself, about Emma's age, when she first heard the rumors about Bitter End. She remembered a schoolmate had told her about the mysterious ghost town, hidden in the hills. She was convinced it'd all been a lie, a story her friend had concocted. Then, years later, when she was wise and mature and all of thirteen, she'd overheard Edwina and Lily Moorhouse mention a ghost town.

Ruth trusted the Moorhouse sisters and had asked them about it. They, too, had claimed it was real and explained that the history of Promise was tied to the forgotten town. Only a few people knew about it, and even fewer knew where it was situated.

Ruth sighed and her hands went idle in her lap. Only one other person had shared her secret—which was that she'd been to Bitter End herself—and he was long dead. At eighteen she'd decided she would find this town. Cocky and self-confident, she'd gone in search of it.

That was how she'd met Jerome Bishop—her Jerry. He was older and had fought overseas toward the end of the Second World War, coming home a decorated hero.

She remembered how curious she'd been about him, how interested. But he was nearly thirty and she was still in her teens. He'd encountered her riding on his land and asked her a few questions. She didn't dare tell him the truth, so she'd fabricated something and prayed he'd believe her.

He hadn't, but said if she was a cattle thief, she was by far the prettiest one he'd ever seen.

Ruth smiled at the memory. A few days later she was back, certain she wasn't anywhere close to Bishop land. But Jerry found her, and in her rush to get away and avoid his questions, she'd let her horse escape and twisted her ankle as she tried to catch the reins.

In his concern about her injury Jerry hadn't plied her with questions, but carefully examined her foot, his touch gentle for such a big man. She'd been half in love with him following their first meeting, but after this, her heart was forever lost.

Naturally such a romance was impossible. He was older, more worldly; she was just a schoolgirl. He didn't kiss her, nor did he chastise her. Instead, Jerry had rounded up her mare, then escorted her almost the entire way home. She'd been too shy to talk much, giving one-word replies to his questions. Before he'd left her, he asked her to forget the ridiculous notion of finding Bitter End on her own—not that she'd ever admitted she was looking for it. He'd gone so far as to suggest she stay home in the afternoons and read books or talk on the phone with her friends. Ruth had smiled politely and said she'd take his advice under consideration.

The next evening he'd stopped by the house to discuss ranching with her father. Ruth had been involved in helping her brothers with their homework. She felt Jerry's eyes on her, and through the whole evening, she feared he'd mention her afternoon horseback excursions. He didn't.

The next time she ventured out horseback riding, Jerry was waiting for her.

"Are you meeting a lover?" he'd demanded.

"No." She'd been appalled that he'd even think such a thing.

She doubted he believed her, but she couldn't bear letting him think she loved another man. Instead, she'd broken down and told him she was attracted to someone who felt he was too old for her. If he'd guessed she meant him, Jerry never said. When he couldn't convince her to forget about finding the lost town, he'd reluctantly agreed to accompany her.

The day they'd stumbled upon the ghost town was one she would long remember. That was when Jerry had first kissed her. Ruth wasn't sure which had excited her more—his kiss or locating the town.

But it was the only time they'd ever been to the town. High on exhilaration, they'd walked down the center of the deserted main street. Soon they realized something was very wrong. It was spring and the hills were blanketed with bluebonnets, yet Ruth noticed not a single flower in Bitter End.

The place was bleak, dark. A huge blighted tree stood at one end of town. Everything was dead.

But that wasn't what had kept them from returning. It was the ugly feeling, the sensation of dread that pressed against her heart, making it almost difficult to breathe. Jerry had kept her close to his side and mumbled something about the town reminding him of the feeling he'd had when he came upon battle-grounds during the war. It felt like death, he'd said.

Whatever had happened was horrible enough to cry out from the land, from the buildings and everything around them. Whatever it was had killed this town and forever marked it for ruin.

They'd never gone back. Never wanted to. Finding the lost town had been their secret, a silent bond they'd shared. To the best of Ruth's knowledge, they'd never spoken of it again.

Afterward there'd been no reason for them to meet. Ruth had missed Jerry more than she could say, but if he missed her, he didn't let on. They met in passing twice—both times in Promise—and exchanged little more than casual greetings. Ruth was miserable, loving him the way she did, and she was sure he cared for her, too. So she decided to take matters into her own hands. It was a brazen thing she did; she smiled at the memory of it and the shocked look on Jerry's face the day she rode over to his family's ranch. She'd figured she had nothing to lose. Her ostensible reason was that she'd be graduating from high school within a few weeks and needed the advice of an older more experienced person about her best course of action.

He'd asked about her options and she'd mentioned two: marrying him or moving to Dallas with a friend and finding work there. Jerry's face had tightened, and then he'd suggested that marrying him was probably the better of the two ideas, but he preferred to do the asking.

She granted him that much and waited impatiently for him to make his move. The day she graduated from high school he stopped by the family home with a diamond ring. Afterward they'd argued amiably about who'd proposed to whom; it was a private joke between them.

A few years after they were married, Jerry's mother had died and they'd inherited the chest.

The very chest that sat in the attic of this house, Jake and Nell's place. She'd gone through the contents once. To a historian the chest would have been a treasure trove, filled with bits and pieces of life in the nineteenth-century hill country. But it was more than that. Ruth had recognized almost immediately that some of the things packed in the cedar-lined chest had come from Bitter End.

She'd looked them over, then closed up the box and never investigated it again. Ruth supposed it was because she'd been so young at the time, and that one

visit to the town had continued to haunt her. She'd
wanted nothing more to do with Bitter End. No link
to it. If she couldn't throw out the chest—and she
couldn't—then she'd hide it away, obliterating from
her mind any memory of that horrible place. Jerry
must have agreed, because once he knew the contents,
he'd never asked about it again.

The time had come, Ruth believed, to reopen that
chest. They had to disclose what was known about
the town, discover its secrets, undo whatever damage
they could. She was too old now for such a task. But
it seemed somehow fated that Travis Grant had arrived when he did.

She would talk to him, show him the chest, whether
Nell wanted her to or not.

That decided, Ruth picked up her crochet hook and
started back to work. The clock chimed nine; Nell
would be returning with Travis soon. She had a good
feeling about those two. They were well matched, the
way Nell and Jake had been.

Yes, the more she thought about it, the more fated
Jake's appearance began to seem.

THE FOLLOWING MORNING, Nell was in the kitchen
preparing the children's breakfast when Ruth came
downstairs.

"I take it you found Travis," her mother-in-law
said, with a slight smile.

"I found him," Nell confirmed.

As if to verify her words, the back door opened
and Travis stepped inside. He looked fresh from the

shower, his hair wet and recently combed. His gaze searched out Nell's and he smiled. "Morning, everyone."

"Morning, Travis," both Jeremy and Emma said at once, and their faces brightened at the sight of him.

"Where were you last night?" Jeremy asked. "I asked Mom, but she said she wasn't sure."

"I wasn't sure, either," Travis replied.

Nell cast him a warning glance. He'd already promised he wouldn't tell the children about Bitter End, but she feared he'd forgotten his word.

"I got...lost," Travis said, keeping his gaze on her. When she stopped stirring the oatmeal long enough to glare openly at him, he winked.

Nell felt the color rush to her cheeks and prayed her children wouldn't notice, but her prayer didn't reach heaven fast enough to include Ruth. She noticed her mother-in-law grinning as she took her place at the table, obviously pleased.

When the oatmeal was ready, she served it with brown sugar and raisins. The toast was from a loaf of the homemade bread she'd baked the evening before. She'd kneaded away her worries about Travis on the dough, and it was some of the lightest fluffiest bread she'd ever baked.

The grandfather clock in the living room chimed eight, and the children leaped up from the table, grabbed their lunches and dashed out the door.

"You finished with your chores?" Nell shouted after them.

They both assured her they were.

"What are your plans for the day?" Ruth asked, directing the question to both Nell and Travis.

Travis glanced at Nell. She dragged in a deep breath. "I'm driving Travis back to where he left his car. We're taking along a five-gallon can of gas," she explained.

"You going anyplace else?" her mother-in-law pressed.

"I've asked Nell to help me find Bitter End," Travis said.

"Will you, Nell?" Ruth searched her face.

"I'm not sure."

"I think you should," Ruth said unexpectedly.

For a moment Nell was too shocked to respond. "You want me to find Bitter End?"

"That's what I said." The older woman nodded. "And once you've located the town and walked through it, come back and tell me. Don't dawdle, either. There's something I have for you—both of you. Something that's been in the attic all these years."

"Ruth?" Nell asked in hushed tones, bending over her mother-in-law. "What is it?"

"Ruth?" Travis knelt down in front of her.

The older woman smiled and gently touched his cheek. "Find the town," she said softly. "Just find the town."

Travis helped Nell clean up the kitchen, then loaded the can of gas in the back of the pickup. She was already in the cab when he climbed inside.

"Thank you," he said.

The man could unnerve her faster than anyone she'd ever known. "For what?"

"For coming with me."

In the light of day Nell was annoyed for responding to Travis's kisses the way she had. It was because of her relief at finding him safe; it must be. She simply hadn't been herself—except she'd used that excuse before.

Despite Ruth's encouragement, she intended to tell him she refused to look for the town. She didn't want to know what was there, didn't care to find it.

"Losing your nerve, are you?" Travis asked.

"No," she denied heatedly, then added, "I'm a rancher, not a...historian."

"And a—"

"Coward," she finished for him. Her fingers ached from her death grip on the steering wheel. What it came down to was fear. Everything she'd ever heard about the town rang in her ears—rumors, warnings, advice. And it all seemed to whisper *Keep away*.

"What's Ruth talking about?" Travis asked once they were on the road.

"I...I don't know," Nell said, which was only partially true. The attic was full of forgotten treasures from the Bishop family. Old clothing, furniture, letters and memorabilia. Seeing that Jake's family, like her own, had been among the original pioneers, it was quite possible that something stored in the attic had come from Bitter End. Anything her parents might have had, however, had been taken with them when they retired to Florida.

"Won't you come with me, Nell?" Travis coaxed.

It took a long time, but reluctantly she decided Travis was right. She had to confront whatever was there, not just for her own sake but that of her family. Her friends. The people of Promise. It sounded melodramatic to put it in those terms, but then it was a melodramatic situation. Certainly an extraordinary one.

"All right," she finally whispered.

"Thank you," he said again.

Had they been anywhere else, not tearing down the road in her pickup, Nell was convinced Travis would have gathered her in his arms and kissed her. Had they been anywhere else, she would have let him.

That was quite an admission for her, she realized. Despite her reservations and doubts, she was falling in love with this greenhorn. Every unmarried rancher in the area had asked her out at some point since Jake's death, but who did she fall for? A writer. A man who was going to break her heart, one way or another.

Nell let Travis do the driving after a while, and an hour later, with Savannah's map spread out on her lap, Nell suddenly cried, "Here!" She pointed to a grove of trees on the right.

Travis brought the truck to a stop.

"We go on foot from this spot," Nell said, rereading Savannah's instructions for the tenth time.

"So I was close," Travis muttered to himself.

They left the truck and started out on foot. Nell could already feel her heart pounding, and not from physical effort, either. It seemed to thunder, *Keep away, keep away,* with every beat.

"Are you okay?" Travis asked her a few minutes later.

"Sure," she lied. "What's there to fear?"

"We don't know that yet, do we?" he said, his expression serious.

They didn't speak for a while as they made their way through heavy brush and over rocky, treacherous ground. When they reached a limestone outcropping, Nell paused to look over the small valley below—and gasped.

She pointed a shaking finger at a charred steeple in the distance. The church was the tallest structure, but she could see others, too.

Travis's gaze followed the direction of her finger. "Bitter End," he whispered.

Nell studied the cluster of buildings. From her vantage point she could look down at them, could see the whole town laid out. Bitter End was divided by one main street with buildings on either side. The church and cemetery were at one end of the town, a corral at the other. Some of the buildings were constructed of stone, others of wood. It surprised her how well preserved everything seemed to be.

"So far, so good," Travis said.

Nell wordlessly agreed and breathed in deeply before they scrambled down the hill and into the town. They arrived near the corral. As they progressed, Nell experienced a feeling of heaviness, of being weighed down, that reminded her of how she'd felt those first few months after Jake's death.

She didn't say anything, but wondered if Travis felt the same thing.

"What is it?" he asked in a hushed tone.

They were on the main street now, their hands tightly clenched. With each step they advanced into the town, the feeling intensified. The weight pressing on Nell's heart grew stronger and stronger until she slowed her pace.

"I...I don't know."

"What's that?" Travis pointed to the saloon and the rocking chair that sat in front of it. Something leaned against the building.

"It...looks like Richard's guitar," she said. "He hid here for weeks before he was found."

"How could he have stood it?" Travis wondered, his voice low and hoarse.

"I don't know." Nell didn't understand why they felt compelled to speak so quietly. He squeezed her hand, and by tacit agreement they moved from the street onto the boardwalk. Savannah was right, she thought with a shudder. There was nothing living here—except the ceaseless wind.

She paused and looked inside the mercantile. A half-dozen bloated cans of food were scattered on the shelves. An old cash register stood on the counter, its drawer hanging open.

"Someone was looking for spare change," Travis remarked.

"Probably Richard." Evidence of his presence was everywhere.

They located the room in the hotel where he'd been sleeping and carefully skirted past the area where the stairs had collapsed. The wood floors were stained with his blood. Debris and empty bottles appeared here and there; magazine pages and food wrappings were blown against the sides of buildings.

"What are you thinking?" Travis asked as they neared the end of the street.

"That I want the hell out of here."

He chuckled, but the sound was uncomfortable. "Anything else you want to see?"

"No." She slid her arm through his and stayed close to his side. The oppressive sensation remained, reminding her even more forcibly of the horrific grief she'd suffered after Jake's death. It had become a part of her, something she lived with day and night. When it finally did ease, it went a little at a time. Slowly she could laugh again, then dream again. She was only now discovering she could love again. She stopped, suddenly struck by an idea.

"Hold me, Travis," she said urgently. They were near the church.

"Now?" He seemed surprised.

"Please."

He pulled her into his arms and she spoke into his ear. "I'd like to try an experiment."

"Okay. What do you need me to do?"

"Nothing," she said, then thinking better of it, added, "much."

She felt his smile against her skin.

Easing away from him, she placed her hands on both sides of his face and touched her lips to his. The kiss was deep, involving, as intense as the kisses they'd shared the night before. When she drew back, she studied his face.

"I like this kind of test," he told her flippantly. "Am I being graded?"

"No."

"Why not?"

"Travis, this is serious."

"I am serious."

She sighed expressively. "All right, I'll give you a B-plus."

"Why not an A?"

"Travis, you won't get an A until you answer my question."

"Fine. What's the question?"

"The feelings. Have they lessened?"

"I'm feeling all sorts of things just now. Which feeling do you mean?"

"The one we felt when we entered the town."

"I won't know until you kiss me again."

"Quit joking! This is important."

"I wasn't joking. I can't tell."

"Never mind."

"Why?"

"I have my answer."

"And?"

"It *has* lessened," she said. "I'm sure of it."

He nodded. "You're probably right."

Holding hands, they walked out of Bitter End. As they approached the outskirts, she felt a sudden sense of release, as though the bonds that constrained her had gone slack. A few steps outside the town, the feeling had all but disappeared.

After that, they concentrated on the arduous trek back to the road and said very little for some time.

"Are you okay?" Travis asked once.

"Fine. What about you?"

"Fine."

Travis followed her in his rental car as she drove back to Twin Canyons Ranch. Ruth sat on the porch with the rocking chair positioned to face the road; she stood and put away her crocheting as soon as she saw them.

"Did you find the town?" Ruth asked when they entered the kitchen.

"We found it," Nell told her.

She nodded. "I figured you would," she said softly. "Travis, would you follow me upstairs? There's something I'd like you to bring down."

Chapter Eight

Travis had one hell of a time bringing the cedar chest down from the attic. It almost seemed as though it was reluctant to give up its secrets, he thought, knowing how whimsical that sounded. Then he needed all his strength to pry up the lid.

Nell stood back, while Ruth edged close to him, firm and purposeful.

With the chest finally open, the first thing Travis noted was how neatly packed it was. The top layer was folded clothes, which Ruth carefully removed and set aside.

They found an old family Bible beneath the dresses and men's shirts. Ruth held it respectfully with both hands. "It's exactly like the one Ellie has," Nell breathed. "Ellie Patterson—used to be Frasier," she explained to Travis. "Ellie owns the feed store in Promise. Her family came here when mine did, and Jake's."

Travis could picture her easily. Ellie, as he recalled, had judged the chili cook-off.

"Ellie found the Bible while she was sorting

through her father's things after he died," Ruth said. "She used the Bible for her wedding ceremony. I was touched that she had, since she was so close to her father." Carefully Ruth folded back the leather binding and examined the title page. "It says this Bible belonged to Joseph Savage."

"Jerry's great-great—there are too many greats for me to remember," Ruth said, "but the family's directly descended from Joseph's, that much I know."

"I'm sure this Bible is identical to the one Ellie owns," Nell said, moving in close and running her finger down the page.

"It wasn't unusual for a salesman to come into town and sell any number of the same item," Travis said. "My guess is that's the case here." In his research he'd come across references to old-time peddlers who rode from one town to the next selling their wares. More often than not, the men who sold Bibles were itinerant preachers, too, performing marriages, conducting funerals and preaching fire-and-brimstone sermons.

The next thing Nell extracted was an aged cardboard box. "Probably more clothes," she suggested. "Someone's wedding dress?"

"Open it," Ruth said.

Nell set the box down and with trembling hands removed the lid. She was wrong; it wasn't a wedding dress, not even an article of clothing, but parts of a quilt made of a cream-colored muslin.

"What is it?" Travis asked.

"The backing and some squares for a quilt, from

the looks of it,'' Ruth said. ''Apparently someone started the project years ago and never finished it.''

''It's not any pattern I've ever seen,'' Nell said. ''Most quilts have an overall design.''

And most were a great deal more colorful than this one, Travis mused. The squares lacked the vivid and varied colors of others he'd seen.

''It looks like each square's a picture of some sort,'' Nell said, and held up one with an oak tree embroidered in the center. The detail was impressive, the stitches minute. She squinted and stared at the square, then shook her head. ''I think there's something carved into the side of the tree,'' she said.

Ruth looked at it and shook her head. ''My eyes aren't what they used to be.''

Travis took a turn, as well, and after staring at it intensely, was able to make out the letters. ''It seems to say, 'cursed'.''

''Cursed?'' Nell repeated. ''Weird.'' She set the square back in the box. They studied the other squares, but again didn't find them particularly attractive. Each had a different image, although it wasn't always clear what that image was meant to be.

Nell returned the pieces to the cardboard box and set it aside. Leaning over the chest, she reached in and said, ''Doesn't this beat all?''

''What is it?'' Travis asked.

''It's a doll.'' Nell pulled out an obviously old rag doll, stuffed tight with a hand-stitched face. It had been made of white linen that had faded to a dull yellow, not unlike the color of the quilt squares. The red calico apron added a splash of brightness.

"I've seen one like that before," Ruth said, frowning in concentration. "Oh, yes! Dr. Jane had one exactly like that in her office not long ago."

"Dr. Jane?" Nell asked. "That seems odd. Are you sure?"

"Positive. She had it sitting on a bookcase. I remember seeing it the last time I was in for my physical. You remember, Nell? You drove me into town yourself. I needed my blood pressure medication renewed."

"How would Dr. Jane come by something like this?" Nell asked. "She's from California."

Travis listened to the conversation and shook his head. A doll identical to one that had come from Bitter End was owned by a California native? He agreed with Nell; it didn't make sense.

"Let's ask her about it," Travis suggested.

"Can't hurt," Nell said, and Ruth nodded.

The rest of the chest's contents consisted of old newspapers from the 1920s through the assassination of President Kennedy in 1963, army discharge papers and the like. Those, too, were neatly filed in cardboard boxes.

As Ruth carefully repacked the chest, Travis helped Nell finish the chores around the ranch. And then, together, they drove into town.

"This is probably a wild-goose chase," Nell said.

"Probably," he agreed, wondering if she'd had

second thoughts about pursuing the significance of their discoveries.

They parked in front of the medical clinic, and once again he noted Nell's hesitation. "Nell," he said softly, "what is it?"

"Nothing," she insisted.

Travis stared at her. Ever since they'd returned from the ghost town, she'd been quiet, withdrawn, speculative. He didn't know what to make of it.

Dr. Jane was with a patient. They sat in the waiting room, and Travis flipped through magazines until the receptionist led them back to Jane's office. Travis glanced around; he noticed no antique doll on her bookcase now.

Jane entered briskly and took a seat at her desk. "Good to see you, Nell," she said. "Hello," she added, nodding in his direction.

Nell introduced Travis and they shook hands. Dr. Jane Patterson's lovely blue eyes revealed a genuine pleasure at seeing Nell—and open curiosity about him.

"Ruth mentioned noticing a rag doll in your office a few months ago," Nell said, getting immediately to the point of their visit.

"Doll?" Jane frowned as if she'd forgotten, but then apparently remembered, because she smiled. "As a matter of fact, I did, but I...no longer have it."

"Would you mind telling us where you got it?" Travis asked.

Jane studied them both. "Is there a particular reason for these questions?"

Nell and Travis exchanged glances. "We found a doll very similar to the one Ruth saw here," Nell explained.

Jane reached for a pen and started making small circles. "Can I ask where you found this doll?"

"Have you been to Bitter End, Dr. Patterson?" Travis asked abruptly. Then he remembered she *had* been. Jane was the one who'd found and treated Richard Weston.

He felt Nell's displeasure with him at the bluntness of his approach. But his curiosity was at a fever pitch. He was looking for answers, and the only way to get them was to ask the right questions. A growing sense of excitement filled him.

The doctor surprised him by asking a question of her own. "Have *you* ever been to Bitter End?"

Nell and Travis looked at each other.

"We were there this morning," Travis answered.

"Did you find the doll there?"

"Not exactly," Travis said. "It was in an old chest in Nell's attic."

"I see." Jane folded her hands and leaned back in her chair. "I don't suppose it would do any harm to tell you how I came to have that doll. Maggie Weston brought it to me."

"Maggie?" Nell sounded shocked.

"This was months ago, before Caroline and Grady were married and he legally adopted Maggie. You might not be aware of this, but Maggie disappeared the same time Richard Weston did. As far as anyone can figure, Maggie must've been hiding in the pickup Richard stole from the Yellow Rose Ranch. For a whole night, Caroline and Grady didn't know where she was. Sheriff Hennessey's the one who put two and two together.''

''It must have been hell for Caroline,'' Nell said in sympathy.

''I'm sure it was. The following morning Maggie reappeared as mysteriously as she'd vanished. She wouldn't say where she'd been, but the sheriff thinks Richard brought her back.''

''Thank God!''

''He'd taken her to his hiding place, then—in the ghost town?'' Travis asked. His jaw tightened at the thought of a five-year-old in Bitter End.

''Apparently so,'' Jane said. ''No one knows exactly what Richard said to the child to convince her to keep his secret. But considering the type of person he is, it's not too hard to guess.''

''Prison's too good for the likes of Richard Weston,'' Nell muttered.

The more Travis learned about him, the more inclined he was to agree.

''While she was in Bitter End, Maggie found the doll and tucked it in her backpack. Later it worried her that she'd taken something that didn't belong to her. She developed stomachaches, and that was when she brought the doll to me.''

''And the reason you had it on your bookshelf,'' Nell added.

"Exactly! I didn't know at the time that the doll was from the ghost town. I'd hoped the rightful owner would see it in my office so I could simply return it without mentioning Maggie's name."

"Where's the doll now?" Travis wanted to know.

"Maggie has it. Once the truth came out, Grady and Caroline decided Maggie could keep it."

"The memory of how she got it doesn't bother her?" Nell asked.

"It doesn't seem to. She believes she saved that doll. So her feelings about it have become quite positive."

"Good," Nell said. "I'm glad such a horrible experience ended well for her."

Jane smiled, then her gaze swung to Travis. "You're visiting Nell?"

"Actually I'm doing research for a story."

"He's my first guest," Nell explained. "The dude ranch hasn't officially opened, but he needed a room and Mary and Phil suggested my place."

Travis didn't like the classification. A guest—a paying one at that. She'd said it as though there was nothing between them, as though their kisses meant nothing. Despite her tone, Travis couldn't make himself believe it.

"I see," Jane said, sounding a little unsure.

She wasn't the only one. "Nell and I are finding out everything we can about Bitter End," Travis explained. "It's time the mystery of that town was solved."

Jane nodded. "I couldn't agree with you more. My

fear is now that the word's out, someone else is going to decide to hide there. If something isn't done soon, there's every likelihood people will get hurt again. Some of those buildings aren't safe for people to explore. It's a wonder they've stood all these years as it is.''

"The entire town should be destroyed," Nell said, her voice raised.

Travis disagreed with a sharp shake of the head. "Bitter End is an important part of Texas history. Why would anyone want to destroy it?''

Nell didn't answer.

CAL AND GLEN took a long-overdue lunch break, letting their horses graze near Gully Creek while they ate their sandwiches. The morning had been spent vaccinating cattle. Cal felt they both deserved a respite while the crew, who'd lunched earlier, finished up.

Although Cal saw his brother every day, they rarely had a chance to talk anymore. Especially now that they were both married. Glen was busy with his life in town; he and Ellie had bought a run-down Victorian that they were fixing up. Cal and Jane were still newlyweds, still learning about each other. A lot had happened in the two men's lives in the past year, more than Cal could adequately take in.

Glen finished his lunch first, then stretched out on the cool grass, shading his eyes with his Stetson.

"Jane mentioned something interesting the other

day,'' Cal said, leaning back and resting his weight on his palms.

"What?"

"Nell Bishop was in to see her with that city slicker guy from New York."

"I wouldn't say that to his face," Glen said, lifting the Stetson and grinning. "I think he wants to be a cowboy. Besides, the guy's bigger than you."

"So what? Hey—I'm a Texan!"

"He went to see Jane? What's the matter," Glen joked, "is he having trouble with the drinking water?"

"No, he's been to Bitter End."

If Cal hadn't gotten his full attention earlier, he had it now. Glen sat up and looked at his brother. "Is that for real? How the hell did he find it?"

"Grady and Savannah drew him a map."

"You're kidding!"

"Nope."

"What gives *him* the right?"

Cal smiled, remembering that his initial reaction had been similar to that of his brother. "He thinks it's time someone solved the mystery."

"Really?"

"I tend to agree with him."

"Fine, but it should be one of us, then, someone from Promise. Don't you think?"

"Why?"

"Because it's *our* town. Our history. Personally I don't like the idea of some city slicker poking around in affairs that aren't any of his damn business. If he wants to uncover a few skeletons, I say let him open his own closet.''

"You willing to do it or not?"

"Dig up the dirt about Bitter End?" his brother clarified.

"Yup." Cal studied his brother. "You know—figure out what went wrong. And why."

Glen expelled a long breath. "I say let sleeping dogs lie. Frankly I don't need to know."

"That's the way I felt, too," Cal told him. "Until recently."

Glen broke off a long blade of grass and stuck it between his teeth. "What changed your mind?"

"Richard Weston."

"What about him?" Glen asked, sounding disgusted.

Cal didn't hold any more affection for Grady's brother than Glen did; Richard had done nothing but embarrass the family and the community. It wasn't common knowledge that he'd stolen from his family not once, but twice—and, as they'd since learned, he'd victimized a lot of vulnerable people in a really nasty scam back East. The news about his arrest and prison sentence had been the talk of the town for weeks. Some people had difficulty believing Richard was capable of committing such crimes. Cal had no such problem. Richard was a lowlife and deserved every day of the twenty-five-year sentence he'd received.

"Richard being airlifted out of Bitter End brought up a lot of questions about the town. Quite a few folks had never heard of it. Others had and wanted to know more. I think it's time we put an end to this speculation and settle the past once and for all.''

''Grady agrees with you?''

''He'd planned to personally take Travis Grant there, until his water pump broke. Even then, he had Savannah draw Travis a map. From what Jane told me, Nell's involved in this, too.''

Glen continued to chew on the stem of grass. His hands were tucked behind his head and he stared up at the blue sky. ''Maybe you're right.''

''What can we do to help?'' Cal asked after a silence.

''You and me?'' Glen seemed surprised.

''We're among the few who've actually been to the town.''

Glen closed his eyes. ''Don't remind me.''

Glen had been there once, Cal twice—most recently with Jane, who'd insisted she wanted to find the town. He'd finally given in and agreed to accompany her, knowing that otherwise she'd search for it on her own.

As it happened, their going into the ghost town precisely when they did had saved Richard Weston's life. The events of that day had shaken Cal considerably. He was accustomed to being in charge, knowing what to do, but if it hadn't been for Jane and her medical expertise, he could have done little but watch Richard Weston die.

''I'm trying to remember what I know about Bitter

End," Glen said, cutting into his thoughts. "What do you think Nell and her friend might want to know?"

Nell and her friend. Cal ignored the question and concentrated on the picture that formed in his mind. He'd seen Travis and Nell dancing at the rodeo not long ago. It had been a shock to see her in the arms of a man, especially since she'd always refused dates and invitations. Once the shock wore off, he'd felt pleased. She'd been completely absorbed in the guy, hadn't even noticed him and Jane.

The ribs he'd injured in the rodeo had been hurting like hell, but he'd managed to talk Jane into staying for the dance. The pain was worth it, seeing as Willie Nelson had unexpectedly shown up. Jane still talked about it; she'd been thrilled.

"A penny for your thoughts," Glen teased. "If they're worth that much."

"I was just thinking about Nell and Travis Grant...."

"What about them?"

"There's a romance brewing."

"So?" Glen said.

"So, I think it's a good idea. I liked Jake—he was one of my best friends—but I'd hate to see Nell grieve the rest of her life away. Jake wouldn't have wanted that, either."

"Is she interested in this Travis character?"

"Seems to be." More than that, Travis Grant was obviously taken with her. Whatever was happening there, Cal hoped it would work out for Nell. She was in line for a bit of happiness.

JEREMY LIKED Travis Grant—so much that it actually worried Nell. Her son was enthralled with him. Several times now she'd been forced to talk to Jeremy about giving Travis time to himself. Like this afternoon, for example. She knew Travis was writing, but the minute her son returned home from school, he'd raced out to see Travis. She didn't know what they'd talked about, but Jeremy had been wearing a silly grin ever since. As if he knew something she didn't.

She'd chastised him soundly for not doing his chores, and he'd left the house in a temper. At dinnertime, when she couldn't find him, she knew where he was likely to be. She hurried over to the bunkhouse and knocked at the door.

"Yeah?" Travis called.

Apparently this was how New Yorkers said, "Come in."

Nell opened the door and was surprised not to see her son there, making a pest of himself despite her scolding. "Have you seen Jeremy?" she asked.

"Not lately." Travis was sitting in front of his computer screen, his brow burrowed.

"I hope I didn't interrupt anything," she said, feeling badly to have barged in on him, considering she'd admonished her twelve-year-old for doing the same thing.

"No problem, Nell." He seemed abstracted and barely glanced away from his work.

She quietly closed the door. Jeremy sometimes liked to escape to the hayloft and read, especially if he was angry with her. She headed in that direction next, hoping to make peace with him.

"Jeremy." She stood in the middle of the barn, staring up at the loft.

"Yeah." Her son peeked over the ledge.

Yeah. Just like Travis. She swallowed the urge to correct him and said, "Time to wash up for dinner."

"Already?" he groaned. He climbed down from the loft and followed Nell back to the house, dragging his feet. He didn't mention the incident earlier that afternoon, and because he hadn't, she didn't, either.

"What are you reading?" his grandmother asked him.

"A book," he said, and set it on the kitchen counter. "When will Emma be back from Girl Scouts?"

Nell glanced at her watch. "Any minute. Kathy's mom is dropping her off. Would you kindly tell Travis dinner will be ready in ten minutes?" She didn't need to make the suggestion twice; Jeremy was out the door as fast as a cartoon character racing across the screen.

"He seems to like Travis," Ruth commented.

"I noticed."

"That worries you?"

It did, Nell thought. Once Travis left—and he *would* leave—her son might well feel abandoned. Initially she hadn't been concerned, but Jeremy's liking for Travis had recently grown into full-scale adulation.

And what about her own feelings? Travis had

shaken up her emotions, made her feel all kinds of things she'd shut herself off from. Like attraction. And…desire.

"Yes," she answered her mother-in-law. "I'm worried he likes Travis too much."

"You seem to like him yourself," Ruth added slyly.

Nell bit her lip, unable to explain or confide.

"Something happen you want to talk about?" The older woman studied her closely.

Nell just shook her head. Fortunately Ruth left it at that, giving her a hug before pitching in to set the table.

Dinner consisted of meat loaf, scalloped potatoes, homemade bread, corn, green salad and fresh rhubarb pie. Emma ran in the back door, shucking off her jacket, just as they were about to sit down.

As usual, dinner conversation settled around the children and school. This evening Nell was more than grateful to let her two youngsters do the talking. Particularly since her adventures with Travis in Bitter End wouldn't have been an appropriate subject. Nor did she want to discuss their trip into town and the chat with Dr. Jane.

"What's that book you were reading earlier?" Ruth asked when there was a lull in the conversation.

"*Prairie Gold,* by T.R. Grant," Jeremy said. His gaze briefly flew to Travis before he helped himself to a second slice of bread. "He's a great writer."

"You've read enough of his books," Nell said in

a conversational tone as she passed the butter to her son.

"You heard of him?" Emma asked Travis.

Jeremy burst into giggles and Nell quelled him with a look.

"You could say we're friends." Travis smiled at Emma, and Nell wondered if he was teasing her daughter. She certainly wouldn't appreciate it if he was.

"I've read all his books," Jeremy stated proudly.

"Every one of them," Nell testified.

"Do you *really* know him?" Emma asked, returning to Travis's earlier statement.

"Travis is a writer," Nell said. "He probably knows lots of other writers." She didn't want to put him on the spot.

Once more Jeremy burst into giggles.

"What's going on here?" Nell demanded.

"Mom, have you ever wondered what the T.R. in T.R. Grant stands for?"

"No," she said. She hadn't given the matter a moment's thought.

"Travis Randolf," Travis supplied slowly, holding her gaze and refusing to let go.

Nell dropped her fork with a clatter.

"Nell?" Ruth said, her eyes showing concern.

"You're T.R. Grant?" Nell whispered, finding it hard to speak and breathe at the same time.

Travis grinned. "At your service."

Chapter Nine

"I told you I was a writer," Travis explained, as though the logic should have been obvious.

"I figured it out this afternoon!" Jeremy exclaimed excitedly.

"But you didn't say *what* you wrote," Ruth said, frowning.

It just so happened that one of the most popular children's authors in the entire country was sitting at this very table, was sleeping in their bunkhouse. Was kissing her senseless every chance he got.

"Nell?" Travis's gaze continued to hold hers. "Maybe you and I should talk about this privately after dinner."

The idea of being alone with him for even a minute was too much. She shook her head vigorously. "That won't be necessary."

Before Travis could comment, Jeremy and Emma immediately bombarded him with questions. At any other time Nell would have cautioned them to mind their manners. But not tonight.

After dinner Ruth went into her bedroom to watch

"Jeopardy" on her television set. Protesting loudly, Jeremy and Emma were sent upstairs to do their homework, while Nell cleaned the kitchen.

She scrubbed the dishes, rinsed them, dried them. She didn't turn around, but she knew Travis was still in the kitchen long before he spoke.

"You might have said something," she told him in a deceptively mild voice.

"Well, I didn't exactly hide it, but I didn't shout it from the rooftops, either." He paused. "Does it change who I am?"

"Yes...no."

"I'd rather you got to know me for who I am first—without muddying the waters with my success."

Although she understood, it hurt that he hadn't trusted her with the truth. But it was just as well. This simply reinforced what she already knew—that she shouldn't expect anything from him.

"You wanted to ask me something?" she said pointedly.

"I want to go back to Bitter End in the morning."

"Why?"

"We're missing something important there, Nell. I can feel it, but I can't put my finger on it."

"I don't have time to waste. I've got work to do around here."

He hesitated. "I need you."

"Why?" she cried again, standing with her back to him. "You know the way now. You *don't* need me."

"I do," he said softly. "But I'll leave it up to you." Having said that, he quietly left.

WHEN MORNING ARRIVED and the children were off to school, Nell had a change of heart. This, she promised herself, would be the last time. From then on, Travis was on his own.

"I'm glad you're coming," he said, smiling as she climbed into the sports utility vehicle beside him.

"We ran into a dead end," she muttered. "And if it were up to me, we'd drop the entire project now."

"You don't mean that."

It was true she didn't, but she refused to admit it.

They parked the same place they had before and made their way into the ghost town. Even before they reached Bitter End, Nell could feel the sensation approaching. Gradually it descended on her, the intensity mounting with each step she took.

"What are we looking for?" Nell asked in a whisper, standing close to his side. She'd prefer to keep her distance, but the town frightened her.

"I don't know yet," he said, his voice low.

As they stood in the center of the street in the middle of Bitter End, Travis surveyed the buildings. "Does anything strike you as familiar?" he asked after a moment, his voice slightly raised.

"No." Nothing had changed from the day before except her anxiety to leave, which had only increased.

"The tree!" he shouted, pointing down the street. He started for it, leaving her behind.

He stopped some yards from the large dead oak with its gnarled, twisted limbs.

"Wh-what about the tree?" she asked, breathless from running after him.

"Nell, don't you remember the quilt? That's the tree! You can tell by the trunk."

Travis walked slowly toward it. "Look. Nell, look."

He ran his finger over the rough crude letters in the dead wood.

Nell's swift intake of breath was the only sound.

There, carved into the side of the tree, was the word "cursed."

IT CAME TO TRAVIS then, in a blinding flash. The quilt squares they'd found so puzzling held the key to whatever had happened in Bitter End.

"The quilt," he said. "The squares tell what happened to the town."

"A story quilt! I hadn't even thought of that." Nell's eyes went bright with excitement. It was all Travis could do not to kiss her right then and there. He resisted, with difficulty.

He might have kissed her, anyway, if he hadn't felt her withdrawing from him. The fact that he was a successful novelist had come to light at the worst possible moment. In retrospect, he realized he should have told her much sooner, but he'd enjoyed the anonymity. He appreciated being accepted and liked for the man he was and not for what he'd achieved.

Then, too, her unawareness of his identity, his success, had given him a chance to know her. His career hadn't intruded on their relationship. They'd simply become friends. Well, more than friends if he had his way.

Unfortunately he'd felt Nell retreating emotionally as soon as she'd learned the truth about him. She believed he'd misled her and he supposed he had, although he hadn't meant to. He'd planned to tell her in his own time. And now...

"Think," Nell said, biting her lower lip. "What else was on those quilt squares?"

Travis tried to remember, but his thoughts were on Nell, not on the quilt. There'd only been a handful, five or six squares. Obviously they weren't enough to complete the entire quilt, which meant some squares were missing, maybe forever lost.

"Okay, the oak tree. And one of the squares showed a grave marker," Nell said, counting them on her fingers.

"One of them showed something that resembled a dry riverbed," he recalled. "But there's no river around here."

"Gully Creek isn't far," she said with a thoughtful frown.

"It isn't unheard of for creeks to run dry," he added.

"What else?" Nell asked.

"A frog?"

"Yes, but a frog doesn't make sense," Nell said.

"If there was a creek here, there could have been frogs."

"Yes, but..." She shook her head. "The quilt sounded promising at first, but I'm beginning to have my doubts—especially about the square with a hangman's noose. What could that possibly mean?"

"I don't know," Travis admitted. Like her, he was feeling some reservations. "You said one of the squares was a grave marker, right?"

She nodded.

"Do you remember what it said?"

"Yes." Nell answered and took a deep breath. "It said Edward Abraham Frasier and there was a Bible reference."

"I don't suppose you remember the Bible reference."

She nodded. "Matthew 28:46."

It didn't mean anything to Travis. They'd have to wait until they were back on the ranch and had access to a Bible.

"'My God, my God, why have you forsaken me?'" Nell quoted in a soft voice.

Travis was impressed. "Great," he said, and reached for her hand, squeezing it gently. He intended to check out the cemetery next to see if they could find the grave marker.

"I...read that passage frequently after Jake's death," she whispered.

Travis remained silent, knowing this was a difficult moment for her.

"Let's go look at the markers in the cemetery here and see if we can find that name," she finally said.

The graveyard was behind the church, surrounded

by a sun-bleached cedar-rail fence. Several markers still stood, crude crosses, a few headstones.

Travis wandered among the graves, but found nothing.

"It's impossible to read the names," Nell protested. "Something might have been etched into the wood, but you can't read it anymore."

Travis knelt in front of one headstone, choosing it randomly. A rosebush bloomed nearby. The irony of it didn't escape him—the only living plants in this town were in the cemetery. God had a great sense of humor.

He could see that a name had once been visible on the simple stone marker, and not knowing what else to do, he ran the tip of his finger gently over it. After a moment he could make out the first letter.

"W," he said aloud.

"Did you say something?" Nell asked, strolling toward him. She stood at his side while he continued to kneel in front of the marker.

"A," he said, his enthusiasm growing. "L...T, I think...E...R."

"Walter?"

"That was his name." Travis glanced up at her. "Try pressing your finger over the inscription," he said.

Nell did as he suggested, kneeling in front of another grave, close to Travis. It wasn't easy; her hands were callused from ranch work while his were more sensitive. The most strenuous activity he used his hands for was tapping computer keys.

"A!" she shouted triumphantly.

"Wonderful," he said. He removed a small notebook and pen from his pocket. Walter E. Bastien was the first name he entered. If he read the dates correctly, Walter had died at age three.

"D...E...L...E," Nell completed excitedly. "Adele!"

Travis moved on to the next marker. They were able to read nine names before they found Edward Abraham Frasier. He'd died at age five. Of the ten names they'd recorded, Travis noted that eight were children, who'd all died before the age of seven.

"Life was hard in those days," Nell said soberly. "My great-grandmother was one of ten children and only five survived to adulthood."

"A fifty percent mortality rate."

"I couldn't bear to lose a child, not after..." She didn't need to complete the thought.

"Well," Nell said abruptly, sitting back on her haunches, "this is all very interesting, but what does it mean?"

Travis didn't know and merely shrugged.

"How can we solve anything? We need to know what happened! Okay, so the quilt is somehow tied in to the town's history, but what does it tell us? Bitter End does indeed have a tree with the word 'Cursed' carved in the wood. And we found the grave marker for Edward Frasier, who's got to be an ancestor of Ellie's but it doesn't mean anything if we don't know all the facts."

"The tree's dead," Travis murmured.

"What else is new?" she said, sounding almost flippant. "Everything in this town is dead."

"I want to know why. What happened here? At one time this was a prosperous enough community, but something went very wrong. Something that no one's ever written about, so we're stuck with no documentation. Except...what about old newspapers?"

"If Bitter End ever printed a newspaper, whatever copies were published disappeared a long time ago."

"We don't know that." His research skills were beginning to kick in. "I'm thinking that if something horrendous happened, it would be reported elsewhere."

"Like where?"

"Perhaps in the Austin newspaper. Maybe San Antonio. It wouldn't do any harm to check it out."

"But how in heaven's name would we ever find that? Travis, it would take weeks of looking through microfilm."

"My dear," Travis said, slipping his arm around her waist, "haven't you ever heard of the Internet?"

ELLIE WAS BUSY reading a cookbook when Glen walked into the kitchen, fresh from the shower. He skidded to a stop when he saw her and pretended to be terrified, shielding his face with both arms.

"All right, all right," she said dryly. "Very funny. But I'm not planning to poison you, if that's what you're thinking." Ellie's limited culinary skills had become a shared joke. She'd learned a few recipes but rarely ventured into new territory.

"Honey, I don't mind cooking."

Ellie knew that was true, but Glen's repertoire consisted primarily of roast beef, beef stew and spaghetti with meat sauce, except that he added ingredients not generally associated with those dishes—jalapeños, green olives and walnuts. He was also inventive when it came to salads.

"Where did you get the cookbook?" he asked.

"The library," Ellie said. She couldn't see investing a lot of money in the project until she was sure she was up to the task.

"Do I dare inquire what's for dinner?"

"Tamale pie, cooked in a kettle." She had all the ingredients assembled on the kitchen counter. Her sleeves were rolled up and she'd tucked a towel into her waistband. If she *looked* capable and in control, she figured she might *feel* that way.

"That's your first mistake," Glen said knowingly.

"What?"

"Following a recipe. Use your instincts."

"I don't have any," Ellie muttered. Her upbringing hadn't been traditional. From early childhood, it was understood that she'd be taking over the family business. Instead of spending time in the kitchen with her mother learning the conventional domestic skills, she'd been with her father learning about types of feed and tools and worming medications.

"You've got instincts," Glen insisted. "You just don't know it yet. Here, let me read the recipe."

"Glen..." she protested, but knew it would do no good. In the months since their marriage, she'd managed to acquire a few skills. Dovie had given her cooking lessons and taught her the basics. Still, Glen continued to tease her.

"Tamale pie," he read over her shoulder. "Look at this," he said with disgust. "There's no mention of jalapeños."

"There's chili powder in the sauce."

"Instincts, Ellie, instincts."

"I'll add jalapeños as soon as I develop some," she said. "Instincts, I mean." She booted him firmly out of the kitchen. "Scoot. Go read the newspaper. Watch television. Worry about the price of beef— whatever—but leave me to my own devices."

He gave a disgruntled shrug, then did as she requested. She'd purposely chosen this recipe because it looked simple enough even for her. If all else failed, she had a frozen entrée tucked away in the freezer.

After reading the recipe twice, she started her task, remembering what Dovie had taught her. One step at a time. Everything went smoothly and she was beginning to think that there might be some Martha Stewart in her, after all. She'd actually enjoyed this, although the kitchen was a disaster. For now, she planned to bask in her success and leave the dirty dishes for later.

The beauty of this recipe was that the entire dinner was cooked on the stove. The cookbook warned against removing the lid and checking on the cornmeal topping until the required time had passed. While she waited, she glanced through the other recipes, finding three or four casseroles that looked tempting. Glen would eat his words, or more accurately, he'd eat her tamale pie and rave about it.

"How much longer?" Glen shouted from the living room.

"Not long."

"Are you making a salad?"

"I was thinking about it."

"Want any help?"

"Oh, all right." She sighed as though she'd made a major concession. In truth, she was pleased. Glen used his much-vaunted instincts to concoct salads, and tossed together the most amazing creations. He started with the traditional lettuce and tomatoes, then added whatever else he could find, including cheddar cheese, shredded carrot, sliced Bermuda onion and even seedless grapes.

"Cal mentioned something interesting the other day," her husband said, his head stuck inside the refrigerator. He reappeared, loaded with ingredients, both plain and exotic.

"Cal is always interesting."

"He said Nell and that reporter friend of hers are looking into solving the mystery of Bitter End."

This was news. "How?"

"He didn't say. At first I was opposed to the idea and said so."

"I'd rather they bulldozed the entire town and set it on fire," she said, not realizing until now that her feelings ran this strong. She'd been there once with Richard Weston, and that had been enough to last her two lifetimes. Never, ever would she return. Of course

it didn't help that her companion had done his best
to scare her half to death.

Richard had started by blindfolding her for the
drive so she wouldn't be able to find the way on her
own—as if she'd want to. When they arrived, he'd
promptly disappeared. Then he'd popped up in front
of her, frightening her so badly she'd nearly fainted.

"At first I felt it was best just to let things be,"
Glen said.

"You've changed your mind?"

He washed the lettuce and patiently tore it into
small pieces. "Cal's right about Bitter End." His tone
was thoughtful. "Ever since Richard was airlifted
from the town, there's been plenty of speculation
about it. Not many people had heard of it, before, but
more and more have learned it's there. Because of
Richard."

"So we have another thing to thank Richard Weston for," Ellie said sarcastically. It infuriated her to
remember she'd actually dated that lowlife. He'd pretended to be enthralled with her, had even proposed
marriage. On the other hand, though, if it wasn't for
Richard, Ellie doubted she would have recognized
how much she loved Glen.

Her husband had been equally blind. When he did
finally figure out he was in love with her, he'd managed to humiliate her in front of the entire town. Naturally Richard had encouraged that. Even worse, he'd
succeeded in convincing Glen that Ellie was going to
marry *him*. That Glen actually believed it was a huge

affront to her pride. But in the months since, he'd more than made it up to her.

Glen was a good husband, and when the time came, he'd make a good father. She loved him immensely, and her love grew stronger every day.

"In this instance," Glen said, "I do think we should thank Richard. Bitter End has been a blight on our history for a lot of years."

"Something horrible happened there." One trip to that awful town had proved it. Just thinking about it made her skin crawl.

"But what?" Glen asked in challenge. "Isn't that the real mystery?"

"Yes," she agreed, but stopped herself from saying more. The timer on the stove went off, signaling dinner was ready. She cast an eye to her husband and sincerely hoped this meal turned out to be as appetizing as the cookbook had promised.

Glen finished preparing his salad, adding last-minute touches of almond slivers, cilantro and goat cheese, tossing everything together with a panache she'd never possess. They carried the meal to the kitchen table, and for a while were too busy eating to bother with conversation. Her tamale pie was pronounced an unqualified success and Ellie was thrilled.

"Aren't you the least bit curious about Bitter End's history?" Glen pressed.

"Yes," she admitted with some reluctance, "but at the same time I'm afraid."

"Of what?"

"Unearthing skeletons I'd prefer remained buried," she murmured. "Suppose it was my ancestors who were responsible? I'd never be able to hold up my head again."

"No one's going to blame you for something that happened over a hundred years ago."

"Don't be so sure."

"It could have been my family," Glen said, resting his fork beside his plate. "Or the Westons. Whatever made Richard the kind of person he is—well, that had to come from somewhere. There could be a whole lot of dirt disclosed."

"You still feel Nell and her...friend should go ahead with this?"

"Yes," he said, "for a lot of reasons. I'd rather deal with some embarrassment than have a kid get hurt out there because he's curious about the mystery." His voice grew uncharacteristically serious. "Secrets are dangerous, Ellie. They lead to fear and repression. Remember what the Bible says— 'The truth shall make you free.'"

"The Bible," Ellie repeated. She'd found one among her dad's things. When she opened it, she'd read the names handwritten in the front. She'd studied the births and deaths that had been listed. One death had occurred in Bitter End. A boy of five, Edward Abraham Frasier. It was what had drawn her to the ghost town. She'd wanted to find his grave, but the markers had been impossible to read. Richard had lost patience and she'd given up, eager to escape the town and the dreadful feeling that had come over her while she was there.

"I found something else in my father's things," she said. "I don't think I showed it to you. A six-inch square of material fell out of the Bible."

"What kind of square?"

Ellie shrugged. "At first I thought it might be part of a quilt, but no one would make a quilt with this picture on it."

"What was it?"

"A giant grasshopper," she said. "Huge. The stitching was all very tiny and neat, but frankly it was quite ugly. For a while I thought of having it framed, seeing as it's so old, but eventually I decided against it. A grasshopper isn't something I want hanging in our bedroom."

"I don't know," Glen said, with a teasing glint in his eyes. "I find it rather romantic."

"Romantic?"

"I'm buggy over you."

Despite herself, Ellie laughed.

Glen laughed, too, but then his expression sobered. "I wonder if you should tell Nell and her writer friend about this."

Ellie wasn't sure yet if that was something she wanted to do.

NELL SQUINTED at the computer screen, amazed that something smaller than a board game was capable of such magical feats. Travis had brought his laptop into the house, and by plugging in a few wires had connected it to her kitchen phone. Afterwards he'd reached the web site for one of the state universities and begun reviewing the files on state history.

After an hour she'd taken over the task. Sitting at the kitchen table, she'd become fascinated by what she was reading. So much information available with such little effort! It astonished her. She had to force herself to remember what they were looking for. She feared that even if she did find the answer, she wouldn't recognize it.

"Mom." The back door swung open and Jeremy appeared. He stopped short when he saw Travis, his delight unmistakable. "Travis!"

"Jeremy, my man, how's it going?" Travis held out his palm, and Jeremy slapped it.

Nell rolled her eyes. Before she could comment, the door opened again and Emma burst in. Seeing Travis, she squealed with pleasure and raced toward him. He lifted her into his arms and hugged her.

In less than three weeks' time, Travis Grant had worked his way into their hearts. And hers.

"I told my teacher who you really are," Jeremy announced on his way to the refrigerator.

"And?"

If Jeremy didn't notice the hesitation before Travis spoke, Nell did.

"She didn't believe me. That's the thing about teachers," her son said with all the wisdom of his years. "They get jaded because so many kids lie these days."

"Give me her name and address, and I'll have my publisher mail her an autographed book."

"Would you?" Excitement flashed in Jeremy's eyes.

"Will you mail one to me?" Emma asked.

"Sure," he said, putting her down.

Jeremy tossed her an apple, which Emma deftly caught. "You want a cookie?" he asked Travis. "They're some of Mom's best."

"Of *course* I want a cookie."

Emma brought a pitcher of milk from the refrigerator.

Soon the three sat at the table, chatting. They were so involved in their conversation, Nell thought she might as well be invisible. She smiled to herself. Despite her fears about Travis's leaving, she'd learned something this afternoon. A lesson from her own children.

Both Jeremy and Emma accepted that eventually he'd return to New York. Instead of fretting about it or complaining that he'd disrupted their lives, they were grateful for his visit. Grateful to have met him.

Nell, too, had plenty of reasons to be grateful to Travis. Not only had he pulled her out from her protective shell, he'd also warmed her heart. She knew what it was to feel passion again, to feel that quickened interest in life. To feel what a woman felt when she was falling in love with a man. Nell didn't flinch from the thought.

Another thing: her children's reactions to him revealed how much they needed a father figure, a male role model. For years she'd been bogged down in her grief and refused to see what should have been directly in front of her.

Dinner that night was an informal affair. Ruth was in town with friends playing bridge, and the kids were content with leftovers. While she assembled sandwiches, Travis showed Jeremy how to play a couple of computer games.

"I want to learn, too," Emma insisted impatiently.

"Wait your turn," Jeremy muttered, not removing his gaze from the screen.

Nell thought to remind both kids that there would be no computer after Travis left, in case they thought she'd run out and buy them one. Fortunately she stopped herself in time. Perhaps in a year or two, when the dude ranch was successful, she'd be able to afford a computer. The technology was fast becoming part of everyday life, and she would need one as her business grew. That, and a dishwasher.

Following dinner, Jeremy and Emma, with their usual protests, went upstairs to do homework. Nell was left alone in the kitchen with Travis. He sat at the table with the laptop while she washed up the few dishes they'd used.

"I owe you an apology," she said, surprising herself.

He lifted his eyes from the screen and she gave him a feeble smile. "I've had a rotten attitude recently."

"I need to apologize myself," he said. "I should've mentioned sooner exactly what kind of writer I am."

"That's your business, Travis, and none of mine. As you said the other night, it doesn't make any difference to who you are as a person." She turned and reached for another dish, drying it by hand. "I want to thank you for being so good with the kids. It's no wonder they enjoy your books so much."

"They're delightful kids."

"I think so," she said.

He pushed back his chair, scraping it against the floor. "You're delightful, too," he said, coming to stand beside her. He removed the plate and dish towel from her hand.

"Travis?" She looked up at him, not knowing what to expect. Then again, she did.

He kissed her just the way she knew he would and she allowed herself to be consumed by it. His hands were in her hair, his fingers buried in her braid.

He sighed heavily when he lifted his lips from hers. "Kissing you could become addictive."

"That's what you said about my cookies earlier." Her small attempt at humor was a gentle reminder that this kiss—in fact, everything between them—was to be taken lightly. As soon as they had the information they needed, they'd be able to work out the details regarding the events in Bitter End. And once the mystery was solved, Travis would return to New York.

And she'd return to life as she knew it, a little smarter and a little more capable of coping with the future.

He continued to hold her until they heard the sound

of footsteps racing down the stairs. They broke apart like guilty teenagers.

Jeremy walked into the kitchen, stopped and looked at the two of them. "Am I interrupting anything?"

Nell denied it with a shake of her head.

"I came for a glass of water," he said. A minute later he was gone.

Travis sat in front of the computer again. Nell sat next to him, reviewing the notes he'd taken and re-reading her own. They'd found a number of references to Bitter End, but nothing concrete that pertained to the mystery.

Not yet, at any rate. Nell had a positive feeling, though; she was really beginning to enjoy this.

"Nell," Travis said, holding his finger against the computer screen.

"What is it?"

"This newspaper article from the *Brewster Review*—it's from 1879."

"But that's a year before Promise was founded."

"My point exactly." He got out of his chair. "Read it for yourself."

Chapter Ten

Nell slid onto the chair Travis had vacated and stared at the computer screen. Excitement bubbled up inside her. Was it possible Travis had stumbled onto the answer already?

As she scanned the first paragraph of the newspaper article, her spirits sank. Travis was looking too hard for a connection. She hated to be discouraging but could see nothing relevant.

"All this reports is the wrongful death of sixteen-year-old Moses Anderson in Bitter End."

"Continue reading," Travis said.

Nell returned her attention to the screen. "It says Moses was defending a saloon girl from an abusive drunk." Nell glanced up at him, a puzzled expression on her face.

"Read on."

Nell did so, mumbling a couple of lines aloud. "And the other men in the saloon sided with their friend." She gasped as she read the next paragraph. "The drunk and his friends dragged the young man outside and—" she looked up at Travis "—hanged him.'' Nell sighed at the brutality of such a deed. The boy was only sixteen. Nevertheless she didn't see how this one act of mob rule was connected to the troubles in Bitter End.

The question must have shown in her eyes because Travis asked, ''Did you notice the teenager was a preacher's son?''

''Yes, but what makes you think this has anything to do with what happened to Bitter End?''

Travis's smile was wide. ''The quilt. We were right, Nell—the mystery is linked to those quilt squares. Who better to curse a town than a man of God? The tree had the word 'Cursed' carved into it, remember?''

Of course she did. ''Wasn't there another square with the hangman's noose? Maybe that's the connection—Moses being hanged.'' Nell's enthusiasm mounted. ''Let's look at those quilt pieces again!''

''Good idea.''

Travis followed her into the living room. She opened the cedar chest and removed the cardboard box. Nell set aside the folded sheet of muslin and placed the squares on the coffee table.

''What in heaven's name do a frog and a word carved in an oak tree have in common?''

Jeremy came down the stairs. ''What are you doing?'' he asked.

''Unraveling a mystery,'' Nell explained absently as she continued to study the quilt pieces.

''Why not put Moses Anderson's name on the tombstone, instead of Edward Abraham Frasier's?''

Travis added, as though he was beginning to doubt his own theory.

"Who's Moses Anderson?" Jeremy asked, leaning forward to get a better look at the embroidered squares.

"Travis found a news article about him in an old newspaper," Nell murmured, concentrating on the squares.

"Off the Internet? Mom, I'm telling you, we gotta get a computer."

"Someday."

"Aw, Mom..."

"The river scene without a river," Nell muttered listening with only half an ear to her son's pleas.

"Did you notice that the stitching on the river-bank's sort of a rusty red?" Travis asked.

"Soil in the area is iron-rich," Nell explained, dismissing any significance in the choice of color.

"Moses turned the water into blood, remember," Jeremy commented. "We read about it in Sunday School last week."

"Moses did indeed," was Nell's vacant reply.

"Moses and his brother Aaron."

"That's it," Travis shouted, and threw his arms in the air. "Jeremy, you're a genius, a living breathing genius. That's it, that's the key." He gripped the boy's shoulders to hug him wildly. Then he reached for Nell, laughter spilling from him like water.

Jeremy and Nell stared at him as if he'd suddenly gone weak in the head.

"What are you talking about?" Nell demanded.

"The curse!" he shouted.

"What's Travis so excited about?" Emma asked from halfway down the stairs.

"I don't know how we could have been so blind." Now that Travis had stopped laughing, he clasped Nell around the waist and danced her about the room. Jeremy and Emma clapped and laughed.

"Travis, for the love of heaven, stop! Tell me."

Breathing hard, he draped his arms over her shoulders and rested his forehead against hers. "I can't believe we didn't see it sooner."

"See *what?*" she cried, growing more and more frustrated.

Travis turned her around so that she faced the coffee table. "Look at the quilt pieces again."

"I'm looking."

"What was the preacher's son's name?"

"Moses," she said.

"After his son was murdered, the preacher cursed the town."

"Yes." Her gaze went to the square with "Cursed" carved in the tree.

"Now look at the frog."

"I'm looking, I'm looking."

"Jeremy, bring me your Bible," Travis instructed. The boy raced out of the room.

As soon as Travis mentioned the Bible, Nell understood. "Moses and the plagues."

Jeremy returned with his Bible and handed it to Travis, who started flipping pages in the Old Testament.

"Somewhere in the first part of Exodus," Nell said, fairly certain that was where the story of Passover was told.

"Here," Travis said, running his finger down the seventh chapter. First there's all this business about turning staffs into snakes, then Moses and Aaron did as the Lord commanded and hit the surface of the Nile with a rod, and the river turned to blood."

"Gully Creek became bloody?" That sounded a bit far-fetched to Nell.

"Maybe the water went bad and they couldn't drink it," Jeremy suggested.

"Or dried up," Travis said.

"What else happened in the Bible that ties to Bitter End?" she asked, eager now, reading over his shoulder. Travis skimmed through several chapters, listing the plagues that had befallen Egypt. The death of cattle, flies, hail and lightning, locusts, boils, crop failures were the ones described first.

"What was the one that came after the river turning into blood?" Jeremy asked.

"Frogs," Travis said triumphantly. "The land was covered with frogs."

"Not if the creek dried up." Someone had to show a little reason, Nell thought.

"I don't think we'll ever completely understand the dynamics of what happened."

"The grave marker," Nell said excitedly. "The five-year-old boy, remember?"

"Abraham Edward Frasier."

"Remember, it was the death of the firstborn sons

that convinced Pharaoh to let the Israelites leave Egypt," Nell said.

"The children." Travis's voice was low. "Of the ten graves we were able to identify, eight were children." He paused. "The last plague was the death of the firstborn sons," he said slowly.

As a widow, Nell knew she could survive any financial trial, bad weather or crop failure, if she still had her home and her land. The one thing she wouldn't be able to stand was losing her children. If *they* were at risk, nothing else mattered.

"That's why everyone left the town," she said confidently. "Their children were dying. The community had withstood everything else—the river drying up, the pestilence, the other trials. But no land, no town, no community was worth the loss of their children."

The phone rang just then and Emma ran to answer it. "Mom," she shouted as though Nell was in the barn, instead of the next room. "It's Ellie Frasier."

WADE McMILLEN sat at the desk in his study and tried to ignore the bright sunshine flooding the room. The most difficult part of his week was writing the Sunday sermon. While he enjoyed preaching, even enjoyed the research demanded in his work, he wasn't particularly fond of the effort that went into composing his sermons. Especially on a day as glorious as this one.

Putting aside his notes, he rose and walked over to his study window, gazing at the tree-lined streets of Promise. It was a changed town from the one he'd come to serve five years ago. And this past year had seen the most dramatic of those changes.

There'd been a number of weddings, sure to be followed by a rush of births. Just last week he'd been out to visit the Smiths' baby girl for the first time. Wade had watched Laredo, as the new father, rock Laura to sleep, crooning cowboy songs, instead of lullabies. The memory of that scene brought a smile to his lips even now.

Recently Grady Weston had proudly told him Caroline was pregnant. Wade was pleased; this was exactly the kind of happy news he'd been waiting to hear. Maggie would make a wonderful big sister. It would be nice, too, for the Smiths' daughter to have a cousin around the same age. Wade recalled how close he was to Les McMillen, a cousin only three months younger than he was. They'd been inseparable. In many ways he was closer to Les than his own brother, who was four years his junior.

It wouldn't surprise Wade any if Ellie and Jane, the wives of the Patterson brothers, showed up pregnant—and soon. He knew from the hints he'd heard Mary and Phil give their sons that the boys' parents were more than ready to become grandparents. Wade didn't think they'd need to wait much longer.

With his thoughts full of weddings and babies, Wade didn't realize he had visitors until he heard the voices outside his door. His secretary buzzed him on the intercom.

"Nell Bishop and Travis Grant are here to see you," Martha announced.

"Show them in." Wade knew Nell had a paying guest staying at Twin Canyons. Nell had briefly introduced him after service a couple of Sundays ago. Jeremy and Emma had been full of chatter about their guest the past few weeks, as well, but Wade hadn't met him yet.

His first sight of Travis Grant revealed a large man with a kind face.

"Wade McMillen," Wade said, and the two men exchanged handshakes. Wade gestured for Nell and Travis to sit down, which they did. Maybe he was getting to be an old hand at such things, but Wade felt he knew the reason for this unexpected visit.

One glance told him they were in love; he knew the signs. It was early, probably too early, for them to think about marriage. If that was what they were here to discuss, he'd feel obliged to suggest a long engagement. Nevertheless, Wade was pleased for Nell, very pleased indeed.

"What can I do for you?" Wade asked, leaning back in his leather chair.

"We've come to talk to you about Bitter End," Nell said.

Wade frowned. That was the last subject he'd expected her to mention. The ghost town that had been the cause of so much trouble lately, what with Richard Weston having holed up there. Sheriff Hennessey and the town council had combined their efforts to keep things quiet, but information always seemed to leak out, anyway.

"You do know about the ghost town, don't you?" Travis asked.

"Yes. Have you been there?" The question was directed at Travis, but Nell answered.

"We both have. Twice," she added.

"Actually three times."

Nell nodded. "Three times."

Good grief, they already sounded like an old married couple.

Nell looked at Travis and her eyes sparkled with excitement and happiness. "We think we've solved the mystery of why everyone left Bitter End."

"The town was cursed," Travis explained.

"Cursed?"

"By a preacher whose sixteen-year-old son was hanged when a mob of rowdy drunks got out of hand."

Wade hated to discourage them. In the Wild West it wasn't uncommon for a preacher to be credited with the ability to rain fire and brimstone down upon the backs of sinners. There were usually logical reason for these supposedly supernatural events, but they were cheerfully overlooked.

"His name was Moses," Nell supplied.

"The preacher's?"

"No, the teenager who was hanged."

The violence of the Old West never ceased to distress Wade, but then all he had to do was take a walk through an inner-city slum to appreciate that, in certain ways, humanity hadn't advanced much.

"When the mob of drunks hanged the boy, the

preacher came to the town and cursed it with the plagues of Egypt,'' Nell said.

''That's our theory, anyway,'' Travis added.

Wade was willing to listen, but he didn't hold out much hope that this was really the reason the town had been abandoned all those years ago. ''How do you know about the plagues?''

''From the story quilt.''

Nell and Travis glanced at each other as if to decide who should explain the role played by this quilt. Apparently it was decided that Nell would, because she continued. ''Ruth had a cedar chest in the attic that was given to her after her mother-in-law died almost fifty years ago. Inside it, we found the makings of a quilt. The backing was intact, but there was only a handful of completed squares.''

''We found only six, but we knew there had to be others.''

''There were,'' Nell said, her face glowing with enthusiasm. ''Ellie Frasier phoned and told us about an embroidered square she'd found in her father's Bible.''

''One with a giant grasshopper,'' Travis explained.

''Locusts,'' Wade murmured.

''Exactly.''

''We're convinced,'' Travis said, pausing to look at Nell, who nodded eagerly, ''that the final plague, the one that drove the families away from Bitter End was some kind of epidemic that killed their children. By now, the residents had endured one tribulation after another—bugs, weather problems, failed crops...''

"The quilt told you all this?" Wade asked.

"Yes," Nell said, "it explained everything. Well, almost everything."

"Go on." Wade motioned to Travis. "I didn't mean to interrupt you."

"When the children started dying, the people who were left panicked, packed up everything they owned and moved. Canned goods still remain on the store shelves, so my guess is they had a big meeting and made the decision to get out together immediately."

"Drought, disease, pestilence," Wade murmured. "I'd leave, too."

"It's an incredible story," Nell said, and glanced at Travis, her pride evident. "Travis is going to write about it."

"This is exactly the type of story I've been waiting to find. For years I've been writing for juveniles and I've searched for the right vehicle to cross over from children's books to adult fiction."

"You aren't going to stop writing for kids, are you?" Nell asked, looking distressed.

"No, they're my audience, and I'll always write for them. But the story of Bitter End gives me an opportunity to make my mark with another readership."

This exchange was lost on Wade. He knew Travis was a writer, but had assumed he wrote for a newspaper. Rather than ask a lot of questions, he narrowed it down to one. "Was there something you needed from me?"

The two of them stared at him as though they'd

forgotten he was there. "We want you to bless Bitter End," Nell said.

"Bless it?"

"That's what the town needs," Travis interjected. "And according to what Nell tells me, Promise will benefit from it, too."

Wade wasn't sure there was anything to this curse business. All the disasters Travis and Nell had described were probably nothing more than an unfortunate set of coincidences. Superstitions ran deep back then, and people put credence in matters they shouldn't. But it wouldn't hurt to bless the town. He'd be happy to do it.

THREE DAYS LATER, Wade stood in the middle of Bitter End. With him were several members of the town council, Sheriff Frank Hennessey, the Patterson brothers and their wives, Grady and Caroline Weston, Nell Bishop and her writer friend, and Laredo Smith. It was unlikely this many people had congregated here in more than a hundred years. Each had come for his or her own reasons. And almost everyone who'd accompanied Wade was related to the original settlers in one way or another.

Bitter End. Not exactly a promising name for a frontier settlement. As Wade remembered it, the town had gotten its name from the first settlers, who'd arrived by wagon train. The journey had been long and arduous, but eventually they'd reached the land of their dreams. Unfortunately, due to the hardships they'd suffered on the journey, many of their dreams had turned bitter.

As soon as he set foot in the town, Wade had felt a gloom and a darkness settle over him, even though the day was bright and sunny. He tried to ignore it and proceeded with the ceremony.

Once everyone was gathered around him, he opened his Bible and read a passage. As he spoke the words, he felt the oppression loosen its grip on him.

If the preacher a hundred years ago had used the Old Testament, filled with its judgments and laws, to curse the land, then he'd bless it from the New Testament. Freedom from bondage and judgment would be his prayer.

Wade's voice rang loud and clear down the lifeless streets. When he'd finished reading, he bowed his head. The others followed his lead. Wade prayed that God would smile down on this land once more and make it a place of love, instead of hate, a home of joy, instead of sadness.

A chorus of amens followed when he finished.

Laredo Smith stepped forward, carrying a bucket, shovel and a budding rosebush. "Savannah couldn't be here today, but she wanted me to plant this close to the tree where the boy was hanged."

"That's a wonderful idea," Nell said. Then she pointed to the charred marks on the church steeple. "That was one of the plagues—lightning and hail."

Wade was fast becoming a believer of this incredible tale. He'd studied the quilt pieces—including a seventh one that had been found by Dovie, an illustration of lightning striking a church. And he'd checked out the Internet sites identified by Travis. The more he read and heard about Bitter End, the more everything added up.

"The feeling's not as strong," Wade heard Ellie Patterson murmur to her husband.

"I noticed that, too," Dr. Jane added.

Wade smiled to himself as the assembled group headed back to the highway where the cars were parked.

Wade enjoyed the way these friends talked and joked with each other, but he noted that Nell Bishop and Travis Grant appeared strangely quiet. They were the ones who deserved the credit for solving this mystery. Over the past few days, they'd been the center of attention, and while Nell seemed to be uncomfortable in the limelight, Travis was clearly in his element.

It was often that way with couples, Wade had observed. One shy, the other outgoing. One sociable, the other private. The law of opposites—the wonderful balance that brought stability into a relationship.

As they approached their vehicles, Travis stepped up to Wade. "I'd like to thank you again for all your help."

"The pleasure was mine," Wade said, and meant it.

"I'll be leaving Wednesday morning, and I wanted to take the opportunity to say goodbye," Travis went on.

That explained Nell's dour look. Travis was returning to New York City, a city far removed from this land of sagebrush and ghost towns and tales of the Wild West.

"The best of luck with your book," Wade said. "Keep in touch."

Travis glanced in Nell's direction and responded with a noncommittal shrug.

Wade couldn't help wondering what had happened between the two. Whatever it was, he felt saddened that they didn't have more of an opportunity to explore their love. Although he was far from an expert in the area of romance, Wade had sensed they were well suited.

"You're leaving?" The question came from Grady Weston.

Travis nodded. "I've been away far longer than I expected as it is."

"You're not going to let him drive off into the sunset, are you?" Caroline pressured Nell.

It seemed every eye turned to the widow. "As Travis said, he needs to get back." Her tone was stiff. Then she turned away.

TRAVIS STUFFED a stack of shirts in his suitcase, not showing any particular care. He was a patient man, but he'd been tried to the very limits of his endurance. Beyond!

Nell acted as though his return to New York was cause for celebration. She'd gone so far as to throw him a farewell dinner party. She'd invited her friends, and the last he heard a dozen people had promised to show.

All day she'd been in the kitchen, cooking up a storm, baking, chopping, sautéing. His last hours in Texas, and the woman he loved had her head buried in a cookbook.

Not that he didn't appreciate the effort. It was a kind gesture, but spending the evening with a crowd wasn't how he wanted it. He'd hoped to have a few minutes alone with Nell, but that wasn't to be. In fact, she'd made it quite plain that she *didn't* want to be alone with him. Fine. He was a big boy; he knew when he'd worn out his welcome.

"Do you need any help?" Jeremy asked as he came into the bunkhouse.

Travis zipped up his bag. "Thanks, but I've got everything packed."

The boy at least had the common decency to show some regret at Travis's departure. Emma, too, had moped around the house from the moment she walked in the door. She followed her brother into the bunkhouse.

"Hey, Emma," Travis said. "Why the sad face?"

Her lower lip quavered. "I don't want you to go."

"He *has* to go," Jeremy answered on his behalf.

"Do you?" Emma asked, her eyes wide and forlorn.

Travis opened his mouth to answer, but Jeremy beat him to the punch. "That's what Mom said, remember? His work and his whole life are in New York." Jeremy sounded as though he'd memorized his mother's response. A very reasonable response, he had to admit—but it wasn't what he wanted to hear.

"Mom said we're going to have lots of guests in the next few weeks," Emma told him.

"She's right," Travis said. Nell would have the dude ranch in full swing before long.

"We're bound to get attached to lots of folks," Jeremy said, again echoing his mother's words, Travis suspected.

Attached. Nell thought the relationship he shared with Jeremy and Emma was just one in a long list of attachments. The woman didn't have a clue, he thought angrily. He loved those kids! Her, too.

And all she saw him as—or *wanted* to see him as— was a paying customer at Twin Canyons Ranch. Which made him the first of many wannabe cowboys.

All he needed was some encouragement from Nell. Then he'd stay. Just one word of encouragement. Two at the most. *Don't go* would have sufficed. Instead, she was so pleased to see him off she was throwing a party. It was hard for a man to swallow.

The dinner guests started arriving at five. Nell had the front yard set up with tables and chairs. In addition to all the food she'd been cooking, her friends and neighbors bought over a variety of tasty dishes— salads and casseroles, pies and cakes.

Once dinner was served, they seated themselves at the tables and ate. Ruth sat next to Travis. He almost had the impression that she was waiting for him to do something—but what? After the meal Travis went around to pay his respects to the people he was just beginning to know. He seemed to hit it off with Grady Weston best. It was a shame to call a man a friend in one breath and tell him goodbye in the next.

Travis didn't know what Nell found so all-fired important, but he didn't see her the entire meal. As far as he could figure, she'd hidden herself in the kitchen where she'd been all day.

Before he could do anything about it, Grady joined him, and they exchanged pleasantries for several minutes. Then Grady grew strangely quiet. "What time are you going back to New York?"

"First thing in the morning," Travis said. His flight was late in the afternoon, but he had a three-hour drive ahead of him, plus the rental car to return.

"Do you…anticipate seeing Richard again?"

So that was where this conversation was headed. "I don't expect I will."

Grady nodded, his look grave.

"Would you like me to check up on him now and again?" Travis offered.

"He's a criminal and he's paying for his crimes, but dammit all, he's still my brother." Grady's voice dropped.

"Hey, no problem, and I don't need to say I'm there on your behalf."

"It isn't on my behalf, so to speak," Grady was quick to correct him. "I just want to be sure—I guess I'm looking for a change in him."

"Is it possible?"

"I pray it is," Grady said. He stood, patted Travis on the back and left the table to return to his wife.

The laughter and chatter continued for a while, and then people packed up their leftovers and were gone. Travis was grateful. Nell couldn't avoid him forever. He gathered up the serving dishes and carried them into the house.

Nell was washing dishes, her arms elbow-deep in soap suds.

"That was a wonderful dinner," he said.

"Thank you."

"I don't think anyone's ever gone to so much trouble to send me off." He realized he must have sounded a little sarcastic, but if she noticed, she ignored it.

"It wasn't any trouble," Nell countered. "Besides, the community owes you a debt of thanks. If it wasn't for you, no one would know what happened in Bitter End."

"You worked just as hard."

"You dragged me kicking and screaming into this project, remember?"

That wasn't *exactly* how Travis recalled it. She'd been reluctant, true, but had willingly enough accompanied him. They'd made a great team.

"I'm going to miss you," he said, and wished to hell she'd turn around so he could look at her. Instead, she stood with her back to him and revealed none of her thoughts.

"Me and Emma got all the trash picked up," Jeremy called from the living room.

"It's bedtime," she told them. "Go upstairs and wash."

"Aw, Mom."

"You heard me."

Nell must have removed the plug from the kitchen drain because he heard the water swish and gurgle. She turned to reach for a towel and beamed him a smile so dazzling it startled him.

"What time are you leaving?" she asked.

"Around six."

She nodded. "I probably won't see you, then."

He was hoping she'd suggest they have coffee together before he left. Just the two of them. No kids. No Ruth. Just them.

She didn't offer.

Travis forced himself to smile. "I guess this is it, then."

"This is it."

They stood and stared at each other for an awkward moment.

"It's been...great." Nell said at last.

He nodded. "I'd like to kiss you goodbye, Nell," he said.

She hesitated, then floated easily into his arms. When their mouths found each other, the kiss was a blend of need and sadness, of appreciation and farewell.

When she slid out of his arms, Travis was shocked by how much he missed her there. He might as well get accustomed to it, for she gave no indication that she cared to see him again. Not one word, not one sign.

"You'll keep in touch?" he asked, hoping she'd at least be willing to do that.

"The kids would love to hear from you."

Her words hit their mark. "But not you?"

"I didn't say that."

"Would *you* enjoy hearing from me?" It was damn little to ask.

She lowered her gaze and nodded.

"Was that so hard, Nell?"

She looked up at him and he was surprised to see tears glistening in her eyes. "Yes," she whispered. "It was very hard."

Chapter Eleven

It did no good to pretend anymore. Nell sat out on her front porch, watching the sunset. Travis had been gone a week and it felt like ten years. She'd fallen in love with a greenhorn. Travis Grant might know everything there was to know about computers, but he'd barely figured out which side of a saddle was up.

"A writer," Nell muttered, staring at the sky. She was thoroughly disgusted with herself. Everything she'd ever wanted in this life she'd had with Jake. But he'd died, and she was so lonely. She hadn't even realized *how* lonely until that New Yorker kissed her. All the men who'd pestered her for a date in the past couple of years and she hadn't felt the slightest interest. Then Travis came into her life and before she knew it she was in love. It felt like she'd been sucker-punched.

"Are you thinking about Travis again?" Ruth asked, standing just inside the screen door.

"No," Nell denied vehemently, then reluctantly confessed. "Yeah." *Yeah.* Now Travis had her doing it. If he'd stayed much longer, she'd sound just like a Yankee.

"You gonna write him?"

"No." Of that much Nell was sure.

"Why not?"

"I can't see where it'd do any good."

"Oh, Nell."

"He's from New York. He wouldn't be happy in Promise and this is where the kids and I belong." The situation was impossible, and the sooner she accepted that, the better it would be for everyone. Travis Grant was a writer who lived in the center of the publishing world. He'd come to Texas to research a book, not find himself a wife and take on a ready-made family.

She was convinced that in time she'd fall in love with someone from around here. Someone who stirred her heart. Travis had shown her it was possible; now all she had to do was find the right man.

"Nell, dear, I still think you should write him a letter." Ruth sat in the rocker next to Nell and took out her crocheting.

Even if she did write Travis, Nell mused, she wouldn't know what to say. Really, what was there to write about? Bedsides, he might misread her intent and assume she was asking something of him.

Eventually she'd get over him and her heart would forget. Any night now she'd stop dreaming about him. Any day now he'd fade from her thoughts.

No, she most definitely wasn't going to write. If he

wanted to continue the relationship, then he'd have to contact her first.

Well...maybe just one letter, she thought. Just to be sure he arrived home safe and sound. And she could always ask him about the book. One letter, but only one.

That couldn't do any harm.

TRAVIS SQUINTED at the computer screen, then yawned and pinched the bridge of his nose. He'd been home all of eight days and he'd already written the first fifty pages of his new book—the book for adults. The words seemed to pour out of him. He couldn't get them down fast enough.

But then, he'd always been able to escape into a story when his life was miserable. It was one of the blessings of being a writer—and one of the curses. His stomach growled in angry protest and he realized it'd been twenty-four hours since his last meal.

He walked barefoot in the direction of his kitchen, surprised to realize it was morning. It was 6 a.m. according to the clock on the mantel. From the view through the windows in his high-rise apartment, he saw that the city was just waking up. In Texas Nell would be—

He stopped, refusing to think about Nell, or Jeremy or Emma. They were out of his life and that was the way it had to be. The way *she* wanted it. That had been made more than clear before he left Promise.

Promise. Yeah, right. They should have named the town Heartache.

His stomach growled again, more insistently this time, and Travis headed toward the refrigerator. It shouldn't have come as any surprise to find nothing he'd seriously consider eating. He was rummaging through his pantry shelves when the apartment intercom buzzed. He muttered under his breath as he heard his ex-wife's voice. Still muttering he waited at the door to let her in.

"You've been home for a week and I haven't heard from you," she said accusingly. "I thought I'd stop by on my way to work to greet the prodigal son." She'd always been an early riser, like him, and generally got to the office before seven.

"I've been working." He might not have been as friendly if she hadn't come bearing gifts. She carried a sack from his favorite bakery and a takeout latte. At the moment he would have thrown his arms around a terrorist offering food.

"You eating?"

He reached for the sack. "I am now."

Valerie chuckled and followed him into the kitchen. She was a lovely-looking woman, but Travis was now immune. Unfortunately she was cold and calculating, and about as different from Nell Bishop as a woman could get.

"So what'd you find out about that ghost town?" Val asked.

Travis quickly devoured two jelly-filled doughnuts, pausing only long enough to inhale. His stomach thanked him, and he settled back with the latte. Between sips, he filled in the details, casually mentioning Nell. He acknowledged her help in solving the puzzle and said nothing about his feelings toward her.

Valerie might have remarried, but she tended to believe that Travis remained stuck on her. He couldn't be bothered setting her straight.

"Who's this Nell?"

Damn, but it was impossible to hide anything from her! "A woman I met."

"You in love with her?"

Leave it to Val to get directly to the point. "Maybe." He licked the jelly from his fingertips rather than meet her gaze.

"Travis," she chided. "I know you, and 'maybe' isn't in your vocabulary."

"She was a...nice diversion," he said, evading her question. If he was truly in love with Nell, he'd walk on hot coals before he'd admit it to his ex-wife. The one who deserved to know first would be Nell. However, at this point, it seemed unlikely that their relationship would go any further.

"Did you meet Richard Weston's family?" Val asked.

Travis nodded. "They're good people."

"Actually Richard's not half-bad himself."

Travis's gaze narrowed. He was surprised she didn't recognize Weston for the kind of man he was. He'd credited her with better judgment. "What's going on?" he asked.

Val shrugged. "Nothing. How can it? He's behind bars."

"You actually like this guy?"

Val crossed her legs and smiled. "I know what he did, and while he isn't exactly a candidate for a congressional medal of honor, I find him rather charming."

Snakes could be charming, too. Frankly Travis didn't like hearing her talk this way. Recently Val had implied that she and husband number two weren't getting on, but surely she wouldn't get mixed up with a prisoner. "Time for a reality check, Val."

Her eyes flared. "You're one to talk," she snapped. "You're in love with some cowgirl widow."

"I didn't say I loved her."

"You didn't have to. It's written all over you."

Travis exhaled sharply. He had better things to do than get involved in a useless argument with his ex-wife. "All I'm saying is be careful with Richard, all right? He's a user."

"Of course," she said, and gave Travis a demure smile. "We both know I'm too self-centered to do anything that's ultimately going to hurt me." She stared at him. "You, on the other hand, might be tempted to do something foolish about this cowgirl of yours."

"She isn't mine." Travis didn't want to talk about Nell.

"Have you heard from her since you left?"

He sighed. "Do you mind if we talk about something else?"

Val's delicately shaped eyebrows lifted. "You really are taken with her, aren't you?"

"So what if I am?"

"Are you going to leave it at that?"

"Probably," he said, his control slipping.

"You could always write her. Or call."

"And say what?"

"Don't look at me—you're the one who works with words. Seems to me you should have plenty to say." She glanced at her wrist and leaped to her feet. "Gotta run. Court this morning. 'Bye darling." She kissed his cheek and was out the door.

He wasn't going to write Nell, he decided. He would if there was anything to say, but there wasn't. It'd be a cold day in hell before he let another woman walk all over his heart. And really, when it came right down to it, he and Nell didn't have a thing in common. Not one damn thing.

Well…maybe one letter to ask about the kids and Ruth. And he did plan to send Jeremy and Emma autographed books. He'd keep the letter short and sweet, thank her for putting him up, that sort of thing. One letter wouldn't hurt. But only one.

NELL'S GAZE fell on the calendar hanging on the bulletin board by the phone. If she'd calculated right, her letter to Travis should arrive in New York City that day. She'd agonized over what to say and in the end had made it a chatty friendly letter. At least that was what she hoped. Her one fear was that her real feelings shone between every line.

Ruth walked into the kitchen. "I picked up the mail while I was in town," she said as she set down her purse and a shopping bag. "Do we know anyone in New York City?" she asked coyly.

Travis. Nell's heart thumped. Because she didn't want Ruth to know how excited she was, she casually reached for the stack of mail, sorting through the various solicitations and bills until she found the envelope. It *was* from Travis.

She stared at it so long Ruth said, "Well, for heaven's sake, girl, open it."

Nell didn't need to be told twice. She ripped open the envelope, her hands shaking with eagerness. Her eyes quickly skimmed the first typed page and glanced at the second. Once she saw how much he'd written, she pulled out a chair and sat down. She read slowly, wanting to savor each word, treasure each line. Like her, he was chatty, personable, yet slightly reserved.

"Well?" Ruth said.

"You can read it if you want."

Ruth looked downright disappointed. "Are you telling me he didn't say anything...personal?"

"Not really." Then again, he had, but it was between the lines, not on the surface. His letter really said that he missed her. That he was thinking of her, working too many hours, trying to get on with his life. Nell identified all this because she'd conveyed identical things to him—in what she'd written and what she hadn't.

"There's a package here, as well, for Jeremy and Emma," Ruth said.

In her rush to read Travis's letter Nell hadn't noticed.

"Are you going to write him back?" Ruth asked.

Nell nodded, but she'd wait a couple of days first. It might look as if she'd been anxious to hear from him if she replied too soon. Despite that, she sat down at the dinner table that night and wrote him a reply. The kids each wrote a thank-you note for the autographed books, and it didn't seem right to delay those. Since she was mailing something to him anyway, and her letter was already written, she sent it off the next morning. It wasn't a special trip into town; she had other errands so it worked out conveniently. Or so she told herself.

Ruth was standing on the porch grinning from ear to ear when Nell returned. "You've got company," Ruth called when she climbed out of the pickup. She glanced at the dark sedan parked near the bunkhouse.

Ruth's smile blossomed as Travis opened the screen door and joined her on the porch.

"Hello, Nell," he said, grinning.

He wore a Stetson, faded blue jeans and rich-looking cowboy boots. He might not be a working cowboy, but he was the best-damn-looking one she'd seen in a very long while. It took all the restraint she could muster not to run straight into his arms.

"Are you surprised?" he asked.

She nodded, afraid she couldn't say anything intelligible.

"I'll leave you two to sort everything out," Ruth stated matter-of-factly, and started toward the house.

Her eyes pleaded with Ruth not to leave her, but the older woman was oblivious to her silent cries for help. Nell didn't know what to think, what to say. Her heart raced, but she was afraid to read anything into Travis's unexpected visit. Maybe he was in the area for more research or for business or...

She walked over to the porch and sat down on the top step.

"Mind if I join you?" he asked before he sat down next to her.

"Of course not."

"You look wonderful," he said softly.

She nodded her thanks for the compliment. "Were you in the area...?" She had to ask.

"No."

"I...I got your letter." She wanted to tell him how excited she was when she saw it, but couldn't manage the words.

"I got yours, too. That's the reason I'm here."

"My letter?" He must have booked the flight out of New York a minute after he'd read it.

"You love me, Nell don't you?"

She nodded slowly.

"I love you, too," he whispered, and reached for her hand.

"But—"

"Hear me out," he interrupted. "You're about to list all the reasons it's impossible for us to be together, but there's nothing you can say that I haven't thought of myself. We're different, but it's a good kind of different. We're good together, a team."

"But—"

"Together we solved a hundred-year-old mystery. There's a lesson in it, too. The people who left Bitter End were looking to make a new life, a new start, and put the pain of the past behind them. I'm offering you the same opportunity—and taking advantage of it myself. We belong together, Nell. You and me and Ruth and the kids."

"But—"

"I'm almost finished," he promised, and drew in a deep breath. "It'll be a new life for all of us. I love you, Nell. I want to marry you."

"I can't live in the city," she blurted.

"You won't have to."

"You mean that?" It was almost more than she dared believe.

"Not if you don't want to. I can work anywhere, you know. One of the benefits of being a writer." He paused. "So?"

"I'll marry you." She'd known that the minute she saw him standing on the porch.

"You don't have any questions?" He seemed almost disappointed that she wasn't going to argue with him.

"Yeah. One." She smiled. "Just how much longer do I have to wait for you to kiss me?"

Within a single beat of her heart, Travis had wrapped her in his arms. His mouth was hard and hungry over hers, and Nell let herself soak in his love. He loved her, really loved her! And he was right that it was time to put aside the past and start again.

"How soon can we arrange the wedding?" he whispered against her throat.

"Soon," she said.

Travis chuckled. "But not soon enough to suit me." Then he kissed her again.

Come to Promise next month—there's going to be a wedding! See what all your friends are up to: Grady and Caroline, Savannah and Laredo, Glen and Ellie, Cal and Dr. Jane...and the rest. Find out what happens when another stranger comes to town, a pregnant woman this time, and Reverend McMillen discovers he's a flesh-and-blood man as well as a man of God. Look for LONE STAR BABY, the last HEART OF TEXAS book, in July.

Take 2 bestselling love stories FREE

Plus get a FREE surprise gift!

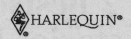

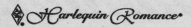

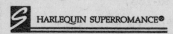

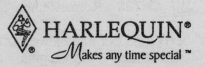